THE MISSION

The Arlin Trilogy: Book 2

THE MISSION

ONDREA KEIGH

ISBN: 979-8-9872442-3-4 (paperback)
ISBN: 979-8-9872442-2-7 (eBook)
ISBN: 979-8-9872442-7-2 (Hardback)

Book Cover by Emily's World of Design

Map by Emily's World of Design

Edited by Laura Ebersole

Published by Lyonsword Publishing

www.ondreakeigh.com/lyonsword-publishing

To those who are struggling.
Keep fighting.
You are not alone.

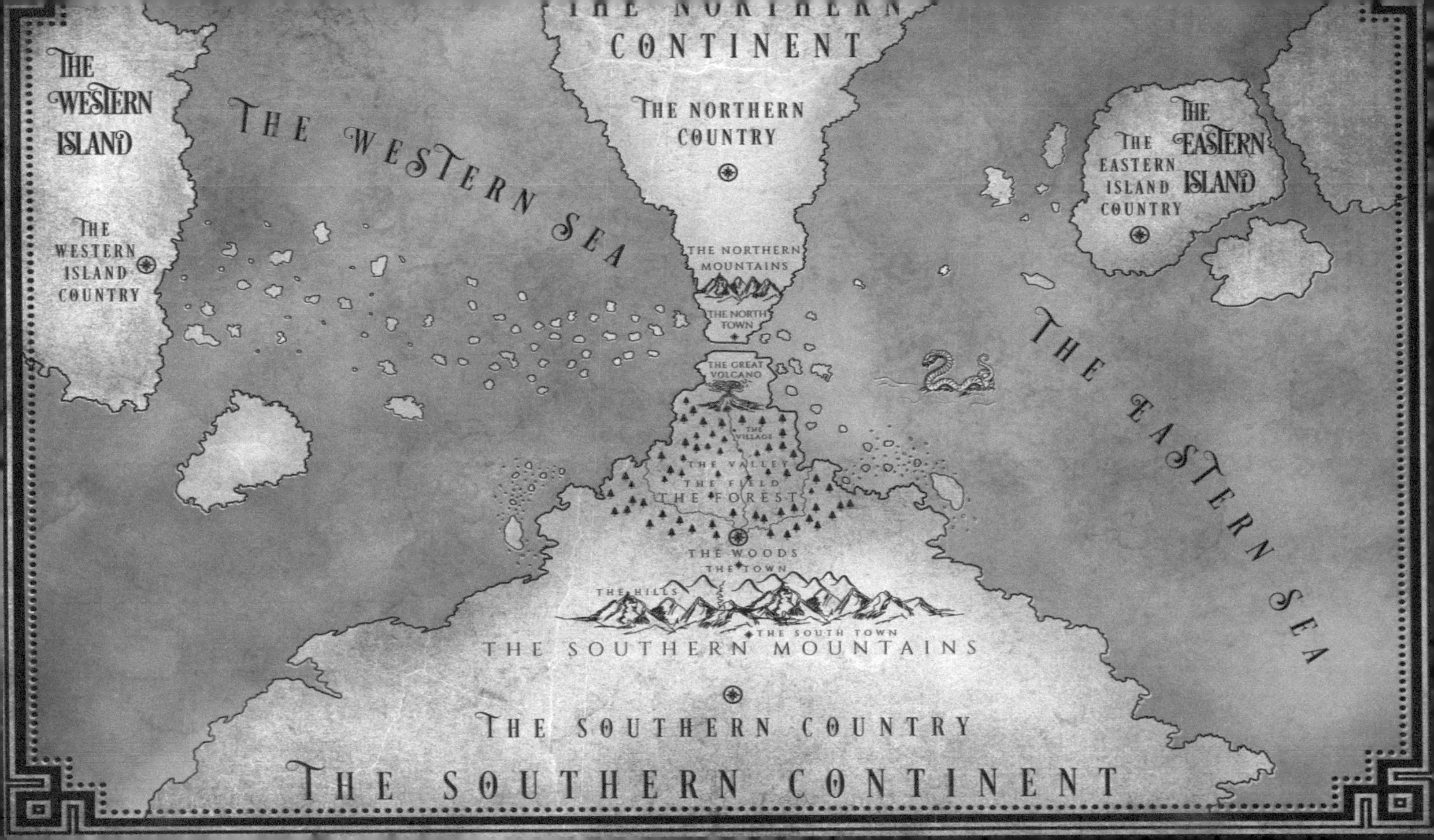

THE EASTERN SEA

THE EASTERN ISLAND
THE EASTERN ISLAND COUNTRY

THE NORTHERN CONTINENT
THE NORTHERN COUNTRY
THE NORTHERN MOUNTAINS
THE NORTH TOWN

THE GREAT VOLCANO
THE VILLAGE
THE VALLEY
THE FIELD
THE FOREST
THE WOODS
THE TOWN
THE SOUTH TOWN
THE HILLS
THE SOUTHERN MOUNTAINS
THE SOUTHERN COUNTRY
THE SOUTHERN CONTINENT

THE WESTERN SEA
THE WESTERN ISLAND
THE WESTERN ISLAND COUNTRY

Chapter 1

WATER WASHED OVER THE main deck as violent waves tossed the *Lyonsword* through the evening's dark waters. The winds wailed and battered the ship in gusts as the ship's bowels creaked under the stress of the raging storm. The crew was working feverishly to tie down the last of the cargo and tools that were exposed to the weather. Doing my best to avoid being trampled by the crew or drenched by a wave, I struggled across the deck toward the captain's quarters with Christopher, the captain's first mate, in tow.

Roughly eight months ago, I had been on dry land working for General Delaney. I had played a crucial part in his efforts to piece the Town back together after the last two wars with the Great Beasts of the Southern Mountains. And I would still be working for the general now, with the next war looming, if I hadn't seen it—the Beast of the Woods. From the day I first saw the Beast of the Woods, my life had changed. At that moment, I was set on a journey that would lead me to discover that an old, out-of-print story about a prince was true, that *The Story*, as we had decided to call it, contained information about a gate that could save our world from the Great Beasts of the Southern Mountains, and that General Delaney was actually working for the enemy.

Now I was on a mission from the Prince himself to take *The Story* to the four corners of the earth, the four countries that were once connected by land bridges, and find the mysterious gate of which it spoke. Though I wasn't entirely sure why *The Story* had to be taken to the four corners of the earth, the Prince had told me to do so, and I felt a strange sense of duty to follow his command. For the past six months, with the help of Captain Nathaniel Bates and the crew of the *Lyonsword*, Solace, Nadia, Ivan, Otto, and I had finished setting up a network of connections established by the person who had originally copied down *The Story*. Ruth, the Prince's betrothed. How she had survived all this time, we had no idea. There were still a lot of unanswered questions. But for now, we needed to focus on the task at hand. The plan was to start by printing copies of *The Story*, since we had no idea where to start searching for the Gate. We would then distribute the books to our contacts in each of the four corners of the earth. After months of planning and working in secret to remain undiscovered by General Delany's army, now I was here, on the *Lyonsword*'s salty deck in the midst of a raging storm, as we rushed to meet with our first contact.

Christopher and I grasped the gunwale as a wave crashed over the ship's port side onto the deck before us, bringing with it a thick gust of salt-scented air. The wave sent the crew scrambling to grab hold of anything that would keep them from being washed overboard. Once the wave had run its course and we could set out again across the soggy deck, Christopher and I fought our way to the door of the captain's quarters and entered, closing the door as fast as we could to prevent the water from following us into the lantern-lit cabin.

"The two halves of *The Story* are together now," said Christopher as we reached for handholds to keep us steady as the ship rolled with the waves. "Though Ben isn't certain he saw every detail during his vision in the Woods, all that Solace and Ben know of *The Story* is written and ready to put in print. All we need is to reach the Eastern Island Country in one piece."

Captain Nathaniel Bates was standing over his map table, hands braced on its edges, his cream-colored blouse free of his night blue captain's jacket. His sleeves hung loose and damp from helping the crew secure the deck when the storm had first arisen.

"Hopefully, accomplishing that task will not get any harder than this storm is already making it," the captain said in a distant voice as he stared at his maps. He gripped the table to keep himself steady as the ship moved below us. "We have just started this journey, and we still have to make it to all four corners of the earth with *The Story*. That won't happen if we all die," he said under his breath, still focused on his maps. His eyes darted over them as if searching for something.

I glanced at Christopher with a questioning look to see if he knew what the captain was looking for, but Christopher just shrugged and whispered, "Don't look at me. I have been out there all day." He gestured to the door and the battle with nature that was taking place beyond its solid boundary.

I turned back to the captain to see his response to our whispering, but he was too focused to hear Christopher's words. In an attempt to see what demanded such attention, I grabbed on to the map table and leaned over to look at the map the captain was so intently focused on. As I was not a sailor, I saw nothing enlightening, so I decided to simply ask. "What's wrong?"

The captain made a sound just short of a grunt and shook his head. "The storm has blown us off course, and we have entered dangerous waters," he explained in an ominous tone. "We need a way out..." He trailed off and was silent for a moment. "But the storm is pushing us further into danger," he mumbled as he ran his index finger over a section of the map he was studying.

"What makes this area dangerous?" I asked, straightening as much as my firm grip on the table would allow. "We are in neutral waters. No one really defends these parts, save a few pirates. But they wouldn't attack in a storm like this...would they?"

"I am not worried about pirates," said Captain Bates, finally pulling his gaze from the maps to look at me. "There is a reason these waters are not claimed by any country," he explained, frowning. "We have drifted into the leviathans' favored hunting grounds."

"The last time we encountered a leviathan was right before we met you," explained Christopher with a slight shiver. "It took us two weeks to repair the damages, and we barely kept our hidden dock a secret because we had to bring in so many supplies. That is why we usually take a longer route to the Eastern Island," he finished with a shrug.

"Only two weeks?" I said. "That doesn't seem like a big fix." I might not be a sailor, but I did know that fixing a badly damaged ship was not an easy or fast job, especially if the hull was damaged.

"It was big for this ship," he said with a confused frown, as if that should be obvious.

I didn't fully understand what Christopher was talking about, but I shrugged and moved on, turning back to the captain. "Do you think we will run into one?" I asked, concerned. "A leviathan, I mean."

"I am not sure," replied the captain. "But if we do, we need to be ready for the fight of our lives. These waters are their home, and it takes a considerable amount of injury to convince one to abandon a meal like a ship full of people."

I let out a heavy breath and leaned over the map table again. *All we need right now is a sea monster added to the growing collection of things that want us all dead,* I thought to myself as I remembered our last encounter with Valdra and his soldiers. Only a sword with power I didn't yet fully understand had driven off my old comrade turned enemy, but we all knew he was coming after us. It was just a matter of time.

"Well," I said out loud, "tell me about the leviathans. I have heard stories, but I have never seen one. Maybe we can put together a plan."

The captain straightened, grabbed a rope drooping from the ceiling, and braced himself in a shoulder-width stance that kept him on his feet as the ship rolled beneath him. "To put it simply, these creatures are essentially indestructible with the tools we have on board."

Christopher placed a hand on the edge of the map table opposite me, leaving his other hand free to steady himself on a beam above his head. "They are massive, aggressive, ravenous carnivores that are extremely territorial and covered in impenetrable scales," he added.

I bent further over the map table to examine the area we were passing through. Now that I knew what to look for, I spotted our general location immediately. I could see that the area of ocean we were traveling through was marked with a small image of a long creature that resembled a wingless dragon. Unfortunately, we were still three days away from the Eastern Island Country, which meant we would have to be extremely fortunate to encounter any ships in a storm like this in this exact location. So, we were on our own. If we got in a fight now, the only tools we would have to fight back with would be what we had on board, which, according to Captain Bates, wouldn't be enough to kill a leviathan.

"Are you sure you don't have anything that can penetrate their scales?" I asked.

"We're sure," replied Christopher. "The scales are thicker and harder than anything I have seen. They can't be penetrated by arrows, swords, or even harpoons," he said hopelessly.

I looked at the captain with raised eyebrows. "Then how did you all survive last time?"

"One of General Delaney's warships showed up, and the leviathan went after them instead," replied the captain. "We barely made it out of there alive."

"The *Punisher*, wasn't it? We saw them on that first trip we took with you and your crew," I said with hope. "If they survived the leviathan attack, then there must be a way to defeat one."

"It is less a matter of defeating one and more a matter of convincing it that eating us all is not worth the trouble," said the captain. He paused for a moment in thought, then asked, "Where is Nadia?"

I gestured toward the door. "Last I saw, she was on deck with the rest of the crew, trying to keep everything from floating away. Why?"

"Tell her I need her in here," the captain responded. "Her and Ivan both. They have good minds for this sort of thing, and we need a feasible plan in case we do run into a leviathan. If we all die, the only copy of the true story will be lost," he said as he met my gaze.

"Yes, captain," I replied with a quick, respectful nod.

Before I could turn to leave, the captain asked, "Has Otto found anything about the writing on the sword?"

The mysterious sword Ruth had given me, which had somehow caused Valdra to retreat from our last encounter without much of a fight, had on its blade a sentence written in a language none of us had ever seen before, and Otto had been trying to figure out what it said.

I shook my head. "Unless something has changed since I last saw him, about an hour ago, he still has nothing," I replied. "The books Otto brought with him came up empty on any trace of the language in history, just like all the other books he has read over the past six months. Solace has been helping him scour every language we have been able to track down, and none seem to be similar enough to help Otto decode the language. Apparently, they came across some small similarities to other languages, but Otto says there's not enough of the language on the sword..." I trailed off. "Well, in short, no," I said with a frown. "And it hasn't helped that Otto has been distracted thinking about returning to the Eastern Island Country without his mother."

"Why?" asked Christopher in confusion.

"Otto is from the Eastern Island Country," I explained. "He left to find his mother, and he is none too happy to be returning without her. I think he is afraid he will run into his father and have to explain that he failed," I finished as Christopher and the captain gave silent nods of understanding.

"Well, how about the Gate? Any success figuring out how to find it?" the captain asked skeptically.

"Nope," I said with raised eyebrows and a shake of my head. "Still nothing."

"Doesn't *The Story* say anything about it?" asked Christopher.

"Yes, but nothing definitive. It says a few things about hope and truth. But we have hope, and we have truth…" I shrugged. "I don't know what to do without Ruth. She is the only one I know who knows anything about this stuff."

The captain nodded as he briefly grasped my shoulder, offering reassurance. "Well, stick with it. If we still can't find her by the time we finish getting *The Story* delivered to our contacts, we will have to figure it out ourselves."

"If it comes to that, we are going to have to go back to the Woods," I reminded the captain. We would need to speak with the Beast of the Woods, the creature that had shown me *The Story* was true and had been present when the events of *The Story* occurred. But the Woods were located in the heart of what we now knew was enemy territory. The Town, right next to the Woods, was controlled by General Delaney.

Captain Bates nodded. "I know." He rubbed his chin in thought. "For now, let's just focus on getting *The Story* out there."

"How are we going to keep track of all the people who have been given *The Story* and those who still want *The Story*?" I wondered out loud as the thought occurred to me.

The captain surprised me with an answer. "I have taken care of that. As you know, once we get a few copies of *The Story*, we will take them to contacts who will ensure they are printed and distributed. I have ensured that those contacts can keep track of anyone who wants a copy of *The Story* without alerting General Delaney."

I grinned. "This is why I chose you to help. You always think of everything."

Captain Bates chuckled. "Never assume I have thought of everything, my friend. One day, I might not be by your side," he said, placing his strong hand on my shoulder.

I smiled. "I hope to never see that day. But I will heed your wise counsel." With a respectful nod, I left the captain and his first mate to map a path out of this storm while I went in search of the Kuzmich twins, Nadia and Ivan.

As soon as I opened the door, I was greeted by a wave crashing across the deck. I pulled my collar up and hunkered down as I followed the gunwale toward the nearest crewmen I could see through the rain. Thankfully, the two figures turned out to be Dan and Casey. They spent the most time with Ivan and Nadia, so they were my best shot at finding the twins without wandering around the dangerously wet and pitching deck.

"Where are Nadia and Ivan?" I yelled over the sound of the raging storm when I reached them.

Casey squinted through his sopping wet, usually shaggy brown hair and thumbed toward the center of the deck as he yelled back, "We got everything tied down, so they went below deck to check on Otto and Solace."

"Is Yuuki down there too?" I asked as I realized I hadn't seen her in a while. She was probably with Solace since that is where I saw her last, but she was an adventurous little girl, and the last thing I needed was her trying to come above deck to watch the storm.

"Sure is!" Dan yelled over the storm as he gripped the gunwale with one hand and wiped his dripping blond hair away from his face. "I saw Solace snag her a few minutes ago just before she made it through the hatch onto the deck. Thought for sure such a young child would be worried about the storm, but she seems to be the calmest person aboard!" He laughed.

Yuuki certainly was a brave little girl at five years old. Solace and I had more or less adopted her to protect her from General Delaney and his soldiers after she had followed us—initially without our knowledge—on our misdirected journey to find a doctor. We had hoped the doctor would show us how to lure the Beast out of the Woods, but it turned out he had been part of a plot to kill us all before we discovered the truth of *The Story*. That journey would have been a complete waste of time if we hadn't discovered General Delaney's treachery. Our discovery of his attempt to lure us to our death in pursuit of the doctor had actually turned out to be the revelation we needed to get us where we were now. And to be honest, we wouldn't have made that discovery without Yuuki.

Rather than trying to speak over the waves and wind again, I just smiled and nodded to Dan and Casey before trudging off toward the hatch that led below deck. Before I reached the hatch, another wave rose above the ship's starboard side and crashed across the deck. As I scrambled for cover and a grip on anything solid and unmoving, I heard a distant call for help.

"Man overboard!" yelled a crewman named Eric as he peered over the ship's port side, searching for the source of the call.

I ran to the gunwale with Dan and Casey right behind me. I scanned the raging waves and quickly saw what I was looking for. One of the crew had been caught up in the wave and washed over the side of the ship, and he was now struggling to keep his head above water. Without hesitating, I stripped off my pistols and my boots and gave them to Dan, making sure I had my knife in my belt just in case. I grabbed one end of a rope that Eric had brought with him when he heard the cry for help, and I tied it around my waist about twenty feet back from one end, leaving enough rope to safely tie to the overboard crew member. "Eric, when I grab him, pull us back up!" I yelled over the salty wind.

Without hesitating, Eric tied down the other end of the rope, and four other crew members stood by, waiting to help pull us back up. I climbed up on the gunwale and dove into the raging waters below. I plunged into the cold waves, my clasped hands breaking the surface first, and was immediately pushed farther under by a wave crashing above me. Fighting the turbulent waters, I swam toward what I hoped was the surface.

As I broke the surface, I heard someone calling out. "Help me! I'm over here!"

I looked toward the sound of the voice just in time to see the man get sucked under the crashing waves. I dove underwater in an attempt to swim under a wave instead of through it and kicked out in the direction of the crewman. As I reached him and emerged from the water, I noted he was more a boy than a man. He looked to be around fifteen and on the verge of severe panic.

Keeping my distance so he wouldn't shove me underwater in a desperate attempt to keep himself above the waves, I called out to him, motioning as best I could with my hands. "I am going to toss you a rope! Tie it around your chest up under your arms. I need you to stay calm, or you will drown us both!" The boy nodded as best he could, and I tossed him the section of the rope I had left hanging from my waist.

The boy had just finished tying off the rope when we were suddenly yanked backward in the direction of the ship. I turned just in time to see the very thing I had wished to never witness. A leviathan erupted from the water near the ship's stern. Its dark green scaled head was enormous, and its jaws opened wide, revealing rows of teeth half the size of Yuuki. It had bumped the ship before breaking the surface, causing the ship to lurch and pull us with it. I suddenly felt another jolt in the opposite direction and turned to see what had caused it. In a panic, the young crewman was attempting to swim in the opposite direction of the ship.

"No!" I yelled. "Come this way. The only place that might be safe is on the ship!" The boy looked at me with panic in his eyes. "What is your name?" I asked in an attempt to distract him from our disastrous circumstances.

"L...Luke," he replied through chattering teeth.

"Luke, I need you to stay calm. Eric will pull us back as soon as he can." The boy nodded as he tried to force himself to relax. Abruptly, we both froze. The cold water below us swirled around our feet. Something was moving beneath us. I looked back at the ship. The leviathan was no longer above water. It had spotted easier prey.

The dark blue, eerily cold water below us suddenly shifted with a new force, and I felt something move dangerously close to my legs. I took a deep breath and then looked below the water's surface. What I saw sent a jolt through my body, and I nearly inhaled water in a brief moment of panic as I, too, had to force myself to stay calm. The leviathan had taken a dive. Its tail had stirred the water below us as it plunged into the deep, cold waters, and soon it would turn, coming straight at us from the dark depths of the ocean below.

I broke the surface and turned to the ship, frantically waving both hands to get Eric's attention. "Eric! Pull us up!" I yelled over the sound of the crashing waves and wind, hoping he could hear my call.

Thankfully, he either heard or saw me, and we lurched yet again as Eric and the crew pulled us toward the ship. As soon as we got to the ship's side, I turned and scanned the water around us for the creature that had pegged us as its dinner. When I didn't see anything, I grabbed the rope connecting me to Luke and pulled Luke close so I could help him move the rope down to his waist. "Place your feet on the side of the ship like I do and hold on to the rope between us," I shouted. "Walk up the side of the ship exactly as I do, and don't slip!" When he nodded in confirmation that he had heard me, I turned around and held onto the rope that extended up the side of the ship. I placed my feet on the side of the boat, and we walked up the ship's hull as we were pulled from the merciless, raging waters, keeping our hips low with each step that took us closer to safety.

Just as we reached the railing of the gunwale, the leviathan burst from the waves again. Salt water splashed in every direction as Eric and the other crew members managed to pull us over the gunwale and onto the waterlogged deck just as the monster's jaws snapped shut on empty air, missing us by a hair. The leviathan hit the gunwale and slipped partially back into the water.

With no time to lose, we all scrambled to our feet, and I untied the rope around Luke's waist before getting started on mine. But as I started on my section of the rope, I heard a growl from behind me that seemed to echo within the monster. I turned to see the leviathan rise over the gunwale for another strike. Abandoning the rope knot, I dove to one side, pushing Luke out of the way and causing him to let go of the tail of the rope that had been around his waist. The leviathan attacked, but one of the crewmen who had helped us aboard couldn't get out of the way fast enough. Just barely missing my feet, the leviathan's head landed on the deck, crushing a section of the gunwale as it sank its teeth into the crewman and the tail of the rope Luke had dropped that was still attached to my waist. Having snagged some prey, the leviathan retreated once again into the waves, the trailing section of the rope still tied around my waist trapped between its bloodied teeth. The nearest crewman jumped forward, trying to grab at me, but he was too late, and the slack in the rope began to tighten.

Frantically, I struggled to untie the rope from my waist, but my fingers were too wet and cold. I could not get a decent grip. As I fought with the knot, the rope's slack was taken up, and I was yanked toward the gunwale once again. I fumbled for my knife and started to saw through the rope as I was jerked and dragged toward the gunwale, and my death. Time seemed to slow, but what happened next probably only took seconds. Realizing where I was headed, I spun onto my back, sliding feet first toward the damaged railing and the water below as I tried to aim for a section of the gunwale that was still intact. I was sawing as fast as I could when my feet hit the gunwale, and the weight of the leviathan jerked my back off the deck. I would have certainly gone airborne, but I pressed my feet against the gunwale and pushed with all my might as I sawed at the rope with my knife. The rope snapped. I flew backward and fell to the deck, landing flat on my back as the rope vanished over the edge of the gunwale without me.

I coughed and gasped for several long seconds, the wind knocked out of me, until I was finally able to let out a complete sigh of relief. I rolled over onto my side and lay still for a moment, catching my breath. But the moment of relief didn't last long as Eric suddenly pulled me to my feet just as a wave crashed over us, and we were sent rolling to the opposite side of the ship. The rest of the crew scrambled to safer positions while Eric and I headed to the hatch that led below deck, and we slipped inside just before yet another massive wave crashed across the main deck.

As the hatch closed and water rained down on us, we both sank to the steps and looked at each other. Soaking wet, I could feel water streaming out of my clothes. Eric's short, curly red hair seemed to repel water, but even he looked as though he had gone for a swim fully dressed. After taking a moment to comprehend what had just happened, we both allowed ourselves a smile of relief that Luke had survived. But the loss of the other crewman seemed to sit heavy on Eric's shoulders.

"Thanks for the save," I said with a smile, trying to take his mind off the tragedy neither of us could change. For now, we would all just have to move on, until there was time to mourn the loss properly.

Eric forced a grin, his blue eyes brightening slightly as his lightly freckled face broke into a smile that could cheer even the grumpiest person. "Any time, my friend. Thanks for getting Luke out of that mess," he added.

"Is he new? I don't remember him from the last time we were on the ship," I commented.

Eric nodded with raised eyebrows. "Very new—"

A loud thump came from outside the ship, and Eric and I were both pulled back into the moment. Reminded that we were still in a fight, and a storm, Eric and I jumped to our feet and ran to tell everyone below deck that we needed all hands on deck to fight the leviathan.

"Get some crew to the oars. Maybe we can help the captain maneuver the ship!" I called to Eric.

But he turned and gave me a confused frown. "What oars? There are no oars on this ship."

"There were oars last time I was on board." But even as I said it, I didn't recall seeing any oars when I had boarded the *Lyonsword* this time.

"Well, they aren't here anymore. Find the twins—they can help," he called before tuning to go ensure that everyone was headed to their posts.

Pushing the ship's mysterious lack of oars from my mind, I went in search of Solace, Otto, and the twins. While Nadia and Ivan usually bunked in the forecastle cabin with much of the crew, when we had set out on this journey, the captain had decided it might be better for Solace, Otto, Yuuki, and me to bunk on the lower deck. Having a space below the main deck gave us a bit more room to work on the books and also gave us faster access to the smuggler holes in the ship's cargo hold where we could hide what we were working on in case of an emergency. Working on the lower deck meant we all spent a lot of time down there, including the twins. Solace and Otto had been using a corner as

Solace checked *The Story*, which I had written down, for any errors and Otto searched old texts for hints about the language and the Gate, and the twins often helped. But, when I checked the lower deck workstation, I didn't find anyone. So, I went down one more level to the cargo hold and found Solace on the hunt for a dry place to stash *The Story*.

"We need all hands on deck, Solace. A leviathan is attacking!" I said urgently.

She spun and looked at me. Though she had no way to know if I had been soaked by the rain or from going overboard, she could tell something had happened. It was a skill she had somehow picked up since we had gotten engaged five months ago, and it had only grown since we had married just over a week ago, the day we had left on this voyage. Having both endured multiple near-death experiences, we had wasted no time in making things official.

"What happened to you?" she asked in surprise as the ship rocked to one side and we both stumbled to grab a handhold.

"It's a long story, and I'll tell you later. For now, grab a weapon. I'll find Nadia and Ivan."

"They are back there." She pointed toward the opposite side of the cargo hold. "They were helping me find a good place to keep the book safe in case this ship gets torn apart by the storm."

I planted a quick kiss on Solace's lips in thanks, then turned toward the bow side of the hold. Before I made it halfway, Ivan and Nadia appeared. "We are needed on the main deck," I said urgently.

"Ya don't say! What was the noise?" asked Ivan. "Did we run into something?"

"Not exactly. More like something ran into us," I said as I led all three of them upstairs, passing Otto, who was hiding in a corner trying to keep his notebooks dry as water dripped through small gaps in the deck above. I paused briefly and told him to keep an eye on Yuuki, who was already helping him. Not waiting for Otto to protest the instruction, I opened the hatch, and we climbed out onto the windy, wet main deck. As Ivan, Nadia, and Solace looked to the waves, they saw what had caused the sound. The leviathan rose above the port side of the ship, its teeth bared, poised to strike yet again.

Ivan and Nadia were immediately at the ready. "The captain wants your ideas on how to stop it," I yelled over the wind. "It has already taken one of us, we have no help, and we cannot pierce its scales with any weapon."

Nadia looked at the massive creature. "Yeah, but we can pierce the inside of its body!" she yelled over the storm.

"How do we do that?" I asked as I lifted my arm to shield my face from the pouring rain.

"We get inside!" said Ivan with way too much excitement.

"You get the harpoon, and Ivan and I will get its attention," yelled Nadia over the wind.

I nodded, understanding, and we got to work. Nadia and Ivan trudged toward the monster with swords held high, and Solace and I grabbed the harpoon with its large arrow almost as tall as Ivan, a massive, barbed metal arrowhead on the tip. Since this animal was essentially unkillable, we just had to convince it to find food elsewhere. To do that, we would have to do some damage. The inside of the leviathan's body was the softest part, so we would have to get inside its mouth. Ivan was crazy enough to go in there himself, but he couldn't do enough damage with his sword, so we would need to be ready with the harpoon.

Ivan charged at the creature, getting its attention just in time to stop it from biting down on the ship. The rope that had been around my waist was still dangling from its mouth, and Ivan grabbed hold of it and started climbing while Nadia distracted the huge animal by firing arrows at it. The arrows simply bounced off its thick scales, but they at least kept the leviathan's attention away from Ivan. As I loaded the only harpoon we had on board, Solace took one of my twin matchlock pistols and started firing at the monster, careful not to hit Ivan. The crew followed Nadia and Solace's lead as the captain kept the ship under control as best he could.

Once Ivan had reached the monster's mouth, he grabbed one of the large scales on its temple and waved a hand in front of its eye. As I finished prepping the harpoon, the monster snapped in Ivan's direction. Its mouth opened, and Ivan jumped directly into it with his sword drawn. The leviathan's jaws locked shut around Ivan, and a moment of tense hesitation fell over the ship.

For an instant, I thought the leviathan would retreat into the waves with its catch as it had before. But suddenly, the leviathan jerked backward in pain and confusion. To my relief, instead of retreating into the water, its jaws sprang open, revealing Ivan standing with his sword over his head, stabbed into the roof of the sea monster's mouth. As the leviathan's mouth opened, it let out a sound that was somehow a deep rumble and an ear-piercing screech at the same time. Without a moment to spare, I aimed the harpoon directly at the back of the monster's throat, and just as Ivan jumped clear of its jaws, I fired. As Ivan slid down the rope, the harpoon sailed through the air and went straight into the monster's mouth, piercing the large U-shaped flesh hanging in the back of its throat. The animal let out another cry, and Dan and Casey immediately began cutting the harpoon's rope to allow the monster to leave. The ship creaked as the leviathan pulled back in pain and swung a clawed fin toward its mouth. Dan and Casey worked at the rope until, finally, it snapped, and the leviathan vanished beneath the waves.

Chapter 2

The storm raged on for the remainder of the evening and through the night. With the leviathan gone, the captain was able to steer the ship back on course. Though we still had to fight the wind and waves, we eventually made it to safe waters. But it was not until morning that the sails were raised, and we continued our voyage on a calm ocean, propelled by a smooth, constant breeze.

As the sun rose before us, we held a moment of silence for our lost crew member. Experiencing such a loss wasn't an encouraging way to start this mission, but it reminded us all of what was at stake. Many of us had lost loved ones in the wars with the Great Beasts of the Southern Mountains. Wars this mission was trying to put an end to. It was a dangerous mission, but failure would trap us in a world where such deaths at the claws of the Great Beasts would become far too commonplace. An outcome none of us were willing to allow. But I couldn't help but wonder, *Are we chasing false hope?*

When the moment of silence came to an end, Christopher and I helped the rest of the crew go through the cargo that was on the main deck and look over the ship to make sure nothing significant had been lost or damaged and the ship could make it to port. I was surprised that we had made it out of the fight with only minimal damage, considering our opponent, and we would have time for repairs once we docked at our secret smugglers' cave on the Eastern Island three evenings from now. However, we would have to spend most of our last three days on the sea fixing what we could and cleaning up the deck.

"What did we lose?" asked Captain Bates as he approached Christopher, Eric, and me.

"Thankfully, not much," said Christopher. "We were able to tie down everything important. We lost a few weapons and a barrel of whiskey. But I think we can do without it until we get to land."

"Any injuries?" asked the captain, his jaw set as he scanned his ship and those still aboard. The loss of his crewman was not something he took lightly.

"Luke has a gash on his head from when he went overboard. It's a miracle he didn't get knocked out," commented Eric. He shrugged. "But he should be fine. Otto took care of it."

Captain Bates nodded. "Keep me appraised and make sure this ship gets cleaned from bow to stern," he ordered.

With clipped nods and a united "Yes, Captain," we got to work as the captain did his rounds, checking on his crew and ship.

As the captain moved on, joined by Christopher, a crew member named Catherine approached. Her dark, almost black hair hung long and wavy, and a few thin braids were pulled back into a small bun behind her head. She was one of the crew's best fighters and well known for her teasing personality. Much like Ivan, she had a knack for lifting people's spirits.

"You two still in one piece?" she asked. "That was quite the rescue, pulling Luke out of the water."

Eric smiled. "It was nothing," he said, standing a little taller.

Catherine laughed. "Yeah, that's because Ben did all the work."

Eric's expression melted into a frown. "Ha ha, very funny."

I grinned at Eric as Catherine walked off, laughing at her own joke. They liked to tease each other, and I hadn't had the faintest idea as to why, until recently. Catherine and Eric were the only couple aboard, apart from me and Solace, but that had been lost on me until Solace pointed it out.

"Why don't you just marry her?" I prompted with a grin.

Eric smiled and shrugged. "Not enough money," he said simply. "We planned on it before we even joined the crew, but to make a life together...we just don't have a place to settle down."

"What do you mean? I know you have enough to pay for the priest and all that," I said with a frown. "Plus, you don't necessarily have to settle down. Solace and I aren't."

Eric nodded. "Catherine wanted to be a farmer before we joined the captain's crew...So did I. But...the land we inherited from our parents was all destroyed in a war," he explained. "We had no choice but to start over."

"What did you do?" I asked, curious. I hadn't asked him about his past before.

"We joined the crew of another ship. A rough bunch led by a man named Gregory Turk, captain of the *Black Siren*. But then Captain Bates caught us stealing from his ship one night. We had stumbled upon his hidden port and decided not to leave empty-handed."

"What happened?" I asked, struggling to imagine how they had come to join this crew after attempting to rob the captain.

Eric pursed his lips and raised his eyebrows. "Well, Captain Bates almost shot us."

"Almost?" I asked.

Eric nodded. "Catherine pulled out her damsel in distress act and got us off the hook." He laughed. "But the captain wasn't as fooled as we thought. He and his crew followed us back to the *Black Siren*, and he paid Turk an unwelcome visit that night."

I placed a barrel back in its rightful corner on the deck and prompted Eric to continue. "I am assuming he didn't take it as a courtesy visit."

Eric shook his head. "Captain Bates told Turk that he didn't take kindly to people stealing from him. The fact that the captain had snuck into Turk's cabin at night without anyone seeing him rattled Turk enough to tell Captain Bates that he would have us executed that night."

I froze. "Really?"

Eric nodded. "We didn't know until two crewmen came and got us. They took us to the main deck where Turk was waiting, but Captain Bates was already gone."

"So, how did you end up here?" I asked with a frown.

"Well, it turns out that Captain Bates is not only good at scaring pirates half to death, but he is also a good man. He told Turk to hang us."

I raised a confused eyebrow. "That sounds like a great thing to do," I said sarcastically.

Eric chuckled. "Yeah, except that he faked our deaths. I don't really know how he did it. He has never told us. We passed out before we even felt the ropes go tight and woke up on this ship without so much as a scratch."

"So, the captain has some tricks up his sleeve," I commented. "Why did he do all that for you?"

"He said he didn't want to waste good talent," said Eric with a shrug. "Whether or not that is the real reason, we don't much care. We are alive, and the captain has been good to us. We have a good life here, and he even pays us when he can. One day we might be able to afford a farm to settle down on because of him." He paused and ran a hand through his hair. "He doesn't run his ship like a soldier, or a pirate, and yet he has been called both," he added with a shrug and a light chuckle.

"And what do you call him?" I asked. In the short time I had known the captain, I had come to see him as a friend. But I did not actually know him all that well. He didn't often talk about his past.

Eric smiled. "Captain."

We chuckled and returned to our work. Figuring out the secrets of Captain Nathaniel Bates would have to wait. The ship was still a mess, and we had been ordered to clean it up. Whether the captain was a soldier, a pirate, or something entirely different, we would gladly do his bidding.

⚜

After two more days of travel and cleaning up the ship as best we could, the deck was finally back in order and there were no more repairs we could do until we reached land. Late that afternoon, Ivan, Nadia, and I left the main deck and headed down to the lower deck in search of Solace and Otto. We found them hunkered over their small table with the book of *The Story* open in front of them. Yuuki was observing from a distance while she played with her rock collection. Otto had his notebook in hand and was looking through *The Story*, writing down what appeared to be the parts of *The Story* that sounded like directions to a gate.

"Have you found anything?" I asked as I sat down next to Solace.

She shook her head. "It talks about hope, truth, faith, and the Gate, but it doesn't tell us where the Gate is," she said with a shake of her head as she rubbed her tired eyes. "It could be in the Woods, but...you said yourself that you didn't see the Gate in the Woods."

"Well, remember, the Prince also told Ben that faith will lead us to the Gate," said Otto flatly. "The problem is that faith is not a map. It can't lead anyone anywhere!" he said irritably, gesturing to the book with both hands, palms up.

"Well, faith can lead you, in a manner of speaking," said Nadia.

"How?" asked Otto.

Nadia rolled her eyes. "It is not literal, Otto. Faith leads people because..." She shrugged as she searched for the right words. "Because they know they can do something."

Otto frowned. "That doesn't make any sense. How would knowing you can do something lead you somewhere or show you a gate?"

Nadia chuckled, and Solace took over. "What Nadia means to say is that when people believe in something, it is easier for them to take action based on their belief in that thing."

"So maybe 'faith will show us the Gate' means that we have to have faith in something, and by having faith in that something, we will be led to the Gate?" suggested Ivan.

Solace shrugged. "That is the only thing I can come up with right now."

I shook my head. "Actually, as I think about it, the Prince said faith would *show* us the Gate, not lead us to it. But either way, what are we supposed to have faith in?"

"*The Story*?" asked Solace.

I lifted my shoulder in a slight shrug. "I don't know. You had faith in *The Story* long before we did, and you've never seen the Gate."

Nadia frowned in thought. "So, faith in—"

The hatch door suddenly opened, interrupting Nadia, and we all turned to see who was coming down the stairs.

"The captain wants to talk to you all," said Christopher as he descended the steps. "We will be docking just after sundown, and he needs to go over the plans with you."

We all stood as Solace put the book away and Otto stowed his notebook in his bed. Once everything was in place, Otto and the twins followed Christopher back up the stairs and toward the captain's quarters.

At the bottom of the stairs, Solace gently pulled me aside and asked, "How have you been sleeping?"

Over the past few months, I had been sleeping sporadically. Ever since my last encounter with the Beast of the Woods, I had been having occasional dreams about the Unseen Lands and the Beast wrapping its tail around my waist to show me the vision of *The Story*. When the Beast of the Woods had wrapped its tail around my waist, just before I saw the vision of *The Story*, there had been a brief flash of an image I hadn't quite understood. An image of a scaled animal giving me what had turned out to be a belt. I hadn't thought much of it at the time since I was distracted by the vision of *The Story*, but then I started having the dreams. The dreams began as just flashes, like when the Beast's tail had encircled my waist. But as we neared the start of this journey, the dreams had grown more vivid, until they showed me the belt in great detail. The belt was made of thick dark brown leather, with a silver metal buckle engraved with small lettering that looked similar to the writing on the sword. The belt looked like it might have been part of a soldier's armor from long ago. Over time, the dreams had been plagued with darkness looming at the edges of the space around me, as well as haunting feelings of guilt. But once we had finally loaded onto the ship and set sail on our mission, the dreams had stopped.

"Not bad, actually," I responded. "Since we started this trip, I have not had any dreams of the Beast or the belt and scaled creature."

"Well, you need to tell me if that changes," she said with concern. "We can't have you exhausted before this mission even properly begins. The journey will be grueling enough as it is, and people already have a tendency to lose their minds on the ocean."

I chuckled. "I will let you know if I start losing my mind," I said, lowering my voice to a comedic whisper for the last three words.

Solace rolled her eyes, but before she could remind me to take this seriously, we were interrupted.

"Benjamin, Solace!" called Christopher. "Let's go!"

We told Yuuki to stay put below deck until we got back, then climbed the stairs and caught up with the others. We entered the captain's quarters to find the captain seated behind his desk, dressed in dry, clean clothes. His night blue captain's jacket was back in place, and he smiled as we approached. "Sorry to interrupt your studies, but we need to discuss a few things before we dock," he said as he stood.

"No problem, Captain," I said. "What is it that we need to discuss?"

The captain moved in front of his desk and leaned against it, crossing his arms. "The contact we are meeting sent out a message. It just arrived by bird."

"I didn't know you had homing pigeons aboard!" said Otto as his face lit up in excitement.

The captain smiled. "There are only a couple on each continent that will come to this ship, and they only come when we are close to port. We developed this method so I could be warned if there was ever trouble waiting at the docks."

"What did the message say?" asked Nadia.

The captain let out a breath. "It explained that Valdra knows we are headed to the Eastern Island Country. He has General Delaney's armies and Martecytes all over the island looking for us. Also, our printing contact has gone into hiding until our meeting date. This message was sent by a friend of mine who has been helping our contact secure supplies."

"Do Valdra and the Martecytes know where we will be docking?" asked Solace with a wince.

"No, but it will be difficult to go anywhere on the island without being spotted. And to make matters worse, Eric found some hidden damage on the *Lyonsword*. He isn't sure how bad it is, but we must get it fixed when we arrive. Though it shouldn't take as long as one might think, it will still add to the list of things we will need to deal with upon arrival."

I rubbed a hand down the back of my neck and paced across the cabin. "We will make it work," I said as I mentally ran through all the things that could go wrong when we reached land. "We will just have to be careful. We need to get these copies of *The Story* made." I turned toward the group. "There is no place that General Delaney and Valdra can't find us. We will be hunted no matter where we go now. We just have to keep going."

The captain nodded. "I am afraid that is not all the message said."

"What was the rest?" I asked, turning abruptly to the captain as I let my hand fall to my side. I didn't want to hear more bad news.

"The printing press we were going to use to print the copies for our contacts was confiscated by Valdra's army. And they have officially convinced the Eastern Island king that we are all criminals," the captain stated calmly.

I heard Ivan groan and Nadia ran a hand over her face in frustration. I scowled. *This is just getting better and better.* "We can still make it work," I said, mostly to convince myself.

Solace stepped to my side and grabbed my hand. "I agree with Ben," she said, looking me in the eye before turning to the others.

Nadia shook her head. "We have never faced anything like this before, Ben. This isn't like having Valdra and his army follow us as he has been for the past six months. This is all of General Delaney's soldiers, all his beasts, all the Martecytes. This is all of them after us in every place we go. It's us against an army," she said intensely. "And we will not be the only ones in danger. Now that everyone thinks we are criminals, we will be putting the people we deliver the book to in danger as well," she said, holding my gaze.

"I don't think it will be all of the enemy, and we will be putting them in more danger if we do nothing," I countered. "The Prince gave us a mission, and it is our duty to carry it out. If we fail, the Prince will have suffered in vain, and we will all be trapped in a land full of darkness, with beasts hunting us every day."

Solace nodded. "The Prince chose us as the last Night Rider. We cannot fail. We have spent the past six months preparing for this. And now we are here. We cannot let Valdra and his Martecytes get in the way of our mission."

Nadia took in a deep breath as she considered the situation. She knew as well as I did that Solace was right. We had been tasked by the Prince and the King to protect *The Story* and spread it to the four corners of the earth. That was the Night Rider's job—to protect *The Story* and those who found hope within its words and, at the command of the Prince, to make the unseen seen.

"I am not saying that I will not fight by your side. I am just saying that we need to be smart about this," Nadia pointed out.

I looked at Nadia. "We will. We can make it work." I let my gaze fall on each person in the room. "But I will not ask any of you to continue if you do not want to."

One by one, they sounded their commitment as Nadia glanced at Ivan. He gave her a grin and nodded. They both turned to me. "We're in," she said.

"Good." I accepted their dedication with a sharp nod. "Let's make a plan then."

"What are we going to do about the printing press?" asked Nadia. "It's old, but it's the only one we could find that Valdra wouldn't be looking for...or so we thought."

"We could steal it back," suggested Ivan.

"I agree with Ivan," said Otto from behind us. We all turned and looked at him in surprise. He never knew what to do in these meetings, so he always sat near the door and watched in silence while we talked.

"Why is that?" I asked in surprise. He rarely agreed with Ivan.

Otto lifted a shoulder in a small shrug, his brown cloak creasing across his chest as he did. "It's just that our options are limited, and even if we do find a different printing press, Valdra's soldiers will just take that one too. While stealing the press would be practically impossible, we don't have much of a choice unless we want to redo all of the planning we've done over the past six months."

I nodded. "He's right," I said, turning to the rest of the group. "If we can find a different one, they can find it too. Plus, we don't have time to go searching for another one if we want to meet up with our contacts on time."

"That might be the case, but if we try to get the press they took, there is a good chance they might catch us and kill us," said Nadia matter-of-factly.

Otto shook his head. "You all are not listening!" he said irritably. "While I do agree with Ivan's brash point of view on this, whether we get caught and killed is a nonissue because one cannot steal a printing press in the first place. Have you ever even seen one? They are not exactly designed to move around quickly or quietly."

The captain considered Otto's point. "That's true, but if we can find where they are keeping it, we might be able to simply use it there rather than take it. But we would likely only have time to print a couple of copies."

The captain's idea seemed to spark something in Otto. "Unless we make sure they have no way of knowing we are there…" suggested Otto in a thoughtful tone.

"How would we do that?" asked Solace.

Otto cleared his throat and, with a pained expression, explained, "There may be something in *The Story* that could help us."

"If it is so helpful, why do you look like you are in pain?" I asked, a little irritated.

Otto pursed his lips. "Well, I am not actually sure how it works, or even if it does anything."

"What is your idea?" Nadia asked, crossing her arms.

"As you all know, Solace and I have been studying *The Story* since we discovered its true form. In my studies, I noticed that it says that the Prince took the corrupted mark of the Chosen and broke it into pieces," said Otto.

I nodded. "Yes, and he made the sword and the shield. What does that have to do with hiding from Valdra's army? We can't fight them while we print books. We'll be vastly outnumbered," I countered.

Otto stood. "No, we can't fight. But there is a chance that we can hide."

"What are you talking about?" asked Ivan, his shoulders slouched. "Just tell us plainly," he moaned.

Solace snapped her fingers. "The shield!"

Otto nodded. "While I have been studying *The Story* for information on what the sword might say and how to find the Gate, I have also been studying the sword and shield's miraculous properties. *The Story* says that the shield will protect you and the sword will help you battle evil. Originally, I thought this was meant literally, but then I remembered the sword's special power. The sword gives its wielder the ability to see the unseen armies of darkness and light, which is necessary in order to fight them. So, what does the shield do?" he prompted.

I glanced at the captain, whose expression seemed to echo how I felt; Otto's point made sense. *If the mark of the Chosen was specially made by the Prince and was broken into pieces, one half forging the sword and one half forging the shield, wouldn't that mean that they both have miraculous properties?* I wondered to myself.

"That is a good point, Otto," I said. From the expressions of the others, I could tell we were all thinking through this new idea.

"If the sword was said to help you fight, it does so by giving you special sight," said the captain. "An army you cannot see is hard to fight against. But it is equally hard to defend against."

"Maybe the shield levels the playing field," proposed Nadia.

"What do you mean?" I asked.

"Well, *The Story* says that it will protect its wielder, right?" We all nodded. "The enemy is protected because we cannot see them. So maybe it will shield its wielder from the enemy's sight!" she exclaimed.

Otto nodded. "Exactly what I was thinking."

I took a deep breath and considered that thought. "That is an interesting idea, but one we have no proof of," I responded.

"Have you used the shield before?" asked Christopher.

"No." I shrugged. "I have never been a huge shield guy."

"Well, you know my solution," Ivan added with a grin.

"Let me guess, to barge into a nest of beasts and see if you vanish under the shield's protection?" suggested Solace with a grin.

We all laughed. But our amusement was short-lived as we realized that Ivan's idea was the only one we had at the moment.

"Well, whether or not Otto's theory is true, we need to focus on first things first," I said. "We need a plan for meeting with our first contact without getting caught by Valdra and his Martecyte army." I turned to the captain. "Is he meeting us at the dock?"

"No, no one but those who make up the Lion's Sword or the *Lyonsword*'s crew know of our secret docking ports," explained the captain with a shake of his head. "But he sent his location in the message. We are to meet him at the old church near the city's southeastern edge."

"I have not been to the Eastern Island Country since I was young, so I am not familiar with its streets or the church," I explained.

The captain nodded. "Solace told me. Otto will have to lead you through town."

I shook my head. "He is the son of one of the most recognizable families on the island. He is too noticeable. Once we get to where we are going, I would prefer he stayed on the ship."

The captain frowned. "And none of you have been there recently enough to remember anything?" he asked, glancing at the others.

"I have never been there," said Solace, while the others just shook their heads.

The captain crossed his arms in thought and leaned back against his map table again.

"We might need Otto, Ben," said Nadia. "He has connections on this island. Whether he leads us to the church or not, I think we should bring him."

The captain nodded in agreement. "She has a point."

"What about Yuuki? She was going to stay behind with Otto," I said.

"She will be fine with the crew," said Captain Bates. "The cook loves having her around to help, and she and the cat have struck up a friendship. I'm sure she will enjoy staying on board with the crew until we get back from the castle."

I frowned. "Okay, fine. Otto can come. But we need to keep him out of sight as much as possible," I said.

"The captain should come too," Otto said worriedly. "What if something goes wrong and we need him, or the contact doesn't let us in? He doesn't know any of us."

"He's not wrong," I said, looking to the captain. "I know we planned this so we could meet the contacts with or without you, but I would hate for things to go sideways with this first one just because you weren't there."

There was a moment of silence as we waited for the captain's reply.

Seeing the captain's hesitation, Christopher politely broke the silence. "I and the rest of the crew will be stuck in port fixing the ship, and we can do that without you."

Captain Bates looked at him and spoke sternly. "I do not wish to leave my crew when we are trapped on an island swarming with the enemy."

Christopher crossed his arms and met the captain's eyes. "Your crew know full well that you would never abandon them."

The captain held Christopher's gaze for a moment. Then he simply nodded to his first mate. "I know." Captain Bates looked to me. "I will come with you and lead you through town. I know of all the secret passages and people who would gladly welcome us into their homes no matter the cost if need be."

I nodded. "Then it is decided. We will dock after sundown and head to the old church to meet the contact with the captain as our guide." I turned to Otto. "You need to stay out of sight. Keep your face covered, and don't talk to anyone."

Otto nodded. "I don't talk much anyway."

Nadia and Ivan grinned at Otto's comment.

"What?" he asked, his voice rising slightly in irritation.

"You definitely talk a lot," commented Christopher with a grin.

Otto crossed his arms defensively. "I only speak when I think you are in need of my assistance."

The captain smiled as the rest of us laughed. "And it is a good thing, too, my friend," he said as he clasped Otto's shoulder with a firm grip. "I am sure we would be lost without you."

Everyone laughed and Otto's eyelids drooped in annoyance.

With the plans in place, we sat down to eat a meal while the sun set and the stars gradually appeared in the ever-darkening sky. As the sun's light faded to only a slight yellow haze on the horizon, the *Lyonsword* approached the captain's secret, hidden docking port on the southwestern tip of the Eastern Island Country, a little ways away from where the main city lay on the southern edge of the island.

The southwestern side of the kidney-shaped Eastern Island was characterized by rocky terrain that provided a sectioned-off cavern large enough to hold a ship of the *Lyonsword*'s size. Once we had docked in the well-concealed port that the captain had long ago set up to accommodate this kind of stop, we waited for Dan and

Casey to check the perimeter while the captain went over the route we would take to reach the church.

"The church we are looking for is located east of here," explained the captain, "just on the other side of the docks. We will need to approach it on foot, because the Castle Guard has a clear view of the water on the southern side of the island. On foot, it will be a bit of a trek, but not too bad. The trail we will be taking is relatively hidden until we get to the edge of town, but we will still have to keep quiet and stay close. Once we get past the docks, the church is concealed near the beach."

I nodded. "When does the contact expect us?"

"He said he would wait until an hour before sunrise. If we do not arrive by then, he will assume we were caught," responded the captain.

When Dan and Casey returned with the "all clear" signal, Solace, Otto, Ivan, Nadia, Captain Bates, and I joined them and headed out, leaving Christopher and Eric in charge of the ship and Yuuki in their care. We stuck close to the water and stayed concealed in the trees and rocks. No one spoke during the journey, and thankfully we made it to the edge of town uninterrupted.

"That was unnervingly easy," I whispered as I crept up next to the captain, who was crouched behind the outermost building of the city.

"Exactly what I was thinking," he said as his eyes scanned the area for trouble. "We need to be cautious."

"What if Valdra has caught our contact?" asked Nadia. "And how do we know the Martecytes won't be waiting for us at the church? It could be a trap."

"We are stuck on this island until the *Lyonsword* is fixed. We can either give up now and go back to the ship or run the risk and hope our contact hasn't been discovered," I said, looking at each person. "You all know what is at stake."

"I say we run the risk," said Ivan.

We all smiled. Typical Ivan. I turned to the captain. "Lead the way, Captain."

Captain Bates pulled his hood up so it cast his face in shadow, and we all followed suit as we entered the outskirts of town. This city was the largest in the Eastern Island Country and was well known for its modest buildings and clean streets. The city was well taken care of and had a booming economy, and the king had a reputation for treating his subjects with respect. However, the city was not free of ill deeds, for though the citizens tried to ignore them, there were plenty of unscrupulous dealings after dark. As in most towns, the area near the docks, where we were headed, was not the most civilized. At this time of night, the only people out and about were either intoxicated or just as keen on staying hidden as we were. Though the streets were relatively empty, we stayed to their edges and ducked down dark alleyways whenever we could.

We followed the captain as he led us through side streets along the edge of town, but as we neared the docks, hiding became more and more difficult. The docks smelled of fish and were full of cargo, some of which was being loaded onto ships by crews from a few of the sketchier shipping companies. Other stacks of cargo were waiting to be loaded in the morning onto ships owned by Otto's father, who ran the leading shipping business on the island.

"Does your father know where you have been?" Solace whispered to Otto as we passed a crate that was labeled "Bilden Shipping Co."

Otto nodded. "For the most part. He knows I went to look for Mother. But he was doubtful that I would find her, and..." His voice trailed off.

"What?" asked Solace.

"I refused his help." He glanced at the shipping label. "I always had a hard time with riches. I got lost in them, and it wasn't until my mother went missing that I realized other things in life were much more important."

"What happened?" Solace asked as we settled behind another crate and waited for the captain's signal to move.

Otto lifted his shoulder in a small shrug. "I was afraid I would get pulled into the world of extravagant wealth again, so I refused his financing and left."

"Did you leave on good terms?" she asked.

Otto pursed his lips. "Not sure," he said simply.

"I'm sure your father is proud of you," said Nadia as she placed a gentle hand on his arm. Otto blushed and swallowed hard before looking away. I glanced at Solace with my eyebrows raised and gestured toward Nadia and Otto, but Solace just held back a smile and shrugged.

"Shh," came a gentle reminder from the captain. "We are about to pass through the busiest section of the docks, so everyone needs to remain silent from here on out," he said.

We all nodded, then followed the captain as he wove his way through the various cargo containers and shipments. The area was dimly lit by a few lanterns, but thankfully the moon was mostly covered tonight by clouds. Suddenly, the captain stopped and held up a hand. We all shrank into the nearest shadow and held our breath as the sounds of two men's voices grew closer.

"Did you hear about the message that General Delaney's right-hand man delivered to the king, *personally*?" one voice asked. From the way he emphasized the last word, it was clear that was not a common occurrence.

"Yeah, something about a group of criminals who tried to kill General Delaney," the second voice responded.

"He thinks they are headed here," said the first voice. "Word is that they are planning to tear down the monarchy. He told the king they will likely try to overthrow him as they attempted to do to General Delaney."

"But General Delaney's is not a king. Why would they go after him?" said the second voice.

"He is the richest man in the world, and he knows more about the beasts than anyone else! He helps finance every war against the beasts and cover the cost of repairs for all the damage they cause. And it was him and his ancestors who found ways to kill the beasts. Without General Delaney, many countries would fall, and their rulers would be overthrown by angry, starving people," the first man explained. "With General Delaney gone, kings from around the world would have no way to rebuild their cities and towns after the wars, and the beasts would run rampant. Life as we know it would cease to exist."

I looked at the captain. It was clear we were both thinking the same thing. If General Delaney had convinced the king and his people that we were a threat to the king's safety, we were in more trouble than we had initially thought.

The two men grabbed some supplies and disappeared around a corner, still discussing the situation. The captain held his ground with his hand raised, waiting until their voices had completely faded before swinging his hand forward, motioning us all to continue following him.

Chapter 3

WE MOVED THROUGH THE rest of the docks relatively quickly and with no more interruptions. When we reached the eastern edge of the docks, the shipyard gave way to a beach about fifty yards long. Toward the far end of the beach, the city ended abruptly at the edge of a forest, which separated the city from the castle property. A thin bank of trees acted as a barrier between the city and the small beach, with the old church nestled up against the tree line, long forgotten and well concealed by years of overgrowth. If we were to continue east through the forest, we would end up at the castle, a magnificent building carved into the cliffs on the edge of the island, where the eastern king could keep watch over both the island inhabitants and the ocean.

The old church had long since been abandoned. Its once white paint was now a dirty, weather-stained brown, pealing underneath vines that had overtaken the church's base and steeple. The windows had all been boarded up, though the front door hung loose on only one hinge.

The captain stopped us at the edge of the beach, hidden in some bushes that had grown up over a long-forgotten trail left by the people who had once attended the church. We waited in silence as the captain scanned the area, and Nadia, Ivan, and I checked behind us. When we were sure we had not been followed and no one was lying in wait, the captain moved out once again. Rather than leave footprints in the sand leading directly to the church, we slipped through the bushes, careful not to leave a readily apparent impact on the overgrowth. We entered the old church through a worn side door whose locks and boards had been broken by some kind of animal that had clawed its way in, likely looking for warmth during the winter.

With the windows boarded up, the church was quite dark, and we all had to be careful not to trip over old pews, fallen boards, and various piles of decomposing plant life, probably gathered as bedding by the animal that had broken the side door. Thankfully, it looked as though whatever had lived here had abandoned the building some time ago. Thin beams of moonlight shone between cracks in the walls and windows and sliced through the darkness at various angles around us, making some corners seem darker than others. The smell of damp wood, dying plants, and the nearby ocean filled the air as Captain Bates signaled us to spread out and check the building for anyone lying wait. Once we were sure no threats were hidden in the depths of the church's darkened corners, we moved through the main room to a door in the back of the church that probably led into some type of back room, perhaps once an office of sorts.

The captain lifted a fist and gently tapped a knuckle on the door before saying, "I am here to see a friend."

From the other side of the door, a voice whispered, "What friend?"

The captain replied, "A friend of the carpenter."

In response to the captain's words, the door opened, and we were all ushered into the room by a middle-aged man in a dark cloak. "I am glad you made it, friend," the man exclaimed quietly as he closed the door behind us before clasping the captain's forearm. The captain returned the gesture with a grin, and they pulled each other into a brief hug like old friends.

As they released their embrace, the captain turned to me with a hand on his comrade's shoulder. "Lance, this is Benajmin Arlin. Benjamin, meet Lance Sather. This old church was once run by his great-grandfather. Lance was taught how to use a printing press by his mother, who used to work for the biggest printing company in the Northern Country. Now, he has agreed to help us out."

I reached out, and we clasped forearms in greeting. "Thank you, we really appreciate your assistance."

"It is my pleasure!" Lance announced, his bright smile framed by long blond hair pulled back in a low ponytail. "When I was still just a boy, my mother was kicked out of her printing job for printing an article on this very story. Her employers hid the truth and spread rumors that she was kicked out for other reasons, and her reputation was ruined. General Delaney has been keeping *The Story* from being printed for decades now. I am happy to help put it back in print."

I nodded, then turned to the others and briefly introduced the rest of the group to Lance. They shook forearms, and Lance greeted Nadia with a little extra courtesy, which I noticed garnered a frown from Otto.

"How hard is it going to be to get the printing press back?" asked the captain, turning to Lance once the introductions had been made.

Lance's expression grew serious. "It won't be easy. It was taken by a group of General Delaney's soldiers, who are still patrolling the city. To the best of my knowledge, they are holding it in the castle's storerooms."

"They are what?" asked Solace in shock. "That is not good. How are we going to get it back? Everyone is looking for us. We just overheard that General Delaney has everyone convinced that we are planning to overthrow the king."

"It must be a trap," said Nadia, rubbing her chin in thought.

"That was my thought exactly," responded Lance. "But the only other option is to copy *The Story* by hand. But if we did that, it would take weeks or months just to get out a couple of copies, not to mention the higher risk of a mistake being made in the text. I do have access to some supplies that would make printing go faster, but without the press, I am afraid they won't be much help."

"We need to get it printed soon. The longer we wait, the greater the chance Valdra will catch us," Solace explained.

"In that case, I can't see any other option than to break in and steal it," said Lance. Then he paused and asked, "Who is Valdra?"

"He is General Delaney's right-hand man. He is very dangerous and probably the commander of the soldiers who took the printing press," I explained.

Lance frowned and nodded. "It will be nearly impossible to steal the press, as I'm sure those soldiers will be guarding it closely," he said thoughtfully. "Not to mention the fact that a printing press is huge and difficult to move..." Lance's voice trailed off as he noticed us all glancing at each other. "What are you thinking?" he asked, looking from one person to another.

"We are not sure, exactly," said Solace hesitantly, "but we might have a solution to the problem."

"What solution?" asked Lance curiously as he leaned forward slightly.

I glanced at the captain, unsure if I should tell him about the sword and shield in my possession, and how the sword, and possibly the shield, had been blessed with the power of an invisible king. The captain nodded, seeming to read my thoughts.

I took a deep breath. "It might be possible to break in, use the press, and leave without taking it with us."

Lance raised an eyebrow. "I'm listening."

"This sword and shield that I carry were forged by the Prince himself," I explained.

Lance's eyes widened, and his jaw slackened slightly with surprise. "How in the world did you find them?"

"Long story short, we know the woman from *The Story*," explained Nadia.

"You know the—" Lance broke off and stared in disbelief.

"It is truly a story too long to tell tonight, Lance," interrupted Captain Bates.

"Right. Sorry," Lance replied, regaining control over his surprise and excitement. "So, how can the sword and shield help us?"

"Well, like Solace said, we are not sure if this will work, so we need to test it. But there is a chance that the shield may have some miraculous properties," I responded. "We think the shield might be able to offer special protection."

"It's just a theory," added Otto, holding up an index finger.

"What makes you think it has miraculous properties?" asked Lance as his eyes squinted in a slightly skeptical expression.

"*The Story* says that the sword will help one fight and the shield will offer protection. That may seem fairly obvious, but I know from personal experience that the sword has special powers. It helps the one who wields it to fight by allowing them to see the Unseen Lands, or at least those who live there," I explained.

Lance's eyebrows raised in renewed surprise and excitement. "There are Unseen Lands?" he asked.

I nodded. "Yes. Anyway, since the sword contains power, we believe the shield might as well. We don't know exactly what the shield might be able to do, but we hope it might hide the one who carries it from the enemy's view. To find out, we would need to test it, though, and if we test it, we might alert the enemy...if it doesn't work, that is," I finished.

"That sounds risky," said Lance, regaining his composure. "If the shield doesn't work, our cover would be blown, and we wouldn't get anywhere near that castle or the printing press."

We all sat in silence for a moment as we thought about how to solve this dilemma.

"I've got it!" exclaimed Otto suddenly.

Everyone turned to him with anticipation.

"Why don't you just ask someone from the Unseen Lands?" he suggested.

"What do you mean? That is the problem we are trying to solve. The soldiers of darkness—" I started.

Otto waved his hands as if trying to erase my words. "No, no, no. I mean someone on our side."

Suddenly I realized what he was talking about. "Otto, you're a genius!" I exclaimed.

"I am well aware of that," Otto responded plainly, and I caught Nadia attempting at holding back a smile.

"What is he talking about?" Lance asked.

"When I went into the Woods—" I began.

"You went into the Woods?" Lance exclaimed, interrupting me.

I nodded. "You should really read *The Story* sometime," I said with a smile. "It explains a lot."

Lance nodded as his eyes lost focus for a second. Then he blinked and began listening again as I continued.

"Anyway, when I went into the Woods and learned that the sword could show me the Unseen Lands, I saw two soldiers, one from the armies of darkness and one from the armies of light. They had both been following me, the soldier of the Lion's Sword protecting me from the soldier of the Creature."

"You could test the shield with your soldier!" said Solace as she understood what Otto and I were getting at.

"I could try, or at least ask him about it. But I have to find him first," I said. "I haven't seen him since that night."

"Well, draw the sword and see what happens," said Solace.

"Do you feel like there is anyone around?" I asked.

Lance raised an eyebrow. "What does that mean?"

The captain smiled. "Solace was healed by the Prince himself. She has an...awareness of the unseen."

Lance let out a breath and leaned against an old table in the middle of the room. "This is a lot to take in!" he said with raised eyebrows.

I glanced at the captain. I didn't need Lance getting spooked and telling the king about us just because he thought we were all crazy. But the captain's nod of reassurance put my mind at ease.

"Don't worry, Ben. I won't tell anyone," said Lance, noticing the look between the captain and me. "I'm just…This is just a lot to take in," he repeated.

I nodded in understanding. "I apologize. I am not used to people being so interested in the truth."

Lance smiled. "If there is one thing my mother taught me, it's that this world is not as it seems." He straightened. "If we are going to figure this out tonight, you'd better get testing," he said as he rubbed his hands together in excitement.

I turned to Solace. "What do you think? Is he nearby?"

Solace took a moment to think about it. "I don't feel much. But he could be. I am still figuring out what it feels like when soldiers of each army are close. But I don't feel like any soldiers of darkness are close, at least."

I nodded. "Okay. I'll give it a go."

Lance suggested we move into the main room of the church to have more space. He explained that he only had us meet in the back room because there were so many soldiers around and the room had a concealed back door. But as long as we regularly checked the perimeter, we should be able to see people coming and just retreat to the secret exit. So, once we returned to the main room of the church, Lance and the captain double-checked the perimeter before returning to tell us we were still all clear, as best they could see. With the others standing around in anticipation, I drew the sword. For the past six months, we had searched for Ruth and focused on getting *The Story* written and building up her small network of contacts who were willing to help spread *The Story*. During that time, I had not needed the help of the armies of light. Since the time when we had chased off Valdra and his soldiers with the help of five soldiers of light, I had not used the sword to glimpse the unseen armies again. That time, all I had done was draw the sword, and the soldiers had appeared. Not sure exactly how the sword worked, I simply stood there for a moment, sword in hand.

"Nothing is happening," I said as I glared at the sword.

"Try to remember what it felt like when you saw your soldier of light that time in the Woods," encouraged Solace from where she stood a few feet away.

I closed my eyes and tried to envision that moment. The soldier had stood just inside the Woods and watched my interactions with the Beast of the Woods as if he were standing watch over me. He hadn't been close enough for me to see him in any detail, but he had been there. As I recalled the moment, I wondered briefly if he was an eternal being, like the ones Solace had once spoken of. As a child, she had thought stars were eternal beings set to watch over us. *I don't even know if eternal beings are real, and I have never met one, so how would I know?* I thought to myself. Whatever he was, I would never forget the moment I first saw him.

"Now try to draw the attention of only your soldier, instead of a whole group of soldiers, as you did last time," I heard Solace tease.

Ignoring her joke, I focused on the soldier of light in my mind's eye. I didn't know his name or where he was, but I silently tried to get his attention as best I could. For a moment, I didn't feel anything. Then I felt something. Something like hesitation. *"Don't!"* The hesitation turned to a warning that rang out in my mind so intensely I almost opened my eyes to see who had spoken. But then I felt something else. Like a ray of light cutting through a cold morning fog, I could feel something unseen and powerful. Somehow, I knew it was reassuring the soldier, and the soldier's hesitation left him. But inside me, my stomach twisted with guilt, and the warning remained heavy in my mind. *What was the warning for?* I wondered. Then the powerful presence left, and I felt as though someone was standing near me. I opened my eyes.

There, standing in front of me, was a regal soldier. He was about my height and had sepia skin and blue eyes. His long hair was such a pure white that I momentarily wondered if he was an elf, a creature I had read about in books and fairy tales. But I quickly saw his ears were not pointy. He also had no wings, or any other unique characteristic that suggested he might be an eternal being. But then again, I didn't know what eternal beings looked like. Under his silver armor, he wore battle-ready garments of the finest linen in a delicate pale blue. A shining silver sword was strapped to his side, and a beautiful, deep sky-blue cloak was draped over his shoulders, fastened in place by a silver pendant of a unique shape that seemed familiar, though I couldn't place it. I could feel his presence, and it felt different from the more powerful presence I had sensed a moment ago. But still, this soldier had the rough, firm strength that one would expect from an experienced warrior.

"What do you wish of me?" asked the soldier, his face unreadable.

"Who are you?" I asked.

"I am Eyethanoff of Woolkar. I serve the King and the Prince as your guardian in this land," he said with a polite dip of his head.

I nodded. *Okay, so this soldier is probably not an eternal being, since eternal beings are most likely not from a place called Woolkar, though I don't know where that is.* "Well, I guess I owe you my thanks then," I responded respectfully.

He gave a small bow and smiled. "It has been my joy to serve at your side. But I must deflect your thanks to my king, for I only have power through him."

It wasn't uncommon for a soldier to pay respect to his king, but this felt different. Almost as if this soldier wasn't deflecting my thanks out of military respect but rather a personal respect for the King. Not sure how to respond, I simply nodded before moving on. "There is something I need to know...I wish to know how the shield works," I said.

Eyethanoff smiled again. "You must have faith, my friend."

"But I need to know tonight. I need to be able to get into the castle without being seen," I urged.

Eyethanoff's long, pure white hair slid off his shoulder as he cocked his head to one side and regarded me. "You do not know? Did you not see *The Story* yourself?" he inquired.

"I saw it. I know the shield is meant to provide protection. But I do not know how it works. I need to test it," I explained.

Eyethanoff paused and watched me as if he were deciding how he should respond. Then he said, "The sword and shield will help you as they were designed to."

I frowned. This was not how I had expected this conversation to go. The Beast of the Woods had explained so many things to me. But Eyethanoff was speaking in riddles. "Why don't you just tell me?" I asked in frustration.

Eyethanoff frowned. "Have faith, my friend," he repeated. "You will find what you are looking for."

"What about the others?" I asked. "They don't have the tools I have."

Eyethanoff's gaze briefly shifted to look behind me, then returned to me. "They will be safe, for the King's Original Power is sufficient," he assured. And with that, Eyethanoff vanished.

I sheathed the sword and stood there for a moment, processing what I had just seen and heard. *Why couldn't Eyethanoff just tell me what I need to know?* I thought as I clenched my fists in frustration.

"What happened?" asked Solace as everyone approached from various corners of the church.

I shrugged. "He was kind of cryptic."

"I imagine most invisible soldiers of light would be," said Lance with a teasing grin.

I smiled. "I guess I just expected him to explain everything like the Beast of the Woods did," I said. I was quiet for a moment as I thought through everything I knew about the shield and the sword.

"Well, what did he say?" asked Ivan, interrupting my thoughts.

"He told me his name and to have faith. He said that the King's Original Power was sufficient to protect us all," I explained.

"Yeah, that's pretty cryptic," said Nadia as she crossed her arms. "What's his name?"

"Eyethanoff," I responded, recalling the unusual name, "of Woolkar..."

"Hmm." Nadia nodded slowly as she contemplated the situation.

"I guess we will have to come up with a different idea for getting into the castle," said Lance.

Solace shook her head. "Ben, I think we should just do it. I think we should go in there and use the printing press without trying to steal it. There is no way to get it out without drawing too much attention. Even if the shield doesn't help, we don't have much of a choice."

I looked at her. Solace's connection to the unseen had saved us a few times since we had first embarked on this mission. But she wasn't just perceptive about when soldiers of darkness and light were near. She also seemed to have remarkable insight. If she thought we should go ahead and try this plan, then I trusted her judgment.

I nodded. "Do you all agree?"

After a moment of hesitation from everyone, Nadia spoke up. "I don't think we have another option, so...I'm in."

I glanced at the others, and they all voiced their agreement as well. "Okay. We will do it. I will bring the sword and the shield. At the very least, the sword will help me see the safest path past any soldiers of darkness."

"What if the shield doesn't work? Or what if the whole plan doesn't work?" said Otto as he gripped his cloak tightly.

I locked eyes with Solace. She had that look. The look that said she would not back down and didn't think anyone else should. A look of determination to follow through on the Prince's mission no matter what.

"We will make it work," I told Otto as I held Solace's gaze.

"Then it is decided," said the captain. "We will go to the castle and print the books there."

I turned to Lance. "Do you know where exactly the press is hidden?"

He nodded. "Their storerooms. They are located down in the cellars."

"How do we get to them?" I asked.

"We must cross the moat first. The cellars are located underneath the main tower. There are two entrances to the cellars. One is a secret entrance that goes underground, but I don't know much about it. The other is through the cellar door. We would have to get inside first to access those. The back entrance to the castle would probably offer the shortest route, but it is guarded. It is accessible via a path that runs the length of the cliff along the base of the castle wall."

"Are there guards posted at all times?" asked Ivan.

Lance nodded. "I have friends in the castle who know a lot about how the guard shifts are scheduled. When I talked to them two days ago, they said there were men guarding each entrance to the castle and all the doors between the back entrance and the cellar door. All of those guards will be a problem. Even if we did manage to get past them all, they would probably discover our plans pretty quickly. The press isn't extremely loud, but it would likely be audible to any guards standing right outside the door."

"How long will it take to print five copies?" asked the captain. "We were intending to print a whole batch to deliver to people while our print contacts print more, but I doubt we will have time to do that now. But we at least need four copies for the printers to reproduce because we only handwrote one copy of *The Story*. And we need an extra just in case something happens to our handwritten version."

"Well, how many pages is the book?" asked Lance.

"*The Story* is not long," I said with a shrug.

"How many words?" Lance asked.

"I really couldn't say. I've never counted."

Otto spoke up. "*The Story* as it was written down by Ruth was much longer. But we do not have a full copy of it since Ruth never got the chance to print more copies of her version, and her copy was given to General Delaney. Ben wrote down what he remembered from his vision, and his version is four thousand three hundred and ten words."

Lance raised an eyebrow at Otto's detailed explanation, then nodded. "The printing press was designed to print small books, called the octavo format. It takes about an hour or so to print twenty-five sheets, and in the octavo format, you get sixteen pages of text per sheet, eight on one side and eight on the other. With a story that short, it would probably fit on, oh...say, one or two sheets," he said, calculating the numbers in his head. "Because my mother was a printer, I have access to some of her old type. I think if we preset the type and bring it with us, we could easily print five books in under half an hour. We also need to leave time for the ink to dry enough that we can move them without smearing the text, though. All that considered, we could probably be in and out in a little over two hours. But that is just an estimate. Because we will be in a cellar, there might not be enough airflow to fully dry the ink. And it doesn't take the covers into account."

I shook my head. "They will just be leather bound, but we won't be dealing with that."

"Then it's just the printing of the text for five copies," he confirmed. Then he frowned. "Why five?"

"We will leave one copy of *The Story* here with a contact who will hopefully still be able to find a press and print *The Story*. We need to keep moving to stay out of General Delaney's sights, so we will deliver the other copies to the contacts we have in the other three of the four corner countries," I explained. "They will take care of the rest."

"Okay, we have to work fast. The more time we spend with that press, the higher the chance of getting caught," stated the captain.

"If the shield works as we think it might, why would we be concerned?" asked Ivan.

"First of all, we don't know for sure what the shield does, Ivan," Nadia said with a frown. "Also, it isn't just the unseen soldiers that we will be sneaking past," she explained. "The Martecytes are just people who have been infected by shadows. They operate in both the seen and Unseen Lands. If the shield works, we will probably be able to hide from the unseen soldiers of darkness, but the Martecytes might still be able to see us."

"Not to mention the other guards," Lance said, apparently choosing not to ask what a Martecyte might be.

We all looked at Lance in unison. "What other guards?" I asked.

"The Castle Guard," he said simply. "The people by the front gate are not part of the Castle Guard." He shrugged. "Maybe they are these Martecytes you speak of. But inside and along the castle walls, the Castle Guard are on high alert because they believe you are a direct threat to the king."

"Right," I said, more to myself than to the group, as I put my hands on my hips. "The Castle Guard. I was so focused on the soldiers of darkness and Valdra that I completely forgot about them."

"How are we going to get past them?" asked Solace in frustration.

I turned to Nadia. "You are our stealth expert. Got any ideas?"

Nadia twirled a lock of her red hair as she thought. "Well, where are they posted?"

"Watchmen are posted on the battlements, and guards are posted around the royal apartments and the king's bedchamber. There are also soldiers in the barracks and on patrol who are ready to come to their aid as soon as an alarm is sounded. If we are inside when they sound the alarm, we are as good as dead," explained Lance gloomily.

Nadia leaned against an old church pew that had vines growing over it. "What about the back door you mentioned?"

Lance nodded. "I wouldn't advise trying to get to it. It is well guarded. We would have a better chance sneaking around in the castle baileys."

"Does the castle have any supplies or anything coming in or going out at night?" Nadia asked. "We might be able to sneak in with them."

Lance thought about that. "No...Not that I know of," he said as he eyed Otto with a look of amusement. Otto, despite his clothes being already rumpled and dirty from his sea voyage, was cleaning off a pew with a handkerchief. He only succeeded in smearing the dirt around before he gave up and tentatively sat down.

"I might be able to help," said Otto from his seat on the pew nearest Nadia.

"How so?" I asked.

He hesitated, wringing his hands, then said, "My father regularly does business with the king. Around this time of year, he brings shipments of winter clothes from the Northern Country for the king and his household to purchase. Usually, they do it in the market. But...I might be able to convince my father to bring them to the castle."

"You think he would listen to you?" asked Solace.

Otto considered the question. "Maybe."

"And what happens if we explain the situation and he doesn't want to help?" asked Nadia.

Otto's expression was tired as he shrugged. "He's a good man. He wasn't happy that I left without his help, but...he won't turn us in. My mother loved to study the Woods, and she once told me of parts of *The Story*, though I now know the version she told was missing many details. My father loved her, and he knew she loved that story. If for no other reason, he would keep our secret in her memory."

I watched Otto as he fiddled with the hem of his cloak. "Why didn't you accept his help?" I asked.

Otto gave me a questioning frown. "Why does that matter?"

"Because if your father holds a grudge against you over this, he might very well turn us all in just to teach you a lesson," I said sternly.

Otto shook his head. "I didn't accept his help because I was afraid I would misuse the money. He offered me everything. Money, resources, people. But...I wasn't just leaving to find my mother. I was leaving because...because I was afraid."

"What were you afraid of?" asked Nadia.

"The last time I spoke with my mother before she left, I...We got in a fight," he said, scratching his head and rustling his black hair. "I wanted more wealth. I wanted everything my father had. She told me I needed to be wise in how I used it, but I didn't listen." He crossed his arms, and his eyes lost focus. "I was so blinded by what wealth could buy me that I took for granted what it couldn't buy. The last thing I said to her was that I hoped she never came back because then I would get her share as well..." Otto's expression twisted in pain at the memory.

"Wow..." said Nadia with a grimace.

Otto nodded slowly. "Yeah." He stared at the ground for a moment. "Anyway, when Mother went missing, I realized what I had taken for granted...I was afraid that if I accepted my father's gift, I would lose myself to greed again, and I feared my father blamed me for her disappearance. He insisted that wasn't the case, but I just couldn't let it go. So, I left. I looked for Mother, but...I didn't find her," he said in disappointment.

Nadia placed a hand on Otto's shoulder. "You've come a long way, Otto," she said with a smile. Otto looked up at her and offered a small smile in return.

"So, you think your father will help?" I asked.

Otto nodded. "He is a wealthy man, but he has never let it change him." Otto smiled to himself. "He always said the most valuable treasure he had the pleasure of sharing his life with was my mother." Otto looked at me. "At the very least, he would never turn us in for something like this," he said with conviction.

I nodded. "Okay. How can we contact him?"

"If they still do things the way they used to, the man who manages the shipments will be at the docks in the morning around sunrise. I can get him a message. Assuming it's the same man I remember, he is just as trustworthy and will deliver a message to Father if I ask him," said Otto.

I nodded. "Do you think we can meet him at the docks without anyone seeing us?" I asked Lance and Captain Bates.

The captain and Lance looked at each other. "If you meet before sunrise, that area tends to be pretty quiet at that time, so no one should notice you hanging around," said Lance as he turned back to me.

I nodded. "Otto and I can go, and we will take Dan." I turned to Otto. "Do you remember the roads?"

"Of course I do," he said confidently. "I don't forget useful information."

Chapter 4

THE DOCKS WERE NEARLY empty. Most people were not yet up, and the cold morning air would keep them inside for at least another half hour. The only people around were like the man we were about to meet—those who managed shipments and arrived at the docks early to ensure everything was in order and nothing had been stolen. Otto, Dan, and I wore dark cloaks that would help hide us in the shadows, and we pulled our hoods up to conceal our faces as we moved through the stacks of cargo.

We reached the section of the docks where Sir Bilden, Otto's father, held shipments before loading them onto the boats. Otto led the way into an alley next to a building with a sign above the front door that read "Bilden Shipping Co.," and we waited in the shadows.

"When he comes out, I will get his attention. He will recognize me," said Otto, his usual matter-of-fact tone noticeably absent. He tugged at his cloak, his hands trembling slightly. The fact that he had returned home before finding his mother was undoubtedly weighing on him.

I grabbed Otto's arm. "Otto. I need you to keep a clear head. I can't have you distracted. If someone spots you, it may draw more attention than we can handle. If we are caught, we will die," I said sternly.

Otto looked at me with a glint of fear in his eyes. He was still unused to being in situations that could end in a swift death...or, in this case, probably a slow one. Despite his fears, Otto nodded. *He has come a long way,* I thought to myself with a faint smile.

We had been waiting for about five minutes when we saw a man exit the building, headed for the docks. While Dan and I kept watch, Otto left the shadows of the alley and approached the man, careful to keep his face hidden from any passersby. I watched as Otto grabbed the man's arm and then stepped back. He waved his hands slightly at waist level in an attempt to calm the man, then pulled him into the shadow of a nearby shipping crate, where they spoke in low voices. I checked the streets around us, keeping a sharp eye out for anyone who might cause trouble. After a few moments, Otto hurried back toward us, and the man disappeared into the shipyards.

"What did he say?" I asked as Otto entered the alley.

Otto shook his head. "I am sorry, Ben, but my father is out of town. It seems he had to make a trip to settle a shipping issue in the Northern Country," he explained, his shoulders drooping in disappointment.

I put my hands on my hips and let out a breath, puffing out my cheeks, as I looked at the ground. *Can anything else go wrong? I* thought. *I probably shouldn't ask myself that, especially this early in our journey.*

"I am sorry, Ben," Otto repeated. "My father can't get us into the castle, but the man I spoke to did say to contact him if there was anything else we needed help with."

I looked up at him. "It's not your fault, Otto," I said as I placed a reassuring hand on his shoulder. "We will just have to figure out a different solution."

"What are we going to do now?" asked Dan.

I glanced around. "We'd better hurry back to the church before the docks get busy."

With that, we left the alley and headed back the way we had come. As we slipped from shadow to shadow, I suddenly felt like we were being followed. A chill ran down my spine, and I grabbed Otto by the arm and pulled him behind a nearby crate as Dan followed suit, careful not to trip me up as he did so. Otto opened his mouth to respond in surprise, but I clapped a hand over his lips and held my breath. I grabbed the hilt of my sword with my other hand and began to draw it from its scabbard so I could see any soldiers of darkness in the vicinity. I let out a controlled breath and slowly released Otto's mouth, placing an index finger to my lips, warning him to remain completely silent. As I drew the sword farther from its scabbard, I glanced around the edge of the crate. But before I could completely unsheathe the sword, I noticed a shadow across the docks that seemed to move unnaturally. I froze. *A Martecyte!* I thought. The man emerged from the shadows, the edges of his cloak moving slightly as if they were made of black fog. *Thank goodness,* I thought. *At least it's an enemy I can see.* Though I could see this enemy, it was still just as dangerous as the unseen soldiers of darkness, so I remained cautious.

The Martecyte let his gaze fall over the crates around the dock, and I pulled back out of sight again. Dan gave me a questioning look, and I mouthed, "Martecyte." He nodded and kept his back pressed against the crate. After what felt like forever, footsteps sounded from the Martecyte's location, moving away from us. I waited a few seconds and then peeked out from behind the shipping crate once more. The Martecyte was gone. But seeing him had made the reality of our predicament all the more tangible. My stomach churned and I grabbed Otto, pulling him after me as we headed back to the old church.

When we arrived at the church, I updated the rest of the group on the situation, and we immediately began to review our strategy. Nadia and Ivan offered ideas on how we might convince the Castle Guard to bring the press out of the castle, making it easier to get our hands on it. But those ideas were quickly shot down due to the fact that this whole thing was most likely a trap, and the chances that they could be convinced to bring the printing press out were slim. Dan suggested that we simply look for a new printing press. But that idea was also shot down because the press in the castle was currently the only one on this side of the island. According to Lance, two more were on their way into the main city and would be here next week. But that clearly would not help us, as we were under a time crunch to meet up with our other contacts. So, we went over the castle's defenses again in search of new ideas.

"Tell us exactly what we are dealing with," I directed, locking eyes with Lance. "Everything."

Lance took in a deep breath and then began. "Okay. The castle was built on a grassy slope directly against the base of a mountain. The back of the castle looks out over the Eastern Sea from the top of a cliff, and the rest of the castle is protected by two main walls, the outer wall and the inner wall, with six towers in each wall and a moat around the outside. There are only three ways into the castle," he said, holding up three fingers. "There is the main gate in front, which is currently guarded by a few of the Castle Guard and probably the Martecytes and soldiers of darkness. Then there is the back door, which grants the Castle Guard access to the cliff that overlooks the ocean. This back entrance is located on a dangerously thin trail along the cliff's edge that leads from one side of the castle, past the back entrance, all the way to the other side of the castle. The back door is normally only guarded from above by soldiers in the rear castle keeps. But according to my sources, there are now also two of the Castle Guard posted by the door itself. Each end of the trail that runs past the back entrance ends at the moat, which cannot be easily crossed." Lance shrugged. "You could potentially make it across on foot, but it would be slow, treacherous going. The moat ends abruptly just before the edge of the cliff at a small strip of soggy earth with scattered bushes and vining plants. However, even if you made it across that thin strip without falling to your death, the guards at the back door would surely see you coming along the trail," he added. "There is absolutely no cover on the trail itself, as it is designed to give an unobstructed view of the ocean in case of attacks from the sea. The third entrance to the castle is through a set of underground tunnels, and no one knows their location except the king's personal guard," he finished.

"Okay," said Nadia slowly as all the details sank in. "So, we have two options," she thought aloud, "the front gate or the back door."

"Some of us could attack the front gate to create a distraction and let the others slip in," suggested Ivan.

I shook my head. "No, we need at least a couple of hours to use the printing press and allow the ink to dry enough to move the pages. We can't let them know we are in there," I explained.

"Is there any way to get across the moat and through the main gate without being seen?" asked Solace.

Lance shook his head. "I don't think so. There are guards monitoring comings and goings very closely, and I have seen what must be your Martecytes there watching the moat. They try to keep things subtle so as not to alert the people. But they are there," Lance finished.

"And that means that there are probably armies of darkness there as well," I added.

"What about shift changes?" asked Otto.

Nadia perked up a bit. "Otto is right. On high alert, they will be doing regular shift changes."

Lance cocked his head to the side in thought. "Yes. I think you are right. One of the people I talked to who lives inside the castle did say they move soldiers around regularly. If I recall correctly, they mentioned that soldiers move through the hallways multiple times in the night, at eight o'clock, midnight, and four in the morning. So, I guess those would be the shift changes you are talking about."

"It is standard practice to do four-hour shifts on high alert," commented the captain. "I would be surprised if that was not the case in this castle."

"Can we trust these people you spoke to?" asked Nadia.

Lance nodded. "They are good people. Plus, they had no idea I was looking for information. People who live in protected castles all their life just like to talk," he said confidently, alleviating Nadia's concern.

"Okay, so let me get this straight," I said, drawing everyone's focus again. "We can't go through the tunnels because we don't know where they are. We can't go through the front because it is too heavily guarded, but the back door is even worse because it is also guarded and is located on a dangerous cliff with one way in and one way out," I said, looking to Lance for verification.

"Correct," he said with a nod.

"We should go through the back door," said Ivan.

I shook my head. "I just said that was worse than the front door. It sounds like a good place to get trapped."

Ivan smiled. "Yeah, but look at the mistake they have made."

"What do you mean?" asked Lance with a contemplative frown.

"You said that most of the guards were in the front, but they did add more security to the back, right?" confirmed Ivan.

"Yes," Lance said slowly, still confused. "Two guards at the back door as opposed to just those keeping watch from the wall."

Ivan nodded. "Which door is closer to the cellars, the back door or the front?" asked Ivan.

"The back," Lance responded.

"Just as I thought," replied Ivan. "They put more guards on the front and only two guards on the back entrance because that is all they think they need. They clearly think we would not be able to successfully make it through the back door, or they would have put more guards by the moat near the back side of the castle."

Nadia caught on to what Ivan was saying. "So they covered the back with two guards because Valdra is smart and knows that the entrance closest to the press would be attractive to us, but they focused on the front because they think the back entrance would be harder to get to without being spotted and killed."

"That sounds complicated," said Lance.

"The words sound complicated, but the concept is simple," said Solace. "They know the back entrance is closer to the press, so they cover it with extra guards because if we do risk our lives to get to the back door, they will see us coming, and it will be covered. Now that the back door is taken care of, they focus on the front door since that is the most likely choice."

"I still don't get it. How does that help us?" asked Lance, his head slightly cocked to one side.

"They are suggesting we go in the back door because, based on the fact that they only added two guards, the king is too confident that the Castle Guard have secured it," said the captain. "It is common for kings to become too comfortable in their castles when they have only fought wars against beasts and not against other humans, and they insist on using the same strategies and defenses. I imagine beasts usually attack the front because they cannot get to the back, so the king has made the dangerous and unwise assumption that we will do the same. Based on the setup, I'd say Valdra wanted to cover the back entrance, but the king was more worried about the front entrance. So, Valdra did what he could at the back entrance and put the rest of his armies in the front at the king's command."

I nodded. "The back is relatively unguarded, especially with Nadia and Ivan on our side," I said with a grin at the twins.

"And what if we are completely wrong?" asked Otto. "What if there are more soldiers back there, but we just can't see them?"

"Well," said Lance, "let's make a plan to go through the back, and if Ben sees with his sword that there are soldiers of darkness back there, then we will regroup and try a different plan."

"Sounds good to me," said Ivan.

"Well then, we need to figure out how to get across the moat. Could we swim or take a boat?" I asked.

Lance raised his eyebrows in thought. "I would definitely not recommend swimming. Moats usually have some dangerous secrets hidden within their filthy waters. As for a boat, I can't see how we could sneak our own boat into the moat without drawing attention. They do keep a small boat at each end of the moat, up out of the water near the trail, for emergencies. That's partially what the back door is meant to be used for. It's for the Castle Guard to defend against attacks from the sea and for emergency getaways if the castle is invaded from the front. The secret tunnels provide one escape route, and the boats provide a second. I suppose jumping off the cliff into the sea below is another option, but it's a dangerous height, and I'm not sure anyone could actually survive the fall. Anyway, each boat is only accessible to those coming from the castle, though. If we made it across the moat in one piece, we could post someone at the boat and use it for a hasty retreat. However, it's not a big boat. It definitely wouldn't fit all of us in one trip."

"Well, we will just have to make do with what we have," I said. I crossed my arms and began to pace. "Okay, so we can leave someone there with the boat. But how do we get across the moat in the first place?" I asked.

"Like I said, there is that strip of land we could try crossing on foot. When the castle was first built, the castle and moat were constructed a little lower than the top of the cliff. This means a natural wall runs behind the castle, at the edge of the cliff. When you are on the trail, that wall is only knee height, just enough to provide a low boundary. But on each end of the moat, the wall is about two meters high because the moat is lower than the castle. I've been told that when they built the moat, they left that thin strip of land along the wall as their original emergency escape route for the royal family, before the boats. To help conceal the narrow trail, they planted some small bushes along it. Over time, though, the bushes became overgrown, and the path began to erode and crumble into the moat. They added the boats when they deemed the path unsafe for anyone to try and cross. It's pretty well hidden, and I guess they figured that if any intruders did try to cross, they would have to go so slow that the Castle Guard would see them coming. Plus, the trail on the other side is overlooked by outposts in the mountain that have a clear line of sight, and it can be easily defended from above by guards in the keeps. If we approach in single file, there's a chance we might be able to make it across at night, especially if Ben's shield works how we hope it does. But we would have to go very slowly. One wrong step, and we could fall into the moat, where who knows what would be waiting."

I nodded. "Okay. Well, this sounds like our only real option. We'll just have to go for it and hope for the best." Solace stepped up next to me and squeezed my hand. I smiled down at her, then turned back to Lance. "Now, tell me what you've heard about the guards posted inside the castle."

"There are three doors that we will need to go through. The door in the outer wall, the door in the inner wall, and the door to the cellar," Lance said as he counted off the three doors on his fingers. "There is a long, empty hallway between the first two doors, over the bailey. The door in the inner wall leads to the inside of the castle, and when we get through it, we will need to take the hallway to the right, toward the cellar. As we know, there are two guards at the outer door, and from what my sources have told me, there are two on the far side of the inner door, and three guards at the door to the cellar. To the best of my knowledge, there are other guards roaming the hallways. However, they are apparently constantly on the move, so if we time our entrance right, we might be able to avoid them. But I worry that they would notice missing guards at the doors, as we would have to take them out to get in."

I turned to Nadia. "What if we put on the guards' uniforms and took their places? Would we be able to do that with all seven guards?"

Nadia considered the question. "If we took advantage of the shift changes, I think we could do it."

"I think this might just work," I said, rubbing my chin in thought as my plan developed. "We will need one more person, so there'd be ten of us total…" I trailed off.

"What are you planning?" asked Lance with narrowed eyes.

I took a deep breath. "Here is what we are going to do," I started. "We will cross the moat along that old, eroded trail and leave one person with the boat for a faster getaway, just in case. Nine of us will go to the back door, which we'll call door one. We will need to get to the door right before the midnight shift change. We will take out the two guards at door one and take their uniforms. Then, when the midnight shift comes, we will take out the replacement guards and take their uniforms as well, giving us four sets of Castle Guard uniforms. Two of us can put on the uniforms and stay by door one. Then the remaining seven of us will go to door two, with two of us in the other two uniforms. The two in uniform will take out the guards at door two and take their place. These will be the new guards, after the shift change, so we won't have to worry about any more replacements coming. At this point, two of the remaining five of us will have Castle Guard uniforms, and we can sneak the remaining three without uniforms through door two and on to door three, take out the three guards there, and enter the cellar, replacing the last three guards with three of our crew. That will leave one person at the boat, two of us in uniform at door one, two in uniform at door two, and three in uniform guarding door three, and the remaining two of us will go in and print the books and have uniforms for the escape."

Everyone considered that plan for a moment.

"I think that could actually work," said Captain Bates as he rubbed his chin in thought.

"Yeah, I think we can pull it off," Ivan agreed.

"What about the exit strategy?" asked Nadia.

"We could just sneak out," said Solace. "No one would be looking for us, and all of us would be in uniform and look just like guards. Do the uniforms include helmets?" she asked, turning to Lance, who nodded. "So we'd also have helmets to obstruct our faces, and the exits would be guarded by our people so we would have a clear path out. Even if someone noticed us and raised an alarm, we could be out before they could catch us."

"Maybe," I said, glancing around at everyone. "We can't get brash. Remember that if this plan goes sideways and we get caught, we will all be executed." I paused for a moment to let that set in. "That being said, I think Solace is right. I think the plan could work."

"Where will we get the extra person we'll need?" asked Solace.

I turned to the captain. "Do you think you could spare another crew member from the *Lyonsword*?"

The captain ran a hand through his hair. "I don't know. We would have to check with Christopher. We need to get the ship fixed as quickly as possible, and the more people available for that, the faster it will go."

I nodded. "That reminds me, we probably shouldn't carry out our plan until the ship is ready and waiting. If we have to make a hasty retreat, we'll need to get off the island quickly, or they might still catch us even if we escape the castle."

"Well, let's go back to the ship and discuss it with the crew and the carpenter. They were double-checking to see how bad the damage is, and they were hopeful that it might not be as bad as we thought. No damage to anything structural," said the captain.

"Okay." I turned to Lance. "Is this church safe for us to operate from, or do we need to go back to the ship and work from there?"

"This place is rarely visited. I would advise caution, but it should be safe to meet here again in the future," he explained.

"Okay, everyone will stay here except the captain and me. We're less likely to be noticed if it's just the two of us. If the ship can be repaired quickly enough that we can go in tomorrow night, we will bring another person back with us and finish planning here. If not, I will come get you, and we can all return to the *Lyonsword* and wait there until the ship is fully repaired." I looked from face to face. "Do not leave this church until we get back. The more we wander around, the more chance we will be spotted. Stay hidden."

Everyone nodded in agreement. As the captain headed to the door, I pulled Solace into a quick embrace.

"Be safe," she whispered into my ear.

"I will," I said softly and planted a kiss on her forehead. With that, I followed the captain out onto the beach and back toward the *Lyonsword*.

Chapter 5

THE *LYONSWORD* WAS NOT as damaged as it could have been, considering the attack it had weathered. However, the carpenter estimated that the repairs would still take about three days, so I retrieved the others from the church, and we did what we could to help. To ensure that we didn't dig too far into the rations for our trip to the Northern Country, Lance snuck us enough food to last us for three days if we rationed it well.

Most of the damage on the ship was to the sails, the gunwale, and upper hull. The mainsail had a tear that was fixed quickly, but there were a few other patch jobs and waterproofing to do, as the gunwale and the hull directly below it had taken a couple of hard hits, and some sections needed to be replaced. The captain and I ensured no one left the ship, apart from a couple crew members who had to go into town to get supplies—a challenge, since no one was supposed to know we were here.

With all hands on deck doing as the ship's carpenter instructed them, we finished in record time. When I commented on how amazing it was that the ship's repairs had again not taken nearly as long as I expected, considering the extent of the damages, Christopher frowned and explained lengthy repairs were not needed on this ship. As to why, I had no idea, and I didn't get the chance to ask, as Christopher was called away to other duties.

When Lance brought the food to the ship, he also brought the necessary tools to preset the type for *The Story*. Whether there was type with the press or not, we weren't sure, but thankfully Lance had access to the old type left over from a press his mother once used. The press itself had since been destroyed during a war with the beasts, but the type had apparently gone untouched in his storerooms. With Lance's type, we loaded the text for each sheet into its own wooden frame with a removable bottom. Then we wrapped each frame tightly with fabric and rope to hold the lettering in place and to conceal them from any passersby on our way to the castle.

After the three days of helping the crew fix the damage to the ship, prepping the type, and Lance teaching me the ins and outs of using a printing press, we finally had everything set. We decided to follow the plan I had laid out, and if the armies of darkness were gathered in the back of the castle when we got there, we would come back to the ship and devise a new plan.

As the sun slipped below the horizon, we gathered what we needed and set out. Lance led the way with Captain Bates, Solace, Nadia, Ivan, Otto, Eric, Dan, Casey, and me in tow. We wove through the outskirts of the city, through the docks, and past the short beach, winding around behind the old church. We passed through the trees that separated the castle grounds from the city and headed to the western side of the castle. As we reached the edge of the trees, the castle came into view. Nestled into a small mountain atop a low hill, the castle was strategically placed so it was protected on three sides, one side by the mountain, one side by the cliff, and the other side by the city. We stopped in the cover of the trees and bushes at the bottom of the gently sloping hill below the castle and waited, checking our surroundings to make sure we had not been followed.

"Are you going to check the dark army's location?" asked Solace.

I looked at her. "Why? Can you feel them all the way down here?" I asked in alarm.

Solace offered a silent nod in response. I turned and looked up at the castle, the base of which was only slightly higher in elevation than the rest of the town. It was said that the first king of the Eastern Island Country was a good man who loved his people. So, even though his castle was situated on a hill for tactical reasons, he had built it close to the level of the city to make it appear more accessible to the people. However, he was not a foolish man and had compensated by growing the ranks of his Castle Guard and ensuring the castle was well fortified. As a result, getting to the castle would not be difficult, but getting in would be a challenge, especially if it was guarded by soldiers of darkness.

I glanced around the group to ensure everyone was on alert, then drew the sword. As the tip of the sword left the scabbard, my grip tightened, and the world around the castle transformed. Soldiers of darkness surrounded the front entrance with swords drawn. As I took in their numbers, I knew we had no chance against them. Without the sword, my companions would be unable to see the soldiers of darkness, who could kill them in an instant. They would never see it coming. *Well, maybe Solace would,* I thought. *No, the soldiers of darkness would much prefer to infect us with shadow, recruiting us into their army of Martecytes.* A shiver ran up my spine at the thought.

I shifted my gaze to the back side of the castle to see what we had to deal with there. Thankfully, the captain was right about the king's overconfidence, but we were also right about Valdra's cautiousness. However, Valdra was smart, and he had taken more precautions than we had expected.

"What do you see?" asked Ivan as he crouched beside me in the bushes.

"We were right. Most of the armies of darkness are by the front gate. But Valdra placed two soldiers of darkness near the back," I explained, "one by the boat and one in the tower above."

"Do we have anything that can kill them?" asked Lance.

I grimaced. "I am still learning how this all works. I have never killed a dark soldier before. All I know is that they don't like the soldiers of light. I can at least fight them with my sword, but I have never tried to fight one with a normal sword."

"Well, then, the sword is what we will use. We can't afford to alert anyone to our presence," said Nadia.

I nodded in agreement. "I will go first. Stay here and stay hidden. If something happens and they see me before I can take them out, run, and I will catch up. We will reconvene at the *Lyonsword* and figure out what to do."

"We can't just leave you to fend for yourself," said Solace.

I placed and hand on her shoulder. "I will be fine. Stay with them, Solace. You are the only person who can protect them without the sword."

"I'm still learning how to do this, Ben," she said, her brow creasing with worry.

"I know, but you have done it multiple times already. Trust your gut," I said with confidence. She nodded with a tight-lipped expression, and I admired her bravery.

With that, I gripped the sword tight and grabbed the shield off my back, holding it in front of me. Keeping a close eye on the two soldiers of darkness near the back wall, I headed down the boundary of trees that lined the base of the hill. The way before me was filled with shadows strewn by the bright full moon. When I reached the cliff, I crouched in the bushes and trees that lined its edge. The soldiers of darkness slouched lazily at their posts, but they still scanned their surroundings regularly. *This will not be easy,* I thought to myself.

After taking a moment to gather my thoughts, I forced myself to leave the shadows in which I had taken refuge. Slowly, I took one carefully placed step at a time, still holding the shield in front of me. I stayed low and moved from shadow to shadow as I approached the moat's edge and the wall that towered over its end. The dark soldier near the boat leaned against the castle wall and swept his gaze across his surroundings. Each time his gaze reached my location, I froze. When his gaze shifted away, I continued my slow, deliberate advance.

As I neared the edge of the moat, shrouded in the shadows of trees, I glanced up at the dark soldier in the tower. His gaze was fixed on the back side of the castle, not bothering to check the moat that his comrade was tasked with protecting. Focusing on the dark soldier near the moat, I inched my way from the tree line to the edge of the wall. Due to the moon's location, unlike the line of trees I had just passed through, this side of the moat was fully in shadow, which would help conceal me even in the gaps between bushes. I crouched as I approached the wall and began inching my way down its length. The ground was soggy, probably from the moat water soaking into what was left of the earth. I proceeded on the muddy strip of ground between the wall and the moat. With each step I took, I carefully lifted and placed my feet as gently as possible so the mud would not make an audible sound. But as I approached the halfway point, I slipped in the wet soil. I retreated backward into a nearby bush, leaned against the wall to keep my balance, and froze, my heart pounding in my chest.

The dark soldier leaning against the castle wall straightened, and his eyes scanned the darkness. I could not go back, and I could not go forward, and he was about to look right at me. With no other option available, I instinctively concealed as much of myself behind the shield as I could and held it steady in front of me. As I peeked around the shield's edge, I saw the soldier look straight at me.

My heart continued to pound as the soldier took a step forward and peered toward me as if he couldn't quite tell what he was looking at. After a full, nerve-racking minute, the soldier stepped back and leaned against the wall again, relaxed.

I couldn't believe it. Somehow, he had not seen me. Though I was in shadow, he was close enough that he should have seen me, but he hadn't. *Maybe Otto is right about this shield,* I thought to myself as I gripped it a little tighter, still not daring to let out a breath of relief for fear the soldier might hear it.

However, there was a possibility that the shadow and my still-ness had kept me hidden. The short bushes around me might have obscured my shape enough to fool the dark soldier's eyes. *But...*I thought to myself, *the shield may have actually hidden me from* *his sight.* I glanced at the dark soldier and then back down at the shield. I took a deep breath and closed my eyes to gather my nerves. I opened them again and gripped the shield and the sword tight as I took my next step.

Each step brought me closer to the dark soldier until I stood at the edge of the wall's shadow. A beam of moonlight was the only thing separating me from the soldier of darkness. *I can't believe this,* I thought to myself. The moment the thought popped into my head, the soldier abruptly straightened and turned toward me as if he had seen something out of the corner of his eye. I gripped the shield and froze once again. *Maybe Otto was wrong after all,* I thought as my stomach twisted in fear.

Frozen in place, I watched as the dark soldier scanned the area before him again. Standing so close to my goal, I watched his gaze fall over my position, searching the shadows for any movement. This time, he didn't let it go. He picked up a stone and turned toward the castle's outer wall. He threw the stone up at the tower above him, and the dark soldier in the tower leaned forward and looked down. They were both looking at me now. I dared not move. I had no idea if the shield was doing anything or not, but I was in no position to test it any further.

The two soldiers of darkness scanned the area until the one in the tower shook his head, signaling that he didn't see anything. Finally, they both returned to their posts. Holding the shield and sword tightly, I took a deep, silent breath and assessed the situation. I had to take out the dark soldier on the ground first and then find a way to take out the one in the tower before he could alert anyone else. I couldn't reach the dark soldier in the tower, and to the best of my understanding, the only thing that could kill him was the sword in my hand, which would be hard to throw at him accurately enough to kill him without making a sound. I couldn't risk testing something that might not work, so there was only one option left. Charge.

Still hidden in shadow, I swung the shield out of my way, then bolted as quickly as possible toward the soldier on the ground. As I ran, I pulled the sword back, then thrust it forward as I reached the dark soldier, plunging it up through his stomach and one lung. His eyes met mine as blood poured from his lips. A thin flash of light registered beyond my field of vision from somewhere above me, but I ignored it and dropped the shield as quietly as I could and finished the soldier off with a small knife across his throat to ensure his silence. I slowly lowered him to the ground and looked up at the guard in the tower. To my surprise, he was slumped over the castle wall. Dead.

In a moment of confusion, I searched the area. *What killed him? Or, more specifically, who killed him?* I asked myself. But I saw no threat, and with no time to lose, I had to move on and take the mysterious win. With both soldiers of darkness now taken care of, I picked up the shield and proceeded to the narrow trail that led from the moat to the castle's back door. At the edge of the castle wall, I peeked around the corner at the guards who stood watch at the back door. They were both slouched at their posts, and one appeared to stifle a yawn. *Good, they are getting bored,* I thought.

I pulled back, out of view of the guards, and looked toward the tree line, where I knew everyone was waiting for my signal. I opened my tinderbox, which was attached to my belt, pulled out the necessary tools, and lit a small flame, doing my best to ensure the sound of my flint stone wasn't loud enough for the guards on the trail to hear. The small orange flame danced as I covered and uncovered it with my hand twice before tossing it into the moat to be extinguished in the water. One by one, everyone exited the tree line and crossed the precarious strip of ground along the wall to my position.

"Nadia, you're up. Please don't kill them," I requested once everyone was gathered at the castle wall. "They are just doing their job."

With a nod of confirmation, Nadia took out her bow. She peeked around the corner of the wall and eyed her opponents. They were sitting roughly forty yards away, well within her range. As she pulled back behind the safety of the castle wall, she drew an arrow from the quiver on her back and nodded to Ivan to get ready.

Nadia nocked her arrow and drew back on the bowstring. "Ivan, go," she ordered.

At that moment, they both quietly stepped out onto the trail. Despite the common perception that Ivan was slow, he was actually one of the fastest people I knew. With Nadia still in motion, Ivan darted out in front of her and charged the nearest soldier, making sure to give Nadia as much room as he could to make her shot along the thin path. As Ivan started his near silent charge, Nadia's right hand found its anchor point at her jaw, and she sighted down the arrow at the guard seated on the far side of the door.

They timed it perfectly, and it all happened within seconds. At precisely the right moment, before the guards spotted Ivan, Nadia released the bowstring, and I watched as the arrow sailed through the air. With the guards leaning back lazily in their chairs, their reaction time was too slow; they didn't stand a chance. Nadia's arrow sailed past Ivan's shoulder, missing him by a hair, and hit its mark in the far guard's shoulder. The arrow drew the nearest guard's attention, and he stood, looking in surprise at the weapon that had just penetrated his comrade. At that moment, Ivan put his head down and rammed into him. But Ivan didn't stop there. Plowing through the first guard like a bull out for blood, Ivan slammed him into the second guard, who was still staring in shock at the arrow in his shoulder. As the two guards collided, their heads slammed into each other, dazing them long enough for Ivan to knock them unconscious with his big fists.

With the first two guards down, we left Otto with the small boat so he could prepare it for our return, and the rest of us headed to the back door. While I tied up and gagged the guards, Nadia and Solace dressed in their uniforms and dragged the unconscious men into the narrow shadow of the low wall along the cliff edge, where they would hopefully not be visible if anyone looked down from the wall above.

Ivan and I took up hiding places in the shadows just inside door one, and at midnight, right on schedule, the shift change came. Two guards entered the second door, continuing down the hall, headed for door one. As soon as they reached our position, Ivan and I grabbed them from behind, wrapping our arms around their necks, squeezing tight just long enough for them to lose consciousness. We dragged their bodies outside door one, then Dan and Casey dressed in their uniforms. Nadia and Solace bound and gagged the guards tightly and put them with the other two unconscious guards, making sure to place them far enough apart that they would not be able to help each other once they awoke, no doubt with painful headaches.

It was decided that Solace would guard the outer door with Nadia, as Solace was the only person other than me who would know if soldiers of darkness were near. Leaving Nadia and Solace at the outer door, the rest of us proceeded down the hallway to the inner door, door two. Captain Bates opened the door and whistled to the guards, as if signaling he needed them to check something out. Through the slightly open door, we heard one guard tell the other that he would investigate. The door opened the rest of the way, and the guard came through, unknowingly passing Ivan as he did. Ivan silently stepped from the shadows and wrapped his big arm around the man's throat, again squeezing until the guard fell unconscious. Captain Bates put on the guard's uniform and helmet, then opened the door partway and beckoned to the other guard as if to show him something suspicious. Again, as the guard emerged, Ivan stepped from the shadows and did the honors, knocking the second guard out before he could utter a word.

The captain and I concealed all of the unconscious guards along the walls of the hallway while Ivan put on the second guard's uniform. The uniform didn't quite fit his large frame, but it would do. Dan and Casey, already in uniform, passed through door two, making sure to appear at ease in case anyone was in the hallway and watching.

Once the captain and I were ready, I opened the door slightly and glanced at Dan. He cleared his throat and cracked his neck, bending his head to the right to signal that a guard was posted down the hall to the right, the direction we were headed. Dan then gave a nod. No one but the guard was in the hallway.

Ivan and Captain Bates took the lead, since they were in uniform, and Eric, Lance, and I fell in step behind them so we would be concealed from the guard until the right moment. We marched down the hall, headed toward a bend in the hallway that led to the base of a tower, which contained sleeping quarters on its uppermost floor. The cellar was located below the tower. Lance had known that the cellar door was guarded by three guards. Hopefully, this guard at the bend in the hallway was one of them. As we marched down the hallway, I caught a slight glimpse of the guard, who looked just as bored as the others we had encountered so far. He was seated in a chair that was positioned to give him a clear view of both the hallway we were in and the hallway to the cellar door.

As we approached, Ivan motioned the guard to come toward us. Thankfully, the guard's boredom seemed to motivate him to seize any opportunity to stretch his legs. He stood to approach Ivan, who, in his guard's uniform and helmet, appeared to be his comrade. Once Ivan was sure the guard was no longer visible to guards down the other hallway, he clocked him square in the jaw, knocking him out with one well-aimed punch. The man never saw it coming.

While Eric and I tied up the guard, Captain Bates and Ivan rounded the corner with confident strides that said they belonged there. A low greeting and some thumping noises sounded from around the corner, so I risked a peek. The last two guards were down. Thankfully, the plan had gone off without a hitch. *So far.*

The captain and Ivan took the uniforms off the last two guards, then took all three guards and stowed them behind door two with the others, making sure they could not escape. When they returned, Eric was in uniform. Ivan took up watch at the bend in the hall, and the captain and Eric stood watch outside the door to the cellar. Lance and I took the last two guards' uniforms with us and entered the cellar, the captain closing the door behind us.

We were in.

Chapter 6

AN UNLIT LANTERN HUNG on the wall to our right. Lance grabbed it and ignited the wick, then held it out, revealing a staircase. Lance and I descended the short flight of stairs to find another door. I slowly opened it partway, unsure of what to expect on the other side. Cold, slightly damp air filled our lungs, and the smell of dirt and musty cloth was overwhelming. But thankfully, as I risked a look into the dark room, I didn't see any sign of people lying in wait to capture us. So, I opened the door the rest of the way and stepped into the damp cellar, pausing to light another lantern on the wall. Sure enough, the room was empty of guards. Lance entered behind me and closed the door, leaning on it as if its solid frame reassured him that we had made it. In the silence, we looked at each other and both let out a deep sigh of relief.

Standing just inside the cellar door, we examined the room before us. Amid stacks of crates, wooden barrels, and bulging sacks, the printing press was positioned in plain sight. *Thank goodness,* I thought. *Lance's information was good.* Without further delay, Lance and I got moving. It looked like the printing press was the last thing to be placed in the room, so it was easy to get to. We put down the bundles of type and other supplies we had brought, and Lance hung his lantern on the wall while I lit two more. Then we quietly repositioned a few items so we would have room to maneuver. Finally, we got to work.

Because we had preset the type, we were hopeful that we could be done printing the five books in about a half an hour, leaving enough time to let the ink set so we could move the papers. While Lance unwrapped the type for the first half of the first sheet, I pulled out the rolled-up paper we had brought and prepared the tympan to place the paper on. I loaded the first sheet onto the tympan, pushing two small pins through the paper, and secured the paper with the frisket, a frame that folded over the top of the paper to ensure that when the tympan was pressed down and lifted, the ink would not print on unwanted areas of the paper and the paper would easily lift off the type without smearing the ink.

With the first sheet of paper loaded, Lance gently slid the first set of type from the base of the wooden frame we used for transport onto the galley of the printing press. Once in place, the type was securely wedged into the cradle, where it would sit while it was inked and the paper pressed on top of it.

While Lance finished loading the preset type into the galley, I took out the ink we had brought and prepped the inking pads. The two inking pads were about the size of small dinner plates and wrapped in padding and an outer layer of leather, each with a short wooden handle. I poured some ink out onto a small, finished wooden plank we had brought for this process. Then I placed the leather-covered ink pads into the ink and rolled them around, covering the leather with the black ink.

Next, we inked the type by blotting the ink pads onto the metal type secured in the cradle of the printing press. Lance had informed me that it was important to blot the ink, not swipe, or the ink would get in the grooves of the letters, and we would end up with a bunch of ink blobs on the pages.

With the paper loaded and the type set and inked, I lowered the tympan with the paper secured by the frisket. Once the paper was in place over the type, I cranked a handle to slide the whole thing under the platan, which would press the paper onto the inked type. While I grabbed the next sheet of paper, Lance pulled a different handle toward his chest to lower the platen and press the page onto the inked type. The platen only covered half the sheet, so Lance had to lift the platan and slide the tympan halfway out so he could press the other half of the sheet.

We repeated this process on five different sheets of paper, draping them over some old chairs nearby to set so less ink would come off when we printed on the other side. We printed what we needed on this typeset for all five books rather than switching between typesets repeatedly. Once we were finished with the first typeset, we placed the next typeset into the press. We loaded the first paper sheet, print side down, making sure to line up the pin holes in the page so the type and margins would be even on both sides of the page. Once everything was again loaded and set up, we pressed this side of the paper with the new typeset. We repeated the process with all the typesets and all the sheets of paper until we had what we needed for five books.

With the pages printed, they still needed to dry before we could load them into a box for transport. But, as I stood there, I realized we might have time to print extras. I glanced at the lamps. I had noticed they were full when we arrived, and based on the oil level now, it appeared we were a little ahead of schedule.

"Should we print more?" I asked Lance.

Lance glanced over the pages that were hung on various objects to dry. "Even these pages will not be fully dry by the time we need to leave. I made the box the exact size of the pages, and I have very thin boards to put between the first five books to keep them from slipping around in the box. But the ink will still be barely dry enough to not smudge." Lance looked at me. "We certainly have time to make a few more copies while we wait for these, though. And I suppose even if they don't dry as much as we would like, they might come out okay. We should save enough blank pages to put one between each sheet to prevent them from smudging against each other, though. It might not stop it completely, but it will hopefully at least keep the text legible."

"Good idea," I said, nodding as I looked around the room at our handiwork. "Well, then, let's get to work."

Lance began resetting the type while I quietly went out the door and up the stairs to let the captain know about our plans. He informed me that the one o'clock bell had rung, so we had about three hours until the next shift change. When I rejoined Lance, we re-inked the first set of type and started again. We would use as much of our remaining time as we could, making sure to still leave enough time to load up the pages and leave before the replacement guards came to their posts.

The work went reasonably quickly, but as we were nearly finished with our fifteenth copy and I had started fanning some of the printed sheets of paper to help them dry, I noticed Lance looking a little distracted.

"You do this kind of thing often?" I asked as I sat down next to a sheet of paper to blow on a particularly wet section.

Lance shrugged. "Not usually in the belly of the beast, if you know what I mean," he said with a nervous chuckle.

I nodded and smiled.

"Do you?" he asked.

I shrugged and returned to using my hand to fan the paper. "I'll admit, this is the first time I have broken into a castle. But I have been in some risky situations."

Lance nodded. "You were a soldier once, weren't you?"

I nodded. "How could you tell?"

Lance offered a small shrug. "Soldiers hold themselves a certain way. One gets good at spotting it after a while."

I nodded in understanding.

"Though I must say it took me longer to see it in you," he added, studying me with a side-long gaze.

"It's been a while," I responded as I inspected one of the first pages we had printed. It looked to be drying pretty well despite the damp atmosphere.

Lance nodded. "You get injured or something?"

"You could say that," I replied without looking up, not wanting to get into the loss of my family, who had been killed by beast attacks. I had been all alone until I met Solace.

Lance pressed the last piece of paper, then lifted the platen and removed the sheet to let it dry. After a moment of silence, he said, "I lost someone too, you know."

I looked up at him in surprise. Although he appeared sad, he didn't seem scarred by loss, as I was. Maybe he was just good at covering it up. A skill I had yet to master.

Lance nodded, his gaze growing slightly distant. "War is a messy thing." His eyes refocused and he looked at me. "People like you have stopped many people like me from losing everything. But I have learned over the last few years that soldiers lose more than we realize."

Unsure what to say, I remained silent. Not many people seemed to care. I wasn't used to this kind of understanding.

"Thank you," said Lance after a moment of silence.

I nodded. He didn't need to say anything else. I knew what he meant. And I appreciated it.

"Well, we have a couple more sheets we could press while we are here and still leave enough to put a blank page between each sheet. Shall we?" he asked, changing the subject.

I stood with a silent nod, and we got back to work.

Once Lance and I were finished and the first set of pages had dried enough to move them, we began loading the papers into the box and prepared to leave. The last few copies we had printed would likely smudge during transport, but hopefully they would still be readable.

While Lance secured the box, I grabbed the shield from where I had set it against the wall nearest to me. As I picked up the shield, the sword slid down the wall, and I reached out to catch it. As my fingers gripped the sword's hilt, something in the corner of the cellar suddenly caught my eye. As I straightened and looked toward the object, everything around me seemed to fade as the object drew my complete attention as if it were the only thing in the room. I faintly heard Lance's voice but didn't fully grasp their meaning.

The sword in my hand felt odd, and for some reason, I couldn't take my eyes off the object. It was as if the sword wanted me to go to the object, so I approached it cautiously, one step at a time.

The object was about as tall as a man and oval, and it stood in the far corner of the cellar, covered by a sheet. As I approached, I found myself reaching out toward it. I grabbed the edge of the sheet and pulled it off. As the sheet was pulled free, a blinding light poured from the object before me, and I had to shield my face with my arm. As I closed my eyes against the light, a brief image of the Beast of the Woods wrapping its tail around my waist flashed through my mind's eye. The image seemed to meld with an image of the scaled animal from my vision in the Woods also wrapping something around my waist, as if the two were giving me a single object. *The Beast's tail? No, it was something else... The belt from my dreams!*

As I lowered my arm and opened my eyes, the brief image disappeared, and I found myself standing before a gold-rimmed mirror. It shone with an unusual shimmer, and something was written around its rim in a beautiful script that resembled the writing on the sword. But that was not what caught me by surprise; it was the reflection I saw in the mirror's clear, shiny surface.

As I turned my attention to the reflection, I saw myself. But my image was slightly transparent, and behind my reflection, looking back at me as if it were inside the mirror, was a great dragon. *The scaled creature from my vision!* I realized. Its scales were almost transparent white, as if they were made of ice, yet they appeared tinged with blue from beneath. It watched me with intelligent blue-green eyes and a regal expression.

"Who are you?" I whispered in awe.

"Be on guard, my friend," she said in a gentle voice, "for your heart is a treasure worth protecting."

As she finished speaking, the dragon reached out of the mirror and placed the tip of her claw on my chest. As her claw touched me, a silver breastplate of armor appeared on me in my reflection, covering my back and chest from my shoulders to my waist. I reached out and touched the reflection of the breastplate, but as my fingers made contact with the mirror, suddenly, the breastplate and dragon vanished to reveal a new reflection. I remained in the new reflection, but a dark shadow appeared behind me. Veins of darkness seemed to penetrate my reflection, spreading throughout my body as the dark being rose, looming over me. Its presence transformed my reflection into a dark version of myself. My skin was pale, my eyes a dull grey, and in my arms I held the limp, bloodied body of the Beast of the Woods, dead, a reminder of the intentions I'd had all those months ago when I entered the Woods.

Startled by the abrupt change and the guilt it inflicted on my mind, I flinched backward, dropping the sword. The dark reflection in the mirror abruptly disappeared, replaced with a normal image of me as the mirror seemed to lose some of its shimmer, and the mysterious words around its frame vanished.

Suddenly finding myself standing in the cellar with Lance, I shook my head and rubbed my hands over my face as the guilt welled up within me, twisting my gut and filling my mind with memories of nearly killing the Beast. When I had entered the Woods about six months ago, I had intended to kill the Beast to save Solace's life, the one thing she had not wanted me to do. I had also intended to kill what I now knew was the last of the King's beasts. That intention had plagued me with guilt since I first made the decision. And I still had not told Solace of my intentions that day—my intentions to put my own fear of losing her over her wish to protect a story I now knew was true. A story she had spent her whole life protecting. *What would she think of me? Would she forgive me if she knew?*

"Ben," I heard Lance say with concern. "Ben, are you okay?"

I blinked a few times but couldn't focus on anything as my mind replayed what I had seen in the mirror. "I...I'm fine," I said, still in shock. "Did you see that?" I asked as I shoved my guilt down somewhere deep within me.

Lance's brow furrowed in confusion. "See what? Ben, we need to leave," he urged. "The guards will be here soon for the next shift change."

I looked at him in surprise. "What? Why didn't you grab me or something?" I asked as I picked up the sword, hoping it wouldn't show me the images again.

"I tried," he replied, "but it was like you were,"—he shrugged—"in a trance or something."

I shook my head, trying to focus once again on the task at hand. "Okay, let's just get out of here. Is everything loaded and ready to go?"

Lance nodded. "Almost. There are just a few more pages to load."

The door to the cellar suddenly opened. My heart jumped into my throat as I instinctively raised the sword in defense, and Lance and I both froze.

"Hurry, up!" commanded Captain Bates in an intense whisper. "I hear movement."

Lance and I let out a synchronized sigh at the sight of the captain and hurried to finish loading the printed sheets into the wooden frame. Since we were sure the ink had not had time to fully dry on all the copies, Lance loaded a sheet of paper between each page and a thin piece of wood between the first five book copies. Once all the sheets were loaded, he placed the rest of the paper on top to weigh down the ones with print and keep them from sliding around. We hoped this would minimize any smearing.

With the sheets loaded and secured in the wooden frame and all the supplies we no longer needed stowed out of sight in the cellar, Lance and I quickly moved as many things as we could back where they had been before. Then we dressed in the guards' uniforms we had brought and headed out the door. As we exited the cellar, I glanced back at the now covered mirror as the images I had seen flashed through my mind and the dragon's words sounded in my ear. *"Be on guard, my friend, for your heart is a treasure worth protecting."* Shaking the images and the fears that accompanied them from my mind, I turned and headed after Lance, closing the door behind me. We ascended the stone stairs and stepped through the door at the top. With the captain and Eric in the lead, we made our way down the hallway, and Ivan joined us as we turned the corner.

With Ivan taking up the rear, Lance and I walked in formation behind the captain and Eric, making sure to conceal the box of pages in case anyone unexpectedly stumbled upon us. As we made our way toward Dan and Casey, who were still stationed at the inner door, the sound of voices echoed down the hall from somewhere up ahead, around another corner. We all froze, uncertain if we should move forward or go back. If it was the shift change, we would be discovered and they would sound the alarm. After a moment of indecision, the voices thankfully faded as the speakers moved on to a different part of the castle.

I glanced at the captain and nodded, signaling that we needed to speed up. We hurried toward the exit, Dan and Casey joining us as we passed through the inner door. Casey closed the door behind us, and we all broke into a run toward the outer door, where Nadia and Solace were waiting. We had to make it to the moat before the next set of soldiers got to their posts.

We sprinted down the hall and through the outer door, where we all took off the guard uniforms and quickly began to change back into our clothes. Nadia finished first, and as we were putting on our last garments and securing our weapons, she headed back into the hallway.

"Nadia," I called out in a harsh whisper as I secured my sword in place. "What are you doing?"

"I'm going to block the doorway with the bodies of the unconscious guards. It won't stop anyone, but it will slow them down," she called quietly before she was out of earshot.

I ran after Nadia, wanting to yell at her, but I thought better of it. Who knew how much these walls echoed.

When I reached her position, she was already dragging a body in front of the door, so I helped. "We need to get going," I insisted.

"The others aren't dressed yet, and this will slow down the guards who come for the shift change. There is no way we will all make it back across the moat in that small boat. If some of us end up crossing on foot again, we are going to need all the time we can get," she whispered.

"If we leave this door accessible, they might not notice anything is wrong until we are across the moat," I pointed out. "These guards along the wall are in shadow, so they might not see them, or we could hide them outside."

She blew a lock of red hair out of her face and frowned. "Do you really believe that? As soon as they see there are no guards to replace, they will know something is up. And if they see us before we get across that moat, there is a good chance they will just shoot us. You know this is our best bet." She suddenly froze.

"What?" I whispered, but she held a finger to her lips.

A sound came from the other side of the door, and I risked opening it just a crack. We stood silent for a moment as we strained to hear whatever had made the sound. Distant voices came from inside the castle, echoing off the walls, accompanied by the sound of footsteps and metal gently clanking on metal. The guards were coming to their posts.

Upon hearing the voices, we dropped one more body in place and turned and ran through the outer doorway. "Hurry, they are coming!" I snapped in a harsh whisper, waving everyone on ahead of me toward the moat as I took a head count.

Spurred on by the incoming threat, we all made a mad dash to the moat, careful not to fall to our deaths over the cliff's edge. When we reached the moat, Ivan dragged the small boat into the water. But the boat couldn't hold us all.

"Captain, take Solace, Otto, and Eric with you. The rest of us will go on foot," I directed.

"We will take Lance as well," said the captain. "They will be looking for the copies of the book and will come after us first if they see we have the box."

I frowned. He had a point. First and foremost, Valdra would want to stop *The Story* from being spread. If he had to make a choice, he would go after *The Story*, leaving those of us on foot with a better chance of escape. "Okay, take Lance too."

I turned to Solace. "Take this," I said, handing her the shield. "I don't know exactly how it works, but at least you will have some extra protection."

"But what about you and the others?" she asked, her brow creasing with concern.

"Have a little faith," I said with a smile and a wink. Solace smiled back and nodded before climbing into the boat, joining Otto, Captain Bates, Eric, and Lance, who clutched the box with the book pages. Nadia, Ivan, Dan, and Casey stayed with me, and we began the precarious journey along the thin strip of land at the end of the moat while the boat made its way across the water as fast as it could.

The boat was full and rode low in the water, but it made it across the moat much faster than the rest of us. While the captain and the others disappeared into the tree line with the book pages, the rest of us inched our way across the slippery strip of land between the wall and the moat.

We snuck along in shadow, the night still quiet. But just as we reached the halfway point, the castle behind us erupted in commotion as an alarm bell rang out. They knew we were here.

I glanced up at the castle wall with the sword in hand in time to see a soldier of darkness leap from the wall, headed straight for us.

"Run!" I yelled to the others, no longer concerned if the enemy heard me.

The armies of darkness charged over the wall with the Martecytes and Castle Guard in tow, spilling from the back door and down the castle walls on ropes. I slashed the first soldier of darkness, killing it, as we scrambled across the rest of the soggy ground as fast as we could. But I slipped in the mud, losing my footing, and began to fall. Just as my feet began to sink into the water, Ivan's hand flashed out toward me, and he grabbed my free hand. But my relief was short-lived when my boot struck something hard in the water. *Spikes!* I realized. The base of the moat was covered in metal spikes. *They must be lining the edge of the moat. It's a wonder the boat didn't run into any. Lance was right about the dangers hiding beneath the surface!*

"Do not fall in!" I called to everyone. "There are metal spikes in the water!"

Ivan pulled me free of the water just as another soldier of darkness reached us. "Go!" I yelled to the others. As they rushed toward the more stable ground on the other side of the moat, I turned to face the castle and lifted my sword in defense as the soldier of darkness attacked with its sword. Metal struck metal with a clang that I briefly wondered if the others could hear. As I glanced over my shoulder, I saw them struggling to get across the remainder of the narrow strip without falling into the moat. Nadia grabbed Eric just in time to keep him from losing his footing and falling into the murky waters, where he would have most certainly been impaled.

As they reached the other side of the moat, I returned my focus to the soldier of darkness. I barely managed to keep my footing as I backed my way toward the safety of solid ground. My mind raced as I blocked the soldier's advances and navigated the treacherous path.

As soon as I reached the other side of the moat, I turned my back on the castle to run, but I slipped again. This time, I managed to pull myself back onto solid ground without sliding into the spike-filled water. I scrambled away from the water's edge as I desperately dodged the dark soldier's sword thrusts. I blocked the blade with my sword, and, in a clean diagonal stroke, I lunged upward and sliced through the front of his neck, killing him instantly.

As the soldier of darkness fell, I stumbled to the side and looked toward the castle in time to see the first few Castle Guards reach my side of the moat. They had brought out more boats—from where, I had no idea—and were quickly swarming across the water. But that was not the sight that drew my attention. Standing on the land between me and the moat, Eyethanoff, my soldier of light, suddenly appeared. He reached for his sword and drew it from his scabbard in a precise, elegant motion. As its tip escaped the scabbard, he raised the sword in a smooth arc, stopping with the blade centered in front of his face. As the armies of darkness approached, he took a smooth step back, landing in position with his feet braced apart. As his back foot found its mark, his sword ignited with a flame so hot it burned blue.

With only Eyethanoff standing in their way, the armies of darkness hesitated. The seen world around them seemed to move in slow motion as the Castle Guard unloaded from the boats, unaware of what was taking place before them.

"Run," commanded Eyethanoff calmly.

I glanced at him, not wanting to leave. But his tone had left no room for argument. He had given me an order, and I would follow it. Trusting he knew what he was doing, I ran toward the tree line. As I dashed through the trees, the Castle Guard and Martecytes followed not far behind, and I wished I had Jeb to carry me to the ship faster.

I darted through bushes and jumped over rocks and downed trees as I sprinted toward the old church. I managed to gain some ground on my pursuers and tried my best to throw them off my trail, but the sound of dogs baying told me they would catch up to me eventually.

When I reached the old church, I stopped to catch my breath for a moment before heading in to find the others hunkered down in the back room where we had originally met. They were hastily separating the freshly printed pages into each book.

"We can't stay here," I said breathlessly, the sword still in my hands. "They have dogs."

"We need to get the book pages to our contact so it can be printed for the people of this island country," said Solace.

"Where are we scheduled to meet the contact?" I asked.

"At the docks on the northwestern side of the island. We were supposed to meet tonight at sunset to drop off the book," the captain replied.

"We can't wait that long. They will find us," I said urgently.

The captain shook his head. "Not if they think we left the island," he said with that focused look he got when he was solving a problem.

"What do you mean?" I asked.

"It only takes one or two people to deliver a book to someone—or two books, now that we have extra copies," he said, frowning slightly. "If everyone but Lance and possibly you or Solace gets on the ship and we make sure to sail out where they can see us sail away, they will think we left the island. Then, late tonight we can double back around and pick up the people left behind."

I nodded as I considered that suggestion. "You might be on to something, Captain," I said, rubbing my chin. "I think it's a good plan. But both Solace and I will have to get on the ship, or Valdra will know something is up."

The captain looked to Dan. "Dan, go with Lance to deliver the book pages. We will meet you both on the northwestern side of the island at midnight tonight."

"Yes, sir," said Dan.

"Both?" I asked.

The captain nodded. "Lance has decided to come along and lend a hand on our mission. We might need him if we lose another press or contact, as he has connections that have helped a lot since before you joined us."

As Dan and Lance headed off in the direction of tonight's meeting, I turned to the captain. "I will provide a distraction and lead the Castle Guard on a chase. Get everyone to the ship, and I will meet you there."

"Unless you get caught," said Solace with a frown.

"I'll be fine," I said, smiling to cover up the sudden guilt that sprang to my stomach as Solace's comment brought back the image of me carrying the dead beast. The Beast had somehow known my intentions when I entered the Woods, and its words had stopped me in my tracks. Now I was here, still carrying that secret—I had not told Solace of my intentions to kill the Beast, and I did not want to face it now. I shook my head to erase the thought. "I'll take the sword and shield and go on a small detour through the city before heading back to the ship," I said as I pushed away the feelings of guilt before turning to the captain. I needed to focus on the task at hand. "When I arrive, we need to set sail right away to make it look like we are running and have no choice but to leave the island."

Captain Bates nodded. "Will do. We should get a move on, or they will catch us here, and this whole thing will end tonight," he said with conviction.

With that, I took the shield back from Solace, and as the rest of the group set out for the ship, I took off through the trees, heading for town. I darted through the docks to make sure people saw me. To my relief, the Castle Guard fell for it and came after me. They pursued me through the city on a wild goose chase until I finally turned and headed back toward the *Lyonsword*.

With the sounds of the Castle Guard's pursuit and the baying of their tracking dogs echoing through the night, I pressed on. I momentarily thought I was lost but soon recognized a landmark and managed to get back on track. I hoped the others had reached the *Lyonsword*'s secret docking port with no trouble and would be ready to leave as soon as I arrived.

Finally, I found the entrance to the hidden docking port. I rounded a big boulder and ran through the small pass-like entrance to the hidden alcove where the ship was waiting. Relief washed over me as I saw the others running about the deck, preparing to disembark. The crew were already beginning to raise the sails as the ship was drifting slowly away from the dock. The captain stood at the gunwale, waving me to keep coming as the ship drifted far enough from the dock that the gangplank between the two fell into the water.

With the sword still in hand, I darted across the beach, throwing a glance over my shoulder. Lights flickered among the rocks as the guards and their dogs closed in. I sheathed the sword and hung the shield over my shoulder as I bolted down the wooden dock just as the Castle Guard spilled into the alcove. Sprinting with everything

I had left, I ran and jumped for the *Lyonsword*. As I sailed through the air, I aimed for the gunwale and grabbed it with both hands, but my boots slipped. Gripping the edge of the railing, I hung off the side of the boat as the sound of arrows being released from bows registered in my ears. The captain appeared over the ship's edge and grabbed my arm just as an arrow hit inches from my hand. Ignoring the arrow, the captain pulled me up and over the edge of the *Lyonsword* as the boat drifted beyond the rocks and the sails caught the wind, pulling the ship out to sea.

The captain and I each let out a heaving sigh, then released small chuckles of relief as we stood on the deck. The captain slapped me on the back with an approving smile, then began shouting orders to the crew to be ready for an attack as I turned and looked at the dock we had just left behind. It was lined with the Castle Guard, but the brief barrage of arrows had stopped. Dogs on leashes barked as their prey sailed away, and men watched us retreat into the night, shaking their heads in frustration. But the words of the dragon in the mirror echoed in my mind, reminding me of the darkness that pursued us, and curiosity got the best of me.

I drew the sword from its scabbard and tightened my grip on its hilt. As confidence in its power flowed through me and it became balanced in my hand, the armies of darkness appeared. They stood among the men and dogs on the dock, invisible to the Castle Guard but ever-present. They watched like shadows with understanding. They knew we would meet again.

Chapter 7

As I STOOD ON the *Lyonsword*'s main deck and watched the Eastern Island drift away, I couldn't help but wonder if I was making a mistake by leaving so soon. The mirror I had found in the castle was clearly connected to the Unseen Lands. *What was it doing in the castle? Do I need to go back? Who was the dragon? And what about the breastplate of armor? What did it mean?* My mind wandered to the flash of darkness and the image of the dead beast that had appeared when I touched the reflection, and the dragon's words echoed in my head. *"Be on guard, my friend, for your heart is a treasure worth protecting."* Chills ran down my spine as I remembered the dark shadow that had overtaken my reflection, seeming to reveal what was really within me.

A small tug on my coat pulled me from my thoughts, and I looked down to see Yuuki standing next to me.

"Did you get the books?" she asked, looking up at me with bright, questioning eyes.

I smiled as I placed a hand on her head and looked back out to the ocean. "Yep. We got 'em."

"Oh. Good. Because I spilled some water on your notebooks," she said with an innocent grin that suggested she was hoping the mission going well would dampen the problem of waterlogged books.

I glanced down as she handed me a partially damp notebook. I took the book and looked through the pages. It wasn't too bad. It was still legible, and the pages would dry in time.

"Christopher said that I should just leave it until you got back so that I wouldn't smear stuff..." She clasped her hands behind her back and absentmindedly twirled her skirt. "Sorry."

I squatted down in front of her and smiled. "Thank you for telling me, Yuuki. You did the right thing. But how did it get wet?"

Yuuki took a deep breath and looked up at the sky for a moment, something Solace said she had learned from me. "I might have spilled some water in your bed," she said as her eyes met mine again.

"You might have?" I prompted as I held back a small smile.

Yuuki was a sweet little girl, and since Solace and I had taken her in, she had gone with us everywhere. But her curiosity often got her into situations like this—something Solace and I had learned to be less frustrated over with each incident. It was often better than her wandering off into some forest, following an animal to its family for a play date, which had also happened on multiple occasions.

"I did spill water," she corrected herself with a sharp nod.

I nodded. "Well, did you clean it up?" I asked with raised eyebrows.

"I was going to pull the water out and throw it in the ocean, but it didn't work," she said with a frown.

"Pull it out?" I asked, confused.

"Yeah, you know, with power," she explained as if I should know what she was talking about.

Yuuki's imagination seemed to get more elaborate the longer we knew her and the more she heard about the Unseen Lands.

I smiled. "Well, I'm sorry it didn't work; maybe we should just let it all dry by itself."

She nodded. "I moved your other books so they wouldn't get wet," she explained. "Also, I found this," she added as she held up a damp piece of paper.

I took the paper and gently unfolded it. I had not seen it before, and the note was not in any handwriting I recognized. "'Meet me at the Smugglers' Road,'" I read out loud. "Where did you find this?" I asked Yuuki as my mind ran through everything that had happened in the past few months that might tell me who this note was from.

"In the place you keep the sword and shield," she said with a shrug. "I was trying to move things to dry them off, and it fell out of the cloak you usually wrap them in," she explained.

The cloak was a black, hooded garment that Ruth had wrapped the sword and shield in when she gave them to me. *Maybe this note is from her,* I thought. The last time I had seen her was when she gave me the sword and shield. I looked down at the note. *No, this isn't her handwriting, and the paper looks old,* I realized.

"Thank you, Yuuki. Why don't you go see if Christopher needs your help with anything? I'll go finish making sure everything is drying out."

"Okay," she said as she turned to leave.

As Yuuki set off to find Christopher, I went in search of Solace. After asking a couple people, I located her below deck. She was sitting near one of our hammocks, folding and cutting the sheets of book pages so they would be ready to bind in leather and hand off to our contacts.

"Solace, did Yuuki show you this?" I asked as I approached her, setting the sword and shield in the corner of the room by our hammocks. As I stepped up beside her, I half expected myself to feel the same guilt that had arisen the last time we spoke. But the feeling didn't come, or at least not as intensely as it had before.

Solace glanced up at me and the piece of paper I was holding up before returning to her project. "No, she just said that she had to tell you something. I assumed it had to do with the wet notebooks," she said with a smile.

I nodded. "Yeah, she told me about that too. Are they damaged?"

"Not bad," replied Solace as she lifted a shoulder in a shrug without taking her eyes off what she was doing. "They will dry."

"Good," I responded.

"What does the paper say?" Solace asked as she put aside her project and stood to look at the damp note in my hand.

"It says, 'Meet me at the Smuggler's Road.'" I glanced at Solace. "Does that mean anything to you?"

She shook her head. "No. Where did Yuuki find it?"

"She said it fell out of the cloak that Ruth gave me—the one I wrap the sword and shield in when I am not using them. I thought it was from Ruth, but I have seen her handwriting in her book, and this doesn't look like hers."

Solace raised an eyebrow. "Do you think she meant to leave it in there?" she asked as she returned to her project.

"I don't know. But it would be worth checking out...if we could figure out where the Smugglers' Road is," I said.

"Maybe Captain Bates knows. He has worked in the smuggling world for years."

"Good idea. I'll go ask him." I looked at the leaves of the books she was working on. "How is the bookmaking going?"

"Good," she replied. "Most of the copies turned out nice. But the last ones you printed need more time to dry, and they have a couple small smudges. But I think we can still use them. Either way, you made extra, so we will make sure at least one good copy gets to each printer," she said as she folded a sheet once the long way and twice the short way and then began cutting the folds until she had eight pages of text. "We are cutting and binding them in leather. Nothing too fancy. Just enough to hold them together until we can deliver them."

"When you are finished, make sure to store them away from Yuuki," I said with a grin.

Solace chuckled. "She didn't mean to spill the water. It happened when the wind caught the sails."

"I know she didn't mean to," I said with a smile. "I'm just teasing. She did a good job cleaning up after herself."

I placed the note in my pocket, careful not to rip it, but before I could leave, Solace put a hand on my arm, pulling my attention back to her.

"Lance mentioned your...encounter," she said, her brow furrowing slightly in worry. "What happened?"

I shook my head. "I don't really know...I saw some things...I..." I shook my head and winced. "Can we talk about this later?" I asked. "I need some time to think through what happened."

Solace cocked her head to one side and examined me. She was a smart woman and not an easy person to hide things from. But to my relief, she nodded. "Yes. Go. Ask the captain about the note. But,"—she looked me in the eyes and held my gaze—"we need to talk."

I nodded, then headed up the stairs to the main deck in search of the captain. When I emerged onto the deck, I saw that we were finally far from shore. The sun had not yet risen, so the land just appeared as a lump of black in the distance, but the sky would lighten sometime in the next hour or so. The crew looked like they were working hard to prepare for something, and there was a tension in the air that had not been there before. Though we did still need to return to the island without getting caught, the atmosphere seemed a little too strained for everything to be going smoothly.

I crossed the main deck and entered the captain's quarters. Closing the door behind me, I turned to find Captain Bates standing near the window facing the island we had just left behind.

"What's going on?" I asked. "What is everyone prepping for?"

Captain Bates responded without taking his eyes off the water. "My messenger thinks they are sending out a ship to pursue us," he said in a distant voice.

I glanced at the map table and saw a small scroll from a pigeon. "Can you see a ship yet?" I asked, joining him at the window.

"No. Not yet," he said. I could tell he was contemplating solutions to this new potential problem. Abruptly, the captain turned from the window and looked at me. "What did you need?" he asked as I followed him to his desk.

"Well, it can wait. We need to make sure we can get back to the island tonight," I said.

The captain held up a hand. "Is what you have brought me important?" he asked, cutting to the point.

I nodded. "I think so." I handed the captain the note. "Yuuki found this in the cloak that Ruth wrapped the sword and shield in when she gave them to me. I am not sure who wrote it, but I don't think she would have just forgotten it or left it in the cloak unless she wanted us to find it."

The captain took the note and wandered over to the map table while he read it. When he reached the table, he placed the note on the edge and began scanning various locations on the map. "Do you know anything of this Smugglers' Road?" he asked, his attention now fully focused on this new mystery.

I shook my head. "No. I was hoping you would know."

"I don't know for sure, but I recall Ruth mentioning a road when we were starting to put smuggling plans in place to move the book around, before I met you. Apparently, she had used the road before and said it was a good smuggling route. But then she disappeared, and you and I joined forces instead," he said as he studied the map.

"Did she tell you where the road is?" I asked.

"No. However, she might have hinted at its whereabouts. She mentioned something about an old symbol. I never got a chance to have her show me what it looked like, but it might be a good place to start."

A symbol, I thought to myself. The shield had a strange symbol on it of intertwined curling lines, which suddenly reminded me of the language on the sword. It probably had something to do with that language. The first time I had seen that symbol was on a pendant the Prince wore when I saw him in the Woods. Then I remembered I had also seen that symbol on Eyethanoff's uniform. The clasp on his shoulder that held his cloak in place was crafted in the shape of the symbol.

When I didn't respond, the captain looked up from the map to catch my expression. "What are you thinking?" he asked as he straightened.

"It might not be related, but there is some kind of symbol on the shield Ruth gave me. It is the same symbol I saw on the Prince's pendant when I was in the Woods. I didn't really think much of it until now, but it looks a lot like the language on the sword."

The captain rubbed his chin as he thought. "Well, there is no harm in starting there, I suppose. At least none that I can think of at this moment."

"I left the shield with Solace. I will go get it from her," I said.

The captain thought for a moment before adding, "Have Otto make copies of the symbol. We can at least start by distributing the copies among the crew and telling them to let one of us know if they see it anywhere else on our travels."

I nodded. "Good idea. I'll let him know." I glanced back out the window. "What are we going to do in the meantime?" I asked, gesturing toward the water to remind the captain about the enemy ship that might be lurking in the dark.

"Eric and Catherine will keep an eye on things this morning from the nest," he explained. "The various armies that are after us don't know exactly where we are going. So, hopefully, we can make it back to the northwestern side of the island and pick Dan and Lance up before the Castle Guard or Valdra's army catch up with us."

"Well, then, what are we going to do after we pick them up? If Valdra is sending a ship out now, they will definitely try to pursue us when we really do leave, or worse, catch us while we are picking up Dan and Lance."

"Like I said, they don't know for sure where we are headed," he said.

"Valdra might know," I said simply. "He probably has spies everywhere."

The captain crossed his arms. "Good point." He pondered the dilemma for a moment before continuing. "Do you think he could catch us before we make it to the Northern Country like he caught up to you at the Town?"

I considered the possibility. When Valdra had come after us the first time, he had pursued us over land through the Forest. This was different. I had never seen him pursue us over water. "I'm still learning about all of this, but to the best of my understanding, even the armies of darkness and the Martecytes interact with tangible things the way we do. Their swords clang against ours, they can pick up rocks, and they lean against things." I shrugged. "I am not certain, but there is a chance they can't do anything like walk on water or fly. It seems that the Martecytes can simply morph between the seen and unseen," I explained. "Then again, at the Woods, I saw some soldiers of darkness in the air...Either way, I don't think it wise to assume they can't outmaneuver us," I finished.

The captain nodded in agreement. "In that case, once we pick up Dan and Lance, we will head for the Northern Country as planned. But we will have to be careful as we get closer. I have a messenger who will alert me by pigeon if any dangers await us on land. But we will have to keep an eye on the water behind us," he said, gesturing to the window.

"Okay." I crossed the room and paused with the door half open. "Once we pick up the others, how long will it take to reach the Northern Country?" I asked.

"About two weeks," said the captain.

I nodded and left the captain's quarters, headed back to our sleeping quarters to get the shield and, hopefully, find Otto. As I entered, Solace was just getting up to take a break from working on the books. "Where did I put the shield?" I wondered out loud.

"Over there." Solace pointed to the corner near my hammock.

"Oh, thank you. I am a little preoccupied. The captain is concerned about Valdra picking up Dan and Lance without getting caught." I gave her a quick kiss, then walked to the corner and pulled the shield from beneath the cloak she had placed over it. The cloak was still damp in places from Yuuki's spill, so I laid it over the top of my hammock to let it finish drying. Then I grabbed the shield and looked over the symbol. It was quite unique. It definitely resembled the language on the sword, but it was not an image I remembered seeing anywhere other than on the Prince's pendant and Eyethanoff's uniform.

"Where's Otto?" I asked, looking to Solace as she climbed into bed. But then I spotted movement from his bed in a corner near the door.

Solace gestured to the pile of blankets and notebooks on Otto's bed. "He hasn't slept much since he started trying to figure out this language. He sat down to work when we got back to the ship and was out like a light," she explained.

I walked over to Otto's bed and stood next to it, hoping he would sense me standing there and wake up. The faint sound of his snoring suddenly grew louder, then subsided again. No luck. *I should know better by now,* I thought to myself as I rolled my eyes. *He has no sense of his surroundings.* I supposed I shouldn't hold it against him, though. He wasn't a soldier like the rest of us.

"Do you think it's okay to wake him?" I asked Solace, concerned that he really did need more sleep. He had been working nonstop for a while now and tended to work through the night.

Solace pursed her lips in thought. "I think it will be okay. He's been sleeping for over an hour, and he did tell me to wake him if he fell asleep. But I wanted to let him get some rest."

I looked at the pile of blankets atop Otto. Since he had adjusted position, I could see some of his limbs now hanging out from under the blankets, and his face was covered in a notebook he had been using to record notes on the language. I puffed out my cheeks as I let out a breath and bumped the makeshift bed with my boot.

Otto exploded from the blankets. "I don't know!" he called out groggily.

Otto's bed was positioned on top of a small landing that opened into storage compartments, and his sudden movement was enough to send him tumbling off his bed with a clamor. I took a step back to give him room to collect himself. In his usual fashion, he scrambled to his feet with his hair sticking out everywhere and a small smudge of ink on his face.

"I don't know!" he repeated as he stood, swaying slightly.

"Otto," I said, waving a hand in front of his face. "Otto, wake up. I need your help with something."

Otto shook his head and opened his eyes wide enough that I could see white all the way around his irises. He blinked a few times and then nodded. "I got it."

"You got what?" I asked, leaning in to get a better look at him and make sure he was actually awake.

Otto blinked again and looked around the room. "Um, never mind," he said as he regained consciousness of his surroundings. Running a hand over his black hair, Otto finally looked at me. "What...what did you say?" he asked with an inquisitive frown.

"I said I need help with something," I repeated.

He nodded. "Of course you do," he said, regaining his usual air of intelligence.

Otto cleared his throat as I turned away to keep him from seeing my smile. When I first met him, Otto had annoyed me to no end. But he had become a good friend, and we had all come to find his unkempt brilliance both amusing and helpful.

I turned back to face Otto and held up the shield. "I need you to draw this symbol and tell everyone on the ship to keep an eye out for it during our travels."

Otto nodded. "I can draw it. But no one listens to me," he complained. "Shouldn't you tell them to look for it yourself?" he suggested.

I smiled. "It'll be good practice for you," I said as I clapped a hand on his shoulder before turning toward the door, leaving him standing there with the shield in his hands and a still half-asleep expression on his face. "And don't forget to rest up over the next few days," I called over my shoulder as I disappeared through the hatch to the deck to look for Ivan and Nadia.

I found the twins on the quarterdeck, which formed the roof over the captain's quarters. The moon was low and bright in the sky, and its light danced across the surface of the ocean. Nadia was perched on the port side railing of the poop deck above, the long tails of her green jacket gently waving in the wind as they hung past the railing. Ivan was at the helm with a guiding hand on the wheel and a smile on his face. He looked perfectly content and free as the wind gently rustled his burly mustache.

"How does it look out there?" I asked as I came up the stairs.

"So far, so good," said Nadia from her perch.

"You two need to remember to get some sleep," I said, glancing between them.

"We're good, Ben," Nadia reassured. "We slept yesterday," she said teasingly.

"Yeah, but not nearly enough," I said, crossing my arms. I didn't need them overtired and losing their touch. "Eric and Catherine are keeping an eye out this morning. You two need to get some sleep if you want to be able to relieve them later." I paused. "By the way, how did you even know to keep an eye out?"

"We talked to the captain just a minute ago," said Ivan.

Nadia climbed down from her perch. "I don't like the idea that Valdra is following us out here, Ben. You know he probably has some foggy black ship that will sneak up on us right when we least expect it," she said, her lips and forehead wrinkling in frustration as she crossed her arms.

"Yeah, but we'll be ready for him," said Ivan with a grin.

"Not if you're both exhausted," I said, only half teasing. "Go get some sleep," I commanded as I turned back to the steps.

"Where are you going?" asked Nadia.

"I just need to check in with Eric and Catherine to make sure they haven't seen anything either."

Nadia's expression suddenly slackened, and her gaze became distant.

"What?" I asked, stopping at the top of the stairs.

"I just had a thought," said Nadia.

"A bad thought, I am assuming, based on your expression," I replied, turning to give her my full attention.

"Do you happen to know if the armies of darkness have ships of their own?" she asked, meeting my gaze.

I raised my eyebrows. "I hadn't thought of that," I admitted as a sudden wave of concern washed over me. "I have no idea."

"Well, you might want to check. We have been on the move for an hour or so now, and we haven't seen anyone even though we have been warned that they are following us. What if that's just because we can't see them?"

I looked out over the dark ocean, its small waves casting tiny shadows on the water that quickly vanished as they moved, and I shuddered at the thought.

Chapter 8

I RETRIEVED THE SWORD and returned to the quarterdeck to find that a small crowd had gathered. The captain was waiting with Nadia and Ivan on the poop deck, and the sun was just beginning to lighten the horizon. I climbed the small staircase to the uppermost deck and took up position near the railing, then drew the sword and looked out over the waters around us. To my relief, I saw nothing.

"No one's out there," I said with a sigh.

The atmosphere on the quarterdeck changed noticeably as everyone relaxed. But the calm was short-lived when Nadia pointed.

"Look!" she exclaimed. "A ship, over there."

I followed Nadia's gesture and saw a ship in the distance, just rounding the southern edge of the island. Not a ship of the armies of darkness, but one visible without the sword. "Who is that?" I asked.

The captain stepped forward and peered through a spyglass. "It's the Castle Guard. It looks like they are just keeping an eye on us."

"How are we going to get Lance and Dan back if they are watching us?" asked Ivan.

"We have been gradually sailing north to make them think we will head past the northeastern side of the island and sail straight out to sea. But if we go too slow, they will know something is up," explained the captain. "We agreed to pick up Lance and Dan around midnight, so we have to wait around until then. But if we act now, we might be able to lose the Castle Guard ship in the two small islands over there." He pointed toward the northeast. "With the sun this low still, we might be able to hide behind an island and convince them to sail past us. Then tonight we can sail back south to the Eastern Island to pick up Dan and Lance. At midnight, you can go ashore in the rowboat to pick them up. We'll just need to stay out of sight of any other ships."

"I'll go with Casey to find the others tonight," I volunteered. "With the sun rising now, we will have to move quickly, or we will lose the shadows that can help us hide among the smaller islands." Turning to the captain, I added, "If they have just been keeping an eye on us rather than chasing us, there must be a reason. What do you think it is?"

"I don't know. It could be they simply want to guard the island from our return. Whatever their reason, we need to keep our focus on getting Dan and Lance back," replied the captain before turning to the crew to dish out orders.

I watched the approaching Castle Guard ship as the *Lyonsword* maneuvered around the smaller islands off the northern shore of the Eastern Island Country. Before the Castle Guard ship could catch up with us, the captain concealed our ship on the northeastern side of one of the islands. With the island backlit by the sun, it would appear to them that we merged with it. As they came around the first small island, the captain and crew expertly navigated the *Lyonsword* around the second one. Thankfully, the Castle Guard did not see us and fell for the captain's trick, turning to head back out to sea to track us down. However, there was no telling how long they would search before coming back or how many other people would be sent to join the search. A few more ships began searching the area around midday, and we just barely managed to keep out of their sight until night. After sunset, we ventured our now nearly invisible ship out into the open ocean toward the Eastern Island Country. Once we were in position, we launched the small dinghy, and Casey and I rowed toward the place where we'd arranged to meet on the northwestern side of the island. As we approached, we kept our eyes peeled for an ambush. It had been a challenge to get away from the castle without being caught, but so far, most of our plans had gone off without a hitch.

No problems had arisen by the time Casey and I reached the shore and pulled the rowboat onto the sand. That was not how this type of thing was supposed to go. Something wasn't right. We could all feel it. With the sword in hand and Casey close on my heels, I crossed the beach and entered the tree line. Casey and Dan had worked out a signal they could use to find each other, so I let him take the lead once we were in the trees. We walked in silence for a few minutes, and then Casey let out a low whistle. The sound was echoed in the dark foliage ahead of us, and Lance and Dan appeared.

"How did it go?" I whispered as they joined us.

Lance shook his head as we all headed back toward the beach. "We almost didn't make it. The Martecytes you spoke of—they were guarding the location where we were supposed to meet the contact. It turns out the guy we were to meet was arrested right after we left the castle."

I stopped in my tracks and turned to face Lance and Dan. "Then where are the pages we sent with you?"

"You wouldn't believe—"

We all froze as the sound of rustling leaves whispered through the foliage. After a moment of hesitation, I decided that whatever had made the sound had probably moved on. But just in case, I held a finger to my lips and waved the others forward. We postponed the discussion until later and headed back to the boat in silence.

As we neared the beach, I had the sudden feeling that someone was watching me, and I paused to look behind me. I scanned the foliage and saw nothing but shadows, reminding me of the mirror and the darkness it had shown me. With a shake of my head, I left my thoughts behind and hurried after the others.

When we arrived at the edge of the tree line, I scanned the beach with the sword in hand but found no one lying in wait to kill us. As I guarded their flank, Casey, Dan, and Lance loaded into the small dingy, and then I pushed us off the beach and jumped in last.

We all stayed alert as Casey rowed the boat over the moonlit water back to the ship. To keep from spending too much time close to the island while people were looking for the ship, the captain had not dropped anchor but continued at a slow pace, so we had to row a little ways northwest to catch them. In silence, we came up beside the boat, and the crew lifted the rowboat up out of the water.

"The captain wants to speak with you all in his cabin," announced Eric as we climbed over the gunwale onto the *Lyonsword*'s deck.

I nodded. "Yeah, we want to talk to him too."

Eric frowned. "Did something happen?" he asked with a concerned expression.

"No," I said, raising my eyebrows, "but that is exactly the problem."

Dan, Casey, Lance, and I headed to the captain's quarters and knocked on his door. When the order came to enter, we did so and found the captain leaning over the left side of his map table, frowning and rubbing his chin. It was an expression he regularly wore when he was deep in thought, and the longer I knew him, the more I realized that was his specialty. Detail. Analyzing every move and every problem.

The captain straightened as we entered. "How did it go?" he asked as he came around to the front of the table. He crossed his arms and leaned back against it.

I glanced at Lance, knowing I had not let him finish his story while we were on the island. "The pickup went great!" I said as I ran a hand through my light brown hair. "Too great, actually."

"No action?" asked the captain.

"Suspiciously quiet," I responded. "But Lance has something to tell us, I think."

The captain looked to Lance in surprise and raised an eyebrow.

Lance glanced at me before turning back to the captain. "We traveled up the island and made good time by hitching a ride on the back of a delivery carriage that was headed to the northwestern shipping yards. But when we arrived, the contact was not there. We waited, but the contact didn't show."

"Someone else did, though," said Dan.

"Who?" asked the captain with narrowed eyes.

"Mr. Bilden's assistant," Lance replied.

"What?" I asked in surprise, looking to Lance.

"It turns out he was a friend of our contact. He explained that he had just left the contact's house when the guards arrested him. The contact had apparently told him he was going to the northwestern docks to pick something up but didn't tell him what it was or why. After the contact was arrested, though, he figured it had something to do with what Otto had mentioned."

"Are you sure it was him?" asked Casey.

"He showed up at the drop point. We were about to leave when two workers spotted him, and they referred to him as Bilden's assistant. He exchanged some casual conversation with them, and then they left," explained Lance.

"We didn't have much of an option, so I risked a look, and it was him," said Dan. "I remembered him from Otto's meeting. It was either move on and not get the papers to anyone or give them to him."

Lance nodded. "We gave him the papers and told him who our backup printer is. He said he could get them to him and hid them in one of his recently offloaded shipments that will be delivered in the same area as where the printer lives. He said he knew the printer we told him about and would make sure he printed the books and distributed them as planned."

"We didn't have any other option, and Otto said we could trust him," Dan explained. "He seemed like a capable guy."

"Sounds like a good solution considering the circumstances," I said as I turned to the captain.

The captain took a slow, deep breath. "You are sure it was him?" he asked sternly as he made eye contact with Lance and then Dan.

"I know what you are thinking, captain," said Dan. "It could have been a trap. But I am certain it wasn't. If it was, they would have taken us then and there."

The captain studied Dan for a moment, then nodded. He looked out the window again at the island we were leaving behind. "It doesn't look like anyone followed you, but we need to be cautious. Things are not as they should be considering our circumstances," he said as he stepped around behind his map table.

"What are you thinking?" I asked.

The captain leaned over the maps again, placing his hands on the edge of the table. "Valdra and his army must be setting some kind of trap ahead of us. It is the only thing that makes sense based on their behavior. Their goal is to get rid of us all and stop us from getting the books to the four corners of the earth."

"So far, they haven't done much to stop us," Casey scoffed. "I mean, they sent ships out to look for us, but only a few. It didn't seem like much of an effort."

"I know. That's what has me worried," said the captain.

I watched the captain as he studied his maps. He had been focusing on the Northern Country, where we were headed next, and he kept running his fingers over the beach line near his hidden docking port. The port was only a mile north of the Channel, which bisected the Northern Continent and the Southern Continent.

"You are looking for an ambush point, aren't you?" I asked as I crossed my arms.

The captain nodded. "The only reason they would act the way they are is if they were pushing us toward a predesignated location. I am thinking they know where we are headed and want us to go there."

"But why wouldn't they just grab us here?" asked Lance.

"I am not sure," the captain said as he straightened again. "But there is a chance that the king of the Eastern Island Country would not be pleased with the idea of us just being executed."

"As I am sure Valdra suggested," I added.

"Why wouldn't the king want us executed if Valdra has convinced him we were planning to kill him?" asked Dan.

"The king might be a bit lax when it comes to castle defenses, but he is a good man. He would most likely want to put us on trial," explained the captain.

"Which is something Valdra and General Delaney would not want," I finished.

"Why not? If we told our story, or *The Story*, the king would probably just think we sound crazy," said Casey with a slight shrug.

The captain shook his head. "Valdra and General Delaney are probably more concerned with what the people hear than what the king hears. If we told everyone about this book and explained our mission, more people would come to know the truth, and that would undermine their plans even if the king did put us to death."

"Okay, so we will proceed as if they know where we are planning on going next," I said. "Do you have a backup docking location?" I asked Captain Bates.

"That is what I have been looking for," he responded. "The problem is that if Valdra knows where we are headed, he might already have our contact in custody, which means he might also have our backup contact in custody. If we get there and find that he does, we will have no one to get the book to. But if we don't go..."

"We will never know if the contacts were compromised. It's the same issue we had here. If we don't go, we could be wasting the only opportunity we have to get this book where it needs to be," I said, rubbing the back of my neck. "We could go straight to the Western Island and skip the Northern Country for now," I suggested. "We would have to reschedule the meeting with our contact, but at least we wouldn't get caught."

"That wouldn't make much of a difference unless we avoid the Channel altogether, which would mean sailing for nine months or so to get around the northern or southern tip of the main continents," replied the captain. "The only way from here to the Western Island is around the continents or through the Channel, which is the perfect place for an ambush."

"Well, taking the longer route and missing a meeting is better than getting captured by Valdra," I replied.

"Not really," Dan chimed in.

"What do you mean?" I prompted.

"You think the waters around here are dangerous? There is a reason people don't usually travel around the main continents instead of going through the Channel."

Casey nodded. "Yeah, the oceans surrounding the Southern Continent are teeming with dark creatures and monsters. Even some of the fiercest smugglers have abandoned that longer route in favor of the Channel, despite being more likely to encounter other smugglers, pirates, and privateers."

"Can we go around the northern tip of the continent?" I asked with a wince.

The captain shook his head. "Not unless you want to freeze to death or die of old age before you reach the other side," he replied. "That is one of the reasons the Channel was built."

Dan and Casey exchanged worried glances.

"What?" I asked as I watched them squirm.

Dan shrugged. "It's just that the Channel isn't the easiest place to sail a ship like the *Lyonsword* in our circumstances," he explained. "I mean, we've done it before, but not in a combat situation. It's an easy place to get trapped. It is open for anyone to use, and it is safe during the day. But at night, with people lying in wait for you..." He trailed off.

"We were already planning on going through the Channel, and it didn't bother you before," I pointed out.

"Yeah, but that was before we realized that Valdra knew where we were headed," said Casey.

"They have a point, Captain," I said.

"We can't take the longer routes because we will miss our meetings, and I think it is safe to assume that Valdra has enough soldiers to cover both our secret port and the Channel. So, at this point, either way, we aren't getting out of this unscathed," the captain said gravely as he met eyes with each of us in turn.

Dan and Casey nodded confidently. "Whatever you need, we've got your back," said Casey with a grin matching Dan's.

"I'm on board," chimed in Lance, who had been listening from the corner of the room.

I let out a breath. "To the Channel it is, then," I confirmed.

"Now, I need you all to get some rest," ordered Captain Bates as he put a hand on my shoulder and looked at each of us again. "We don't know what exactly is going to happen on this trip, and I need you all alert."

With that, Dan, Casey, Lance, and I left the captain in his cabin and dispersed to our sleeping quarters. It was only when I arrived at my hammock below deck that I realized how tired I was. I took off my coat and boots, and instead of joining Solace in her hammock, I climbed into my own so I wouldn't wake her. Since we had been married, we usually slept together, but we kept separate hammocks for days like this when I got to bed much later than she did.

I settled into my hammock, thinking that maybe the Lion's Sword could help us get to the Northern Country safely. *Maybe Eyethanoff can help.* As I began to drift off to sleep, a strange feeling fell over me. One I couldn't fully identify. Whether it was dark or light, I wasn't sure. Maybe it was both, or maybe just indigestion. Then I remembered the feeling I'd had on the island. The feeling that someone was there, watching me. I had felt that when this all first started, and I had learned it had something to do with a dark soldier that seemed to keep an eye on me. I looked over at Solace to see if she stirred, but she lay still. Yuuki slept deeply as well, curled up in her own little hammock next to Solace's.

I looked back up to the ceiling, then closed my eyes. The ship swayed beneath me, rocking my hammock gently from side to side. As I let myself be lulled by the motion, for a moment, the sounds of the ship faded as I felt myself start to fall asleep. But then I felt it again, the feeling that I was being watched. I snapped awake and sat up to look around. I scanned our sleeping quarters, which were dotted with barrels of supplies. Only sounds of the ship on the ocean and people snoring broke the silence. Nothing. There was no one there...that I could see.

In a last-ditch effort to figure out what was going on, I closed my eyes and reached for the sword. As my grip tightened around its hilt, I tried to get Eyethanoff's attention, but I got no response. As I tried again, exhaustion finally overtook me, and everything faded to black.

⁂

I stood with the Beast of the Woods, surrounded by the Woods' thick foliage. I turned to the Beast, and it reached toward me with its silky black tail, wrapping it around my waist like a belt. Once again, I was met with a briefly clear image of the Ice Dragon placing something around my waist before it grew hazy as *The Story* began to play out around me.

As *The Story* unfolded, the dragon touched the Beast's tail, and it turned into a belt. I heard the dragon say, "Have hope, my friend, for the truth is a treasure worth knowing."

Unlike in past dreams, this time, the vision of *The Story* faded into the background, and the dragon lifted her claw from the belt to my chest. As she placed her claw on my chest, the breastplate from the mirror appeared, and the dragon's words rang out. "Be on guard, my friend, for your heart is a treasure worth protecting."

I reached up and touched the breastplate, wanting it to stay, but suddenly it vanished, along with the dragon, and the world around me turned dark. A faint image of the Woods surrounded me on all sides, and I saw beyond the edge of the Woods two soldiers, one dark and one light. The dark soldier's expression now became clear. His eyes were filled with cunning intent, and a sharp-edged smile curved his lips. His coat moved like black fog around him, and he watched me as if he were waiting for me to exit the safety of the Woods.

I struggled to pull my eyes away from the dark soldier. His gaze sent chills down my spine, though I knew I was now dreaming. But as I tried to ignore him, it was as if he became even more real. His foggy coat contorted wildly and seemed to fill the space around him, growing as his smile turned to a laugh. Though he stood outside of the Woods, his eyes told me he would do anything it took to get to me. I tried to close my eyes to the fearsome image, but it did not help. I could not look away.

Suddenly, the faint image of the Woods vanished into near-total darkness, and the dark soldier lurched for me. His hands grew claws and his eyes turned wild like those of a Great Beast of the Southern Mountains as the image of my darkened reflection, holding the lifeless body of the Beast of the Woods, flashed before me like lightning.

⁂

I jerked awake in a panic and released the sword's hilt as if it had burned me. I half rolled, half fell out of the hammock, landing on my hands and knees before pushing myself up onto my feet as the faint echo of the dragon's words rang in my head. *"Be on guard, my friend..."* Thankfully, the sword had landed on a pile of blankets near my hammock and did not wake anyone. But I stared at it as if it might jump up and attack me. *"...for your heart is a treasure worth protecting."*

Breathing hard, my heart pounding, I shook my head and forced myself to calm down. *Maybe whatever just happened was just a regular nightmare,* I told myself. But I knew deep down it wasn't. The dreams were back. Something about what I had seen in the mirror had triggered them all over again.

I grabbed the sword and tried again to get Eyethanoff's attention to ask for help, but still, there was no answer. Anger flared within me. We lived in the same world, side-by-side. To the best of my knowledge, there were only two things that separated us. The fact that he was part of the Unseen Lands and the fact that he wielded Original Power. Each time I had seen him, it wasn't a vision. He had actually shown up in flesh and blood. But suddenly, he had decided not to respond to my call. *Why won't he come help me?* I thought as frustration grew in the pit of my stomach.

I put the sword back in its sheath and strapped it around my waist before heading toward the stairs and the hatch that led to the main deck. I had to clear my head. As I closed the hatch behind me, I took a deep breath of fresh, cool air. It was still dark, so most of the crew were either at their night posts or asleep.

I walked over to the gunwale and looked out across the water as I leaned my elbows on the rail and ran my fingers through my hair. The water shimmered in the moonlight, and I felt myself grow calmer. After a moment, I heard a sound behind me and looked back to see Solace climbing through the hatch. She wrapped herself in a blanket and came to my side, slipping her arms around my waist as I let my arm rest over her shoulders.

"What's wrong?" she asked sleepily.

I shook my head. "A dream," I said, attempting to brush it off.

Solace frowned. "Was it the same as before?" she said, looking up at me with concern in her brown eyes.

I lifted my arm from her shoulders and placed my elbows on the railing again as I took a deep breath, then let it out in a sigh. "Not entirely," I said as I fidgeted, a hint of guilt returning to my stomach. "Like Lance said, on the island, I...I saw something."

"Okay. What did you see?" she asked, suddenly fully awake and attentive.

I took a deep breath. "There was a mirror there, in the cellar. The sword..." I shrugged, not fully understanding what had happened. "The sword seemed...attracted to it." I let my gaze drift over the calm waves as I pictured the mirror. "There was writing around the edge, like the writing on the sword, and it showed me the scaled animal from my dreams...an ice dragon."

Solace's eyebrows raised. "What happened?"

"She gave me something...At least, I think that's what she was doing. It was similar to the first dream when she touched the Beast's tail, and it became a belt. But this time, it was an old armor breastplate. It was just in the reflection, though. When I tried to touch it..." I paused as I remembered what I had seen in the mirror.

"What?" Solace prompted.

I looked at her for a moment as I thought about the darkness I knew was in me. The things I had done before I met her. The things I had intended to do despite what I knew she would have wanted. All the people I had killed while working for General Delaney, and that night I had intended to kill the Beast of the Woods despite knowing it completely opposed Solace's wishes. All the memories came flooding back with an overwhelming feeling of guilt that twisted my stomach. Part of me wanted to think that these transgressions were too small to make me this guilt-ridden. I had only wanted to kill the Beast to save Solace. Surely that wasn't so bad. And I had only killed others because I was following orders. But I knew those were just empty excuses.

"Do you know what I did before I met you?" I asked, holding Solace's gaze.

"You worked for General Delaney."

I nodded. "I killed people for him," I said plainly, watching for her reaction.

Solace nodded, and her expression remained calm. "That was not the only thing you did...but I know."

I watched her, trying to gauge her feelings. "Solace, I am not a good person," I said as I realized I had to come clean.

Solace shook her head. "Ben, that is not true—"

I interrupted her. "That mirror forced me to see something I have been ignoring since this journey began. When this all started, I was literally executing a man for General Delaney because he refused to give up the book's location. Solace, I was one of the ones who came after people like us," I said as I straightened.

"You didn't know what you were doing," she said, trying to reassure me.

"Really?" I asked defiantly. "Do you really believe that? Because, as I recall, I chose to be there. I chose to do that job. Solace..." I sighed as my frustration faded into exhaustion.

"What?" she asked.

I looked into her eyes. *I have to come clean.* "That is not all," I said as the memory of the night she had almost died sat heavy in my stomach. She had believed the Beast could protect the spoken version of *The Story* her family told, and she had been determined to complete her mission even if it meant she would die from an incurable disease. I had selfishly plotted to kill the Beast to keep her alive. Thankfully, things had not gone as planned, and everyone, including the Beast, was still alive. But my intention to murder the one thing Solace thought she needed most spoke volumes about who I really was. I had put my own fears first. I had been willing to sacrifice what Solace valued for what I valued. Now we were married, and I still hadn't told her. *Will she still want me once she knows the truth?*

I took a deep breath and looked down at my hands. "The night the Prince saved you, I...I entered the Woods...to kill the Beast," I confessed. With that admission out, the rest came easily, almost without my permission. "I was going to kill the one thing you were counting on the most because I was too afraid to lose you. I was going to sacrifice your mission to protect what I wanted," I said as I met her gaze. "I am not a good person," I repeated.

Solace stared at me for a moment. I could see from her narrowed eyes and lips pinned together that she was still processing what I had just told her. But then her expression went blank. "Why didn't you tell me this sooner?" she asked in a steady tone.

I hesitated, then frowned. "I was afraid..."

"Afraid of what?" she asked as a flicker of anger crossed her face.

I looked into her eyes, pushing past the pain of seeing just a hint of her displeasure. "Losing you."

Solace looked away, then said, "And what does this have to do with your vision at the castle?"

I paused for a moment to consider her surprisingly calm response, then shook my head as I replied. "When I tried to take the piece of armor the dragon was offering me, an image of my darkness got in the way. I just...I thought this was my purpose. To do what the Prince told me to do. But what if I am wrong?"

"What do you mean?" she asked, keeping her expression neutral.

I looked out at the ocean again. "*The Story* speaks of a place where all this darkness won't rule over us. The Great Beasts won't roam and cause wars we cannot win. We will be free of the Creature's influence. The world will be different. Better."

"And...?" Solace prompted. Something in her tone told me she was using this conversation to keep her anger in check.

I took a deep breath. "What if we are tied too closely to this darkness?" I turned to her again. "Solace, that mirror reminded me of things I have been pushing aside for a while now. But I can't hide from them anymore. I don't deserve to be part of this. I have done awful things...and what if that is the reason Eyethanoff has not answered me? What if that is why the mirror showed me those things? To tell me I am not worthy."

"Eyethanoff hasn't answered your calls?" she asked, her blank expression still masking her anger.

I nodded, and we both fell silent.

"I know the things you have done," said Solace after a moment, her tone still carefully controlled.

I looked at her, trying to gauge what she was thinking. A silent battle raged in her eyes. She wanted to be angry with me. But for some reason, she was fighting it.

I shook my head and let the regret show in my eyes. "You know *The Story* even better than I do, and people like me—we don't live with the King. We live with the Creature." I looked away, not wanting to face her.

Solace took in a deep breath, then let it out. To my surprise, her posture softened. She reached up and gently turned my head toward her. Her eyes locked with mine and I could see that silent battle still raging, but she pushed it aside. "Ben, do not let this world lie to you. Whatever this is, whatever you think that mirror showed you, remember that the King has a plan, and we need to trust that he knows what he is doing. The Prince asked you to be part of this. He brought you into his army. He would not have done that if he thought your past was too dark for his power to handle." She released my face and turned away again. "And as for Eyethanoff not showing himself, he probably has a good reason."

I frowned. I could no longer hold in my confusion. "Why?" I asked, watching her carefully. "Why are you not letting your anger flare? I deserve it. I should have told you before we were married."

Solace sighed and leaned on the gunwale. "Because this isn't about me, Ben." She looked at me, her eyes intense and her brow furrowed, my question stirring her well-capped emotions. "This is about the mission we have been given to accomplish. There is something here that I know that you still do not understand!" Her voice rose slightly as she struggled to control her anger. "And it is something I cannot teach you. I know because I have tried!" She lowered her voice again and rubbed a hand over her forehead. "I can only do what I promised, and that is to complete this mission and love you, no matter what." She paused and shook her head, looking away. "You were right to think I wouldn't approve, and you are right that you should have told me before we married." After a moment she looked at me, and pain filled my chest as I saw she was holding back tears. "I don't approve that you put your needs ahead of my mission. I don't approve that you would have sacrificed what I fought so hard for to keep what you thought you needed. I don't approve that you refuse to let go of how you think things should work!" She sucked in a sharp, shaky breath. Then she let it out slowly. "But I do understand…"

Each of her words dug deeper than the last, making my chest grow tighter and tighter. I knew I had failed her, and I knew I should have told her everything before we were married. But then, those last four words struck me like a hammer. They took me completely by surprise. I opened my mouth to ask her why, but nothing came out. I took a moment to replay all her words in my mind, then finally asked, "You do?"

Solace turned to me, giving me her full attention. She looked me in the eyes, took in a deep breath, then let it out. "I know what it is like to fear losing someone you love. I understand the drive to do whatever it takes to protect them. And if I am being honest, some of my anger is because it worked for you. You know my story. You know I once selfishly went against someone else's wishes, putting their mission at risk, and now they are dead." She closed her eyes, causing a tear to finally break away and slide down her cheek. But when she opened her eyes again, she smiled. "If you had not gone in there with that intention, I would have died." She wiped the tear from her cheek. "Maybe this was why we were brought together. Maybe both of us together are the last Night Rider because each of us can make decisions that the other can't, or won't."

I was baffled by her, by her willingness to forgive. "But…you are angry with me," I said.

Solace nodded. "I am angry, Ben. But that's no reason not to forgive you. And it doesn't change how I feel about you. We all make mistakes. What matters is that you are telling me now."

I shook my head in disbelief. I had been prepared for her to scream and throw me off the ship. But this I hadn't seen coming. Then Ruth's words came back to me. *"Thankfully for us, true love does not depend on what we deserve."* I kissed Solace on the forehead as I wrapped her in an affectionate hug. "You never cease to amaze me. I don't deserve you."

Solace rested her head on my chest. "I learned from the best."

I could only imagine she meant the Prince.

I let out a breath. Maybe this would be the end of the darkness I saw in my dreams. But something within me would not let go of those images I had seen. Though Solace forgave me, the mirror was clearly connected to the Unseen Lands. I found my mind growing distracted with unanswered questions. *Whose mirror was it? How did it work? Was the mirror showing me the reality I feared? That I would forever be stuck in this world and never be free of darkness?*

I shook my head. "I am not so sure you are right about Eye-thanoff. He answered at the church. I saw him. But he hasn't answered my calls since, and I keep feeling like he doesn't want to," I said in frustration.

Her head still resting against my chest, she responded, "Just because you can see something doesn't mean you have all the in-formation." She yawned. "Have a little faith. It will all work out in the end."

As we stood there in each other's arms, my mind briefly wandered, once again, to the image I had seen in the mirror of my body infested with darkness. Solace believed that one day I would be welcomed into the Kingdom described in *The Story. But I am not like her. She will go, and I will not. We will be separated forever by my darkness,* I thought in sorrow. I hugged her a little tighter.

The sword had led me to that mirror, and I knew the sword only showed the truth. *The truth is...I don't deserve to be part of that world.*

Chapter 9

We spent the next few days of travel catching up on sleep and trying to decide what to do when we arrived at the Northern Country. The ocean on this side of the Channel was known for being much rougher than on the other side, but thankfully, the waters remained relatively calm. As a result, catching up on sleep was unexpectedly easy, at least for everyone but me. However, the planning was not.

As the days passed and we entered our second week of travel, we found ourselves talking in circles, unable to settle on a plan. We were more or less convinced we were headed into a trap but had no other options and a deadline to meet. Adding to our frustration was the fact that Solace and Otto had run out of information they could use to analyze the language on the sword and the symbol on the shield, and they had gotten almost nowhere with what little information they did have. There were too many problems and not enough solutions.

The biggest problem we were facing was Valdra and his armies. We had all agreed that he was very likely waiting for us with the intention of taking us down quietly. As the captain had suggested, that seemed more logical than taking a risk by allowing us to tell *The Story* publicly in front of a royal court and plead our case as to why *The Story* should be put back in print. Getting the book back in print would not be that hard if we could convince a king to do it. But the rulers of the four corners of the earth were unaware of General Delaney's plot to keep the book, and the truth it contained, away from the people. The last thing General Delaney and Valdra needed was someone telling the four kings about how they were helping an ancient dark being known as the Creature perpetuate the cycle of wars against the Great Beasts and maintain an illusion that kept the people in continual fear and darkness. Even if the kings didn't believe our tale, they would probably be curious as to why a powerful man like General Delaney was so concerned about one book being in print. So, we were certain the general would want to ensure we did not live long enough to speak to any of the kings.

The second biggest problem we had to solve was where we would dock once we arrived near the Channel. There were a couple options. We could use the dock we had originally planned to use, which was concealed in the rocky terrain on the northeastern side of the Channel. There was a chance that Valdra did not know the docking port's exact location, and we could slip in unnoticed. However, Valdra had two armies—the Martecytes, who could be seen, as they were simply people infected with shadow, and the soldiers of darkness, who could not be seen, except by someone wielding the sword Ruth had given me. With these two armies at his disposal, Valdra could patrol a large portion of the shoreline near our hidden dock, as well as the shores we would have to pass along the way. The other option was to skip docking and go right through the Channel. If we did that, we would more quickly reach our contact in North Town, which was near the Channel's halfway point, but we would be very exposed in the Channel and risk getting ambushed and caught.

After a week and a half of mulling over these issues, I started to see a plan take shape. One afternoon, several of us gathered on the quarterdeck, and we reviewed our options once again.

"We are just going to have to go for it," I told everyone. "As I said before, we have no choice unless we want to abandon our mission completely."

"I agree," said Solace.

"If we dock at the hidden docking port," I continued, "we might have more time to check for threats and try to find a safer route to our contact, but we would risk drawing Valdra straight to the secret dock, eliminating yet another port for use in the future. Of course, that is assuming Valdra doesn't already know where the docking port is and have soldiers guarding it. So, I say we go straight through the Channel."

"We could get a different ship to take us to the Western Island Country," suggested Nadia from her perch on the stern's gunwale near the ship's main boom. "No offense, Captain," she added, looking to Captain Bates respectfully.

The captain shook his head. "None taken. I had the same thought. But we have no way of knowing if anyone will take you with Valdra on your tail, especially on short notice. I know of a few smugglers I could connect you with, but at this point, I'm not sure that is a wise idea," he warned. "The ones who would be willing to take you on this journey just happen to be the ones who would sell you out at the drop of a hat."

I nodded. "We will keep that idea in our back pocket for now."

Captain Bates nodded. "Then through the Channel it is. What did you have in mind for dealing with Valdra?" he asked me as he kept a hand on the helm.

I leaned back against the gunwale from my seat on a barrel and clasped my hands behind my head. "Our contact is in North Town, at the base of the Northern Mountains. I think we can sail straight there through the Channel—the town is only about two miles inland. Once we get there, Ivan, Nadia, Lance, Solace, and I will deliver a couple of books to our contact while you continue to sail the ship through the Channel. That way, if one group gets captured, some of the books will still be safe, either on the ship or with those of us going to meet the contact."

Otto frowned. "You mentioned that idea a few days ago. It still does not solve the problem of getting to the Channel or through it without being seen."

I glanced at Solace and then back to the others as I unclasped my hands and sat up. "I am going to see if the Lion's Sword will give us a hand."

"Remind me who the Lion's Sword is again," inquired Lance with a confused wince. "Isn't that the name of this ship?"

The captain smiled. "This ship was named after the Lion's Sword, yes, but the Lion's Sword is the army of the King of the Unseen Lands."

"The people we can't see but who are on our side," clarified a shirtless Ivan from where he lay on the deck, half dozing in the sun.

"Oh. Got it," Lance responded with an understanding nod.

"So, you think you can get them to provide a distraction?" asked the captain. "That would definitely alert the armies of darkness that we are nearby."

"I know. But…" I looked at Solace for support and was glad to see she was nodding along with me. "I think we should try. We just need to get through the Channel to the Western Sea. Then we will be in open ocean again and have a completely different problem on our hands."

"What problem?" asked Otto in surprise.

"They will be chasing us instead of waiting for us," said Solace.

"Oh," he said simply.

The captain looked at me. "What about the shield? Do you know if it worked that night at the castle, or was that just luck?"

I shook my head. "Honestly, I don't know. But I don't think we should rely on the shield to hide us."

The captain nodded. "Did you contact your soldier?"

"His name is Eyethanoff, and I have tried. But I haven't gotten any response so far, so no guarantees about the distraction," I said with a frown.

"Well, if we can't get a distraction, then what are we going to do?" asked Otto.

"We could send out an attack party before us!" suggested Ivan. "Take a third of the crew and send them out in boats. They attack before we get there, then the rest of us show up and overwhelm the enemy."

Nadia rolled her eyes. "We can't overwhelm them, Ivan. They have an army."

"Actually, they have two armies," Otto reminded us.

"Well, we could still try it," said Ivan, glaring at his sister.

"What do you think, Ben?" asked Nadia.

I thought about it for a moment. With our limited numbers in comparison to Valdra, attacking would be risky. But it might be our best option if the first plan failed. "I think it could work...but only if we surprised them." I turned to the captain. "Do you think you could spare some crew members if I can't get Eyethanoff's help?"

The captain nodded. "We could make do with a few less. I would advise that Ivan and Nadia go with the surprise attack team while you and Solace stay on the ship. As was the case on the island, Valdra will most likely be keeping a closer eye on you two and might know something is up if he somehow discovers you are no longer on the ship before we reach the Channel."

I nodded. "Sounds good to me."

"Ahoy!" We were suddenly interrupted as Eric yelled from his perch in the crow's nest. "Captain, we have an incoming ship," he said as he pointed to the east.

The captain ran to the ship's starboard side and extended his spyglass. "It's the *Ghost*," he said ominously.

"Who's that?" asked Otto, his voice rising slightly in alarm.

"The *Ghost* is Dead Man Jackson's ship," replied the captain.

"Dead Man Jackson?" I asked. "That doesn't sound good."

"He and his crew are a wild bunch," said Casey with a nod. "Jackson is still young, but they are some of the most accomplished thieves to ever sail the Eastern Sea. There are many theories as to how the ship got its name. Some say it is because when they raid another ship, it disappears with no trace. Others say it is because of Jackson. He got his name from the fact that he has supposedly been executed twice and should be dead."

I felt my eyebrows raise in surprise. *This is definitely not good.*

"We have done a good job of avoiding them so far, but it looks like our luck has run out." Casey frowned. "Not that I believe in luck," he mumbled to himself.

"Everyone to your posts!" Captain Bates yelled to his crew. But then he suddenly stopped, a thoughtful expression on his face. He turned to me. "Hide Otto, Lance, and Yuuki below deck with the books. Just in case we do not get out of this unscathed, we need to give them the best chance we can to carry on without us. Tell Solace to go with them. She can protect them with the sword and shield."

"What about the rest of us?" I asked.

"Blend in. If they board the ship, I don't want them finding out who you are or what you are doing," explained Captain Bates.

"But, sir, are we really going to let them board this ship? We have cannons. We could fight them!" I suggested, confused at the captain's willingness to give up so easily.

The captain looked at the approaching ship, his expression distant. "No...we let them take us..." The captain turned back to me before I could respond. "Benjamin, no matter what happens, follow my lead. I have an idea."

After a moment of hesitation, I decided to trust him. "Yes, Captain," I said respectfully. I turned to the others and waved them to follow me. As we descended the stairs and crossed the main deck, I dished out orders. "Solace, take Yuuki, Otto, and Lance below deck. Grab the sword, shield, and at least one copy of *The Story*, and hide. If these people have been in contact with Valdra, they might have soldiers of darkness with them."

"But you will need the sword!" Solace replied.

I shook my head. "You need to keep those pages safe. You can use the sword and shield to do that," I said, grabbing her shoulders and looking her in the eye. "Keep them safe," I repeated emphatically.

Solace nodded. "What are you going to do?"

"I am going to hide with the crew," I responded. Turning to the twins, I continued, "Ivan and Nadia, you both need to blend in as well. We need to be prepared for them to board the *Lyonsword*. Nadia, you and Catherine should dirty yourselves up a bit. I don't want these people noticing your good looks and trying to take advantage of you. You'll end up cutting off their heads and starting a war." The twins both nodded and got to work as I stopped mid-deck and turned to Christopher, who was barking orders at the crew. "Why aren't we going to fight them?" I asked.

Christopher smiled. "We don't run from a fight, my friend! But things aren't always how they look. Trust the captain—he never does anything without a reason," he said with a grin. But I could see worry in his eyes. Dead Man Jackson and his crew were not to be trifled with.

Casey's words echoed in my mind. *"They are a wild bunch."* I shook my head. Wild meant unpredictable. Unpredictable meant a whole different kind of dangerous.

As the *Ghost* drew near, the *Lyonsword* attempted to outrun her. But for some reason, Captain Bates seemed set on getting caught and didn't give them much trouble. It didn't take the *Ghost* long to maneuver us into a choke point between two rocky islands. Even though we were allowing them to take us, their skill and speed were still impressive.

Now in range for a full-scale assault, the *Ghost*'s crew prepared to board the *Lyonsword*. Ropes flew through the air, grappling hooks catching on the gunwale and anything else they landed on. As the two ships were pulled together, Captain Bates ordered everyone to fight back but not kill anyone. Whatever the captain had planned, I hoped we made it out alive.

The *Lyonsword*'s crew fired arrows and flintlocks at the enemy ship, but not in time to stop them. Planks appeared between the ships as the crew of the *Ghost* charged onto the *Lyonsword* with their weapons at the ready. A young man in an extravagant captain's hat stood on the *Lyonsword*'s gunwale and pointed to Captain Bates. "You've got nowhere to run! Surrender, or I'll kill your crew, one by one!"

The young captain and his band of rogues looked like they were enjoying the confrontation, their eyes wild with glee. Their ship was filthy, as were they. Their clothes were a variety of expensive, mismatched items that had been worn ragged on the seas. Clearly, the crew had stolen them from some unfortunate nobleman's ship.

"And who might I have the pleasure of speaking with?" asked Captain Bates in a smooth, polite tone, pretending not to know the famous pirate.

"Captain Dead Man Jackson of the *Ghost*, at your service!" the young man called out proudly as he offered a bow.

Captain Bates looked to Jackson and replied with confidence, "I guess you leave us with no other choice. But I must explain that we are on an important mission and cannot be interrupted," he added in a worried tone.

I stood with the rest of the crew, watching the exchange. I had taken off my black duster, rolled up my sleeves, and rustled my hair to make myself look more like the crew—clean, but not military clean, as I often was. I stole a glance at Christopher, who, to my surprise, had a hint of a smile on his lips. I looked back to the captain as he descended the stairs from the quarterdeck. As we briefly made eye contact, he winked, then looked away. He was up to something.

"Ah, well, whatever mission you are on, my friend, has just ended," said Jackson as he leaped onto the *Lyonsword*'s main deck, his crew spilling in around him. "I have captured the Jewel of the Sea," Jackson said in a loud, playful voice. "And you,"—he pointed his matchlock at Captain Bates—"can do nothing to stop me!" The *Ghost*'s crew whooped and hollered at their captain's words.

Jewel of the Sea? I wondered. *What is he talking about?*

With a cruel grin that revealed a few gold teeth, Jackson added, "Though I am curious about your important mission."

Before Captain Bates could respond, Jackson gave some unspoken cue that threw his crew into action. First, they took our weapons and began to split us up into groups, making us sit in four different sections on the deck and keep our hands where they could see them. Then, after instructing his men to watch us closely, to my surprise, Jackson gestured for Captain Bates to lead the way to his quarters on the *Lyonsword*, leaving us to await our uncertain fate.

"Tell me, Captain, what is so important about your mission?" Jackson asked as they disappeared into the captain's quarters.

With Jackson gone, I hoped the *Ghost*'s crew would get lazy. That was often the way of pirates like these. As soon as their captain left, they would all lose interest in following his orders.

As I kept an eye on our captors, I also scanned the deck in search of each person I knew would be able to help if we ended up in a real fight, noting where they were and who they were sitting with.

Ivan and Nadia were in separate groups, but thankfully Christopher was with me. Dan and Casey were in the group nearest the captain's quarters, and Eric and Catherine were in Nadia's group near the bow.

The crew of the *Ghost* searched the ship for any other crew they had missed and, to my relief, came up empty-handed. I had no idea where Solace and the others had hidden, but I had learned soon after meeting her that she could handle herself.

When I was sure none of the *Ghost*'s crew was watching, I leaned over to Christopher and whispered, "What is the captain planning?"

Christopher stole a glance at our captors and then whispered back, "He didn't have time to tell me everything, but so far, this is similar to a trick we pulled a while back. These guys are thieves. But they are not above ransom. As a matter of fact, they have ransomed or sold entire crews before. The captain is convincing him that we should be ransomed. That way, they will at least keep us alive."

"Do you think he has a plan beyond that?" I said as I glanced around the deck at our unwelcome visitors. I couldn't imagine that the captain would give up his ship and crew so easily unless he had a plan for getting them back.

Christopher chuckled. "The captain always has a plan."

After we'd sat in the hot sun for about an hour, the door to the captain's quarters finally opened, and Jackson exited with Captain Bates in tow. A man followed close behind the captain and kept a pistol trained on his back, but I took it as a good sign that the captain looked unscathed and was not restrained. Captain Bates glanced around the deck to make sure his crew were all in good shape. So far, the worst of the injuries were a few black eyes, and no one had been shot or thrown off the ship. So far, so good, all things considered.

"Which one is he?" demanded Jackson.

To my shock, Captain Bates gestured to me. My heart sank. *Did he just rat me out?* Of all the people on the ship, I couldn't believe that the captain would be the one to betray me. I frowned at him as one of the pirates guarding my group grabbed me and brought me over to where they were standing.

"This is him," said the captain, refusing to meet my questioning gaze.

"So, you are the man worth so much." Jackson grinned and looked me up and down. "You thought you could escape on a smuggler's ship to avoid execution for attempting to kill the king of the Eastern Island Country?" he asked with a hint of admiration in his voice. "I almost wonder if I shouldn't keep you," he said with a laugh that was echoed by his crew.

Relief washed over me. The captain had not turned me in. *It's just a part of his plan. I hope.*

"He is worth a lot of money to the king and General Delaney," announced Captain Bates.

"Well, then, we will just have to take him to the king," said Jackson with a sly grin.

The captain's expression turned thoughtful. "That might not be the wisest idea."

Without warning, Jackson turned and threw a punch at Captain Bates, but to my surprise, the captain blocked it. In an instant, Jackson and the captain had knives at each other's throats, and the sound of pistols being cocked and swords being drawn swept across the deck as Jackson's crew prepared to defend their captain. The ship went silent.

"Stand down, Captain," said Jackson in a low, threatening voice. "You would not want me to start killing your crew, now would you?"

Captain Bates held Jackson's gaze for a moment, and I saw in the captain's eyes that he was calculating. Thinking through his options. Finally, he relaxed slightly and lowered his knife. "My apologies. Old habits," he said with a tense smile.

"That's better," said Jackson as he and his men lowered their weapons as well. But I could see that Jackson had suddenly realized that although the captain may have surrendered, he was no coward. And not only that, but he had nearly gotten the drop on the famed Dead Man Jackson.

Maybe the captain has more control over this situation than I thought.

Regaining his confidence, Jackson narrowed his eyes at Captain Bates. "Do not order me around, Captain," he said in a chilling tone. "Your crew will suffer for it."

Captain Bates dipped his head slightly in submission. "I only meant to point out that this man may be worth more in the Northern Country."

Though I was not quite sure what the captain's plan was, I could see at least part of it involved the *Ghost* taking us to the Northern Country. I was operating with only half the picture, but the captain had told me to follow his lead, and that was precisely what I would do.

"My family is wealthy," I interjected, drawing Jackson's attention as one of his men began to guide me back to my group.

Jackson looked at me and held a hand up to stop his crewman. "So is the king," he said simply.

"Yes, but the king wants you dead too, doesn't he? He is not a fan of pirates," I pointed out.

Jackson watched me suspiciously. "That is a fair point," he admitted. "But I have my contacts within his shipping yards—people who could bargain on my behalf without the king knowing. And the king pays better," he said, cocking his head to the side. Jackson was definitely younger than me, probably in his early twenties, and I could tell he was sizing me up. "Where does your family live?" he asked.

"Near the Channel, at the edge of North Town," I explained, briefly registering the captain's subtle nod at my comment. I was on the right track. "They will pay handsomely to have me returned," I added, doing my best to sound nervous and inexperienced without overplaying it.

"How do I know you are telling the truth?" Jackson asked with a frown.

"You don't," I said simply. "But your only other option is to go to the king."

Jackson suddenly lunged forward and held a knife to my throat. "Or I could kill you all and take this ship and its cargo," he said with a grin.

I nodded slowly, careful to keep the dirty blade from slicing my neck. "You could. But it would be more lucrative for you to trade me for money. Then you would get this ship and all it can offer, plus the ransom money, without running the risk of getting caught by the king. His money has no worth if you are executed."

Jackson watched me for a moment with a flat expression, and I felt the tension on the ship rise, as though even his own crew could not tell if his stillness would erupt into joy or violence.

Jackson was a greedy man, and the temptation of extra wealth was tantalizing. Finally, he abruptly relaxed and said, "Lucky for you, we were already headed in the direction of the Channel." Jackson pulled away and waved at his crewman to return me to my group. "So, for now, my men will pilot this ship, and we will take both ships to port in the Channel. Then we will figure out what to do with you."

With that, he shoved Captain Bates to another group before climbing the steps to the quarterdeck. He spun around to face his men, throwing his arms out wide. "I am captain of the *Ghost*!" he yelled. "And this ship is now mine! The Jewel of the Sea has been captured!"

The crew of the *Ghost* erupted in cheers and howls. Then Jackson began giving orders to prepare the two ships to sail. He instructed his crew to move some of us to the *Ghost* and go through our belongings in search of anything valuable. I glared at the dirty crewman who was stroking my twin pistols with wide, greedy eyes, but I followed the crew's example and didn't fight. Captain Bates had given an order to stand down, and if his crew trusted him, so did I. The captain, Christopher, and I were taken to the *Ghost*, along with about a third of the *Lyonsword*'s crew, while a couple dozen of the *Ghost*'s crew remained on the *Lyonsword*.

On the *Ghost*, the three of us were taken down to a dark, damp corner of the cargo hold, away from the rest of the crew, and restrained with chains secured to our ankles. One man slouched at the base of the stairs that led to the hatch to the main deck, left to guard us. We listened to the sound of footfalls above us as the *Ghost*'s crew finished taking over the *Lyonsword* and arranging people between the ships. We dared not speak yet. I hoped with everything I had that they didn't find Solace and the others. Though I knew she could handle herself, my stomach flipped as my mind filled with thoughts of what might happen to her and her companions if they were found.

After the guard dozed off, I finally turned to the captain and whispered, "What was all that back on the *Lyonsword*? What are you planning?"

The captain smiled. "Good job playing along. I am sorry I didn't have time to explain, but Jackson is our best bet at making it through the Channel. He is a wild man, but he is also selfish and greedy. If we play our cards correctly, we can ensure that Valdra will attack this ship, and then we can sneak out onto the *Lyonsword* during the battle and sail away."

"What if we can't get out?" I asked.

The captain smiled again reassuringly. "Don't worry, Jackson's crew are easy to manipulate."

"We have done it before," said Christopher. "Though they don't know it was us," he said with a grin.

"Then why did you look so worried when they showed up?" I asked Christopher.

"I was just playing along for your benefit," he said with another grin. "Last time we did this, someone caught on because it turned out that our guest was not a good actor. We needed you to be at least a little nervous," he finished with a shrug. "Plus, these are dangerous people. There was still a risk."

I frowned, and Christopher chuckled.

"Where are Solace and the others?" asked Captain Bates, bringing us back to the reality of our situation.

"I don't know," I replied. "But the *Ghost*'s crew checked the ship and didn't find them. I just hope they can stay hidden. We still have three days of travel left before we reach the Channel."

"Does Otto know about the secret smugglers' hole?" asked the captain, turning to Christopher.

Christopher smiled. "Of course he does. The first thing he asked when he boarded our ship the second time was to learn everything there was to know about it. The man is like a sponge."

The captain turned back to me. "If they are in there, they should be okay as long as they grabbed food and water on their way down. It was designed to smuggle people to safety and is very hard to find if you don't know what you are looking for."

"Where is it?" I asked.

"I think it is better that you don't know. Just in case something happens," the captain said.

I nodded. "Let's just hope Jackson doesn't sink the *Lyonsword*," I muttered, mostly to myself.

The captain and Christopher shared a glance, then Captain Bates looked at me and smiled confidently. "He won't sink it. It's too valuable."

"Shut up!" yelled our guard. He was far enough away that all he could hear was the low murmur of our voices, but we fell silent anyway. I glanced at the captain, wanting to ask him why the *Lyonsword* was so valuable, but he shook his head, telling me to wait. I nodded, and we hunkered down and readied ourselves for three long days in the dark.

Chapter 10

For the next couple of days, we were essentially left alone, apart from the guard yelling at us if we started talking. We were fed meager portions, and on the second day, the ship was caught in a storm that kept us awake that whole day and night. Though the others complained, I didn't mind not sleeping. The dreams I had been having were getting more intense and detailed. Every time I closed my eyes, the vision of my darkness consumed me, as if trying to trap me forever.

The belly of the *Ghost* was miserable throughout the storm, as water rushed down through the hatch every time it was opened, until we sat in a couple inches of water that sloshed around as the ship was tossed in the waves. We managed to get as comfortable as we could, though, and eventually our guard was called up to help on deck. With the guard gone, I finally had a chance to ask the captain about the *Lyonsword*.

As I looked over at the captain, I could tell by his slight smile that he knew what I was going to ask. "What did you mean when you said the *Lyonsword* is too valuable for them to sink?" I prompted.

The captain took a deep breath, gathering the dregs of his energy. "Because some believe it is the result of a miracle," he explained simply. "The Jewel of the Sea," he said with a tired smile. The storm rocked the ship from side to side, sloshing the water up against the hull and sending it splashing over us. A story was just what we needed to get through this.

I raised my eyebrows. "That's what Jackson called the *Lyonsword*—the Jewel of the Sea," I said, looking at Christopher. He nodded, an amused smile brightening his tired face. I turned back to the captain. "Why did he call it that? Why do people believe it's a miracle?" I asked.

The captain considered the question for a moment before responding. "Because of how it came to be," he said with a reminiscent smile.

I frowned, perplexed. "How did it come to be?"

The captain adjusted his position and began to explain, "Despite how it looks, the *Lyonsword* has been around for hundreds of years. Legend says it was made with Original Power."

"What do you mean?" I prompted further.

"You have seriously never heard this story?" clarified Christopher with a raised eyebrow.

I shook my head. "No. I had never heard of the *Lyonsword* until the day I met you all."

"That explains all your odd questions about repairs and the oars," he commented.

The captain nodded. "I guess I should tell you the story then," he said with a smile and a twinkle in his eye.

Christopher leaned against the hull behind him and got as comfortable as he could, and I did the same. The captain sat opposite us, leaning against a wall that separated us from some cargo. Taking in a deep breath, he let it out slowly and then began his story.

"Many years ago, when people first started sailing the seas, there was a man by the name of Darius. Darius was a sailor, and he lived on the high seas in a ship with no name. After the Creature set the Lie in place, the land and seas became full of darkness and danger. Unbeknownst to Darius, a man endowed with special powers was watching over Darius's travels. This man was said to be able to wield an ancient power, which we know to be Original Power." The captain smiled. "We all have come to know him as the King of the Unseen Lands, who is the source of Original Power. The King loved Darius and decided to help him as the seas became increasingly volatile once the Lie was in place. Without Darius's knowledge, the King assigned Darius an invisible guardian whose name was said to be Seafrah."

"Who was probably a soldier of the Lion's Sword, like Eye-thanoff," commented Christopher.

The captain nodded and continued his story. "One day, Darius was sailing on the high seas and a leviathan attacked his ship. Darius was all alone, as his ship was quite small, and he had no crew. The leviathan was said to be the biggest leviathan in history, and it damaged Darius's ship severely. As the leviathan ravaged Darius's ship, attempting to kill him, Seafrah saw that Darius was in danger and came to his aid. Seafrah stepped between the massive animal and Darius, stabbing the monster in the mouth as it attempted to grab Darius. Seafrah's sword pierced the animal's soft tongue, and it pulled away in pain.

"Seeing the leviathan pull away in pain, Darius was confused, as he could not see what had hurt it. But being a man of the sea, he had seen many strange things in his life. Things that were hard to explain. Though Darius was unaware of the Lie, he had heard stories of the rise of darkness, and he knew that there were things out there—beings—that he could not see and did not understand.

"With no other option, Darius called out, hoping that what he had seen was not just a dream and someone was actually there and could hear him.

"The King was pleased by Darius's attempt to communicate with his rescuer and wanted to preserve Darius's faith in the unseen, so he told Seafrah to do whatever it took to protect Darius. As the leviathan attacked the ship once more, Seafrah again came to Darius's aid. Seafrah climbed between the ship and the leviathan, holding it back with his feet and a great deal of Original Power, which gave him strength. Darius could not see Seafrah. What he did see was inexplainable. He saw the leviathan dive for the ship but stop short as if something were blocking it. In that moment, Darius chose to take a leap of faith. Choosing to fully believe that someone was there, protecting him, Darius was filled with confidence, and he rushed the leviathan. Though he could not see Seafrah, Darius fought side-by-side with him that day in a battle to remember.

"Suddenly, an enemy of the King appeared and attacked Seafrah. This enemy, most likely a dark soldier, or perhaps even the Creature himself, did not want anyone to know of the King and how much he cared for his people, for the Creature was afraid it might ruin his plans. Instead, the enemy wanted Darius to fall prey to hopelessness.

"With confidence that someone was out there helping him, Darius fought the leviathan, and Seafrah protected him from the unseen enemy. The two battles waged on until Darius vanquished the leviathan, but Seafrah was injured. The enemy saw that the monster was killed but also that the ship was destroyed and Seafrah was gravely wounded. So, he left Darius to his fate, certain that Darius would die at sea, hopeless and alone.

"But Seafrah, heeding the King's instruction to do whatever it took to protect Darius, used the last of his strength, along with the Original Power granted to him by the King, to fix Darius's ship so that Darius would not be lost to the sea. As Seafrah mended the ship, he spoke to Darius, and Darius heard his voice. Seafrah told Darius who had sent him. He told Darius that his faith in the unseen had saved him, and he explained everything that had happened that night. Seafrah told Darius to use the ship for good and that, in the words of the King, the ship would carry him and his descendants over the oceans in safety.

"When Darius asked the voice its name, Seafrah told him and explained that he was a member of the Lion's Sword, an army that fought for the King. He told Darius to never forget what the King had done for him that day. With that, the King funneled his power through the armor Seafrah wore and into the ship, completing its repair and creating the ship you see today. Darius named the ship the *Lyonsword* in memory of the King and his army and the miracle that saved him that day."

"Do you think the story is true?" I asked.

The captain smiled. "I am a descendant of Darius. According to my father, who was captain of this ship before me, the *Lyonsword* has some unexplainable attributes. For one thing, she has not aged a day. Though we do still have to take care of her and patch her up when she gets damaged, she is in as good a shape as she has always been, and repairs always go miraculously faster than they should. My father also said that she changes to fit the needs of her captain.

That's why the ship sometimes has oars and sometimes doesn't. There are also accounts of her moving on her own when her crew is in danger, helping them reach their destination much faster. Some even say the ship sailed itself until Darius found a crew."

"That's why you have always believed," I said, suddenly understanding the captain's dedication to this mission a little better.

The captain nodded. "Not everyone in my family has believed that *The Story* is true. But I have seen things similar to what Darius witnessed. I cannot explain them, save that there is something at work in this world that we do not yet understand." As he spoke, he smiled, let his head lean back against the wall behind him, and closed his eyes. "When I heard *The Story* for the first time, I knew it had to be true."

As I pondered the captain's words, I closed my eyes as well, and we sat in silence, the ship swaying and rocking beneath us.

"We'd best try to sleep," said the captain. "We will need all the energy we can muster when it comes time to escape."

⁕⸱⁘⸱⁕

I stood in the woods. The Beast reached its tail toward me, wrapping it around my waist like a belt. Around me, the vision of *The Story* played out, but it faded into the background, and I found myself face-to-face with the Ice Dragon.

She touched my chest with her claw, and the breastplate appeared. I reached up to touch it once again as her words sounded around me. "Be on guard, my friend, for your heart is a treasure worth protecting."

When I looked up, the dragon was gone, and I saw my dark reflection before me. I had seen it so many times now that I found I was finally able to really look at it. I knew it was there, and I could not hide from it. So, I examined it.

Since I confessed my guilt to Solace, the Beast's dead body had vanished from my dreams. But that was all that had changed. The darkness that filled me from within was still there, reminding me of my past actions. It originated from my chest, spreading through my body like an infection. Around me, darkness kept *The Story* in shadow, like a reality I could not access. But as I looked closer, I saw something in the distance. Something stood out in contrast to the darkness. A light. Not a light from me, but a light beyond me. As I focused on the light, *The Story* around me became clearer and brighter.

Suddenly, my dark reflection lunged toward me. Veins of darkness began growing from within my reflection, corrupting my very soul. Each one with a word on it, "murderer," "liar," "coward." As I read the words, I heard them whispered out loud, as though someone were speaking in my ear. The pit of my stomach twisted as all the terrible things I had done in my past flipped through my mind like pages in a book. I began to breathe hard, and my chest grew tight as I felt myself start to panic. Suddenly, a dark soldier burst from within my dark reflection's chest, its hands outstretched toward me as it let loose an angry cry.

I jolted awake, my heart pounding in my chest as I frantically searched my surroundings for the dark being that had attacked me. The captain and Christopher stirred and opened their eyes.

"You alright?" Christopher asked groggily.

But I could not answer as my mind raced through the images I had just seen. *It was a dream,* I told myself. *Right?* But I knew it was more than that.

"Was it a dark soldier?" asked the captain as he sat up straighter and ran a hand through his damp hair.

I shook my head. "I...Yes...but it was not just that," I said, my breath still coming in gasps.

The captain's eyebrows rose slightly as he anxiously awaited my explanation. "What?" he asked.

"I...I didn't tell you before, but...I had a vision at the castle," I said as I forced myself to take a slow, deep breath.

"Lance told me something happened," said the captain. "What was the vision about?"

"It was about...a dragon. An ice dragon. And a breastplate of armor. I have been having dreams ever since," I explained. "But this time, it was different. There was something else there...A dark soldier. I saw *The Story*, like before..." I shook my head. "But there was also a light."

"What does it mean?" asked Christopher, leaning forward slightly.

"I don't know," I said, rubbing my hands over my face.

"What brought on the vision at the castle?" asked the captain.

"There was a mirror. It was made of gold, but the reflection was different."

"Different how?" asked the captain, his analytical eyes locked on me.

"It wasn't a reflection of me…It was like it was showing me who I really am." I shuddered at the thought of the darkness within my dreams.

"How did you find the mirror in the castle?" asked Christopher.

I shrugged. "It was the sword…It was like it was attracted to the mirror…and so was I."

"It sounds like the sword was leading you somewhere," the captain pointed out.

I nodded slowly. I hadn't really thought of it like that. "That's a possibility, since the sword has a connection to Original Power. But where was it leading me? And why?"

Suddenly, sounds of shouting and metal clanging on metal erupted from the deck above. All three of us stood and listened intently. It wasn't just the storm. It sounded like a battle.

"We have likely reached the Channel," said the captain as he stared at the ceiling intensely, suddenly fully awake. "We've probably been down here for about three days now."

"Who would attack us in a storm?" asked Christopher.

"Valdra," I said irritably. "We need to get out of these chains right now!"

"What about that?" said Christopher, pointing to the captain's sword sitting across the hold in the pile of the weapons that had been taken from the *Lyonsword*'s crew.

The captain shook his head. "These chains aren't long enough for us to reach. But I lifted this off Jackson while we were in my cabin," he said, holding up a knife.

"That won't do anything—the weapons pile is far out of our reach," I said.

The captain smiled, reached up, and unscrewed the large pearl on the end of knife's handle. Out slid a key. "I saw him conceal this key in the knife while we were in the office. He hid it in his desk, and I managed to replace it with a replica without him noticing."

My jaw fell open. "How in the world did you end up with a replica of his dagger?" I asked in shock.

"I once heard he had a master key for all the locks on his ship. This is—" he started to explain.

"I hate to interrupt," said Christopher, "but you will have to tell that story some other time. The fighting is getting worse, and we need to get out of here."

Just then, our guard returned to grab some of the weapons. *Perfect timing.* But before I realized what was happening, the captain seized the moment and kicked a bowl he had eaten from that morning. The bowl slid across the floor and the man tripped over it. His right hand snapped out to catch his fall, and he barely managed to keep from hitting the ground face-first. In a split second, I realized the captain's game. To kill the guard, we needed him to be closer, and the best way to draw him closer was to pick a fight. The guard was almost on his feet again. I had to act fast.

Following the captain's lead, Christopher and I grabbed our bowls and threw them at the crewman. One hit him on the head, and the other hit his leg. The man tried to protect his head with one hand as he pushed himself the rest of the way up with his other. Coming to his feet quickly, he shook his head to clear it from the blow, then glared at us. Christopher smiled and shrugged, spreading his arms out wide in a challenging stance.

There was no need for Christopher to say a word. In anger, the guard lunged at him. Christopher managed to dodge the man's punch and crack his forehead on the bridge of the guard's nose, breaking it. Dazed, the guard swayed backward, holding his bloody nose, before the ship rocked him forward, bringing him just within our reach again. I grabbed him and pulled him to my chest, spinning him around so he was facing outwards, and wrapped my arm around his neck. He struggled as the captain took his weapons, but he was dazed enough that he didn't put up much of a fight. Now all I had to do was hold on tight. As soon as I felt him go limp, I loosened my grip just enough to make sure he wasn't faking it. When I was certain he was out, I lowered him to the ground. The captain unlocked our chains, and I grabbed the guard's final weapon from his belt. Then we headed to the stairs to the upper decks, pausing to grab some weapons from the pile. There weren't many, and most were only small daggers, but the captain made sure to get his sword.

At the top of the stairs, I cracked the hatch and peeked out at the chaotic scene we would soon be entering. It was night, but lanterns and moonlight made it all visible. The *Ghost*'s crew were headed to the *Lyonsword*, which was being towed behind the *Ghost*.

"It looks like someone is attacking the *Lyonsword*," I whispered. "Valdra, I'm sure. You got a plan for this part?"

"We go up there and do everything we can to show Valdra that we are on this ship, not that one. And we pray that Solace has not been found," the captain responded.

"Have you been making this up as we go?" I asked.

The captain smiled. "The key to a great plan is to plan for not having a plan."

We all chuckled. Then I took a deep breath and opened the hatch, and we climbed up onto the deck. As I stood on the *Ghost*, I could see we were at the mouth of the Channel. Valdra's Martecytes had attacked the *Lyonsword*, but there were fewer of them than I had expected.

"Christopher, go find Solace and tell her the plan," I said. "The captain and I will take care of things on this end."

Christopher looked to the captain for confirmation, and the captain nodded.

With that, Captain Bates and I began attacking the crew of the *Ghost* in hopes it would draw attention away from Christopher's mission and convince Valdra's soldiers to come over to the *Ghost*. The nearest crew member of the *Ghost* turned and spotted me before I could launch a surprise attack. As soon as I was within range, he swung his cutlass at my throat, and I dodged it, stepping to the side. As I came to bear on him, I noticed that the crewman fighting with the captain had just drawn a pistol. My pistol. Attached to a strap slung across his chest was the other pistol.

I ducked an attack from my opponent and reengaged him. I noticed he had an injured leg, which I could use to my advantage. In one quick move, I thrust my dagger toward him, dodging the attack I knew would come. I ducked under his swing and delivered a blow to his wounded leg with a closed fist. He went down fast, and I plunged the dagger into the back of his neck, killing him.

Spinning to face the crewman with my pistols, I found him sprawled on the deck in a puddle of his own blood. The captain had moved on to a new target. It was clear he was skilled with his sword. I grabbed the pistols and checked to see if they were loaded before returning them to their rightful place. Only three rounds between the two of them. I could make do with that.

As we waged war with the crew of the *Ghost*, I saw the Martecytes begin to switch targets. They had seen the captain and me on the *Ghost* and began fighting their way through the pirates to get to us, just as we had hoped. As the Martecytes headed toward us, the *Ghost*'s crew on the *Lyonsword* followed to defend their ship, leaving the *Lyonsword* open for us to take back.

As I defeated another crew member of the *Ghost*, firing my last round into his eye socket, I saw Valdra out of the corner of my eye. He was making his way across the *Lyonsword*'s deck, headed in my direction. Most of the *Lyonsword*'s crew had yet to be freed and were still below deck on the *Lyonsword* or the *Ghost*, so Valdra's path was mostly clear. Thankfully, Ivan had been brought to the *Ghost* and had managed to free himself, and he joined in the chaos, attacking the *Ghost*'s crew and the Martecytes as they came aboard. I could count on him for backup.

As the ships continued to sail through the channel, Valdra finally made it across the *Lyonsword* and began pulling himself up a rope that hung down the side of the *Ghost*. He climbed over the *Ghost*'s gunwale and headed straight toward me. Without my sword, I could not see how many soldiers of darkness were around, and I felt out of control. I was also out of bullets, so I had nothing but the small dagger. But I turned to Valdra, hoping that Christopher had made it to Solace and they were working on a way to get the *Lyonsword* out of the Channel.

"You look awful!" snarled Valdra with a sly grin, in mockery of the comradery we once shared. We had both worked for General Delaney, and it was clear Valdra saw me as a traitor.

"Really? I feel great!" I said with false bravado.

Valdra's smile faded at my response, and he charged me, gripping his sword with both hands. I raised the dagger in defense, and Valdra's sword clanged down on it, its small crossbar preventing his sword from slicing my hand off. Valdra pulled back and swung again, but I dodged his sword as it slashed past my knees, the tip slicing through my pantleg. Seeing an opening, I stepped forward and grabbed Valdra's wrist, holding his sword at bay while I plunged the dagger down from above. Valdra released one hand from his grip on the sword and grabbed my wrist before I could plunge the dagger into his neck.

Standing open as I was, I knew I was vulnerable to an attack to my midsection and face. To prevent Valdra from getting enough leverage to let go and attack without being injured, I pushed into him, forcing him to push back and tighten his grip on me as I did on him. As we grappled, he maneuvered his sword hand until his sword was at my throat. Using his own pressure and position against him, I dropped my weight and stepped back with one foot. Dropping the dagger, I used my newly freed hand to grab his wrist and twisted to my right, pulling him past me and toward the ground. Taking advantage of his vulnerable position, I struck his midsection with my hip as I pulled, knocking him off his feet. Valdra hit the ground on his side and let out a grunt as the wind was partially knocked out of him, then continued the roll until he was back on his feet. I spun to face him.

"We once fought side by side, my old friend," growled Valdra. "You betrayed us for this? Death wherever you turn?" he taunted.

"I recall you trying to kill me first," I replied through gritted teeth.

In anger, he lunged at me. As we fought, I was barely aware of the battle around us. The *Ghost*'s crew and the recently freed crew of the *Lyonsword* were both fighting against Valdra's soldiers. But for a moment, I thought I could feel something. Something was different about this battle, but I didn't know what. *The armies of darkness?* I wondered. But the only way I could sense the armies of darkness was through Solace or with the sword. *It must be my imagination,* I thought as I refocused on my fight to survive.

Suddenly, Valdra looked past me, and his eyes widened briefly as something caught his attention. Then he looked back at me and charged, growling in anger. He rammed into me, shoving me backward, and knocked me off my feet. Now on the ground, I kicked his sword free of his grip and scrambled to grab my dagger as Valdra came after me. We rolled across the *Ghost*'s deck as we struggled over my dagger, ending with him on top of me. All I saw was the glint of the dagger and the evening sky behind him, the battle moving around us like a frame around Valdra and the dagger poised above my face. Blood splattered from someone nearby onto Valdra and me as we struggled. Neither of us dared to flinch in response, for one slip would spell the end for one of us. My hands gripped Valdra's wrist as I desperately held the knife at bay, its point coming within inches of my eye. But Valdra had the leverage, and I could feel my arms giving way. The sharp steel blade grew closer and closer.

Just when I thought my strength would fail, Ivan appeared out of nowhere and plowed through Valdra, knocking the knife from his hands. All in one motion, he rolled over him and sprung to his feet, picked up Valdra like a sack of potatoes, and launched him over the side of the ship.

I scrambled to my feet and grabbed the knife as I heard Valdra splash into the waters below us. As I stood and took in my surroundings, I saw what had drawn Valdra's attention. The *Lyonsword* was sailing past the *Ghost*, headed for the end of the Channel. Christopher and Solace were on its deck, fighting off the remainder of the Martecytes and the *Ghost*'s crew alongside the rest of the *Lyonsword*'s crew. The Martecytes were overrun by the two groups and were starting to pull back to land in rowboats I hadn't noticed before.

"Ben!" I heard the captain yell, and I turned to look behind me. "Go! You need to make the meeting! I'll tell Solace and Nadia to meet you on shore," he called before running and jumping off the bow of the *Ghost*, landing in a graceful tuck and roll on the quarterdeck of the *Lyonsword* as it sailed past the *Ghost*.

Ivan and I ran for the starboard side of the *Ghost* and loaded into a small boat. I cut the rope, and we splashed into the water below just as Jackson appeared at the gunwale and slashed with his sword, narrowly missing my head. As Jackson yelled angry threats from above, Ivan took to the paddles and rowed us to shore. We landed on the beach just as the *Lyonsword* reached the end of the Channel, sailing close along the edge of the Northern Continent. I could just barely catch the shadows of Solace, Nadia, and a much less graceful Lance as they jumped from the ship into the upper branches of the trees that lined the shore.

I threw a look over my shoulder and spotted another small boat pursuing us in the darkness. I had no idea who it was, whether it was a Martecyte or something worse, but I wasn't going to stick around to find out. On the *Ghost*, the pirates continued battling Valdra and the rest of his Martecytes, forcing the remaining few back into their rowboats and to the safety of land. Before Ivan and I disappeared into the trees along the shore, I spared one last glance at the now moonlit *Lyonsword* as it set sail into the Western Sea.

Chapter 11

Ivan and I met up with Solace, Nadia, and Lance as we ran through the woods, headed to the meeting we had set up months ago.

We sprinted between the trees, racing toward North Town at the base of the Northern Mountains. Solace handed me the sword and shield as we ran, and I kept an eye out for anyone behind us while she concentrated on making sure no one was lying in wait ahead of us. I spotted two figures following us, possibly those from the rowboat, but it wasn't clear who they were. Thankfully, we were able to outrun them, so we did not have to cross swords with them.

When we reached the edge of town, we forced ourselves to slow down. Frantically running through town would only draw more attention that we didn't need. Lance had the book pages and knew where the contact lived, so we continued on our way with Lance in the lead. We arrived at our contact's home just in time and were waved inside by the owner as she glanced cautiously up and down the street behind us.

Once we were all inside, the woman's husband led us to a back room, where he lifted the carpet to reveal a trapdoor. He opened the trapdoor and led us all down a ladder to the cellar. Then he lit a lamp and gave his wife a quick kiss before disappearing back up the ladder and closing the trapdoor behind him. There was a soft thump as the thick carpet fell back in place overhead.

Lance turned to me. "Ben, this is Jean. She will be printing and distributing the books in the Northern Country." He turned toward our contact. "Jean, this is Benjamin Arlin," he said before briefly introducing Ivan, Nadia, and Solace.

I stepped forward and shook Jean's hand. "It's nice to meet you, Jean. Thank you for your help."

She smiled, her grip firm as she returned my greeting. "I am just glad you made it here. There have been men patrolling the Channel for days now."

The rest of us glanced at each other with wry smiles. "Yes, we did run into them. But thankfully, we still made it," I commented.

Lance handed Jean two sets of book pages. "Here is the book we need you to copy, print, and distribute to those who want it. We were able to make some extra copies, so here is a second copy just in case you need it."

"Thank you! We will make great use of these," she assured.

"You must be careful, Jean," warned Lance. "These people who want to destroy *The Story* are not to be trifled with. They will try to kill you."

She nodded. "I know. If I get caught, no one else will get hurt. No one else in the Northern Country knows that we will be printing the books, and they won't find out. We have set up a secret drop point just as Captain Bates instructed us to." Jean ran an affectionate hand over the book pages. "I believe this story as you do. My father used to tell parts of it to me and my siblings when we were little," she said with a smile. "If more people knew the hope that this story offered, we might be able to rise up and defeat these beasts one day and be rid of their destruction."

"That is our hope as well," I responded, wondering if she knew how much hope *The Story* really contained…and how much truth. "Thank you for your assistance. It was wonderful to meet you, Jean, but we must be on our way."

Lance nodded. "Yes, thank you again for your help," he said. "And stay safe!"

"You are welcome," Jean said politely as she led us back to the ladder up to the trapdoor. But we all stopped short when we heard several thumps from overhead, as if someone were pounding on a door. Jean turned to us, holding an index finger to her lips as we all listened to the sound of the front door opening and muffled voices coming from above.

"How may I help?" I heard Jean's husband say.

"We are doing inspections," said a male voice. "Multiple fugitives from the Eastern Island Country were spotted near the Channel earlier, and we believe they are hiding somewhere in town."

Lance and I glanced at each other as I grabbed the sword's hilt and drew the weapon from its scabbard. There were no soldiers of darkness down here, but when I glanced at Solace, I recognized the look on her face. They were nearby.

Heavy footsteps sounded from above as multiple guards entered the house. I snuffed out the lamp, and we all stood stone still, pressed against the wall underneath the ladder just in case they found the trapdoor. We practically held our breath as the footsteps moved closer.

"I am not sure what exactly you are looking for, but there is no one here," said Jean's husband.

"Where is your family?" asked a new, gruffer voice. "Who else lives with you?"

"Just my wife. She is staying at her sister's house tonight," came the reply.

There was a tense silence in the cellar as one set of footsteps approached and stopped directly above the trapdoor. The other footsteps moved throughout the small house as the guards checked the other rooms.

After a moment, more footsteps approached, and someone spoke to the guard standing above us. "Doesn't look like anyone has been here," he said so quietly I could barely make out his words.

After a moment of hesitation, all the footsteps moved back toward the front door. "Thank you for your time," said the first intruder. "If you see anyone with this symbol on their shield, please report them."

"Thank you, I will keep an eye out for them," replied Jean's husband.

The sound of footsteps faded, and then came the thud of the front door swinging shut. Ivan immediately started to move next to me, but I felt Jean's arm flash out to stop him. We all froze again, still enveloped in darkness.

After a few tense moments, the trapdoor opened, and Jean's husband appeared. "They are gone, but you need to leave now. There is no telling when they might come back," he said urgently as he helped his wife through the opening.

We all quietly filed out of the cellar and to the back door of the house. Jean's husband checked the streets for any threats, then led us out the back door and to the edge of town, where he grasped Lance by the forearm and gave a firm shake. "Be safe," he whispered as they parted, then waved as we all headed back to the *Lyonsword*.

We ran through the trees once again, toward the low, rocky cliff edge of the nearby western shore. According to the captain, the edge would be just the right height for us to jump aboard the *Lyonsword* without the ship docking. *Unless we are late.* We had no time to stop and catch our breath as we raced through the woods. Thankfully, there were no soldiers following us this time.

As we rounded a corner, following a trail lined with rocks and trees, something in the trees to my right suddenly caught my attention. As the others continued, I slowed to a stop and searched the tree line for whatever had caught my eye. Just then, I felt the sword grow weightless in my hand. I glanced down to see the lettering on the blade shining with light. Then I heard something in the distance—a voice.

The voice was so soft I almost thought I'd imagined it. I looked up at the foliage. The trees seemed to draw me in, or more accurately, they seemed to draw the sword, and me with it. Something was there. I didn't know why, but I felt a strong urge to find out what it was. Leaving the trail, I moved toward the trees, one step at a time.

"Ben! Come on!" I heard Solace yell, but her voice was like a distant echo. The sword was reaching out to something, and I couldn't help but follow. I gripped the black leather-bound hilt as the voices of the others faded into the background. As I neared the trees, a light gust of wind parted them before my eyes, and a dirt path appeared before me. As if in a trance, I stepped forward, following the sword's call to wherever it was leading me.

As I walked through the trees, I heard the faint voice grow to an audible whisper. "Be on guard, my friend," the voice said.

With each step, I became vaguely aware that the ground seemed to get harder. I followed the path to a small clearing in the trees. As I took another step, I realized that there was no longer just dirt beneath my feet. I stopped and looked down. There was something under the soil.

I slowly squatted down and brushed the dirt away to reveal an old stone path. The path was peppered with sparkling silver flecks as if something shiny had been ground down and mixed into the soil between the stones.

In awe, I reached out toward the shiny flecks within the path. They seemed to produce their own small glimmers of light, since the moon was hidden behind the trees and there was no other light source that would cause them to glimmer so brightly. As my fingers grazed the sparkling silver pieces, an image of the Beast of the Woods suddenly flashed before my eyes. I stood up so abruptly that I stumbled back a step as I saw the Beast's tail wrap around my waist and turn into a belt. The vision of *The Story* that always accompanied the Beast of the Woods erupted around me in a flash, and then, just as fast, it faded to reveal the Ice Dragon. My breath caught as I found myself standing face-to-face with the majestic being, her massive form no longer contained within the mirror. *Is this real?* I wondered.

The dragon glanced down at the belt around my waist, then reached out and touched my chest with a claw. The breastplate appeared once again.

"Be on guard, my friend," she said, "for your heart is a treasure worth protecting."

As I stood before her, I suddenly remembered what the captain had mentioned on the ship about the sword leading me somewhere. Taking a chance that the captain might be right, I reached up, and instead of touching the breastplate, this time I grabbed it. "I will," I promised. The metal was cool to the touch, and as the dragon released the breastplate, it seemed to mold itself around me. As it settled into place, a bright light briefly shone from the piece of armor. I let my hand drop, and the breastplate remained in place, covering me from my shoulders to my waist. Its presence felt surprisingly reassuring, protective in a way I hadn't known I longed for.

Then the dragon stepped aside.

With the dragon no longer obstructing the path, I saw before me the vision of my dark reflection, but now I could see past it. Something in the distance glowed amidst the dark vision around me, the twinkling stone path laid out before me as a guide.

"Be ready, my friend," said the dragon, "for *The Story* is a treasure worth following."

As the dragon spoke, the sparkling silver in the path grew brighter, as if showing me the way out of the darkness around me. I stepped forward to follow it.

Suddenly, the dark soldier from my dreams leaped from the darkness of the vision, landing on the path before me, just a few paces away. My heart slammed against my chest, and I lifted the sword in defense. I took a deep breath to calm my nerves and remembered the dragon's words. "Be ready, my friend, for *The Story* is a treasure worth following," I repeated. It seemed the captain had been right about the sword leading me somewhere, and since the sword was made by the Prince, I figured I should find out where it was leading me.

"Okay...*The Story*..." I mumbled to myself as the dark soldier stood before me with that cruel smile upon his lips. "*The Story*...What does *The Story* have that can help me?" I asked myself. "*The Story* says that Ruth betrayed her beloved," I said as I took a step, not really sure of what I was doing. "It says that he still loved her despite her betrayal." I took another step, moving to the side of the path to step around the dark soldier. "And it says that he loved her so much he gave his life to bring her and her people back." Step. "It says that darkness will not reign forever, for the Lion will return and vanquish the Creature one day." Step.

With each step and reiteration of the truth *The Story* contained, I noticed a feeling that something was forming around my feet. I looked down to see shoes of silver armor. They were the same shiny metal as the breastplate and were buckled on with leather straps that seemed to match the leather of the belt. As I looked closer, I saw that there was writing engraved on the metal. It was the same kind of writing that had been on the mirror, but the words looked different. It was the same script as that on the sword and shield. Recognizing a pattern, I looked at the belt and breastplate and found that they, too, had writing on them. They were all connected. *Okay...maybe I am on the right track,* I thought. *I know the real story, the story that light overcame dark.* I nodded to myself and let out a long, controlled breath.

Pulling my attention from the mysterious writing, I moved forward, letting the shoes themselves guide my steps. I walked past the dark soldier and my dark reflection and found myself standing in the clearing of a different forest—one strangely familiar, though I didn't know why. Just as I was beginning to grow calm, the image of my darkness crept up from behind me like a predator and morphed into a dark storm around me. Soldiers of darkness appeared and surrounded me, threatening to take hold of me. Darkness was everywhere. Hazy visions of war, death, and evil swirled like a dark cloud around me. But in the distance was the glow of light, surrounded by darkness that threatened to overwhelm me once again. Yet, despite that darkness, I saw where I needed to go. Glittering and showing me the way, the path still shone bright, cutting through the darkness and filling me with a peace I did not understand.

For the first time since the nightmares had started, I put aside my fear, and I followed the path.

As I reached the end of the path, to my relief, I saw the source of the light. Standing before me was a door with no handle. The door was transparent but had an ornate design. Small images around its frame depicted the events of the story of the Prince and Ruth, and in the center of the door was a symbol I recognized. It was one of the symbols I had seen on the Prince's pendant in the Woods. Two ornate 'S' shapes, tall and thin. My heart beat faster with excitement—why, I wasn't quite sure. But my joy was short-lived. Before I could identify the source of my joy, I heard someone whispering from behind me. I spun around, holding the sword at the ready. What I saw before me sent chills down my spine.

I stood, facing my dark reflection from the mirror, the door behind me already forgotten. I stood amidst the darkness, veins of fog speaking words of my failures as they had in my dream. But then I realized the words were not coming from the fog but rather were the source of the fog. For behind me, and yet within me, the dark soldier from my dreams and visions loomed, whispering the words "murderer," "liar," "guilty," "lost," "unworthy."

The vision of the dark soldier within me grew until my dark reflection vanished under its overwhelming presence, and the darkness became like a thick fog around me, even darker and denser than before. In fear, I gripped the sword tighter and braced myself for what might come. But I felt the sword in my hands pull me back toward the door.

As I turned, I saw that the door was glowing, and I got a glimpse of what was on the other side. There stood the Prince, watching me as I stood, desperately grasping the sword, between the light and the dark. The two realities stood opposed, repelling each other. I stared at the light on the other side of the door. I longed for the land on that side, but I could not open the door, for it had no handle. I could not escape the darkness around me. I knew this because I had come to realize that my worst fear was true. *I am darkness!*

As an overwhelming feeling of guilt washed over me, I felt a hand wrap around my ankle, and panic sprang up within me as I felt myself being pulled to the ground and dragged away from the door to be engulfed in the inescapable darkness around me.

In desperation, I stretched a hand toward the door and saw the Prince reach for a handle that had appeared on his side of the transparent barrier. He grabbed the handle, and the engraved images of *The Story* on the frame lit up with white light as he began to open the door. But a terrible thought seized my mind. *What if the Prince is coming to kill me because of my darkness?* As the thought filled my body with dread, I saw the door before me turn to solid wood, and the vision of the door was overtaken by shadow before it all suddenly vanished.

"Ben! Ben!" I heard Nadia yelling. "Ben, I don't know what has gotten into you, but we need to go now. They are coming! I can hear them," she said urgently as she appeared by my side.

Still scrambling backward, away from the dark soldier, it took me a moment to realize he was gone, along with the rest of the vision. I shook my head, desperately trying to grasp what was real and what wasn't.

Finally, I nodded. "C-c-coming," I said as Nadia pulled me to my feet, and I looked around me.

I was still in a small clearing of trees, but the door was gone. Confused, I reluctantly turned to follow the others. As I forced myself to focus on the here and now, I shook my head again in an attempt to rid my mind of all thoughts of the vision. We had to make it off this continent, and then I could sit and think about what I had just seen.

We ran up a slight hill toward the cliff that faced the Western Sea. But as we reached the cliff's edge, we saw that we had taken too long to get there, and the winds were blowing harder than we had thought. The *Lyonsword* was now north of our position, where the cliffs were much higher. We quickly turned right and ran along the edge of the cliff, chasing after the ship and looking for a safe way down.

Then I heard it. The sound of people shouting and dogs braying in the distance. *Great, more tracking dogs,* I thought. Ivan and Nadia immediately picked up the pace, followed by Lance and Solace, and I took up the rear with the shield and sword in hand. We kept low and moved as quickly and quietly as possible, considering the rocky, forested terrain. But despite our best efforts, once we finally caught up with the *Lyonsword*, our pursuers were too close for comfort.

As we came within view of the *Lyonsword*'s crew, Eric spotted us from the ship's crow's nest and waved urgently, beckoning us to jump. We were now higher than we had initially planned, just above Eric's position in the nest. The captain maneuvered the *Lyonsword* parallel to the cliff face, and Nadia made the first jump. She landed gracefully with Eric in the crow's nest and immediately vacated it and began making her way down the rigging so the next person could jump. Ivan went next, then Solace. But Lance was less experienced and hesitated.

Just as Lance finally made his move, the *Lyonsword* was forced to jerk away from the cliff to navigate around a boulder. As Lance flew through the air, Eric desperately leaned over the edge of the crow's nest, barely catching Lance by the arm. With a panicked grip on Eric, Lance swung past the nest like a pendulum, propelled by his jump and the motion of the *Lyonsword*. As Lance scrambled to get his feet in front of him to stop himself from crashing into the mast, Ivan halted his descent down the rigging and climbed back up to help pull Lance to safety.

As I watched Lance get pulled over the edge of the crow's nest, the *Lyonsword* continued sailing north. Suddenly, a shout rang out behind me. One of our pursuers had spotted me, and I ducked as arrows started flying. Out of range and out of time, I swung the shield over my shoulder, hooking it on to a strap over my back, and took off north at a sprint. As I ran to catch up with the ship, I saw that the cliff came to an end a short distance ahead, leaving me with the choice—jump to the *Lyonsword* or turn and fight my way through the woods back to town. I chose the *Lyonsword*.

Arrows whizzed past me, striking trees and dirt and bouncing off the shield as I ran for the cliff's edge up ahead. The *Lyonsword* would have just enough space to maneuver right in front of me before it would need to turn back out to sea to keep from running aground. I darted farther inland to try and get some of my pursuers off my tail and give the captain a moment to get the *Lyonsword* into position. But we were all running out of time. With no other option, I ran straight for the cliff edge. The *Lyonsword* was not in position, but I could see Ivan waiting for me in the crow's nest. If I timed it right, he could catch me. Anything was better than getting captured by the enemy.

Sheathing the sword, I ran for the cliff as the thought that I was much higher than before attempted to eat away at my confidence. With no other way out of this, I pushed the fear aside and pressed on. But, as I broke the tree line near the cliff edge, one of the tracking dogs was let loose by its handler, and it broadsided me. The dog clamped its strong jaws down on my arm, and I grabbed at its mouth, struggling to get it loose, but the cliff was too close. In my attempt to escape the dog's jaws, we both went over the cliff edge.

As I fell over the cliff, I was briefly aware that I was falling to my death, well out of reach of anyone on the *Lyonsword*. But suddenly, something hit me. The dog released my arm and yelped in pain, as though struck by something I could not see, and I was pushed toward the *Lyonsword* as if by a gust of wind.

With no time to think, I reached out in the direction I hoped was the crow's nest and was relieved to feel Ivan grab my hand. Arrows and flintlock fire erupted from the cliff above, hitting the nest, mast, and shield hooked to my back. A barrage of well-aimed arrows struck the shield before the archers shifted their aim toward Ivan. As Ivan pulled me up toward him, I thought I saw three flashes of light out of the corner of my eye. But before I could look for what had caused the flashes, Ivan pulled me aboard, and the *Lyonsword* veered away from the cliff just in time to avoid crashing into the rocky shore.

As the *Lyonsword* sailed out to sea, Ivan and I ducked down behind the wall of the crow's nest and looked at each other. "What just happened?" he asked in shock.

I glanced back at the cliff and the rock-filled water below, where I should have landed, and I briefly recalled the captain's story of how the *Lyonsword* came to be. "A miracle," I said breathlessly.

Ivan and I remained in the crow's nest until we were out of range of the arrows. Once we were back on the deck, Solace and I embraced, happy that we were both still alive.

When she finally released me, her expression turned serious. "Before you do anything, you need to get this wound cleaned," she said, inspecting my arm.

"I need to talk to the—"

"No." Solace turned to Ivan. "Take him to get this cleaned," she instructed before turning back to me. "Then you can go see the captain. He is not going anywhere in the next five minutes."

I sighed and gave in to Solace's demands. Then, after being patched up, I went in search of the captain. I found him still at the wheel, guiding the *Lyonsword* west toward our next stop.

As soon as I set foot on the quarterdeck, the question that had been burning in my mind since I had boarded rolled off my tongue with more intensity than I intended. "It is true, isn't it?" I said, referring to the story of Darius and the *Lyonsword*.

The captain seemed to know what I was talking about and smiled. "There are things at work in this world that we don't have the tools to fully understand." He took his eyes off the moonlit waters to look at me. "You, of all people, should know that by now."

The captain handed the wheel off to me and left, slapping a hand on my shoulder as he walked by, still smiling. For a moment, I watched him go, then I let out a sigh and chuckled to myself. He was right. I should know that by now. I looked out over the waters around me and thought through the incident at the cliff. *I wish I could talk to Ruth. She would be able to explain all of this. Especially since Eyethanoff seems too busy to answer.* Sighing, I decided to take the win and let the events of the day fade from my mind. I grasped the wheel and looked out over the ocean around me. The moon shone overhead, full and bright. As I stared out at its beams dancing across the water's surface, I forced myself to let out another breath and relax.

Time passed as I watched the moonlight reflect off the peaceful ocean. It had a strangely calming effect on me after all the chaos of the mission. But as I looked closer at the moonbeams, something about them held my attention. Though they looked normal at first glance, something about their movement seemed unusual. I blinked, assuming my eyes were playing tricks on me, but the closer I looked, the more they appeared to dance strangely above the water as if they were alive.

Curious, I reached for the sword and began to pull it from its scabbard. As my grip tightened and I focused on the waters before me, something dark suddenly flashed before my eyes. I let go of the wheel completely and drew the sword into a defensive position as the dark soldier from my dreams suddenly appeared before me in a momentary burst of darkness. Simultaneously, I heard Eyethanoff's voice behind me. "Listen to her." I spun in search of Eyethanoff, but there was no one there. I looked around for the dark soldier. He was gone.

I called out, "Eyethanoff, I know you are there! Answer me!" But there was no answer. I was alone.

I must be losing my mind, I thought. Standing there with the sword at the ready, I took a deep breath and let it out, then repeated the process to calm my racing heart. I cautiously scanned my surroundings again. When I still could not find any sign of Eyethanoff or the dark soldier, I lowered the sword and rubbed my eyes. *I seriously must be losing my mind,* I thought. *Maybe these visions are not even happening, and I am just imagining everything the sword seems to be showing me.* With one last paranoid glance around the ship and surrounding waters, I sheathed the sword and turned my attention to steering the *Lyonsword*. Just then, Ivan came up the stairs to join me on the quarterdeck. He plopped down on his favorite napping spot and looked at me with a raised eyebrow.

"What?" I asked after a moment of waiting for him to speak.

Ivan shrugged. "Nothing...It's just that you look awful, like you desperately need some sleep."

I rolled my eyes, but when I looked at him, I could see behind the teasing he was serious.

"I'm fine, Ivan," I said. But as I answered him, a partial thought about the visions began to form in my mind, twisting my gut, but I didn't want to discuss it. I shoved it aside, hoping my expression didn't give any of the new fear away. I sighed and ran a hand through my hair as I realized I really did need a break to recover from whatever it was that was happening to me. I didn't want to admit that to Ivan, though.

Ivan nodded with a smile. "I know. You are always fine."

I chuckled. He knew me well. There was never any hope of covering things up with him around.

"Solace told me you have been having nightmares and that you had another vision. Something about a mirror in the castle," he said in a more serious tone.

"What's your point?" I asked, uncertain what vision he was referring to but deciding not to ask.

He watched me for a moment. "Ben, I have been through hell and back with you. I have seen you on your worst days. But this…" He sighed. "I saw what just happened," he explained.

I tensed, and my stomach flipped at the idea that he may have seen my fight with an invisible dark soldier that may or may not have been real. When I looked at him, I couldn't tell if he was referring to the incident on the cliff or my brief battle with the dark soldier just moments ago. Either way, I could tell he was almost as concerned as I was. *Almost.*

"That wasn't normal. Even for a guy who is dealing with invisible armies and kings and the like."

Pretending I knew which incident he was talking about, I found myself responding out of irritation. "And how would you know?" I asked, my jaw slightly clenched.

"Because you were planning on not telling anyone about it," he said plainly. Then he leaned forward. "That means you are concerned. And when you are concerned, so am I."

I looked at him. He wasn't wrong. "Ivan, I'm just tired. And for all we know, that was not what we think it was," I said, hoping he was talking about the cliff. Me fighting something invisible was pretty much exactly what we thought it was. A bad sign.

"So, you do think you are going crazy?" he asked, crossing his arms.

I let out a frustrated sigh. "Ivan, I..."

"Ben, do not lie to me!" he said, raising his voice. "You know as well as I do that a soldier without clarity of mind is dangerous."

I closed my eyes. *Maybe this is about the dark soldier I just saw.* It didn't matter. He was right. As much as I did not want to admit it, I wasn't sure if I was of sound mind at this point.

"After I saw the vision in the Woods, I began having dreams about it. But then the dreams stopped. They didn't start again until after I saw the vision in the mirror at the castle. Now my dreams are back, but they have changed. They are...darker. Like the visions," I admitted. "And I haven't seen Eyethanoff in person since the castle..."

"You are worried that none of the visions are real?" he clarified, relaxing slightly now that he had gotten me to admit my worries.

I nodded as the thought I had not wanted to discuss came to mind once again. "Or worse...that they are distractions sent by the enemy to pull us off course."

Chapter 12

Darkness swirled around me like fog. The dark soldier's image flickered before me as lightning flashed and thunder boomed. But then a voice sounded all around me. "Guard your heart, my friend, for your heart is a treasure worth protecting." As the words sounded, the dark soldier grew even darker, and I saw that he stood behind my dark reflection, an ominous smile upon his lips as he whispered in my reflection's ear, though it sounded as though he were whispering in my own. "Murderer. Failure. Liar. Coward."

I felt frozen, as though I could not move, but everything in me told me to run. I reached for the sword, but it was not there. I searched for the shield, but I could not find it. Then I felt a presence. The door. I could feel it somewhere nearby, and I wanted it, like water in a desert. But no matter how hard I tried, I could not take my eyes off the dark being before me.

Panic began to rise within my chest as the dark soldier moved closer, though he did not take steps. His eyes were like pools of darkness with flaming red irises. His teeth glinted, and I thought I saw a set of small fangs.

Frantically, I tore my eyes away from him and searched for the door until I finally glimpsed it in the distance. The Prince was standing in the open, transparent doorway.

"*Tsahreyethah Meye,*" he breathed with gentle care.

But I could feel the darkness grab me from behind and I spun around to face the thing I feared most. My own darkness. The dark soldier's smile grew until he burst out in laughter as he consumed my dark reflection. Then, suddenly, the dark being's laughter turned to anger, and he lunged at me.

⁂

I snapped awake with the image of the dark soldier still clear in my mind but the faint words of the Prince echoing in my ears. "*Tsahreyethah Meye.*" Sweat poured down my forehead, and my heart pounded in my chest. Solace and I had fallen asleep on some blankets below our hammocks, and she shifted beside me as I bolted upright. As I tried to catch my breath, I glanced at her to make sure she hadn't woken.

"What's wrong?" Solace mumbled.

My throat dry, I forced myself to swallow and managed to whisper, "Nothing. Go back to sleep." Solace closed her eyes, and within seconds her breathing returned to a steady rhythm.

I lay back down next to her and stared up at the ceiling framed by the edges of our hammocks that were now occupied by Ivan and Nadia, who usually slept in the forecastle but had fallen asleep down here after chatting with Otto about the language on the sword. The ship moved below me, rocking gently on the calm waves outside. I closed my eyes, and almost immediately, the image of the dark soldier reappeared in a flash. My eyes snapped open as I tried to erase the image. Rolling over onto my side, I tried to focus on Solace's breathing instead. *Why is this happening?* The dreams

I had grown to expect. But each one grew more intense than the last. *And more real.*

As I listened to Solace's breathing, I calmed a bit, and a question came to mind. *What did those words mean?* I asked myself. *Tsahreyethah Meye.* The Prince had said those words, so I knew they must be good, but I had no idea what they meant. *Maybe the Prince showing up and speaking in the dream means I am on the right track with following the sword,* I wondered. Then again, it could all just be bad dreams brought on by the exhaustion of ocean travel and being captured by pirates twice.

As I considered whether I was going insane or not, I looked toward the sword and shield. They were propped up in the corner against the wall, Ruth's cloak draped over them to create a tent, or "cave," as Yuuki called it, that Yuuki slept under. The black cloak mostly concealed the symbol on the shield. But I knew it was there.

As I lay in bed, unable to sleep, I wondered what the symbol meant and if the Prince's new words were connected somehow. As I pondered what little we knew about the language on the sword, I thought of Eyethanoff. His name had similar sounds to the words I had heard in my dream. *I wonder if they are of the same language,* I speculated.

Suddenly overcome with curiosity, I quietly climbed out of our pile of blankets and snuck over to Otto's bed. He was sprawled out and snoring loudly. As usual, he had fallen asleep mid-work, so his notebooks and writing utensils were strewn about his bedding. The notebook I wanted was still in his hand and I reached out to grab it. As my fingers wrapped around it, Otto shifted and rolled over, pinning the book beneath him.

I frowned and released the book, letting my head fall to my hands in frustration. I glanced at Solace, wondering if I should just go back to bed. But I really wanted to look over what Otto had found so far. With everything that had happened, I needed to know what the writing on the sword meant now more than ever, and I wanted to understand the Prince's words.

I looked at the book and decided to give it one more try. I grabbed the edge of the notebook and gently pulled on it while resting my other hand on Otto's shoulder. To my surprise, he didn't even flinch. I frowned. Apparently, he still had a long way to go in developing awareness of his surroundings. As a soldier, I'd had to learn to wake at the slightest noise or touch.

As I pushed gently on Otto's shoulder, he eventually shifted again with a grunt, rolling away from me and freeing the notebook. I slipped the book out from under him and uncrumpled its pages as I sank to the ground right beside his bed so I could use what little light was left burning in the lantern still hanging above his head.

I paged through the notebook and scanned Otto's almost illegible handwriting in search of information on the language he had been trying to decode. I finally came across something that looked promising and began reading.

"Today we are still sailing through the Eastern Sea in hopes that we will reach the Eastern Island Country in time for our meeting with our first contact. As I sit in the belly of this damp, cramped ship, I have realized two things. First, I dislike ocean travel. It is wet. Not that I did not know that, but I have concluded that the captain and his entire crew have sustained some form of brain damage. Why else would anyone want to live in a place like this, constantly wearing damp clothes and facing disease and certain death?

The second thing I have realized is that this language is quite unique. I have no idea what this language is called, but it is the most beautiful script I have ever seen. The text on the sword seems to be written with no spaces between words, and, as far as I can tell, there do seem to be similar endings on some of the words, potentially indicating conjugated verbs, though I can't be certain at this juncture.

I have no idea what any of the words mean, but I am starting to think I have found each letter, or symbol, and where they begin and end. However, it is hard to tell for certain as there are small additions to each symbol that are sometimes connected to other letters and sometimes not, making it difficult to distinguish which letters they belong to. As to whether this is important, I am not yet sure."

I flipped through a couple more pages before finding another section that looked like it might be helpful.

"I have been able to separate the words into what I believe are their individual characters. It appears that each word starts with what looks like a capital letter, which is fascinating because of how old this language probably is. Capital letters were first introduced with the invention of the printing press, indicating that whoever used this language had some understanding of printed language. Unless these 'uppercase' letters hold some other meaning.

Despite being able to distinguish individual letters, I have yet to determine what the phonology might sound like or if the symbols could even be categorized as letters. Thus, translation will be nearly impossible without different sentences for comparison or more information regarding what the symbols represent and how the sentence and grammar are structured."

I searched through the rest of the pages but didn't find anything that would tell me if the Prince's words had anything to do with this language. I tossed the book back on Otto's bed and stood, placing my hands on my hips. *If we are ever going to translate this language, I am going to have to find Otto some more information.*

I glanced at Solace and shook my head; I couldn't go back to sleep now. I was too awake. So instead, I headed for the hatch leading up to the main deck and exited the ship's belly. As I emerged from the dim interior, I was greeted with the first hints of dawn on the horizon. I leaned against the gunwale and thought through the dreams and visions I had been having and my mysterious encounter with the dark soldier while steering the ship.

As I pondered my dilemma, I was vaguely aware of the crew moving about on the ship, taking advantage of the morning breeze, which they expertly harnessed to propel the *Lyonsword* in the right direction. I kept thinking that I should try to call Eyethanoff again. But so far, that hadn't worked very well. Ivan was right, this could all just be in my head, which was not the most comforting thought. I let out a breath as frustration built up inside me. I was lacking all the pieces to this puzzle but still trying to put it together. Not an easy task.

If I really thought about it, I supposed Eyethanoff probably had a good reason for not showing up. He had at least shown up at the castle to help hold off the soldiers of darkness. I wasn't sure if we would have escaped without him. But he had not given me anything to go on in reference to finding the Gate and learning what the sword said. And Otto was dead in the water, so to speak, with translating the sword. It would seem my only option was to keep moving forward. I needed to set aside these problems for the moment and focus on the next step of our mission—meeting our contact on the Western Island.

For some reason, that thought reminded me of our journey to find the doctor at the Great Volcano, the trip that had led to this whole mission. During that trip, Solace and I had spoken many times about truth, and I began thinking, *What is true?* I nodded slowly to myself as I began reviewing all the visions and dreams I'd had. *The truth is that the Prince saved Solace's life. The truth is that Valdra clearly feared the sword, and I saw* The Story *play out that day in the Woods; I am sure of it...The truth is that* The Story *is true.* I hesitated. *Do I know that without a shadow of a doubt, though?* Again, I thought about the things I had seen. The vision in the Woods. The Prince. The visions I'd had on this trip. The strange flashes of light on the ocean. The soldier of darkness who now walked among my dreams and my visions. If I was being honest with myself, I was the only one who had seen them. I had no way to say for certain if they were real or just figments of my imagination. I shook my head and let out a frustrated breath.

Accepting the fact that I would not solve this problem simply standing here staring at the water, I pushed my concerns from my mind and joined the crew to busy myself.

⁂

Over the next one and a half weeks, we sailed through the chain of islands that stretched from the Northern Continent to the Western Island, encountering all kinds of weather. It was said that at one point in history, the two had been connected by a land bridge, which had been destroyed—how, I couldn't remember. My father had told me once, but it was a long time ago. I should have paid more attention to his stories. However, I did remember him mentioning that the Eastern Island had apparently once been connected in the same way, but after the land bridges collapsed, the smaller islands in the east vanished, leaving only occasional large islands on that side.

But this side of the Channel presented a sharp contrast to the eastern side. Far different from the forests on the Eastern Island and much of the main continents, the Islands, as they were known in the west, were a tropical paradise warmed by the sun's light during the day and bathed in moonlight at night. Even the Western Island itself was known for its more tropical climate.

Early one morning, as the sun fully broke the horizon, warming the air and sparkling across the crystal-clear, turquoise waters, we passed the first of the tiny islands toward the end of the island chain. The crew's spirits lifted, and those who weren't busy with their regular duties turned to swordplay and card games for entertainment. As more and more islands came into view, the crew grew more playful, and many expressed a longing to visit the white sandy beaches that dotted the ocean like shimmering jewels. The *Lyonsword* rarely sailed through the Western Sea, so when the wind died down, slowing the ship's progress, the captain agreed to let us take the two rowboats out or swim from island to island as the ship threaded its way through the narrow channels between the tiny islands.

I smiled as I looked at the collection of small, tropical islands spread out before me. The trip from the Eastern Island had been long, and it was oddly refreshing to see land, even if most of the Islands weren't much bigger than the *Lyonsword*.

As we readied the boats to row to one of the Islands, the captain came to oversee the process. "I haven't been this far west in a long time," he said. "I forgot how beautiful it is," he commented as he gazed over the Islands with a far-off look in his eye.

"Yeah, the last time you were here was before I joined the crew," commented Eric.

Christopher nodded. "That was a crazy trip."

"Why?" I asked.

"Pirates," he said with a chuckle. "Lots of pirates."

I frowned. "Great."

The captain laughed. "Don't worry about it. Enjoy the break while it lasts."

"So, you don't think we will run into trouble?" I asked.

The captain smiled. "I always expect to run into trouble."

We all shared a good chuckle before the captain sent us off to enjoy ourselves on the Islands.

The first island we visited was simply a plot of sand with a few palm trees. As the *Lyonsword* sailed slowly past each island, we took turns taking the small boats out and hopped from one patch of sand to the next, gathering shells, building sandcastles, and, at Yuuki's request, searching for shiny treasures.

After three hours of exploration, we came to our third island, and I stopped to take in the scenery and let myself relax. It had been a fairly rough trip so far, and it was nice to have a break. But the calm was soon broken when Luke suddenly started shouting and waving his arms, drawing everyone to the spot where he had been searching for seashells.

"What did you find?" I asked as I ran up to the group gathered around him and tried to push my way through.

"That's it!" I heard Otto exclaim.

"What is it?" I asked as the crew parted to let me in.

When I arrived in the center of the circle, an elated Otto spun around to face me, holding a piece of an old clay pot. "Ben, you won't believe what Luke found!" he exclaimed.

"Well, what is it?" I asked again, more urgently.

"It is the symbol!" he said as he thrust the piece toward me, showing me the bottom.

The pot had been broken in two, leaving only half of the symbol visible. But the unique image was still easy to identify. *The symbol from the shield!* As excitement rushed through my body, I gently grabbed the broken pottery and examined it.

"What is it doing way out here?" asked Ivan, scratching his bald head.

"I don't know," I said in wonder. "We'd better take it with us," I said, handing it back to Otto. "Get this back to the ship and tell the captain. We will continue to search for more pieces."

The crew immediately spread out and began looking, but we came up empty-handed, so we decided to search some nearby islands as well. As we continued to the next island, the captain left the ship to join us, with Otto in tow. Their rowboat landed on the beach shortly after we did.

"Otto showed me the pottery," explained the captain as he stepped from his boat onto the white sand. "Have you found anything else yet?"

"Nothing," I replied with a disappointed shrug. "I think anything else that might have been here has long since been washed away. These islands are quite small. The water would easily make it up high enough to do that, especially in a storm."

Otto clambered to the front of the boat behind the captain. "That may be the case," he said as he stepped one foot onto the sand, stumbling as his back foot caught on the edge of the boat. "However, these islands were once much bigger. There was probably a whole society living here at one point, even after the land bridge collapsed."

"How do you know that?" I asked with a confused frown.

"Well, it's just a theory. See, when the land bridge collapsed, it supposedly left much larger chunks of land than there are now. But then things changed. My mother once recounted how she studied an interesting phenomenon. She heard about someone who theorized that seawater around islands pulls away dirt and rocks and moves the sand around. The idea was that, over time, small sections of land might get smaller and change shape," he explained as he tugged his shirt straight. "There is a chance that these islands were once bigger than this. As I said before, that means that there could have once been whole societies living here, but the living spaces they left behind were swallowed by the ocean over time."

The captain and I glanced at each other and shrugged. I supposed it was possible. It was essentially a more dramatic version of my theory of a storm washing things into the ocean. I would keep it in mind.

"It is just a theory, though," clarified Otto as he stopped next to us, having finally made it safely over the apparent obstacle that was the edge of the boat.

Without responding to Otto, the captain turned his attention to the landscape. "This island would be easy to get to for anyone using it as a meeting place but hard to attack without being seen from a ways off," commented the captain, raising a hand to shield his eyes from the sun. "Someone might have used it for a temporary hideout or a secret port and left a few things behind."

"But who would have something like that out here? And why would they have the symbol? Few people know about the Unseen Lands," I said.

"According to Ruth, there was a time when many people remembered the Unseen Lands," said Otto. "There is a chance someone left the pot with the symbol there shortly after the Lie was put in place."

"Well, let's keep looking," I said. "If we keep up our current pace, will we still make it to our meeting on the Western Island?" I asked the captain.

"Oddly enough, since we went straight through the Channel, we made it out of there a little ahead of schedule. But we cannot go much slower than this, or we might miss the meeting," responded the captain.

"Well, I would hate to leave anything behind if it can help us figure out what the writing on the sword says or the location of the Smugglers' Road that note referred to," I said.

The captain considered the situation for a moment. "Okay. You, Solace, and the twins can keep looking, and you can take Otto and Lance too if you want, but the *Lyonsword*'s crew will need to come back to the ship. As we mentioned, there are pirates in these waters, and we need to be on guard. If any of them know about the Unseen Lands and discover that we have something this rare, they will definitely become a problem."

"You think any of them would know about that?" I asked, surprised.

The captain nodded. "I know a few who have heard the stories. There are some collectors out there who would pay a lot of money for something like this, and I know of at least two pirates who would sell to them."

I nodded. "Understood, Captain."

As Captain Bates and his crew returned to the ship, I gathered Ivan, Nadia, Otto, Solace, and Lance and assembled teams to search the remaining islands in the area. As usual, Nadia and Ivan were paired up, then Otto and Solace, and then Lance and me. Yuuki decided to stay with us to help look for more pieces of pottery, joining Lance and me in the search. We sifted through the sand all over the beaches and combed under any trees or plants and rocks.

At one point, with Otto's theory in mind, Nadia and I even dove into the warm waters and searched the ocean floor. We found some plain unmarked pottery, evidence of homes now occupied by fish, and even old cart wheels and a cannon. But throughout the whole process, we still didn't find anything else related to the symbol or the language on the sword.

After searching various small islands, we eventually arrived at a much bigger one. Though still insignificant in size compared to the Western Island, where we were headed, this one was large enough to hold a small cave system within its rocky terrain covered in trees and bushes. Since this island was much bigger, we each fanned out, going off in our own directions, except Yuuki, who begged to stay near me, stating that she wanted to search the water with Nadia and me. I told her she could watch from land, and after a moment of respectful bargaining, we reached an agreement. She would watch from up the beach, and I would bring her something special from what we found. With Yuuki watching excitedly from the water's edge, Nadia and I dove in while the others scoured the beach. We searched the ocean floor and found empty bottles, destroyed huts, wheels, and pieces of pottery, but nothing with the symbol or language from the sword on it. However, I did find a large pink conch shell, which I delivered to Yuuki, who ran off to show the others. Before going for another dive, I spotted her join the search with Solace, apparently satisfied with her new treasure.

After searching for nearly an hour, it was Yuuki who finally found something. As Nadia and I exited the water, Solace approached me and handed me a rock. "Yuuki found this."

I took the rock and spotted the unique shapes immediately, and I hastily ran my wet hand over the surface to make the carving clearer. It looked like part of a sentence or word, written in a mysterious language that resembled the one on the sword. "Where is Otto?" I asked.

Yuuki piped up. "He went over there," she said, pointing toward a cave entrance. Lance was crouched just outside, still sifting through the sand.

Solace, Nadia, Ivan, Yuuki, and I approached and stopped at the mouth of the cave.

"Where is Otto?" I asked Lance as I peered into the cave's dark interior.

Lance stood. "He went to search the cave."

"What?" exclaimed Nadia, her eyes widening with displeasure.

Lance looked confused. "Why, what is wrong with that?" he asked.

"For a natural philosopher, Otto has less than no sense of direction," exaggerated Nadia. "He will get lost and die in there if we don't find him," she said as she stomped off into the cave.

I glanced at Ivan. "What's wrong with her?" I asked.

Ivan raised both hands as if fending off an attack. "Don't look at me. I don't pretend to know how her brain works."

Solace rolled her eyes. "You two are clueless," she said as she set off to help Nadia search for Otto, with Yuuki on her heels.

I glanced back and forth between Ivan and Lance. They both shrugged in confusion. With a shrug of my own, I dropped the stone into my pants pocket and ran to catch up with the others.

The cave floor descended slightly, then split into two dark tunnels. We made ourselves two torches using sticks from around the mouth of the cave and thin strips of cloth torn from the lower hems of our shirts, lighting the fabric with the help of the contents of my tinderbox attached to my belt. I held my torch close to the ground and scanned for footprints, but the cave floor was mostly stone, with only small patches of sand and dirt and moss. I saw nothing to indicate which way Otto had gone, so Nadia, Ivan, and Solace took one tunnel while Lance, Yuuki, and I took the other. The passageway was tall enough for us to stand up straight, with space still above our heads. The rock walls were slightly damp, the smell of wet earth filled the air, and as we traveled further, plant life gradually disappeared along with any remaining sunlight.

We followed the tunnel for several minutes, calling out for Otto, until we eventually came to another fork in the path. Three options lay ahead of us. Without hesitating, Yuuki took off toward the tunnel on the left, and I just managed to grab the back of her dress to stop her.

"You will be staying with me, Yuuki," I said firmly.

Yuuki stuck out her bottom lip and looked toward the tunnel she had been about to go down. "But, I can go."

I smiled. "Says who?" I asked.

She considered the question. "Says...the King?" she said with what I assumed was her best grin of innocence.

"Nice try," I said, returning her grin.

Her shoulders slouched.

"Should I take one?" asked Lance, gesturing to the three paths.

I shook my head. "The last thing we need is for everyone to get lost. We need to stick together."

Deciding at random, I picked the middle route, and we continued. The tunnel got a little smaller before opening up into a colossal cave that ended at what I assumed was the other side of the island. A small beam of light shone through a crack in the ceiling, illuminating the cave's center.

"It doesn't look like Otto is here," said Lance.

I glanced around the large cavern. "Well, since we are here, let's take a look and see what we can find."

Lance and Yuuki searched the middle while I took the torch and searched the shadowed edges of the cave.

As I looked around, I sifted through some dirt in search of anything that might relate to the language on the sword or the symbol on the shield but came up empty-handed. Lance and Yuuki called out to Otto with no reply. After searching most of the cave, we headed back the way we had come, but we were stopped short when a scream rang out, echoing off the walls from somewhere in the distance.

Chapter 13

Lance and I looked at each other. "That was Otto," I said as I grabbed Yuuki and took off down the tunnel we had entered through.

"How do you know?" asked Lance as he followed.

"I just do," I said, remembering the day I had first met Otto. His scream had caught my attention, and I had come to his aid only to find him scrambling away from some harmless stray dogs that were after the food in his pack.

We ran through the tunnel back the way we had come until we reached the point where it had branched off in three directions. The others arrived shortly after we did.

"Where did that scream come from?" I asked.

"Not from where we were," said Solace. "There was only one tunnel, and it just led out to a different part of the beach."

"It must be one of these, then," said Lance, gesturing between the other two tunnels.

We chose the one on the right but were met with a dead end within a few turns. So, we headed back and tried the last option, the path Yuuki had almost taken. We ran through the spacious tunnel, our torchlight dancing over the stone walls, and soon came to another open cave. As I entered the cavern, I looked to my left and found Otto with his back firmly pressed against the slightly damp rock wall, looking rather shocked. When he saw us, he relaxed somewhat, cleared his throat, and stood up straight as he offhandedly brushed some imaginary dirt from his shirt.

"Otto! What happened?" asked Nadia with concern as we all crowded around him.

He cleared his throat again. "Nothing," he said as he smoothed his shirt. "I was simply...caught off guard," he explained in a forcedly even tone, attempting to brush off our concern. He looked a little pale, though.

"Caught off guard by what?" asked Ivan.

Otto pointed. "By that," he said as he gestured behind us.

We all turned and looked toward the far side of the moderately sized cave. Sitting propped up against the damp wall was a skeleton, its clothing mostly decomposed.

"Eeeeew!" exclaimed Yuuki.

I reached down and covered her eyes. "Lance, take Yuuki back to the ship and tell the captain what we found."

Lance nodded and grabbed Yuuki's hand. "Come on Yuuki, let's go see if the cook will let us have an orange."

Yuuki frowned and narrowed her eyes as she followed him. "I know you are just trying to distract me," she said.

Lance chuckled. "Of course you do," I heard him respond as their voices faded down the tunnel.

With Yuuki gone, I turned back to the skeleton. We all approached it and began inspecting the clothes.

"It's definitely been here for a long time," commented Ivan.

Otto frowned. "I would think that is obvious," he said, sounding confused.

Ivan rolled his eyes. "I was just making a comment."

Nadia held a hand up. "Let's stay on topic, boys." She turned to me. "Do you think he had anything to do with the piece of pottery we found?"

I squatted down next to the skeleton and took a closer look at the clothes. They were rather plain, and the cloak that was draped over the shoulders was probably once a dark brown and just as plain. "I don't know," I replied. I was no expert on old clothes or pottery. "The sleeves are straight with no cuffs…That isn't a style I have seen outside of history books." I turned. "Otto, how old do you think they are?"

Otto grimaced in disgust as he moved a little closer. "That straight-sleeve style was once much more common in this area, but probably over eight hundred years ago or more. I would say these clothes and the pottery are both from around the time when the Channel was built and the continents were separated."

I looked at him in surprise. "Really?"

He nodded. "The pottery looked to be of a design used by a prominent family that lost their fortune when the Channel was built, and then they all died of some disease." Otto shrugged as he stepped back. "The design went out of style because people thought it was cursed."

"And the clothes?" I asked, straightening.

Otto gestured to the cloak, "See that stitching pattern on the hem of the cloak, pants, and the small section left of the shirt collar?"

We all nodded.

"That stitch pattern shows that the shirt, pants, and cloak were all made by the same person or company."

"Well, then, this guy had a terrible tailor," said Solace. "From what's left of it here, I can see that the stitching was sewn crooked, and the fabric looks like it wasn't very comfortable. This part here isn't as damaged as the other parts, and it feels like rough wool of some kind."

Otto nodded. "Exactly. Usually if someone has one person or company make all their clothes, they pay a lot of money for them, as they are tailored to fit that person. These, on the other hand, are plain, made of heavy wool, and as Solace pointed out, the stitching was sloppy at best. That kind of work, done by a single company, would be consistent with what was worn by the workers who dug the Channel," he explained.

"How do you know all this?" asked Nadia.

"I read," he said, turning to her with a slack expression of annoyance. But as her eyes met his, he almost choked on his words. He cleared his throat, and I gave Solace a questioning look. Solace rolled her eyes at me as Otto added, "As I am sure you do as well." He directed a slight, awkward bow toward Nadia in what was probably an attempt to be courteous.

Suddenly understanding their behavior, I cleared my throat to get their attention. "Excuse me, but can we gaze romantically into each other's eyes later?" I asked.

Nadia let her face fall into her hand, Otto's eyebrows shot up in surprise, and Solace groaned.

"Why would we be gazing romantically into each other's eyes?" asked a confused Ivan.

I looked at Solace, noting the deep frown on her face. "What did I do?" I asked in genuine bewilderment.

She squeezed her eyes shut and pinched the bridge of her nose. "Nothing, Ben. We will discuss it later," she said tersely, gesturing to the skeleton to draw my attention back to the issue at hand.

"Right. Otto, the clothes," I reminded him.

He cleared his throat again, his cheeks flushed a bright pink. "Like I said, the clothes look like the kind given to the people who worked on the Channel. Many of them were prisoners and people who couldn't pay their bills. Countless died during the Channel's construction."

"Yeah, but if this guy worked on the Channel, how did he get way out here?" asked Nadia.

"That's a good question," I said. "Otto, is there anything you know about how the Channel's construction was run that would explain him being this far out in the Western Sea?" I asked.

Otto considered the question. "I don't know for sure," he said as his face twisted into a frown of thought. "It could be that he was captured by pirates. Or there is a small chance he was marooned out here as punishment for some crime. But there is no reason a worker would be working this far from the Channel, at least none that I can think of at this point."

"Could he have been out here for any other reason completely unrelated to the Channel's construction?" asked Solace.

Otto shook his head. "I doubt it. To get this far out, he would have had to have permission, and based on what I know of the relationships between the workers and taskmasters, that was not something they would have given him. The workers were not treated well. They were kept close by and overworked."

The sound of rocks bouncing across the ground came from behind us, and we all spun, weapons drawn.

"Shoot me, and you'll end up just like your friend there," said Captain Bates with a smile.

"How did you get so close without any of us hearing you?" asked Nadia in surprise as we all let out sighs of relief.

The captain shrugged. "Practice," he said simply.

But I got the distinct impression there was more to the explanation that he chose not to share.

"Lance tells me you made a friend," said Captain Bates jovially as he approached the skeleton and squatted down next to it. "What have you found so far?"

"We aren't sure," I said. "Otto thinks he was alive around the time the piece of pottery we found was used. He also thinks this guy was a worker on the Channel. But we have no idea how he got all the way out here," I explained.

The captain nodded. "Well, there is a possibility that he got caught spying."

We all looked at him. "What do you mean?" asked Ivan.

"The Channel was a political move. At the time, there was one king who inherited rule of the land just south and north of where the Channel is now. When his brother opposed him for the throne, the Channel was built, splitting the main continent into two halves and creating two kingdoms along the Channel instead of one. It also destroyed the land bridges that connected the main continent to what are now the Eastern Island Country and the Western Island Country, though that is a whole different story," the captain explained with a wave of his hand, standing up straight and stepping away from the skeleton.

"Why didn't we know about this?" asked Nadia.

"The wars with the Great Beasts of the Southern Mountains have captured everyone's interest. The history books focus on when the beasts came into play, which was shortly after the Channel was built. Most people don't remember what life was like before the main continent was divided," explained the captain.

"How do you know? I asked.

"My family comes from a long line of sailors, and stories are part of our way of life. The story of the Channel wars has been passed from generation to generation," he explained. "I doubt even the well-educated Otto Bilden knows the details of those wars."

Otto shrugged. "I have heard of them, but you are correct that I do not know the details," he confirmed.

The captain nodded. "The stories say that when the Channel was first built, there were two kings who fought for power during the Channel's construction. and they both sent spies to gauge the strength of their opponent. Some of these spies disguised themselves as workers so they could cross the Channel more easily."

"Do you think there is any chance this skeleton has anything to do with the symbol we found on the pottery and the stone?" I asked.

"What stone?" he asked.

"Oh, I forgot—we also found a stone with writing on it," I added, pulling it out of my pocket and handing it to him.

The captain examined the carving in the stone for a moment before replying. "I don't know," he said with a shrug. "I don't know enough about the Unseen Lands to know if they would have had spies running around during those wars." He glanced back toward the tunnel. "We can continue this discussion on the ship, though. We had best be going if we're to make it to the next meeting on time."

I nodded. "Let me just take one last look to make sure we didn't miss anything," I said. I squatted back down and began checking the skeleton's clothes for anything that might tell us more. The pants didn't have pockets, and the shirt's pockets looked like they had mostly fallen apart as the seam disintegrated. But as I gently lifted the skeleton's faded brown cloak, I discovered a small pocket concealed near the seam that ran from the armpit to the bottom hem. The pocket was expertly sewn into the fabric so its contents would be hard to find, even in a pat down.

"Wait," I said as everyone began to leave. They all stopped. "There is a hidden pocket here, and I can feel something in it." Locating the now easily accessible opening, I gingerly reached into the pocket and pulled out its contents, then stood to show the others.

"It looks like a book," said Solace.

"Or a journal," added Otto.

"Yeah, but the writing is mostly illegible," I said as I opened it, some of the pages falling apart. Handling it gently, I examined the cover and what pages were left.

"Wait," said Solace, reaching toward the journal. "What was that?"

"What?" I asked.

"Let me see it," she said as she gently took it from me.

We all leaned in closer as Solace gently turned to a page that still had some legible writing on it. "Look!" she exclaimed. "Does anyone recognize that writing?"

We all looked closer. "It...it looks like the writing on the sword!" I breathed.

"And look here, the parts written in our language. Does that handwriting ring a bell?" she asked with a grin as she handed the journal back to me.

I examined the writing. Then it clicked. "The note Yuuki found!" I announced. "This is the same handwriting! That means this person might have known Ruth! He had to have been connected to the Unseen Lands!"

"That is exactly what I was thinking!" said Solace before leaning back over the pages to examine them more closely. "It looks like there are a couple notes on the edges of the pages that are written in the language from the sword!" she said with excitement. "Otto, you might be able to use this to help figure out what the sword says!"

"Maybe. It still doesn't tell me what the words mean, but I might be able to work out something," he said with a shrug. "It probably won't help much, but it's better than nothing."

"Ben, look at this," said Ivan.

We all turned to Ivan, who was examining the body again.

"What did you find?" I asked as I handed the book back to Solace and moved to Ivan's side.

"Right here." Ivan pointed to a dagger that was next to the body. I hadn't noticed it before because it had been lying on the ground beneath what was left of the cloak. But Ivan was now holding the cloak back with his own dagger, revealing the weapon.

"That right there is not the type of dagger a worker would have owned," claimed Ivan. "That kind of custom work costs a fortune now," he said, pointing to the silver hilt's intricate design, which resembled a tree with tiny blue jewels inlaid like blossoms in the branches. "And back then, it was probably even more."

"A worker on the Channel would not have been able to afford that," I said, understanding Ivan's point.

"Definitely. This guy had to have been rich or saved up for a long time to get something like that," he commented.

"Or he got it as a gift, as Ben did his pistols," suggested the captain.

Ivan nodded. "That's possible, too. But still, if he were a worker, he would have used it to pay for his freedom. Or, alternatively, the people running the Channel dig would have confiscated it."

"You're thinking this is another indication that he wasn't actually a worker but a spy?" I asked, rubbing my chin in thought.

Ivan nodded again. "Even though he is dressed like a worker, with that book and this dagger, he was most definitely not a worker. I'd bet my life on it; he was a spy for someone. And taking into account the note Yuuki found about the Smugglers' Road and the writing in that book, I'd say he was not spying for the kings of the Northern Continent or Southern Continent."

"You mean he could have been spying for the King of the Unseen Lands?" asked Nadia.

Ivan shrugged. "Could be. Maybe Ruth would know."

"Okay, so we have a spy with an expensive dagger and a book with notes written in the language of the Unseen Lands." I looked at Solace. "And then the note Yuuki found." I considered it all for a moment. "I can't think of any other explanation than that he was a spy working on something related to the Unseen Lands...maybe even working for Ruth. But what exactly was he doing?" I said thoughtfully. I turned to Otto. "Otto, when we get back to the ship, I need you to learn everything you can about this book and see if any of it can be of use to you or if it has any more information on who this person was and what they were doing."

"I will do what I can," said Otto with a nod.

I checked over the body one last time and found nothing more, so we all headed out of the cave and back through the tunnels. We still had a meeting to make on the Western Island.

When we stepped back out into the bright midday sun, it took a few moments for our eyes to adjust. But soon we were across the beach and piling into the boats. As we got moving, I looked over Otto's shoulder at the book as he scanned its delicate pages.

"Don't do that!" he snapped, waving me off. "I don't want to risk getting it wet! This book is already falling apart," he whined.

"Sorry," I said, holding up my hands.

Ivan rowed us back to the *Lyonsword*, and we were on our way shortly after boarding. Otto immediately went below deck and ensconced himself amidst a pile of notebooks and writing utensils to try to work out what he could use to translate the writing on the sword.

At first, the rest of us tried to help him, but he promptly explained that we were all incompetent when it came to language translation, and he disliked us breathing down his neck. He wasn't wrong about our linguistic skills, so we left him to work in peace and attempted to busy ourselves elsewhere.

However, we quickly grew impatient, desperate to know if he had found anything. So, after about an hour of waiting, we started sending Yuuki below deck to see if anything had changed. But, after a while, we realized that there was no real reason to rush the process, and Otto would work better if he were undisturbed.

While Otto worked, Lance, Nadia, Ivan, Solace, and I helped out around the ship. But after only a couple hours of sailing through the islands, the wind stopped, and we ended up dead in the water. So, we headed back out to explore the small islands that we passed along the way. By the time we returned to the ship about an hour later, the wind was back, but Otto was gone from his workstation below deck.

"Where is Otto?" I asked Eric as we came back above deck.

"He just went to the captain's quarters," he said, gesturing across the deck to the captain's door.

We headed over, passing Yuuki chasing the ship's cat across the deck, and I knocked on the door.

"Come in," came the reply from the captain.

Nadia, Ivan, Solace, Lance, and I entered the room to find Otto sitting at the captain's desk, the journal in front of him.

"Ah, Benjamin," said the captain, "Otto was just telling me about what he has found in the journal so far."

"Did you learn anything about the language?" asked Solace as we gathered around.

Otto sat up straighter at the sight of Nadia. "I was able to use some of the notes to verify most of the letters and possibly what groups of them form words. However, that is not what we are discussing," he explained.

"What are you discussing, then?" I asked, crossing my arms as I awaited his response.

"Otto was reading through some of the journal—the part that is in our language. It turns out the man was indeed a spy, as we thought, and Otto has a theory as to what his mission was," the captain said with a smile.

"What do you mean?" asked Nadia.

Otto shifted in his seat. "It seems that the man was a spy for someone who was not on either side of the war that was going on, as we discussed in the cave."

"Ruth?" Ivan and I asked at the same time.

Otto nodded. "I think so."

"But why?" I asked. "What did Ruth have to do with the Channel wars?"

The captain raised an eyebrow and smiled. "Otto seems to have a theory about that too."

"I'm listening," I said curiously, returning my attention to Otto.

"The journal documents this man's life working on the Channel. I wouldn't have thought much of it until I read the last few pages," explained Otto. "In the last few pages, it is clear that he knew he was going to die. But not from starvation. It appears that he was stabbed or seriously injured in some other way. I am not sure exactly what happened due to the damage to the book. But he says something about bleeding badly."

"How did he get all the way out here then?" I asked.

Otto gave me an annoyed frown and replied impatiently, "I would tell you if you would stop interrupting me."

"Sorry," I said, pulling back a bit and giving the captain a questioning look. The captain offered a slight smile and held his hands up, as if to say he didn't bother trying to figure out Otto's moods.

Ignoring our silent exchange, Otto continued explaining the journal's contents. "In the last few pages, the man explains that he failed to give someone, whom he just refers to as 'her,' a message that he had. Because of the note Yuuki found, my theory is that 'her' refers to Ruth. According to the journal, the message was related to something he had recorded earlier in this journal. So, I investigated the previous pages again—the ones that still had legible text—and found some interesting poems that I think were a code," explained Otto.

"Wha—" I started.

Otto held up his hand to stop me from interrupting again and continued, "The poems are about working on the Channel, and the code is hidden in the text. For example, look here." Otto pointed to a passage on the page that was open before him. "He says, 'The workers' watchmen eye the land. The dirt sighs. Death is at hand.' This text is near the beginning of the book, and, based on the previous text, the writer seems to have been writing about the state of the Channel. It seems that he was communicating to someone that the Channel's completion was at hand."

"Why would Ruth need a spy to tell her about the Channel dig?" I asked in confusion.

"Wait, how do you even know that is what he was doing?" asked Nadia. "If you could figure it out, then anyone else could."

Otto shook his head. "First of all, this is just a theory. Second, I figured this out because I know the legend of the Channel Treasure," said Otto. "At the time this was written, the story of that treasure had not yet become a legend."

"What is the legend of the Channel Treasure?" asked Solace.

The captain smiled. "There are two theories about why the Channel was built, one that is widely accepted and one that I always thought was just a myth pirates have been chasing for centuries. The first was the one I mentioned in the cave. The Channel was built because two kings wanted the same land, so they divided it into the two continents and, thus, two kingdoms."

"The other theory," said Otto, "is that the Channel was built to uncover a treasure known as the Channel Stone or the Channel Treasure."

"I've never heard that story," I admitted with a thoughtful frown.

"That is because you are unlikely to hear the legend of the Channel Treasure these days unless you are a pirate or grew up on the seas," explained the captain. "Based on what Otto has found in this journal and what we know of General Delaney, I would say that the general is responsible for that. Ruth once mentioned that it wasn't just *The Story* he wanted to get rid of. I assume now she was referring to the legend of the Channel Treasure."

"Why would General Delaney care about that?" I asked.

"Otto?" said the captain, turning back to him.

Otto nodded. "The legend of the Channel Treasure tells of a stone that supposedly held the land together and filled it with life. It was said that when the stone was removed, the earth died, causing the collapse of the land bridges between the continents and the big islands. The author of this journal essentially describes some of the details from the legend of the Channel Treasure. In multiple places, he explains how the dig was affecting the 'joy of the earth,' turning it to rubble and extinguishing its glow of life. In the passage I read to you, he says, 'The dirt sighs. Death is at hand,' possibly referring to the land's dwindling prosperity due to the stone being removed. Based on what I have read in this book, he was keeping someone updated about the progress of the Channel's construction and the stone's discovery."

"Does he say what happened to the Channel Treasure at the end?" asked Nadia.

"Not specifically," Otto responded. "I can only assume from the passages I just mentioned that it was discovered and moved. This would match what the legend says about the land bridges crumbling to create the islands we have traveled through in both the Eastern Sea and the Western Sea. That is probably how he got stuck out here, actually. If that little island was once part of the land bridge, he could have easily traveled here and gotten stuck when the land collapsed. But I have not read the whole journal yet."

"Maybe that is what he failed to tell Ruth—that the stone was taken," I suggested as I began pacing in thought. "If our theory about her is correct."

"It is possible. I would also say that this stone might have a connection to the Unseen Lands. That is the only place I can think of that a stone with any sort of miraculous purpose, like filling the land with life, could come from," Otto pointed out.

"That would explain why Ruth was involved. But is this stone important to our mission?" I asked, more to myself than to Otto. "I just wish we knew where Ruth was," I said in frustration as I brought my pacing to a stop. "She would know."

Solace nodded. "That is true. But we can't let it hold us back. We need to continue with our mission."

"I agree," I said hesitantly. But I couldn't shake the feeling that there might be something out there we needed to find. "We do need to press on. We will have to figure it out as we go." I turned to the captain and asked, "If we need to come back here to investigate the Islands more after we deliver all the books, would you be able to help?"

"Of course," said the captain with a nod and a smile.

I looked to Otto. "Then, Otto, keep looking into this journal while the rest of us stick to getting the book to our next contact."

Chapter 14

I KNEW THE CAPTAIN would keep his word about coming back to the Islands after our mission was complete. But I was afraid that if there were more clues in the Islands, someone else might find them first, or they might end up in the ocean and we would never find them. I just couldn't wait.

Before I could voice my concerns, a knock sounded on the captain's door.

"Enter," the captain said, and Eric stepped into the room. "What do you need, Eric?" asked the captain.

"You asked me to inform you when we reached the third marker island," said Eric respectfully.

"Thank you," replied the captain. Eric nodded and disappeared, closing the door behind him.

The captain turned back to us. "We have about four days left before we reach the Western Island Country."

"We should comb the Islands for any more information now," I suggested, hoping I didn't sound like I was telling him how to run his ship. "I hate to bring it up again, especially after you promised to bring us back here. But what if there is something important out there? It could be gone by the time we finish our mission."

The captain considered the idea. "Just because these islands were once part of the land bridge that connected the main continent and the Western Island, that doesn't mean we will find anything else that will help us. The journal we found has not told us much about the language. And we can't risk missing our next meeting on a hunch."

"If Otto is right, the author of the journal knew about the Unseen Lands and was communicating with Ruth. But we don't know where Ruth is. So, if there is anything else out here that can help us, we need to find it," I pushed respectfully.

"Have you tried asking Eyethanoff?" asked Nadia with a raised eyebrow.

I glanced at Ivan, remembering our conversation. I had not really tried to contact Eyethanoff for fear that I was losing my mind and all these visions and dreams of the dark soldier were just hallucinations to pull me off track from the real mission. I shook my head. "I don't want to distract him from whatever it is that he has been doing."

The captain looked at me. "Benjamin, we only have so much time." He took a deep breath. "But if you think this is important, you can go. However, you must be back on the ship by nightfall."

"I understand," I said with a clipped nod.

With that, Lance, Ivan, Nadia, Solace, Otto, and I filed out of the captain's quarters and back into the bright afternoon sunlight. The ship dropped anchor so we could have one last look at the Islands. Instead of joining us on another beach search, Lance stayed behind to help out on board and Yuuki accompanied the cook to help prepare for dinner. The rest of us piled into one of the ship's small boats and rowed to the nearest island, which was larger than any of the others we'd seen so far. It would probably take the remainder of the day to search the entire island, and with the sun setting in the next four or five hours, we wouldn't even have time to be thorough.

We scanned the beach first, sifting through the sand and wading through the shallow water around the main beach. When we didn't find anything, we headed inland, into the jungle of tropical trees and plants, which hid rocks and caves. As we continued, we fanned out, staying within eyesight of each other as we scanned the foliage before digging into the ground and searching among the roots of trees to see what we could find. Finally, after about four hours of searching, Ivan spotted something.

"What is it?" I asked as he waved me over in silence.

He held a finger up to his lips, then pointed to the ground, and we all gathered around to look. Fresh footprints. Or, more accurately, boot prints. Someone else was here.

I waved a hand to Nadia and Solace, telling them to fan out again, then turned to Otto and whispered, "Stay put. No matter what happens, stay quiet." I held his gaze to make sure he knew I was serious. He nodded and retreated into some nearby bushes for cover.

I glanced at the others; each held their weapons at the ready and nodded to me as I drew one of my pistols and checked to ensure its three revolving barrels were loaded. We set out, following the boot prints, and quickly came upon a beach on the island's eastern side. We crouched in the bushes that lined the beach and watched the scene that played out before us.

A group of pirates stood in the sand. One had his weapon drawn and trained on a woman standing near them, her hands in the air.

Her brown leather duster covered a cream blouse and black pants. Her black hair fell past her shoulders, with the sides pulled back in a small ponytail, a single braid hanging from the ponytail with a worn yellow ribbon woven into its strands.

"I told you. I don't know exactly where it is!" she snapped in irritation at the pirate standing before her. "I only have as much information as you do," she said as she dropped her hands and placed them defiantly on her hips.

The pirate took a step closer. "You'd better find it, or you are not getting off this island alive!" he snapped back.

I glanced at Ivan and jerked my head back the way we had come. Ivan nodded and passed the message on to the others, and we retreated into the jungle back to where Otto was hidden.

"Otto, we have to leave now," I said as I passed him, grabbing his sleeve to pull him along with me.

"What? Why? Who was there?" he asked urgently as he followed me.

"Pirates!" I replied.

"How did the *Ghost* get here so fast?" he asked, his voice cracking a little in surprise.

"I don't think it was them," I said. "I didn't recognize any of the pirates."

"But if they don't know we are here, then we have time," he protested as he followed us through the foliage.

"Otto," I began as I stopped abruptly and turned to face him, "if we get caught now, we will never make it to the meeting."

"But what about the woman?" asked Solace.

"What woman?" inquired Otto.

"They had a woman with them. She looked like she was in trouble," said Nadia, keeping her eyes locked on mine.

"Yes, but she also looked like she could handle herself," I pointed out.

"Just because she can handle herself doesn't make a crew of pirates versus one person a fair fight," Nadia retorted as she crossed her arms.

I let out a heavy sigh. "We—" I was interrupted by the sound of voices coming through the trees. "Move. Now," I commanded in an intense whisper. "We need to get to the ship before they realize we are here," I said as I pushed Otto forward.

We ran through the jungle back toward the *Lyonsword* but came to an abrupt halt when a loud boom suddenly echoed through the jungle.

"Cannon," said Ivan, glancing at me.

"And it came from the direction of the *Lyonsword*," added Nadia calmly.

We broke out in a sprint and skidded to a halt when we arrived on the beach. Directly ahead, the sun was approaching the horizon. To our left was the *Lyonsword*. To our right was a new ship. A pirate ship. The evenly matched vessels had fired at each other, but why, exactly, I was not sure.

Another cannon was fired, and the two ships continued exchanging fire back and forth just as a pistol shot rang out behind us. A bullet hit a tree only inches from my head, and we all instinctively ducked. With nowhere else to go, we dashed out onto the beach but stopped when the pirates on the deck of their ship spotted us. An alarm was raised, and we suddenly found ourselves under fire from both directions. Trapped between a battle on the water and a battle on land, we had nowhere to run.

A cannon fired in our direction, and we took cover in the jungle as the ball hit the beach, spewing sand in every direction. We raced back the way we had come but immediately came face-to-face with the pirates we had seen earlier.

The pirate who looked to be in charge held his pistol aimed at my chest, the others standing behind him, weapons at the ready. I froze and raised my hands. "Easy there. We don't want any trouble," I said with what I hoped was a non-threatening smile. Cannon fire sounded behind me.

"Is that so?" the pirate said with a grin, revealing mostly decayed teeth. "Then what are you doing on my island?" he asked.

I pointed to the ground. "This...this is your island?" I asked, feigning stupidity.

The pirate jabbed his pistol at me. "The treasure is mine, and it's on this island, so that makes this island mine!" he growled.

I laughed and nodded. "Right. The treasure." If I could get him one step closer, he would be within reach. Then I would just need to distract him. I glanced at Ivan, silently signaling with my eyes to play along. His nearly imperceptible nod told me he understood. "I could...tell you where it is. If you let us go, that is," I suggested.

The pirate smiled and regarded me with narrowed eyes. "Okay...where is the treasure?" he asked skeptically.

I subtly stepped forward and gestured behind him. "That way."

His smile twitched with irritation as he kept his gaze locked on me. "We just came from that way, and there was no treasure."

I shook my head. "No, not that way. That way," I said, pointing in the same direction I had before and hoping that he would be confused enough to look.

He frowned. For a moment, I thought he was going to turn his head, but still he hesitated. "Really?" he asked as his eyes narrowed again.

I nodded. "Lead the way," I said, briefly gesturing behind the pirate again, then letting my hands fall to my sides to prepare for what I hoped was about to happen.

The pirate took a deep breath, then turned his head to speak to one of his men. That was all I needed. I thrust my left hand upward toward his pistol hand, slamming my hand into his wrist as I jumped forward, crashing into his chest. The impact on his wrist sent his aim high, and the jolt of me hitting him caused him to fire a round into the air as we hit the ground. With that, everyone jumped into action.

I did not see the woman from the beach, so there were seven of them and five of us. Ivan aimed for the biggest guy while Nadia gracefully took out the two pirates closest to her. Solace landed a kick in one guy's stomach, sending him sprawling and leaving a clear boot print on his already filthy cream shirt. Solace then dodged the blade of a skinny pirate, grabbed a rock, and launched it at the pirate she had kicked, striking him in the temple. I scrambled to my feet, leaving the pirate in charge lying on his back. I turned to send a fist into one of his men, who wore nothing but pants and an open vest, and my first blow knocked him out cold. I spun to find my next opponent and saw that the pirates' leader had recovered and was coming after me. I threw a punch, but he was fast. I missed my mark, and my fist glanced off his cheek, leaving him with what would soon become a bruise but still conscious. He came at me again, this time with his sword. I had left my sword on the ship, so I grabbed one from a fallen pirate and blocked the man's blow with his own comrade's cutlass. Ivan, having dispatched the big guy, threw a swing at the skinny pirate who had tried to chop off Solace's head, but I didn't see what happened as I locked blades with the pirate captain. I managed to land an elbow strike to the pirate's temple that dazed him enough for us to make a break for it now that all but one of his men were down. As we turned to run, I spotted the skinny pirate retrieving his sword.

The fight had pushed us toward the beach, and we broke the tree line. Exposed to the pirates on the water, we were quickly spotted again, and they dedicated some fire toward us. A cannonball hit the ground only a few yards in front of us, showering us with white sand. Attempting to keep my footing on the soft ground as I skidded to a halt, I turned slightly and placed my hand on a nearby rock, spinning around to find the last pirate looming behind me. His sword was held high, and I knew I couldn't get out of his way in time.

Suddenly, a shot rang out, and the man before me jerked slightly. He stood motionless for a moment as blood trickled from his lips before his knees gave out, and he crumbled to the ground, dead. Standing behind him, just inside the tree line, was a figure hidden in the shade of the jungle. As the figure stepped into the evening light, I recognized her. *The woman from the beach.*

"Hurry!" she said as she ran toward me. "We have to get out of here now, or they will kill us all!"

As I stood upright, she grabbed the sword off the man lying at my feet, and we ran for the rowboat. The others had already made it partway across the beach and were zigzagging their way to the boat, dodging the flying bullets and cannonballs.

Otto stumbled, and the woman ran up to him and grabbed his elbow. "On your feet, Otto! Let's go!" she said excitedly. "Isn't this fun?"

Otto glanced at the woman and then did a double-take as she half dragged him to the awaiting boat. He stared at her in shock as we all clambered into the small boat, and Ivan started rowing us to the *Lyonsword* as fast as the little boat would go while some of the *Lyonsword*'s crew laid down some cover fire to protect us.

The woman turned to Otto. "Well, isn't this a wonderful surprise!" she announced. "What are you doing here?"

Otto stared in shock at the woman who had practically dragged him onto the boat. "M-M-Mother?" he finally croaked.

Everyone froze except Ivan, though the boat slowed momentarily as he registered what Otto had said.

"Otto, this is your mother?" I asked in confusion.

"But..." Otto said, ignoring my question as he shifted a little closer to her.

"Hello, dear," said Otto's mother. "I am glad to see you are doing well. And you have made some friends!" she said excitedly.

"M-M-Mother!" Otto repeated. "Wha—what are you doing? I mean, I can't..." Otto stumbled through his words.

"Otto, snap out of it!" Nadia whispered in his ear, causing him to stiffen.

He swallowed and looked at Nadia with wide eyes and a blush. After a moment, he shook his head and turned back to his mother.

"You're alive!" he finally announced.

Otto's mother raised her eyebrows. "Yes," she said. "Was I dead?" She looked around, slightly confused.

As we neared the *Lyonsword*, a cannonball flew past overhead and slammed into the ship's gunwale.

"Let's save this discussion for later," said Ivan. "We need to get on the ship and get out of here!"

"Agreed," said Otto's mother. "Otto, we will discuss this shortly, but now is not the time."

Ivan got us to the ship, and we hastily hurried aboard once the boat was lifted out of the water.

"What happened?" I asked Christopher as soon I was back on the *Lyonsword*'s deck.

"They just showed up and started firing at us," he explained. "They were behind the island when we spotted them, but you weren't on board yet, so we had to hold our position. We are not sure what they are after, as they don't seem to want to board our ship."

"Tell the captain we are aboard; we need to get out of here!" I yelled over the sound of pistol shots and cannon fire. "I think they would rather defend the island than board our ship."

Christopher ran off to tell the captain as we all took up defensive positions. Thankfully, the captain was ready, and we got out of there quickly. The pirates chased us for a short distance but soon turned back to guard the island they had decided belonged to them.

As the sun set, we gathered in the captain's quarters once again, this time with Otto's mother as well.

"We are out of danger, as the pirates seem to be staying with their beloved island," the captain announced, "but I don't want to rely on things remaining that way." He looked toward Otto's mother. "Are you going to introduce me to our new guest?" he asked with an inquisitive yet slightly tense smile. I knew he must not be entirely happy that we had brought someone seemingly associated with these pirates on board without his permission.

We all looked to Otto to introduce his mother, but his mouth fell open and he stuttered for a moment, so I took over. "Captain Bates, this is apparently Otto's mother. Otto's mother, this is Captain Nathaniel Bates of the *Lyonsword*."

The captain's eyebrows shot up in surprise as Otto's mother stepped forward with an outstretched hand. "It's nice to meet you, Captain. The name is Beatrix. Beatrix Bilden. But most people just call me Trixie," she said with a confident swagger.

The captain stood and shook her hand as he dipped his head in a slight bow. "It is nice to finally make your acquaintance. Otto has told us so much about you," he said with a polite smile.

Trixie smiled. "Do the stories involve me dying?" she asked with raised eyebrows.

"You disappeared!" announced Otto suddenly. We all fell silent. "And with all the beast attacks, we just assumed…"

Trixie turned to her son. "You didn't get my letter, did you?" she said, her tone caring and her eyes soft.

Otto's mouth fell open again, and Nadia nudged him slightly. He snapped his mouth shut and blinked a few times. "No. I…We didn't get anything," he said in confusion.

Trixie sighed. "Otto, I sent letters as soon as I found out the beasts were headed toward the Woods. I thought they were sent. But...I guess they must have been lost."

"Where have you been?" he asked, holding back tears.

"I have been around. I hid in the Forest and spent most of the recent war conducting research there until I heard that a beast was headed to the Great Volcano. Then I went to the Town and met a woman who said I could stay with her until things cleared up," Trixie explained. She must have noticed Otto's emotional state then because her voice took on a more sensitive tone again. "I sent the first letter before I went into the Forest and then another when I met the woman in the Town," she clarified as she took a step toward Otto and grabbed his shoulders. "I am sorry, Otto. I thought you received them."

"Why? We would have written back," he said, still blinking back tears.

Trixie shook her head. "I said in the letters that there was no need to write—that I made it to safety and would stay with someone during the war. I wrote other letters, but I'm afraid I lost them before I could find someone to send them." She looked Otto in the eyes. "Otto. I would have never stayed out here if I thought you and your father didn't know I was alive," she said softly. "I am so sorry," she finished, tears welling up in her own eyes.

Otto stared at her for a couple seconds, then said, "I did make friends." Everyone but Otto and Trixie exchanged surprised expressions.

"I am proud of you for it," Trixie said with a smile as she wrapped him in a long-awaited hug. Otto smiled and hugged her back as he wiped some tears away.

The captain cleared his throat tactfully. "It is very nice to see that you are safe and alive, Trixie, but I think you should explain what was going on with the pirates," he said in a firm tone.

Trixie and Otto parted, and Trixie offered a clipped nod to the captain and got to business. "Yes, well, as Otto has probably told you, I am a natural philosopher. But I have a fascination with rarities."

Otto piped up. "She used to work with a team of researchers studying lost historical items."

"I thought you studied plants," said Ivan, his brow furrowed.

Trixie turned to Ivan and smiled kindly. "I mean no disrespect, but who are you?" she asked.

"Ivan Kuzmich, at your service, milady," he responded with a bow.

Trixie grinned and shook his hand before turning to the rest of us. "Come to think of it, I don't believe I know any of your names," she said politely.

"I apologize for that. With everything happening, it must have slipped our minds," I said. "I am Benjamin Arlin, this is my wife, Solace, and this is Lance, and Ivan's twin sister, Nadia."

"It is nice to finally meet you all," she said as she offered a bow in greeting. "As for your inquiry, Ivan, I study all fields of natural philosophy. Life is a very fascinating thing," she said with a smile as she pushed her brown leather duster aside and placed her hands on her hips, exposing the pistol secured to her belt. Trixie must have seen everyone looking at the weapon because she asked in confusion, "What? What did I do?"

I shook my head. "Nothing...You're just...different than we expected," I said, glancing around the group.

Otto frowned, clearly trying to figure out why we were all so surprised by Trixie's adventurous and free-spirited personality.

The captain cracked a smile at Otto's confusion but cleared his throat to move on. "You were saying, about the pirates?" he prompted Trixie.

"Right. Anyway, we met a few months ago when they captured a ship I was traveling on. To secure the crew's safety, I promised the pirates I would find the Channel Treasure for them. It was something I had studied and wanted to find, but at the time, I just figured I could fake it long enough to escape." She shrugged. "My plan worked, more or less. Things didn't quite go their way, and they have been after me ever since."

The captain sat down in his chair and leaned back with a sigh. "Will they come after us with you on board?" he asked, holding her gaze.

Trixie pursed her lips as she considered the question. "To be honest with you, I would have to say yes. I was able to convince them the treasure they seek is on that island. But when they don't find it, they will come for me."

The captain looked at me and held my gaze for a long moment. "Thank you for your honesty, Trixie," he said as his gaze momentarily landed on her before washing over the group. "I need to think. Why don't you all go get some rest and we will discuss this tomorrow."

As the others filed out of the room, the captain grabbed my arm. "Come back at first light. I need to discuss something with you."

"Why not talk now?" I asked.

The captain wandered over to the window. "I need some time to think...and you need rest." He turned to me abruptly. "As I said, come back at first light—we will finish this discussion then."

With a nod, I turned and left to follow the others.

⁂

The next morning, as the sky was just beginning to lighten, I did as the captain instructed and met him in his cabin. I waited, my hands clasped behind my back, my feet set shoulder-width apart in a habitual position of attention I had picked up in my days as a soldier.

The captain was silent for a moment as he gathered his thoughts. "You might have brought someone onto my ship who could put our whole plan in jeopardy," he said coolly.

I frowned. "Would you rather that I left her behind?"

The captain regarded me with an unreadable expression before letting out a sigh. "No," he said simply as he rubbed a hand over his forehead. "But you have to realize that we now have yet another group of dangerous individuals to add to the list of people trying to kill us," he explained, sounding more tired than angry. "Because of this ship's camouflage at night, the pirates were at a disadvantage. But now that it is almost daylight, they will be able to find us again."

I relaxed and sank into a seat near the captain's desk. "I know," I said with a heavy sigh.

We both sat in silence for a moment as we contemplated our growing dilemma. "We can't leave her out here," I finally said.

The captain nodded. "I agree." He stood and walked to the map table. "The wind has been unreliable. We were dead in the water for half the night and didn't make it as far as I would have hoped. We are still a little less than four days out from our destination. I know the pirate ship. We are closely matched, which means a chase is not in our favor."

I joined him by the maps, and we looked over the collection of islands we still had to pass through. "We could stay in the Islands and use them for cover. That way, if they did catch up to us, we would have some tactical options," I pointed out.

The captain nodded. "That was my thought as well. The Islands are safer than the open ocean right now," he commented. "We just need to pay more attention to who else is using them. We can stay to one side and cross between them if anyone comes up behind us." After staring at the maps for a moment, the captain's expression suddenly lifted, and he began stroking his chin as his mind analyzed an idea from every angle.

"What are you thinking?" I asked, crossing my arms and gently leaning against the table.

"Having these pirates after us is not ideal," he finally said aloud, "but since they are, I can't help but wonder if we would benefit from speaking with them."

"You mean like last time?" I asked jokingly. But it wasn't entirely a joke. The captain had that analytical look in his eye. The look that told me he was developing one of his great plans.

"In my experience, Ben, there is no way to 'talk' with pirates unless you happen to be a prisoner on their ship," he responded with a distracted frown.

"So, we are going to get captured...again? Is this how you normally handle these situations?" I asked.

The captain chuckled. "Sometimes the belly of the beast is the best place to find an exit strategy," he said with a smile.

Before I could respond, a boom sounded from outside the cabin, and something rocked the ship.

Christopher burst through the door. "Captain, we are under attack!"

Chapter 15

W E A L L R U S H E D O U T of the captain's quarters and were greeted by the sun's first rays as a second cannonball hit the water just short of the *Lyonsword*'s port side. The *Lyonsword*'s crew were scurrying to their posts even before the captain started barking out orders.

The pirate ship had rounded an island, surprising us, and was well within range. The captain ordered return fire as he took his position at the wheel and maneuvered the ship around the next small island, attempting to use it as a barrier between the ships.

I joined the captain on the quarterdeck and stood next to him just as Trixie appeared on his other side. "Maybe staying in the Islands was not such a good idea," I commented.

The captain shook his head. "They were going to come after us no matter where we were," he said with certainty. "We can use the Islands to our advantage." He set his jaw, and I had the distinct impression that there was something else on his mind. Something I hoped didn't have to do with "the belly of the beast" he had mentioned.

Trixie glanced at the captain. "If I may, Captain?" she began. He nodded for her to proceed. "As you have probably observed, that ship is the *Sea Beast*, Captain Draco Roberts' ship. Fighting might not be the best option."

The captain frowned in thought.

"Who is Draco Roberts?" I asked.

"He is one of the most prominent pirates in these waters," said the captain. "Has been since he was young. He gathers any and all wealth that he can find from here to the Channel and sometimes beyond." For a moment, I thought I saw a small smile tug at the corner of the captain's mouth, but then it was gone. "He is a greedy, ruthless man," he added as he looked at the attacking ship.

Great. Into the belly of the beast we go.

"We have dealt with pirates before," I pointed out, trying to bolster my own confidence. "We can deal with these as well."

The captain shook his head. "These pirates are different."

"How so?" I asked as I dodged a crew member running past with a cannonball.

"The *Ghost* is known for raiding ships and stealing whatever they find on board, selling it off, ransoming any wealthy passengers, and so on. But these pirates are more calculating. Draco Roberts doesn't let anything get between him and his money. They scour for rare treasures, not just capturing any ship they run into. They don't often take prisoners, and they don't take ships to sell them. If they win, they will sink this ship and everything on board if it means keeping us from getting their treasure," he explained with remarkable calm.

Trixie nodded. "Their ship is of a similar type to this one. We are well matched at close quarters, but an open ocean chase would probably not end well for us. They would most likely be able to keep up with us and might end up trying to sink us in deeper water, rather than here where we could potentially survive in the islands if something goes wrong. Plus, there's their competition."

We both looked at her. "What competition?" I asked.

Trixie shrugged. "I may have incited a war between a few pirate crews the last time I tried to escape," she said in a matter-of-fact tone.

"Are they on their way here?" asked the captain.

Trixie nodded. "I would be surprised if they didn't show up soon. I was stalling on the island, hoping they would turn up and get in a fight, but you beat them to it."

I looked to the captain. "What are we going to do? We can't get stuck in the middle of a pirate war; we will miss the meeting."

"What meeting?" asked Trixie.

"We have to focus on what's at hand," said the captain, ignoring her question. "One problem at a time." The captain maneuvered the *Lyonsword* out of range of the *Sea Beast* behind the next island before turning back to Trixie. "They want you to tell them where the treasure is, right?"

Trixie gave the captain a suspicious look. "What are you implying?"

Captain Bates shook his head. "Not what you are thinking. I just need to know where Draco's head is at."

Trixie relaxed a bit. "They do want me," she responded. "If we trick them into thinking that we all are searching for the treasure, we may be able to make a deal with them to help search for the treasure in exchange for our lives."

"Would Draco hold to that kind of deal? Would he kill the crew anyways?" I asked.

Trixie considered that question. "He might."

"What about the *Lyonsword*?" I asked. "Are you sure he wouldn't try to take it? It is, in fact, a rare treasure," I pointed out.

Trixie looked over the ship. "I know of the legend. He might know of it as well." She seemed to turn the question over in her mind. "We might be able to use it as a bargaining chip. He is not above negotiating if it means he gets something this rare. But I can't say for sure," she finished.

I looked at the captain. "What do you think? They might not take ships normally, but if he knows about this ship, he might try to take it."

The captain shook his head. "He won't...He doesn't like things he doesn't understand," he responded coolly. "The *Lyonsword* fits that description. Draco is a superstitious man. For now, we need to deal with the problem at hand—surviving this attack. We will use the Islands for cover and try to keep them from getting behind us. If we can keep them on their toes, they might pull back."

"But not for long. If these pirates operate as you say, they won't stop coming until they have Trixie," I pointed out.

"One problem at a time, Benjamin," repeated the captain.

I got the sense he knew something about this Draco Roberts that I didn't, so I decided not to push it. Trixie and I took up defensive positions as the captain maneuvered the ship around another island, providing some cover and time to ready our return fire. When we came out on the other side of the island, we were ready for the pirates. They fired the first shot, but their aim was off, and the cannonball sailed past the bow, just missing the base of the bowsprit.

Trixie and I joined the gunners operating the few cannons on the main deck to help prep and fire cannons. We had never fired cannons before, so a gunner, whose name I could not remember, ran us through the steps as fast as he could.

"Powder, wad, cannonball, in that order," he said, pointing out the tools. "Each is rammed into the barrel with the rammer, then we stand back." He pointed to Trixie. "You, grab the cannonballs and be ready to load them." He turned to me. "You, load the powder and the wad. I will work the rammer, and Nancy here will fire the cannon," he said as he indicated the crew member next to him. "No matter what happens, do not stand in front of or directly behind the cannon. I cannot stress how important that is," he said sternly.

Trixie and I nodded and got to work. I loaded the powder, then the gunner rammed it down with the rammer. Next, we repeated the process with the wad. My job done for the moment, I stepped back and glanced around the deck. Ivan and Lance were helping operate a cannon closer to the bow, and Solace and Nadia had taken to the arrows. Otto, to my surprise, was not hiding in the hold; instead, he was nervously adjusting cannons to increase their accuracy. *He never ceases to surprise me,* I thought to myself as I turned back to my cannon.

As Trixie loaded a nine-pound cannonball, the gunner to my left fired his cannon—something I had not experienced from this close before. The sound seemed to penetrate my body like an invisible wave. The cannonball shot from the cannon in a hail of sparks as the big weapon jerked backward against the thick ropes that tethered it to the deck. The cannonball missed its mark, but the gunner to my right fired shortly after. His cannon had been aimed with the help of Otto's exceptional understanding of angles and wind, and it landed its mark. The cannonball penetrated the *Sea Beast*'s gunwale, spraying a volley of wooden shrapnel in all directions, causing the crew to scatter for cover.

The *Sea Beast* returned cannon fire, and the ball clipped the top of our gunwale. Just as the *Sea Beast's* crew had done, we all ducked as wood splinters flew from the ship's wound. Thankfully the ball hadn't fully connected, leaving only a shallow U-shaped chunk of wood missing from the railing. The splinters left small bloody cuts on the nearest crew members, but thankfully no one appeared to have any serious injuries.

When Otto had finished aiming our cannon, Nancy fired our round, leaving a hole in the *Sea Beast's* upper hull. In an attempt to protect themselves, the *Sea Beast* took refuge behind a small island, giving both crews the opportunity to reload and plug holes.

As we scrambled to load cannons, bows, and any pistols or long-barreled flintlocks we had on board, we rounded the southwestern side of the island. The moment the two ships were in range again, the firing resumed. We exchanged cannonballs, arrows, and bullets, and even though Otto seemed to be able to help us aim better than the *Sea Beast's* crew, the *Lyonsword* sustained some damage. But thankfully, it was all above the waterline.

As I shoved a wad down the cannon again, a sound from the ship's port side behind me drew my attention. I spun in time to see the last thing we needed. Three of the *Sea Beast's* crew were climbing over the gunwale. I instinctively reached for my triple-barreled revolving pistol and fired a round. The bullet hit the closest pirate in the left shoulder, and I quickly shifted to the next barrel before firing the second pre-loaded round. By the time I had fired the third round, two more pirates had boarded the ship, but thankfully, others on the *Lyonsword* had noticed.

While I reloaded, Ivan charged the pirates with his sword raised as Nadia threw an expertly aimed knife. As Ivan engaged in a swordfight, Nadia's blade penetrated a pirate's neck, spewing blood on the ship's deck as he collapsed. The crew members who could be spared from the cannons joined me in a rush to defend against the intruders. As we reached the port side gunwale, I saw that the *Sea Beast's* crew had piled into invader boats and snuck up from behind.

With the *Sea Beast* still firing its cannons and what I guessed was about half its crew of around forty men now invading our deck, we were spread thin. To make matters worse, the wind shifted, and the *Lyonsword* became stuck in a vulnerable position. Now that we were no longer moving, the *Sea Beast* landed a couple good shots as it sailed closer and closer to the *Lyonsword*.

Once the ship was within earshot, the *Sea Beast's* captain yelled to Captain Bates, "Surrender, or I will tear your ship apart and leave you here to starve! You are dead in the water, and we have the wind to our advantage!"

Captain Bates held up a hand to stop the fighting on the *Lyonsword's* deck, and we all froze, poised to resume at his slightest signal. Captain Bates looked at me with a surprisingly calm expression. Confused by his seemingly unbothered demeanor, I watched as he glanced at Christopher, who nodded. The rest of the crew remained at the ready, but they appeared to relax slightly, likely reassured that their captain had a plan. He was up to something. *Not again,* I thought.

Anger at the unseen armies arose within me as I wondered, *Why aren't they here helping us?* But I pushed the question aside as Captain Bates turned to the *Sea Beast's* captain.

"What is stopping you from tearing us apart if we do surrender?" Captain Bates asked. "The great Draco Roberts does not leave ships above the waterline," he stated in a calm but menacing voice.

Draco laughed. "You know your pirates, I see, Captain Nathaniel Bates!"

Their exchange of names seemed like a war in and of itself. Two men, two captains. Evenly matched ships and evenly matched brains, yet they were opposites in every other way. Opposites who each knew the other's skill was not to be taken lightly.

"You have something I want," said Draco.

"And what would that be?" said Captain Bates coolly.

Draco smiled. "Your new passenger belongs to me, my friend."

"How's that?" asked the captain in what seemed like a half-hearted attempt to draw out the conversation.

Draco's expression darkened. "Hand her over, Captain," he said sternly, "or I will put you in your place."

Captain Bates cocked his head to one side. "Your crew has taken my deck; I am not a stupid man. I know when I am beaten," he said calmly.

I frowned. This was the second time this month that the captain had given in to a fight. I knew fighting on the sea was different from fighting on land, but if it weren't for the conversation we'd had earlier, I would have wondered if this was his policy.

"What is it that you want with our new passenger?" Captain Bates asked, studying Draco.

By now, the pirates had placed a plank between the two ships, and the *Sea Beast*'s crew spilled onto the deck of the *Lyonsword*. *Not again,* I repeated to myself as I closed my eyes and shook my head. *This can't be happening again.*

Draco crossed the plank and stepped onto the deck of the *Lyonsword*. Where Captain Bates was polished and refined, Draco was rough and rugged. But his eyes held the same cunning danger I often saw in Captain Bates. They stood face-to-face, two sides of one coin.

Draco took his time answering the captain. "Your passenger knows where to find something that belongs to me," he said calmly. "She will show it to me, or I will begin to kill your crew...One. By. One."

Trixie put down her sword and stepped forward from the group that was still poised to resume fighting at the behest of their captain. "I will show you where the treasure is if you promise to let this crew and their ship go," she offered.

Draco turned to Trixie and smiled. "Nice try. But you are not in charge here." He turned back to Captain Bates. "I am."

Captain Bates returned Draco's steely smile. "We have been exploring these islands for weeks," he lied. "We know more about the treasures that lie here than you and your crew could possibly know."

Draco frowned. "I have been sailing this sea my entire life. I know it better than anyone."

"Hmm," responded the captain. Draco's expression wavered slightly.

The two men studied each other, seeming to read each other's minds for a moment, and I suddenly wondered if they had met before. Their entire conversation had seemed odd, and now I could see both a familiarity and a challenge in their eyes. It was as if they had once known each other, maybe even been close, but now were both testing the other to see if they met some unspoken expectation. I could be completely wrong. Still, something about their interaction felt like some kind of strange reunion.

Suddenly, Captain Bates held his hand up. "Stand down, everyone!" he commanded.

I glanced at the *Lyonsword*'s crew and was surprised to see them surrender. When they had faced the *Ghost*'s crew, they had surrendered reluctantly and a trifle nervously. But this was different. This time, they obeyed as if the captain had told them to swab the deck, showing no worry or hesitation. Once again, Draco's expression wavered.

Watching Captain Bates out of the corner of his eye, Draco turned to his crew and ordered, "Take her."

"No!" Otto gasped.

Trixie looked at her son. "Otto. It's okay. Stay here!" she said confidently.

"But—" Otto began, and I grabbed his arm as he stepped forward toward his mother. Looking into his eyes, I saw his worst nightmare coming to life—losing his mother so soon after learning she was alive. I shook my head, warning him to calm down. Nadia stepped forward and clasped one of his hands in hers.

We all watched as Draco's crew led Trixie away. But as she began to cross the plank to the *Sea Beast*, Captain Bates spoke up. "Since you know these islands so well, Captain Draco, then I am sure you are aware of the man who died looking for the Channel Treasure."

Draco looked at the captain with slight surprise.

"Your treasure hunter told us what you are after," said Captain Bates with a small smile. "We have been looking for it as well."

Draco's expression hardened with confidence. "I know of the skeleton in the cave," he said dismissively.

Captain Bates nodded. "Then you must know of the symbol," he responded, narrowing his eyes.

Draco frowned and glanced at the man closest to him, whom I assumed was his quartermaster. They conversed in hushed tones for a moment before Draco turned back to Captain Bates. His cunning eyes studied the captain for a moment. "No," Draco admitted, "I do not know of the symbol."

Captain Bates raised an eyebrow slightly.

Draco smiled. "But you will give it to me," he said as he drew his flintlock.

Captain Bates shook his head. "I am afraid I cannot," he said simply. "See, I did not take it with me when we left that island," he lied again.

Draco laughed. "You expect me to believe that you left a symbol of the treasure on one of these islands instead of taking it to help you look for the treasure?" he exclaimed. His expression suddenly grew dark, and he approached Captain Bates and leaned in close. "Do not take me for a fool, Captain. I am far from it!" he said in a low tone.

Captain Bates smiled. "I am well aware that you are no fool."

Draco eyed him suspiciously. "Explain yourself," he demanded.

As I watched the two captains, it struck me that they seemed to be dueling, not with swords but with words. Like they were speaking their own language. *There's definitely something going on here that I don't understand,* I thought.

Captain Bates took a deep breath and seemed to relax as he gathered his thoughts. "I propose we make a deal," he began, his tone almost lazy, though his eyes were calculating. "We will show you what we know and help you find the treasure, and in return, you and your crew will let us—and Trixie—go."

Draco let out a small chuckle. "And why would I let you go? You would just come after me for the treasure," he pointed out.

Captain Bates pursed his lips. "On my honor as a captain of the *Lyonsword*, I will not," he said, lifting his chin slightly.

Draco raised his eyebrows. "And why should I believe that you know anything about this treasure?" he asked, apparently content with the captain's promise.

Captain Bates held Draco's gaze. "Because you know I do," he said, his tone almost foreboding.

Draco watched him carefully. His expression still skeptical, Draco finally nodded and held his hand out to the captain. "Deal."

Captain Bates smiled and shook Draco's hand. I had no idea how the captain had done it, but he had just negotiated with one of the most ruthless pirates on the seas. It was an odd negotiation, one that was starting to convince me there was a backstory between the two men that I didn't understand. Nevertheless, I let out a sigh of relief. *Perhaps odd negotiations are typical for the captain,* I thought. Whether or not that was the case, I was relieved that, at least for the time being, we would not be prisoners in a damp cargo hold again.

Draco stood on the quarterdeck and announced to both crews, "I have taken over this ship, and my quartermaster will remain in command until we have found the treasure. The crew of the *Lyonsword* will be held here until the rest of us return with the treasure." He then looked to Captain Bates. "Are we agreed?" he asked, raising a challenging eyebrow.

Captain Bates nodded. "We are," he responded with a steady expression.

The captain and Draco locked gazes for a tense moment, then both relaxed a bit and began working out who would come on the hunt for the treasure. Eventually, they decided to sail both ships back to the skeleton cave island. With Draco at the helm of the *Lyonsword* and his quartermaster at the helm of the *Sea Beast*, we set out back the way we had come. The wind was slow at first, but it picked up and we made good time. It was a shame to lose all that ground, but there wasn't much we could do under the circumstances.

When we arrived, after three hours of sailing, the captain, Solace, Trixie, and I were chosen to come with Draco and a few of his men. The rest of the *Lyonsword*'s crew would stay aboard and, at the captain's orders, refrain from causing any trouble.

The two ships were left anchored near the island, and we piled into two rowboats with Draco and two of his men. Five more of his men accompanied us in a third boat, and we headed to the island with the cave containing the skeleton.

Once we were on the beach, I sought out the captain. "What is the plan here?" I asked quietly, keeping a suspicious eye on the pirates as we trudged through the white sand. "Do you know Draco? Is that why you were so willing to negotiate with him?"

The captain glanced back at Draco but ignored my questions. "Draco thinks he knows these islands better than anyone," he said.

I nodded, letting his evasion go for now. "Well, he probably does," I replied.

The captain nodded back. "Yes, he knows them well," he confirmed. "He grew up here." A small smile tugged at the captain's mouth, and he looked at me with a mischievous twinkle in his eye. "But so did I."

Chapter 16

I raised my eyebrows in surprise as images of a young Captain Bates flashed through my mind. *Did he and Draco know each other back then?* If the captain thought he could outsmart a man like Draco Roberts, then he must have something up his sleeve. It was not in his character to be overconfident.

I looked to Captain Bates. "So, you have a plan, then?" I clarified.

He nodded. "We need to buy some time. I need to talk to each of you in private, away from Draco and his men. There is some information that Draco might have that I need to get. It might be helpful to us. But once we have what we need, we need an exit strategy. And we need to put it together before we get inside the caves."

I nodded, unsure what information Draco could have that would help us but deciding to run with it for now. I didn't really have a choice. "Follow my lead," I said. Captain Bates gave a curt nod, and I slowed slightly until I was next to Trixie. "I need you to convince Draco that we must search the beach. The captain needs to talk with us without Draco knowing."

Trixie nodded. "I'm on it." Without warning, Trixie spun around to face Draco and held her hands out to each side. "Here we are, Captain," she said, gesturing around her.

"Nice try," said Draco with an irritated smile. "I know the skeleton is in the caves, not out here. And you have been with me for days. How would you know where it is?"

Trixie nodded. "I have never been here before, but they told me all about it. You know how much I love a good story! When I spoke to them on their ship, they said they found the symbol here in the sand, not in the cave," she lied.

"Then show me where it is!" he demanded, turning to face me.

I scratched the back of my head and grimaced, putting on a show of regret. "Well, see, we kind of got in an argument and...lost it...in the sand. We decided to leave and come back for it later. We have a meeting to make, and we figured no one else knew about it, so it would be safe."

Draco held my gaze for a moment before glancing at Captain Bates, who maintained an unreadable expression. "Fine," relented Draco. "You four spread out and look for it," he said before turning to his men. "Make sure to keep them in your sights. Surround them and shoot if any of them makes any sudden moves!" he commanded. His suspicious gaze fell on Captain Bates yet again as the pirates spread out around us.

As we began to search the sand, the captain slowly made his way over to Trixie. He spoke to her for a moment before moving on, careful not to draw any attention from Draco and his men. Then he sifted through the sand in silence for several minutes before gradually making his way toward me.

As soon as the captain was within earshot to whisper, he said, "Trixie is going to tell Draco a story. I need you to help set him up to believe it by telling him about odd sounds in the caves and a weird feeling you got while interacting with the skeleton. He needs to believe you, but don't try too hard to convince him. Just tell the story as if you're recounting what happened to us earlier. Got it?"

I nodded. "Got it. But why Trixie? She wasn't there when we found the skeleton."

"Trixie can hold Draco's attention better than any of us. I haven't known her for long, but she seems to have the personality for it, and I need his attention off of me. Plus, she has tricked them before, and she is confident she can do it again. Also, no matter what happens, stay on mission," he said, holding my gaze intently for a moment.

I nodded in confirmation that I understood.

Next, the captain turned and surreptitiously approached Solace to explain the part she would play in the plan. Once we all had our instructions, the captain gave a barely perceptible nod toward Trixie.

Trixie suddenly stood up. "Ha! I found it!" she said, holding up the piece of pottery we had found earlier. I guessed the captain must have given it to her.

Draco immediately lurched forward and grabbed the pottery from Trixie. He turned the small piece over in his hands and studied the partial symbol on it.

"What does it mean?" one of the *Sea Beast*'s crew asked as they all crowded around.

Draco shook his head. "I am not sure, but it is beautiful." He looked to Trixie. "What now?"

Trixie put a hand on her hip and gestured toward the cave entrance. "We gotta go in there. One of their crew, who knows about these kinds of things, has a theory that this symbol is a key of sorts.

The dead man carved a map in the cave." She pointed to the piece of pottery in Draco's hand. "That should tell us how to read it."

Draco smiled. "Lead the way."

As we headed toward the caves, Captain Bates looked at me and gave a subtle nod. I responded by leaning over to Solace. Speaking loud enough that Draco could hear but quiet enough that it wasn't obvious, I said, "I don't want to go back in there."

Solace nodded. "Me neither," she said, adding a shiver for good measure.

"Do you think it will happen again?" I asked, slowing my steps. "The strange sounds...and that feeling when we were near the skeleton. It was unlike anything I've ever felt before."

Solace suddenly stopped and started shaking her head. "No! I mean, no, I can't go in there!" she said dramatically. I gave her a hard glare, warning her not to overplay it.

Draco turned and frowned at her. "What is your problem? There is nothing in there but the remains of a man long dead."

Solace gave Draco a worried expression, and I gently took her hand. "It's okay. Trixie's story is just a story," I said, hoping I was putting on a good show of trying to be strong in the face of fear.

Solace nodded and feigned reluctance as she followed me into the caves while two pirates made torches to light the way. Draco herded us ahead of him, and I caught him glancing into the darkness with concern in his eyes.

As we wound through the tunnels and caves, Trixie positioned herself near Draco. When a slight sound came from the cave behind us, we all whirled in surprise. But nothing was there. I glanced at the captain, but he didn't look at me. If I was not mistaken, I might have said he looked slightly worried. Hopefully, he was just a good actor.

We walked in silence for several minutes until one of Draco's men finally asked Trixie about the story I had mentioned.

"Oh. It's just a story," Trixie replied. "Everybody knows ghosts aren't real," she said with a wave of her hand.

The man froze. "Ghosts. What ghosts?"

Trixie looked at him with feigned surprise. "You don't know?" He shook his head. "Well, basically, the dead man was the first person to steal the Channel Treasure," she said, her tone matter-of-fact. "A band of pirates attacked him, so he hid the treasure. But they caught him and marooned him on this island." Trixie shrugged. "The legend says that he drew a map in the cave and left the symbol somewhere in the Islands. He then died here. But his ghost still haunts the caves, on the lookout for the souls of any pirates who might try to steal the map and the treasure it leads to."

One of the other pirates spoke up. "If that were true, we would have heard of that legend long before now," he said.

Trixie shook her head. "Long ago, a pirate found the treasure. To keep the discovery a secret, he left the treasure where it was, and then he killed his crew so no one would tell the tale of how and where he found it. He only left one record of the treasure's location—that one I was studying when you met me," Trixie explained. "But that pirate disappeared. No one knows what happened to him," she said ominously.

The man swallowed. "Why does the ghost only hate pirates?" he asked, clutching his pistol tightly.

Trixie shrugged again. "Aren't you listening? It was pirates who marooned him on this island, and he died here. I'd be mad at pirates too." The man glanced around the caves nervously. Trixie smiled. "Don't tell me you believe in ghosts."

The man shook his head. "Of course not!" he said with wilted confidence.

Suddenly, Draco snapped at Trixie. "Shut up! Just take us to the map!" he said irritably. I had been watching Draco as Trixie told her story. His expression had gradually shifted from bright-eyed greed to a slackened look of concern, which he was attempting to hide. But it was clear that the story had rattled him. While I hadn't heard what Captain Bates had said to Trixie, this little ghost story had garnered such an interesting response from Draco that I had the distinct feeling it was the captain's story, not Trixie's. If I was reading this situation correctly, the captain seemed to be playing Draco like a puppet, and his crazy charade was looking less and less crazy by the second. *But to what end?*

We were silent for a few moments as we continued traveling deeper into the caves, but I gradually became aware that the captain had slowed until he was just ahead of Draco. "How does it work, the treasure?" he asked, keeping his gaze focused on where he was stepping.

Draco sighed as if he had been waiting for the question. "It is just a valuable rock," he replied. "It does nothing."

Captain Bates shook his head. "The legend of the Channel Treasure is missing a detail, I recall, but I can't remember what it is," he said, glancing back to watch Draco for his response.

Without looking at the captain, Draco finally said, "A lesser-known version of the story of the Channel spoke of a war between two mysterious powers. One man wanted to steal the stone to use its power. The Channel was dug after the stone was buried by those tasked with protecting it."

The captain nodded. "Ah, yes, I remember now. Dragons," he said simply. But his brow furrowed in thought as Draco continued.

Draco nodded. "Dragons are just a myth. No one really knows how the stone got there." He paused for a moment, then admitted, "But I did once hear a version of the legend that said the stone's location was compromised when one of its guardians, a dragon now known as Zath, was corrupted. With the dragon's help, the Channel was dug to find it and take control over its power."

"What was his name before he was corrupted?" I asked, unable to control my curiosity.

Draco shook his head. "No one knows. Apparently, 'Zath' means 'death' in some old language." Draco frowned, seemingly annoyed at himself for becoming so talkative. Then he flinched as a slight sound echoed through the tunnels. "Everyone shut up!" he snapped.

We walked in silence for the next few minutes until we reached the point where the tunnel split off in three different directions. Trixie stopped and shifted nervously, but to my surprise, it was Captain Bates who spoke. He glared at Trixie. "Don't tell me you've already forgotten which cave the skeleton is in," he said irritably.

Trixie opened her mouth, but Draco interrupted her. "Nice try," he said in a slow, deep voice before turning to Captain Bates. "I am no fool. I know what you are up to, Captain."

Captain Bates frowned. Then, with a slight sag in his shoulders, he nodded to Trixie to lead the way. Shaking her head, Trixie set off down the left-most tunnel. Apparently, the captain had already told her which way to go. As we finally exited the tunnel and came out into the open cavern, Draco took the lead, grabbing Trixie by the elbow as he passed. He led her to the skeleton and shoved her forward. He scanned the walls around the human remains, but they were bare. Slowly, he turned to look at Trixie. "Where is the map you promised me?" he said in a menacing tone.

Trixie cleared her throat. "He's, um, sitting on it," she said, gesturing to the ground beneath the skeleton.

Draco looked down at the skeleton slumped against the cave's stone wall. He smiled, then turned back to Trixie. "Why don't you do the honors," he ordered, gesturing with feigned courteousness.

Trixie let out a frustrated breath and squatted down next to the skeleton. She reached forward with both hands but stopped short of laying them on the remains. "Sorry," she apologized to the dead man. Then, she placed both hands on the skeleton and pushed him over.

Out of the corner of my eye, I saw one of the *Sea Beast*'s crew glance behind us and suddenly go stock-still. His eyes widened, and his mouth fell open, but no sound emerged.

Oblivious to his crewman's strange reaction, Draco stepped forward, holding the pottery in one hand, to look at the ground the skeleton had been covering, but he suddenly froze when a gasp sounded from behind us. We all spun to find Solace standing near a dark portion of the wall. Something black had snaked around her neck and was choking her. Her eyes widened in shock, and she clawed at her neck as she attempted to gasp for air.

As everyone began slowly backing away from the skeleton with wary glances, panic filled my stomach, and I lunged toward Solace. But she was suddenly pulled backward, vanishing into the darkness, and I crashed into solid rock, right where she had just been. "Solace!" I yelled, banging my fist against the stone. *No! I thought, filled with dread. What is going on?*

"Where is Nathaniel?" demanded Draco as he shoved the pottery into his pocket and raised a pistol.

My mind briefly registered that Draco had used Captain Bates's first name as we all began frantically looking around the cave. The captain was nowhere to be seen. My gaze fell on the crewman who had behaved so oddly. His mouth opened and closed, and he finally managed to speak. "He was there!" he said, pointing to the place where Solace had disappeared. "He was there, and then it took him!" he yelled.

"What took him?" demanded one of the other crew members.

"The ghost!" he said, his eyes wide and skin nearly as white as a sheet.

Draco took a deep breath and glanced around the room, his eyes frantically darting from dark corner to dark corner. "There is a logical explanation for this. There is always a logical explanation," he said, more to himself than to anyone else.

I had no idea what was going on, but I needed to find Solace. Suddenly, the captain's words echoed in my head. *"No matter what happens, stay on mission."* With that in mind, I tried to keep up the charade as I turned to Draco. "We need to find them," I said, hoping that Draco would agree and letting my very real fear add weight to the story we were supposed to be convincing him was real.

But just then, a sound drifted through the still, dank air, seeming to come from everywhere. The sound of whispers. Quiet and silky, the whispers moved through the cavern around us, echoing off the walls. Suddenly a scream reverberated through the cave.

"It's true!" yelled the crewman who had first asked Trixie about the story. "This place is haunted!" he whimpered as he backed farther away from the skeleton.

"No! It is just a trick!" yelled Draco. "Pull yourselves together!" He turned to Trixie. "Where is the map?" he yelled, rage filling his wide eyes. "If you do not show me the map right now, I will kill you and all of Captain Bates's crew!"

Before Trixie could respond, the skeleton suddenly lurched. Everyone jumped back and stared at it in shock and terror. The whispers grew in intensity, and Draco's men began to panic.

I grabbed Trixie and pulled her along behind me as I headed for the cave's entrance. "We are getting out of here," I said firmly, still attempting to play my part.

"Yeah, I thought the captain was joking when he told me this story," Trixie said as she reluctantly followed with a wide-eyed look that seemed to imply she would rather study and record the situation than leave.

Before we could make it out of the cave, Draco cut us off. "Where do you think you are going? Don't tell me you believe in ghosts," he said, repeating Trixie's words with a grin.

Seeing that Trixie was about to lose focus due to her fascination, I glared at her in an attempt to remind her to stay on mission.

Trixie caught my glare, and I saw her act return in full force. "I don't know what the heck is going on here. But whatever it is, I didn't sign up for it," said Trixie. "Captain Bates didn't say anything about this," she yelled as she pointed back toward the skeleton and moved around Draco to leave.

"I knew it was a trick," Draco responded, torchlight flickering across his pale face.

"Yeah," said Trixie as she leaned toward him for effect, "it was. But now it's real, and I am out of here. If you all want to get killed by a dead guy who hates pirates, be my guest!" With that, she turned and headed for the beach.

I ran after her and grabbed her elbow. "We can't just leave without finding the captain and Solace. They could be in danger!" I said sternly.

Trixie looked at me. "I don't want to leave them either. I'm not that kind of person. But we can't do anything for them if we get taken too." Something behind me suddenly caught her attention, and her eyes widened. I spun around in time to see one of Draco's men vanish into the wall, just as Solace had.

Draco's remaining crew members turned to him, and one of them pleaded, "C'mon, Captain, we can find the treasure a different way. We never needed a map before. Or maybe, if she has seen the map, she can draw it for us."

Draco grabbed Trixie by the arm again and shoved me to the ground. In the tussle, I spotted Trixie slip the pottery out of Draco's jacket and hide it in her sleeve. "Get her to the ship!" Draco yelled to one of his men as he pushed her toward him. "We will figure this out later." Without another word, they all ran out of the cave, taking the torches with them and leaving me behind in the dark.

I scrambled to my feet and ran along the wall, groping for the spot where Solace had disappeared. There had to be an explanation. I ran my hands over the rock in search of any cracks or crevasses that she could have fit through. Nothing. I felt the ground for any signs of where she might have gone. Still nothing. *They have to be on this island,* I told myself. I got to my feet and ran toward the entrance, my hand on the wall to guide me through the darkness, following the passages back out to where the three tunnels met. I checked the other two tunnels as fast as I could but still didn't find any sign of Solace or the captain. With nowhere else to search but outside, I ran for the beach, all the way into the daylight, where I slid to a stop, squinting after the darkness of the tunnel.

As my eyes adjusted to the late morning light, the scene I saw was far from what I had expected. Before me was chaos. Solace was not only alive, but she had somehow gotten to one of the rowboats and managed to row herself back to the *Lyonsword,* where she had armed enough of the crew to fight the pirates. On the beach before me, the captain was fighting with Draco and his crew, somehow holding his own despite the odds. They all seemed to be fighting their way toward the second boat. But just as Captain Bates reached the water, a cannonball crashed through the rowboat's hull. As shrapnel and fragments of wood flew through the air, he hit the sand, covering his head instinctively. With a frustrated glance at the sinking boat, he scrambled to his feet as Draco and his men arrived with swords raised.

Trixie was in the third boat, on her way to the *Sea Beast.* Thankfully, everyone was too preoccupied to have noticed, and she approached unchallenged. As she came alongside the *Sea Beast,* a rope was tossed over the edge, and I glimpsed Nadia at the anchor housing. She pulled Trixie up to join her, and they both disappeared into the anchor room. Whatever they were doing, I had no idea.

Leaving them to their job, I ran to join the captain and give him a hand in fending off the pirates.

"What happened?" I asked as the captain tossed me a cutlass, and I blocked a blow from one of Draco's men.

The captain laughed. "What do you mean?" he asked jovially. "The ghost did it!"

I shook my head with a grin as I blocked another blow. Now I understood. It had all been a trick. How he had pulled it off, I did not know. Just when I thought I knew him, Captain Nathaniel Bates still had some surprises up his sleeves.

As the captain and I fought along the water's edge, Ivan and a crew member from the *Lyonsword* arrived in a small boat to pick us up. We loaded into the rowboat, and Ivan quickly rowed us away, leaving Draco yelling at us from land. As we distanced ourselves from the screaming pirate, a shot rang out and the crew member next to Ivan slumped to the bottom of the boat. Captain Bates immediately scrambled over to the man and attempted to stop the bleeding, but he was already dead. The captain's shoulders sagged, and he closed the man's eyes and took a deep breath. Then he stood and looked back toward the beach. Draco was standing there, his pistol raised, and, to my surprise, a look of dread on his face, as if he had not meant to kill the man. I looked up at the captain to find him frowning, his face a mask of grief and anger, as though some sacred agreement had been broken.

Suddenly, a loud boom came from the *Sea Beast*. We all looked toward the big pirate ship, and I felt a grin spread across my face. Someone had set off a charge of black powder on the deck of the *Sea Beast*. An instant later, another charge went off, and the crew left on the *Sea Beast*, who had been lowering a rowboat to retrieve their captain, abandoned the task to begin frantically putting out fires. For now, Draco Roberts was stranded on the island.

As Ivan, Captain Bates, and I neared the *Sea Beast*, Nadia and Trixie dove off its edge into the water. We picked them up and rowed to the *Lyonsword*. As we approached, the *Lyonsword*'s crew launched a cannonball that left a hole in the *Sea Beast*'s upper starboard hull.

Once we were back on board the *Lyonsword*, we were met with a battle scene. The *Lyonsword*'s crew were still locked in combat with the *Sea Beast*'s crew. Nadia, Solace, Trixie, and I each gripped our weapons, but the captain fought his way to the quarterdeck and yelled, "Hold!"

Some people from each crew paused their fighting, but many did not. The *Sea Beast*'s quartermaster turned and aimed a flintlock at Captain Bates. A gunshot rang out, and those nearby gasped and froze. Everyone except one man. The effect seemed to wash over the deck as the rest of the crew realized what had happened. The *Sea Beast*'s quartermaster collapsed, dead, a bullet hole in the middle of his face. We all turned to Captain Bates, who stood motionless with his matchlock pistol still raised, its barrel smoking.

He glared at the *Sea Beast*'s crew. "You will leave my ship now, or every last one of you will face the same fate!" he said menacingly.

Whether it was the fact that they were nearly outmatched, the fact that their own crew needed their help on the *Sea Beast*, the fact that one of their leaders had just fallen, or the fact that Captain Bates's confidence in his ability to shoot them all was quite convincing, they ran. The pirates began jumping from the ship as the *Lyonsword*'s crew pushed them back and let loose with a cry of victory.

As the *Sea Beast*'s crew swam for their own ship, the crew already on board, who had finally gotten some of the fires put out, fired a cannon. The cannonball broadsided the *Lyonsword*, and everyone scrambled to load cannons and return fire.

Ivan and I loaded a cannon while Eric grabbed the light stick. Otto positioned the cannon for the shot, and Eric fired it. The cannonball hit the *Sea Beast* just above water level, leaving a gaping hole they would need to patch as soon as possible, or their ship might sink.

Cheers rang out from the *Lyonsword*'s crew as the captain began maneuvering the ship away from the damaged *Sea Beast* and toward the Western Island once again.

⁂

Once we had put some distance between us and the damaged *Sea Beast*, the captain went to his quarters, waving for me to join him. I followed after briefly pausing to ask Trixie to take the pottery piece she had retrieved from Draco back to Otto.

Leaving the others, the captain and I entered his quarters, and I closed the door behind us. "What happened back there?" I asked. "You knew Draco, and you knew he would fall for that story. Not to mention that you somehow pulled off that whole disappearing trick, leaving me in the dark about Solace's role, I might add." I crossed my arms.

The captain smiled. "That is a story for another time, my friend." He filled two mugs with ale and handed one to me. "I got what I needed. As for Solace, you know as well as I that she can handle herself. For now, we need to get on our way. We will have to find a safe place to stay so the carpenter can patch the damages." The captain looked at me over his mug. "We need to get back on track. I am afraid we might miss our meeting," he said, shaking his head. "This next contact will not be at his own house. So, if we are not there within the time we said we would be, he will have to leave, or someone will get suspicious."

"Can you send a pigeon when we get close?" I asked.

The captain nodded. "I definitely intend to. However, we need to come up with a backup plan. Do you know anyone on the Western Island who might help?"

I nodded. "I fought in the war with the king of the Western Island back when I first joined General Delaney's army. I still have a friend from that time. If need be, we can contact him for assistance. But there is no telling if he will be able to help. He does work for the king." I shrugged. "The message could get intercepted."

"What about the price on our heads? Do you think he would turn us in?" asked the captain.

I smiled. "No, sir. He might work for the king, but he is not part of the Western Castle Guard, if you know what I mean."

The captain nodded with a slight smile. "Good. I will let you know what happens when I send the pigeon, and we will go from there. For now, see if Otto has learned anything more about the symbol, then get some rest."

I nodded. "Yes, Captain."

Chapter 17

WE CONTINUED SAILING UNTIL the captain was sure we were not being followed by the *Sea Beast*. Around noon, once he was certain we were free of them, we docked at a small island to patch up the ship. While the carpenter got to work, the rest of us cleaned up the ship and all the weapons we had used during our run-in with the pirates.

By the end of the day, we had a time estimate on the ship repairs, and we knew for sure that we would miss our meeting by nearly a full day. We were still about three days out from the Western Island Country, and though the *Lyonsword* seemed to partially heal itself, it would take almost all night just to patch the parts of the ship that were essential for sailing.

The next morning, we were back on the waters headed for the Western Island Country. We sailed all day without stopping, most of us helping out around the ship or waiting for Otto to discover something useful in the journal. After an evening of sparring that even the captain joined in on, the captain returned to his quarters, and Solace, Yuuki, the twins, and I huddled below deck, watching Otto as he continued to review the journal and see what he could find out about the language on the sword and the skeleton we found.

"What's everyone up to?" We all jumped and turned to find Trixie leaning over the group, trying to catch a glimpse of what Otto was working on at his makeshift table. We all let out a collective sigh.

"Otto has been helping us figure something out," I responded.

Otto glanced over his shoulder at his mother. For a moment, it looked like he was going to ignore her, but then he said, "Maybe you can help."

We all parted, creating space for Trixie to sit down next to Otto as he cleared his throat and set the journal aside to pick up his notebook. "This sentence here," he said, indicating a line in his notebook where he had carefully written down the sentence from the sword, "is what I am trying to translate."

Trixie leaned forward and studied the carefully drawn letters that formed the intricate sentence. "Oh, wow! Where did you find this?" she asked in awe as she picked up the notebook. "That's Eeffraylick!" she said in excitement.

We all looked at her in surprise. "What?" I asked.

"Eeffraylick," she repeated. "The language that was spoken in Eeffrayldour, the Original Kingdom—a kingdom that is said to have been made by an eternal being but is now unseen. It's just a legend, though," she said with a shrug.

I stared at her. "You know about the kingdoms made by the King?" I asked incredulously.

Trixie nodded. "I discovered them when I was studying the Forest," she explained. "Or, more accurately, I discovered someone who knew about them."

"Can you translate the sentence?" asked Otto excitedly, all trace of his previous hesitation gone.

"I can try," responded Trixie. "I was only able to study it for a short time," she said as she leaned forward and examined the sentence. "Hmm, well, that first word means 'when.'"

Otto started writing in his notebook as she spoke.

"'When truth be known...'" Trixie rubbed her chin in thought. "This is ancient Eeffraylick, which was traditionally written in verb, subject, object order...So it will take me a moment to reorganize it in my head. I think that right there means 'strengthened'...Yes, 'When truth be known has strengthened thee, the...' Hmm..." Trixie rubbed her chin as her expression contorted in confusion.

"What?" I asked, leaning a bit closer to see what had her stumped.

Trixie pointed to a word toward the end of the sentence. "That word is unusual...It seems to be multiple words in one." She leaned closer to study it more carefully. "Yes, I think six words." She paused. "Well...it could be three words," she said, almost to herself.

"What do you mean?" asked Ivan. "How is that possible?"

Trixie lifted a shoulder. "Well, see how each letter in that word looks slightly different from the other letters in the sentence?" she said, gesturing to the page. "The first one is bigger, as it would be in a name in our language. But the rest are small, like lowercase letters. That is how all the words in this sentence are written. However, in this word, these smaller letters are written in capital letter form," she pointed out, "almost as if this word is...possibly referring to multiple entities?"

"So, what do you think it says?" asked Solace.

Trixie examined the word. "Well, I am not sure how to approach this kind of word, but it appears to say 'Lion,' but in the possessive form...I think."

I raised my eyebrows in surprise. "Did you say 'lion'?"

Trixie nodded and looked up at me. "Why?"

"Have you heard the story of the Prince?" asked Yuuki with a smile.

Trixie pursed her lips in thought. "I do remember the woman who taught me about this language telling me a story about a prince. Parts of it I had heard and even told to others before. But much of her version I didn't know. In her version, the Prince died saving his people from an evil creature. But we got interrupted, and she never finished the story," Trixie explained. "Do you know the rest of it?"

I nodded. "Long story short, the Prince came back to life through his father's power. Then the enemy of the King, called the Creature, cast a lie over the land that made the Forest Kingdom, which was a kingdom made by the King, invisible. The Woods house the King's beast, who can show you the truth if you enter—the truth being this very story—and that there is a gate that can set the unseen free, making the unseen visible once again. I know it all might sound a bit confusing with all the kingdoms and beasts, but it is true."

"It is also why we find the word 'lion' so interesting," explained Nadia. "*The Story* refers to the King, the Prince, and their power as the people's Lion," said Nadia.

Trixie nodded in excitement. "That would make sense."

"Why?" asked Otto.

"Because the Eeffraylick word for father is *lahiidreye*, the Eeffraylick word for son is *iiffeye*, and the Eeffraylick word for Original Power is *ffneyer*. The first two letters of each of those words are in this word. If you take those letters, *lah-ii*, *ii-ff*, and *ff-n*, and put them together, it spells out the Eeffraylick word for lion, which is pronounced *laheefn* in Eeffraylick."

"Wow!" said Solace. "So, what does the rest of the sentence say?"

Trixie returned to examining the page. "Okay, 'Lion' I think is possessive here...I think. Possessives always stump me in this language." She examined the word. "This letter here is confusing though...It is in the capital form...but it is small..." Trixie seemed to lose herself in the translation. "I might need to..." She scratched her head without finishing her sentence. "...which would make this next word say 'word,' not 'sword,'...It's so interesting...These two words are only one letter off in both Eeffraylick and our modern language..." she mumbled to herself.

I looked at Otto with an impatient frown, but he didn't catch my gaze and kept his eyes locked on the language his mother was struggling to explain. It made no sense to me, so I hoped she really did know what she was talking about.

Trixie shook her head. "No, I am pretty sure it says 'sword,'" she concluded. "It just confused me because this word here has another small capital letter. That letter might be attached to 'Lion,' but it looks like it could be attached to the following word...But this little mark on this letter here means this word belongs to the word before it. But these letters all have these decorative markings on them, so it is hard to tell if it means something or is just a fancy mark. If I am right, though, I think it says 'sword.' So, 'When truth be known has strengthened thee, the Lion's sword...will...' Um..."

"What?" asked Otto, his eyes wide, as if translating a sentence was the most exciting thing he had ever done.

"I always have a hard time with the verbs, but I think that part says 'to let go of' or 'release.' I think in our language, it would most likely be translated 'to set free.' And that word there means 'you.'"

"When truth be known has strengthened thee, the Lion's sword will set you free," repeated Otto as he wrote it down in his journal.

"What does that mean?" asked Ivan, stroking his mustache in thought. "And, if it says 'Lion's sword,' which is it talking about? The ship or the army?"

"Or the actual sword," pointed out Solace.

"We need Ruth. She will know what it means," I said, running a hand through my hair before crossing my arms.

Trixie's eyebrows raised. "Ruth?"

I nodded. "She is a friend. Someone who knows about this stuff," I explained with a wave of my hand.

Trixie tilted her head to one side. "Small, elderly, seems to know more than she is letting on?"

We all stared at Trixie in surprise before exchanging confused glances. I looked at Solace, who shrugged.

I turned back to Trixie and asked. "How do you know that?"

Trixie gestured toward the notebook. "She taught me about the language," she explained.

"You know her?" I asked in astonishment.

"She is the one you discovered while studying the Forest!" concluded Solace with a snap of her fingers.

"Yes. After I heard that a Great Beast was headed to the Great Volcano, I traveled to the Town to find out if anyone knew anything about the animal's history, and I ran into her. She was selling tapestries in the square. I ended up living with her for a while. She knows so much about the Forest and this language," Trixie explained with a twinkle in her eye. "It was incredible to learn from her."

"Do you know where she is now?" I asked with excitement.

Trixie shook her head. "I am afraid not. I haven't seen her since I set out to look for the Channel Treasure," she explained. "Ruth said if I wanted to understand more about the Forest and why it began to dwindle away, I needed to find the treasure...She was quite supportive, but she seemed to be holding something back about the treasure. But, if you know her, you must know she only divulges exactly what is needed—no more, no less."

I nodded. "True...but what does the treasure have to do with the Forest? Did she tell you that?"

"I did ask her," said Trixie. "She didn't give me much of an answer. The Forest is getting smaller as time passes, and I was determined to know why. She told me that the two were connected somehow." Trixie shrugged. "That was it, really."

"Did you find it?" asked Otto in awe. "The Channel Treasure?"

Trixie smiled. "Sure did!"

We all shifted a little closer and began to barrage her with questions.

"Where did you find it?" asked Otto with wide eyes.

"What did you do with it?" Yuuki asked.

"What did it look like?" I asked.

"What did you find out about it?" prompted Solace.

Trixie hesitated, leaning back a bit with raised eyebrows at the sudden questioning. She hesitated for a moment, seemingly trying to decide who to answer first, then chose Solace, maybe because she was closest. "Well, the Channel Treasure, as Otto knows from stories when he was a kid, was a stone that, when removed during the Channel dig, was said to have caused the collapse of the land bridges between the Western and Eastern Islands," explained Trixie. "When I found the stone, it turned out to be just a medium-sized rock, not much bigger than a cannonball," she said, lifting her shoulder halfheartedly. "But I also found this!" she announced, pulling a medallion from inside her leather duster to show us.

The medallion had a unique design mirrored on both sides. One 'S' shape, much taller than it was wide, was carved into the medallion's silver surface. The image looked familiar for some reason, but I couldn't put my finger on it.

"I thought it was a nice little trinket, so I kept it," she said with a shrug.

Ignoring the medallion, Yuuki looked up at Trixie. "Was the stone warm?" she asked.

Trixie chuckled at Yuuki's odd question as she put the medallion away. "No. It was just like a normal rock—cold, dirty, damp. Though it did have a small crown with a circle around it carved into it, like the legend says."

"Was it made of gold like in the legend?" asked Otto with wide eyes.

Trixie shook her head. "Nope."

I frowned in confusion. "So, what does an ordinary rock have to do with the Forest?" I asked as I began to pace.

Trixie shrugged. "I found some old records that seemed to indicate that the stone was related to the health of the Forest. I was on my way back to find Ruth and ask her, but then I got caught up with the pirates."

"Do you think it is true, what the records and legends say?" asked Otto, poised to write in his notebook again.

Trixie contemplated the question for a moment. "Well, the rock was located near the Channel itself, which is in line with the legend saying that it came from the Channel. A version of the legend said that the Forest started dying when the stone was removed." She paused, thinking. "When I was in the Forest, though, it didn't look dead."

Ivan shook his head. "Nope, definitely not dead. It might actually be too alive," he said with a shudder.

Otto sat up straight, then shuffled through his scattered papers on the table. Realizing the journal was by his elbow where he had placed it, he picked it up and handed it to Trixie. "Maybe this has something in it that can help us both out."

"What is this?" she asked as she carefully took the old journal in her hands.

"It is the journal of a spy," said Solace.

Trixie's eyes widened. "The skeleton in the cave?"

I nodded. "There is writing in there that I think must be Eef-fraylick, and according to Otto, the spy was trying to keep someone, we think Ruth, updated about the Channel's construction and how close they were to finding the stone."

"Is this where you got the sentence about the Lion's sword?" asked Trixie as she gently turned the pages.

I pursed my lips. "Actually, no." I looked at Nadia and gestured toward the sword, which was propped against the wall just behind her. She grabbed the sword and handed it to me, and I drew it from its scabbard before laying it across Otto's table so that Trixie could see the inscription.

"Wow!" Trixie whispered in awe as she set the journal aside. "Where did you get this?" she asked, her fingers delicately dancing over the writing.

"Ruth gave it to me, along with a shield," I explained.

Trixie ran a gentle hand along the sword's hilt as she admired its simple yet beautiful design. The pattern on the hilt resembled a tree that branched out to the ends of each crossbar. The majority of the grip was wrapped in black leather, a green leather ribbon adding some color just below the crossbar. As I watched Trixie examine the sword, I noticed for the first time that something was concealed beneath the leather wrap. I leaned forward to examine it closer as Trixie turned to the others.

"Where did Ruth get it?" she asked.

"The Prince," responded Solace.

Trixie stared at her. "You mean, the Prince from that story you mentioned? The one who died, but you say came back to life?"

Solace nodded. "Ruth was the woman from that story," she explained.

Trixie's eyes opened wide in surprise. "But that story is hundreds of years old!" she said in shock. "Ruth is old, but no one can live that long!"

"I know...We haven't figured that out yet either," I mumbled as I moved the leather wrap on the sword to see what was under it. There, built into the design of the grip and pommel, was yet another symbol.

"What did you find?" asked Ivan, peering over my shoulder.

"I don't know…Another symbol, I guess," I mumbled as I turned the sword to look at the rest of the hilt. The images of what looked like three doors wrapped around the hilt, and each door had a different image in its center. One had a crown, the second had a flame, and the third had a circle. The images all looked familiar, yet I couldn't think of where I might have seen them before.

"Wow." Solace ran her fingers over the hilt. "What do you think these symbols mean?"

Nadia took a turn examining them. "They could be a crest of sorts. If the Prince made this sword, maybe it is his crest?"

"I don't know…" I pondered the new images. *I have seen a door in my dreams and visions, but no crown and no flame, and no circle,* I thought. "Maybe there is something in the journal about them?" I said hopefully. But then, a faint image came to mind. "Wait…I have seen these images before! When I saw them, they were combined into one single image—that's why I didn't recognize them at first. When I met the Prince, he had a pendant that bore three different symbols. These three images combined made up one of them." The pendant flashed through my mind as I tried to recall the other symbols. "It also had the symbol from the shield, as well as a symbol I saw on a door in the vision of the shoes of armor!" I shook my head. "But I have no idea what they mean or stand for."

"There is a symbol on a shield?" asked Trixie with a confused frown.

I nodded and retrieved the shield. "This is the shield Ruth gave me with the sword," I said, adding it to the things on the table. "We thought the symbol had something to do with the unseen kingdoms, so we began keeping an eye out for it. Then we found it on that piece of pottery, so we began to search the Islands until we found the skeleton," I explained.

Trixie nodded. "Well, if I am not mistaken, that symbol is made up of two overlapping Eeffraylick letters, both in capital form. Maybe it stands for something?" she suggested.

"Well," said Nadia, "do you think you can take a look at what the journal says about all this? Maybe it has some answers."

Trixie nodded. "Let's give it a go!" she said confidently. "What exactly would you like me to look for?"

"For now, let's work on figuring out what this sentence on the sword actually means," I instructed, propping the shield back against the wall and pushing the sword to the edge of the table, out of the way. "At least the first part. We can look for answers about the stone, the Forest, and these symbols later. We keep finding more questions and not enough answers. Let's find some answers," I said with a nod to Trixie.

"Sounds good to me. But why just the first part of the sentence?" asked Trixie.

"You said the word for 'Lion' was possessive, right?" I clarified.

Trixie nodded. "Yes, the 'Lion's sword.' As if the sword belonged to—" She stopped abruptly, and her eyebrows raised in realization. She turned to me slowly and pointed. "The sword you have—I mean, you have the sword!"

I nodded. "Well, I know those words that mean 'lion' and 'sword' are not referring to the ship because the word '*Lyonsword*' is not possessive and is actually one word. Therefore, it has to be referring to either this sword or the soldiers of light."

Trixie raised her eyebrows. "Soldiers of light?"

I nodded. "The King's army. We were told they are also referred to as the Lion's Sword."

Trixie nodded. "Okay, well, based on what I know of how capital letters work in Eeffraylick, this sentence is probably referring to an actual sword, not a group of people."

"What do you mean?" asked Solace.

"It's a bit hard to explain, but in ancient Eeffraylick, capital letters were not what we think of as capital letters. Ruth actually referred to them as large form letters. They were usually only used in formal Eeffraylick, a form of the language that was typically only utilized by royalty, often to convey a command or communicate something of great importance. In those cases, each word would begin with a large form letter. Outside of that context, it would have been rare for people to use these large form letters, except occasionally to indicate names and locations or to emphasize one word or the concept that word was communicating. I have never seen a word that uses small versions of all large form letters, like this word on the sword for 'lion.' And the word for 'sword' that follows it starts with another small large form letter, so 'Lion' and 'sword' could be two different words or one word. As I said earlier, it is not clear to me whether that word means 'sword' or 'word,' since the Eeffraylick words only differ by one letter and because I am not sure what the rules are for these strange small large form letters. Plus, it doesn't seem to have a thirtieth letter."

"A thirtieth letter?" asked Otto.

Trixie nodded. "It is a letter with no known name that was usually used to indicate association with royalty, such as a member of the royal house or the King's family. In cases like this, where we know this is probably referring to royalty due to the formal form, indicated by the large form letters at the beginning of each word, the absence of the thirtieth letter at the beginning or end of each word would probably indicate an object that has a connection to royalty, rather than a living being. Personally, I would run with the idea that it is referring to a very special object that belongs to the King or his son—an object like the sword. Plus, the King doesn't strike me as someone who would identify his army as an object that belongs to him. It is more likely that he would refer to them in a familial sense, based on how Ruth described him, in which case, he might use the thirtieth letter...or just the one large form letter per word...It's a little confusing, I know. But that would be my guess based on what I know about the language."

"Wait." I stopped her before she could move on. "You said this symbol on the shield was made up of two overlapping capital—or large form—Eeffraylick letters."

Trixie nodded. "Yes."

"Could it stand for the Lion's Sword, as in the army of the King?" I asked.

Trixie's eyebrows raised. "Yes...Yes, it could. And that would explain why it is on that armor—something a soldier would use," she added.

Solace turned to me. "So, you think this symbol is simply the identifier of the King's warriors?" she asked.

I shrugged. "Well, it would make sense. Ruth served the King, and it was her armor."

"Good point," said Solace.

"One symbol down, two to go," said Nadia.

I smiled, then nodded to Trixie to continue.

Trixie turned her attention to the journal. "Okay, 'When truth be known has strengthened thee, the Lion's Sword will set you free,'" she mumbled as she leafed through the pages of the journal. She continued to murmur to herself as she searched, and we all watched in tense anticipation.

After a couple minutes of scanning pages and flipping back and forth between different passages, she finally came across something. "Ah-ha!" she exclaimed, so suddenly we all jumped. "Right here...Otto, have you studied these poems? Would you agree that some of them contain coded messages?"

Otto nodded. "Yes, I believe they do. The ones I have read seem to be explaining the state of the Channel dig and someone's search for the stone."

Trixie nodded, then looked up at me. "It seems that the stone and your sword might be connected after all," she said with a smile before returning to the text. "Listen to this poem: 'I beg thee halt, for stone and salt. The fire he breathes has come to fault. For dirt and sand have melted down. The battle's lost, as such, the crown.'"

"What does that mean?" asked Ivan, his shoulders sagging at yet another mystery.

"Well, to the average reader, this poem seems to be about the transition from working in the winter to working in the hot summer. In the first line, stone and salt seem to be referring to hard work. Then the writer mentions that fire has come to fault, meaning it has become too hot to burn fires regularly. The third line suggests that the ground has 'melted' or thawed after the winter. Then the last line, 'The battle's lost, as such, the crown,' seems to refer to a point in time when the Channel dig triggered a war between two brothers. They had taken up residence on either side of the Channel, but only one of them was strong enough to hold that land and take control of the Channel."

"The Channel wars," said Nadia.

Trixie nodded. "Exactly. During that time, the king of the Northern Country made all the workers work twice as hard, even during the hot summer months. The king of the Southern Country wanted to free them. But he lost the war; thus, the workers lost hope."

"There were many poems similar to this that were written by other workers during that time," added Otto.

"That's awful!" said Solace with a slow shake of her head.

"You said that was what the poem would sound like to the average reader...What did you mean by that?" asked Nadia.

Trixie nodded. "The legend of the Channel Treasure."

We all stared at her blankly.

"I mean, the poem takes on a different meaning if you know the legend. Well, more accurately, if you know the story behind the legend," Trixie clarified.

Otto frowned. "I don't follow. I don't remember anything from the legend that would relate to this poem."

"That is because you don't know the story that Ruth told me. A story of those who were created to protect a collection of artifacts Ruth referred to as the treasures of Eeffrayldour."

"The detail missing from the legend of the Channel Treasure!" I said to myself. I must have said it out loud, though, because everyone looked at me.

"What?" asked Nadia.

"The captain asked Draco about a detail missing from the legend of the Channel Treasure, but I can't remember what he said." I rubbed my chin as I spoke.

"Dragons," said Yuuki matter-of-factly.

I snapped my fingers. "That's right! Draco said something about dragons guarding the Channel Treasure. One was corrupted, which was how the stone became vulnerable enough to be removed."

Trixie grinned. "Spot on! The dragons were creatures whose sole job was to protect the treasures of Eeffrayldour, including the Channel Treasure. According to Ruth, two dragons were assigned to protect the stone. One was the Dragon of Fire. The other was the Dragon of Ice. They were the mother and father of all dragons and were given special titles—names I do not know."

"'The fire he breathes has come to fault. For dirt and sand have melted down,'" I muttered. "That must be about the Fire Dragon and the Ice Dragon."

Trixie nodded. "According to Ruth, when the wars decimated the dragon population, the King gave the last two dragons special disguises to help them hide so they could more easily protect the stone. But an enemy of the King found a way to corrupt the Fire Dragon because the dragons' hidden form was weaker than their dragon form. Once the dragon was corrupted, he helped the enemy of the King take the stone. With both her beloved and the stone gone, the Ice Dragon disappeared. Since then, no one has seen or heard of either of them. It is possible that the 'dirt and sand have melted down,' which on the surface refers to the ground melting from summer heat, could actually be referring to the Ice Dragon's disappearance. But I am not sure."

"Okay, so how does that help us with the sword?" asked Solace.

"Yes, and what does that have to do with the sentence?" I asked.

"Well, after this poem there's another poem that I find very interesting in light of what we know about the dragons and the sentence on that sword," said Trixie.

"What does it say?" asked Otto curiously.

Trixie pointed to the bottom of the page and began reading, "'Cursed is this land of pain; the way has gone from the plain. For ice has scattered pieces far. Now only sword can strengthen...'" Trixie stopped and looked at Otto. "The rest I can't read because the book is damaged, but I think I know what it is talking about!"

As Trixie spoke, an epiphany had been growing in my mind as an image of the dragon from my visions flashed through my thoughts. The Ice Dragon's words echoed back to me. *"Have hope, my friend, for the truth is a treasure worth knowing. Be on guard, my friend, for your heart is a treasure worth protecting. Be ready, my friend, for* The Story *is a treasure worth following."*

"Ben?" Solace's words sounded faint at first as her voice pulled me from my thoughts. "Ben, are you okay?" she asked.

With a slight nod, I stared at the sword still lying on the table. "Trixie...did Ruth tell you anything else about the dragons and the treasures they protected?" I asked.

Trixie nodded. "That is why this is so interesting! This poem seems to line up with the rest of the dragons' story. See, Ruth explained that before she vanished, the Ice Dragon took a special artifact known as the Armor of Eeffrayldour. The armor has a special connection to the land of Eeffrayldour, and the King's enemy was determined to use it to end all things good so he could rule over all. So, the Ice Dragon scattered the pieces of the armor at the four corners of the earth, keeping only two pieces. Ruth said that only those two can reveal the locations of the other pieces."

I looked at Trixie. "The sword and shield!" I said as I remembered how the sword, and the Beast's tail, which gave me the belt, had both shown me the truth in the Woods. After that, the sword led me to the mirror and the path. *The dragon gave me pieces of armor in the visions—they must be the armor Trixie is talking about!*

"Are you saying the sword and the shield are part of the Armor of Eeffrayldour?" asked Ivan.

I let out a sigh. This changed everything. Up until this point, I had been on the verge of chalking my visions up to sleep deprivation and losing my mind. But now...*Could it really be?* I looked at Solace, then Ivan. "Do you remember the visions I have been having?"

Their expressions lit up. "The dragon!" they said in unison.

"Ivan mentioned you have been seeing a dragon," said Nadia with a frown. "What does that have to do with the sword and shield?"

"The sword was...drawing me to them," I explained.

"To what?" asked Nadia.

"Armor!" I said excitedly. "In each vision I have had, the dragon has tried to give me a piece of armor! You can't see them—I can't even see them all the time—but she has given me three, a belt, a breastplate, and shoes."

"But why now?" asked Nadia. "Why didn't Ruth get them when she had the sword?"

Otto raised an eyebrow. "*The Story* says that the Kingdom had the light of life in it. Maybe that is what the stone is. Maybe it was what was holding the land together. When the dragons fell, the stone was removed, and things began to decay, fall apart, or fade because there was no Original Power feeding the land..." Otto's voice drifted off and he paused for a moment, thinking. "Or maybe it has something to do with time..." He began scribbling in his notebook again. "Maybe Ruth still has a connection," he said, more to himself than to us.

"Otto!" I said, trying to get his attention again. He frequently rambled on about things that seemed totally irrelevant. But I had come to learn that there was usually a point to his rambling; I just had to get him to focus enough to speak plainly.

"Yes?" he asked, looking up from his notebook with a slightly surprised expression, as if he had forgotten that we were all there.

"Are you going to explain what you are talking about?" I asked.

"Oh, right." He cleared his throat. "I don't know," he said plainly.

I sighed. "What were you just so excited about, then?"

"Oh, that," he said. "I was just thinking that the stone might have been some kind of conductor."

"What is a conductor?" asked Ivan.

"It is an object that something else can be transferred through," explained Otto. "There is a man I read about recently who discovered that bone can conduct sound. Maybe this stone can conduct Original Power. When the dragons fell, the Creature took the stone, which allowed him to finish setting the Lie in place and make Eeffrayldour completely unseen and outside our awareness, thus keeping anyone from finding the Gate to Eeffrayldour that *The Story* mentions," he said, his excitement returning.

"But the lack of Original Power running through the land caused the sword's power to go dormant!" exclaimed Trixie. "And that is why Ruth didn't get the other pieces."

Otto nodded. "Yes, that is what I am thinking as well...but this is all speculation. We would have to find Ruth to verify if I am correct on any of this."

I nodded. Otto was right. We were just guessing. We had to find Ruth. As I pondered where she could be, I noticed Solace frowning in thought. "What?" I asked.

Solace looked at me. "Ben, *The Story*...I think it is only part of our mission. The Prince told us to find the Gate as well...Could it be that he sent us to the four corners of the earth not just to spread hope with *The Story* and find the Gate but to find the armor as well?"

I nodded. "I think it is definitely possible."

Chapter 18

"WHAT DO YOU MEAN?" asked Trixie. "What mission?"

"The mission the Prince gave us when I saw him in the Woods," I said as I crossed my arms in thought.

Trixie's jaw dropped and she slowly turned to Otto. "Did you...see the Prince too?" she asked.

Otto shook his head. "Only Ben did. But I did see Solace essentially come back to life in a matter of seconds. I have no logical explanation for what happened to her. And since then, I have seen other things." He shook his head. "Things that I cannot explain," he added, sounding slightly frustrated.

Trixie watched him for a moment. "Okay," she said, slowly turning back to me. "Let's say we are right about the stone, the sword, and the armor. What does that have to do with your mission?"

"When I met the Prince in the Woods, he told me his father wanted us to take *The Story* to the four corners of the earth and find the Gate." I shrugged. "At the time, I didn't know why it was so important to go to the four corners of the earth. But he said that in doing that, we would find what we needed, so I thought he meant we would find the Gate along the way. Now I wonder if he wasn't talking about the Gate. Maybe he was talking about this armor."

Solace nodded and smiled. "See, I told you. Have faith. The King knows what he is doing."

"But why would we need the armor?" asked Otto.

"Maybe it will lead us to the Gate?" Solace suggested. "I mean, we have no information on the Gate's location. So far, this mission has uncovered nothing to help us in that area. But it has brought Ben to the armor. So maybe the two are connected," she pointed out.

I recalled the most recent vision with the shoes of armor. "You might be right, Solace. There was a door in my last vision. Maybe it was the Gate or related to the Gate somehow."

I turned to Otto. "So, let's say you and Solace are right about the stone and the armor. In my vision, the door I saw had no handle, so I couldn't open it. But in my most recent dream, it was open. The sentence on the sword says that 'the Lion's sword will set you free.' That seems to me like it is saying that the sword opens the Gate, like a key of some sort. But why would we need to open it if it is already opened?

The image of the transparent door in my dream flashed through my mind, and I remembered the Prince saying something. *What were those words I heard?* I looked toward Trixie. "Trixie, can you actually speak Eeffraylick?"

Trixie nodded. "Only about as well as I can read it, though."

"If I told you something I heard, do you think you could translate it?" I asked.

Trixie pursed her lips in thought, then nodded. "I could at least try."

"I think it was something like...*tsareyetah my*," I said, attempting to get all the sounds right.

Trixie nodded. "Oh yes, *Tsahreyethah Meye*. Ruth said that to me once when she led me past a beast on our way back to her home. It means 'trust me.'"

Solace turned to face me. "Why? Where did you hear that?"

"In my dreams. The Prince said it to me," I explained. It seemed that amidst the feelings of guilt and fear of facing our dark enemy alone, even when darkness had reared its ugly head, the Prince had been telling me to trust him.

"Okay, well, what are we supposed to trust the Prince with?" asked Ivan with a shrug.

"I think with our lives..." I mumbled, remembering how the dark soldier had been close to taking me when the Prince spoke those words. I rubbed my temples as I finally began to let myself see that I had not been trusting the Prince or the King. These visions, the dreams, they all just seemed too...confusing. I didn't know how to trust the Prince and the King. I just couldn't see it.

"Wait," Nadia said, interrupting my thoughts. "I am still confused about the Gate. Let me see if I have this right. There is a gate, which only Ben has seen, and it was open in your dream. But now we are thinking that the sword is leading us to the armor of Eeffrayldour to open that gate...which is already open?" asked Nadia.

"The Armor of Eeffrayldour is said to have a strong connection to the King and his kingdom," said Trixie. "And if you take into account Ben's dreams, the sword could just be the key to finding the Gate, rather than opening it, but it's not entirely clear," Trixie said.

"Okay, but if the stone powers the armor, how is this all happening if the stone is not in place?" asked Nadia. "You said that the sword was likely dormant because there is no Original Power in the land because the stone was removed.

Trixie shook her head and explained, "Well, that isn't exactly the case..."

We all looked at her.

"What do you mean?" I asked.

"Did something change to let Original Power come back?" asked Nadia.

"Like I said earlier, I found the stone. But I also moved it."

"You moved it?" asked Nadia. "Where?"

Trixie nodded. "I found it in a cave, and I didn't know where to hide it because I couldn't carry it with me without being noticed, so I put it in the one place I thought no one would expect to find it," said Trixie.

"Where?" asked Ivan.

"In the Channel. Well, in the mud and rocks along one side of the Channel. I didn't just drop it in the water."

Ivan laughed. "Well played!" he said, nodding in approval at her "hidden in plain sight" strategy.

Trixie grimaced. "I thought it was quite clever myself, but as I was leaving, some unscrupulous-looking soldiers in dark uniforms picked it up," she explained. "They did, however, put it back. I have no idea if they knew what it was. I don't know why they would, as it simply looks like a normal stone." Trixie shrugged. "Unless they saw the symbol on it...but it is pretty small, so if they weren't looking for the stone itself, they might have missed it," she mumbled.

"So, the stone is back where it belongs," I pondered out loud. "Hopefully. But, if that is the case, why don't I know where the

Gate is? When I have seen it in dreams and visions, it is surrounded in...darkness. I couldn't even begin to look for it...Maybe those soldiers did take the stone, and the sword isn't working correctly now."

Otto mumbled something, and we all looked at him. He was bent over his notebook, studying the sentence from the sword again.

"Otto, what did you find?" I asked. When Otto didn't respond, I raised my voice. "Otto!"

Otto flinched and looked at me. Then his eyes darted from person to person. "What?" he asked.

"You were mumbling to yourself, dear," said Trixie, patting him on the arm.

Otto looked confused. "Oh. Sorry." He turned back to his notebook and continued writing.

I rolled my eyes and looked at Nadia for help.

"Otto, what were you mumbling about?" asked Nadia.

Otto raised his eyes to us again. "Oh. I was just wondering why this word has a squiggly line near it when the line does not appear near the same letter in other words," he said, pointing to the page.

Trixie peered at the sentence. "Oh, that is the word for truth."

Otto frowned, still confused. "So why is that line there?"

Trixie leaned back. "In Eeffraylick, there are a couple reasons why a word would have that line or similar markings added to it. Sometimes markings like that mean that word is a name or refers to a place. Other times it is used to indicate royalty that is not a close relative of the King or something the writer needs someone to pay close attention to. If it is referring to a close relative of the King, the word usually has a large form letter with that mark and a thirtieth letter. Though, to be honest, I am not clear on all the rules. I only studied with Ruth for a short time."

"So why do you think that word has that line?" I asked.

"Well, there is no thirtieth letter, so...I would say this is the name of someone, something, or somewhere, probably connected to the King in some way, but not a relative." She bit the inside of her cheek. "The word is 'truth'...Do you know anyone named Truth?"

I shook my head. "No."

"Anyone? Or maybe a place...maybe a nickname or..." Trixie said, trying to jog our memories.

"Ben..." Nadia raised her eyebrows. "Ben, the Beast of the Woods. I know this isn't really a name, but it did show you the true story of the Prince and the Creature. Maybe that has something to do with this?"

My mind flashed back to the Ice Dragon's voice I had heard in the Woods that I hadn't really noticed until the dreams started after we were on the run. *"Have hope, my friend, for the truth is a treasure worth knowing."* "Nadia, you might be right. When I saw the Beast, that was the first time I heard a message from the Ice Dragon. I just didn't know it at the time. That message said that truth is a treasure worth knowing. What if it was referring to the Beast itself? When I was there, I somehow knew the Beast's name." I shook my head. "What was it...? Adournath!" I looked at Trixie. "Do you know if that means anything?

Trixie raised her eyebrows. "Oh, I don't know. I don't know all the meanings of Eeffraylick names, but I do know that the word for 'truth' on the sword is *adoornah*."

"That must be it! If the belt was the first piece of armor, the first piece was the truth—the true version of *The Story*."

Trixie nodded. "That could be it. The word could easily be referring to a special artifact."

"Then you have all the parts to the sentence," said Solace. "You know the truth—*The Story*—and you have the sword, so you should be able to find the Gate!"

"If we have everything we need, then why is the sword still showing you armor pieces?" asked Ivan.

I shook my head. "I don't know. That's a good question. As for the Gate, like I said, I don't know where it is. It is always standing in darkness—too much darkness for me to see where it might be located. I don't even know if it is a real gate. I could see through it, and it looked more like a door than a gate..."

"Well, how many pieces of armor have you found?" asked Otto, his eyes glued to the journal.

"I don't really know...I don't have any on right now that I can feel or see, but in my visions, I have encountered...three, I think."

Otto nodded. "Well, then, we don't have everything we need to find the Gate."

"What do you mean?" asked Nadia as she came to stand next to him so she could read over his shoulder.

"Toward the end of the book, the writer records what his mission was in case anyone finds his journal. He says, 'It is no longer a secret, even to the Creature himself, that the armor was scattered for protection. For if the Creature were to find it all, he would be able to bind the Gate, making his lie permanent.'"

"Permanent," said Solace. "That sounds bad."

"That information would have been helpful earlier when we were trying to decipher the poems," mentioned Ivan, rolling his eyes.

Trixie shrugged. "We were right about the armor, though. At least partially."

"Stay on task, everyone," I said. "Otto, what is your point?"

"Well, if this is true, it implies that the armor pieces must all be together for the sword to show you the Gate," said Otto. "If you haven't seen where it is, maybe that means you don't have all the pieces."

"Does it say how many pieces there are?" I asked.

Otto scanned the pages. "No...I don't see any details like that. Too much damage to the book."

Just then, the hatch to the main deck opened, and the captain descended the steep steps. "We are coming up on the last section of the Islands," he announced. "The wind is good, so if it stays that way, we should be docking at the Western Island by tomorrow night," he said as he glanced over our work scattered across the table. "Have you found anything interesting?"

"It turns out that Trixie speaks this language," I said, gesturing to Otto's notebook. "Believe it or not, she apparently learned it from Ruth."

The captain looked surprised. "Really? Well, what did you find out?" he asked as he placed his hands on his hips and leaned over Otto to look at his notes.

"The visions I have been having—you were right," I said. "They are the sword leading me to something, we think to an old artifact called the Armor of Eeffrayldour. Based on what we have found, and some assumptions, we think that we must have all the pieces of armor to find the Gate. Then, according to the sentence on the sword, the sword itself will help free Eeffrayldour, potentially by opening the Gate, once we find all the armor." I shook my head. "I still wish Ruth were here. We are making a lot of assumptions. She would be able to tell us if we are right."

The captain nodded. "We will find her, Ben," he said, placing a reassuring hand on my shoulder.

I nodded. "I know."

The captain smiled, then turned to the others. "Well, it sounds like you've made some good progress today. It's getting late, though, and we'll have plenty to do tomorrow. We need to put together a plan for when we arrive on land. We will need a new contact since we're going to miss our meeting. So, everyone, get some sleep tonight, and tomorrow we will reconvene and figure out our plan."

With that, we all parted ways and headed off to bed, Trixie joining us while the twins went to the crew's sleeping quarters.

⚜

That night was calm, though the next day, the winds picked up to almost storm levels. But the ship held together, and the following night, with one day of travel left, the wind died back down to an ideal speed. The ship moved silently over the quiet ocean, the breeze carrying us along at a consistent pace. Yet the mood among the crew was dampened by frustration as the idea of missing our meeting loomed in all our minds. We were uncertain how we would address the issue, as we had no backup contact on the Western Island. I tried to sleep, but my mind swirled with thoughts, not just about our ruined plans. I played over the events of this trip and the dreams I had been having. I couldn't quiet my mind no matter how hard I tried. As the others drifted off to sleep, I found my way to the gunwale to watch the ocean drift by. I had spent more time on the sea over the last few months than I had ever wanted to, and it had changed my life. I had once thought that the only thing to do in this world was fight beasts and wait for the next one to attack. Now, I traveled the world on a mission that most didn't understand and many wanted to terminate.

Frustration still ate away at me, though, and questions filled my mind. *Why didn't the Prince just come and fix this problem of evil, or at least make the solution easier to understand? Why didn't Eyethanoff stay and help or show up when I needed him the most? Why can't one of them just tell me where the Gate is? If the Prince wants me to trust him, why doesn't he help me?* I grumbled to myself, yet no answers came to mind.

I watched as the moonlight danced over the water, shimmering on calm ripples. I remembered the night when it had looked like the moonbeams danced all on their own, as if they were alive. Then I remembered the dark soldier that appeared. Now, looking out over the sparkling ocean, I realized that something about the moonbeams made me tense. *Maybe I am just worried because of what happened last time,* I thought.

Suddenly, a flash of moonlight blinded me. I lifted my arm to shield my eyes and took a step backward. Confused, I lowered my arm as the light faded. *What was that? Was it the water?* I wondered. But something inside me knew it was not. I glanced around. I thought of the dark soldier, and worry began to stir within me. Suddenly, I felt like I was being watched, and I spun around to scan over the ship's main deck. Some of the crew had fallen asleep in hammocks, and a couple more were playing a game of cards. Apparently, they hadn't seen the flash of light. Other than the crew, the deck was empty. Nothing was there.

I turned back to the water and warily observed the moonbeams dancing across its surface. But the feeling of being watched returned, this time more intense than before. I whirled around, my heart racing, and searched the deck but again found nothing out of place. The image of the dark soldier flashed through my mind once more, his intimidating features filling me with doubt and the sudden fear that, in the end, I would not be able to accomplish my mission but would instead be overcome by the enemy. An enemy that scared me beyond all logical explanation.

I slowly turned toward the bow and rested my hand on the gunwale, pausing to take a deep breath in an attempt to slow my pounding heart. But I just couldn't calm down. I decided to head below deck and abruptly turned toward the hatch, nearly colliding with the ship's carpenter. "S-s-sorry," I sputtered, my heart still pounding and my mind racing.

The carpenter smiled. "No harm done." He gave me a closer look. "You seem a bit on edge tonight, though. Something on your mind?"

I swallowed, focusing on his question in hopes it would divert my attention from my fears. "Um...no. Well, yes. I'm just distracted is all."

"Hmm." The carpenter nodded. "The eyes can do that to you. And when they do, they often take the heart along with them." He glanced over the ocean. "Fear and doubt are powerful distractions." He looked at me. "But remember, seek truth, always. It is worth more than you realize. For it is not you but truth that will set you free." He smiled. "Just have faith, my friend."

I frowned. "People keep telling me that. Apparently, I don't have enough," I replied as all the unanswered questions began swirling in my head along with the constant fear and the unsettling doubt that I still had my sanity.

The carpenter placed a hand on my shoulder and leaned in like he was going to tell me a secret. "You don't need 'enough' faith," he said. "You just need it in the right place. The rest is taken care of." He patted my shoulder, smiling, then strode off toward a still damaged section of the gunwale.

As he walked away, taking the welcome distraction of conversation with him, all my fears returned to their original intensity. My heart still pounding, I made my way below deck in search of Solace. As I entered the makeshift room Solace and I shared with Otto and Yuuki, I spotted Solace sitting on the edge of the pile of blankets under our hammocks that occasionally served as our bed. Her eyes were closed, and her brow furrowed in a deep frown.

"What's wrong?" I asked as I sat beside her, trying to forget my doubts and fears.

Solace opened her eyes and shook her head. "I...I feel something," she said, looking at the ground, her complexion pale.

I stiffened. "You feel what?" I asked.

Solace looked up at the wall across from us. "Them," she answered. Her gaze suddenly turned to mine. "They are here, Ben. I can feel them. The dark soldiers are here!"

"Where exactly?" I asked, my fears surging with fresh intensity. "Here on the ship?"

Solace closed her eyes in a pained expression. "I don't know," she said, her voice filled with worry. "I just feel them. It's like...they are here for us..."

"What do you mean?" I asked, grabbing her shoulders and turning her to face me.

"Ben, the enemy is near. We must be on guard!" she urged sternly. "The Prince is warning us. You know he is the reason I can sense these things. It is a message from him!"

I closed my eyes as the image of the dark soldier's grin filled my mind's eye. "I believe you," I said, nodding. "They are here."

Suddenly, the boat lurched so hard that Solace and I almost fell over, and Otto tumbled out of his bed. Trixie sat up in her hammock, pulled from her sleep by the sudden movement. Solace and I looked at each other, then burst into motion. I grabbed the sword while Solace helped Otto to his feet and Trixie scrambled out of her hammock. Then we darted for the door, but Solace froze. "Ben, where is Yuuki?" she asked in a slight panic as she realized Yuuki was not curled up under the shield as usual.

I glanced around the room. "I don't know. C'mon, maybe she wandered up to the deck."

On the main deck, we found that everyone was gathering at the bow, murmuring and pointing to something in stunned amazement.

"What...?" Ivan said in confusion as the captain joined us, and we pushed our way through the crowd to the gunwale. Before us lay the Western Island. The island we were not scheduled to arrive at until tomorrow night.

"How...?" I started. *Maybe the* Lyonsword *moved on its own,* I thought as I recalled the captain's story of the ship's miraculous history.

Solace glanced around. "What just happened? And has anyone seen Yuuki?"

"I'm right here," Yuuki said, pushing her way to us.

"Oh, thank goodness!" said Solace, crouching and wrapping her in a hug.

"I don't know what just happened, but I think we should take advantage of it." I turned to the captain. "So much for having a day to plan. What now? Do you have any ideas?"

The captain nodded. "Well, we are on time now," he said with a shrug.

I raised my eyebrows in surprise. "What?"

The captain smiled. "We were a day behind schedule, but if we go now, we can make the meeting."

We all stood motionless for a moment, still not fully understanding what had just happened. Then we jumped into action. The captain and crew expertly docked the *Lyonsword* at their secret docking port, which we had somehow ended up close to when we mysteriously arrived at the island. The rest of us prepared the pages of the book to carry to our contact. Once we were all ready, the captain sent Lance with Solace, Ivan, Nadia, Otto, Trixie, and me to deliver the book and make sure things went as smoothly as possible.

Solace told Yuuki to stay aboard the *Lyonsword*, making the captain promise to keep an eye on her. Then, we left the ship and headed inland toward the outskirts of the main city on the island. We arrived within an hour, thankfully not running into any problems, and Lance led the way to the house where we were to meet the contact. Once we arrived, he knocked on the door and said, "A friend of the carpenter is here."

The door opened a crack, and a man peered out, taking a moment to examine us before hastily waving us all inside. "You are late. I was about to leave!"

Lance nodded. "Just be thankful we made it at all," he said, glancing at me.

I let a smile spread across my lips as I briefly marveled at everything that had happened on our travels that had led us here, as well as the mysterious circumstances surrounding our arrival at the island. Seemingly out of nowhere, I remembered the flash of light I had seen at the castle when the soldier of darkness in the tower was killed. Then, as we were escaping, Eyethanoff had shown up to defend us. *Is it possible?* I wondered. *Could it be that Eyethanoff was—*

"I don't want to know," the contact said, interrupting my thought. "Let's see those book pages." Lance handed him a box with the pages in it, and the contact opened it and looked inside. "Well done," he responded. "We will print these and get copies out as quickly as possible."

I stepped forward and handed him two more boxes. "Just in case, here are two more copies. We ended up being able to print some extras. We were hoping you could keep one just in case the rest get damaged and give the other to another printer as planned," I explained.

The man nodded. "I will get right on it," he said as he took the boxes and placed them on a nearby table. Then he opened a large barrel and removed the contents, revealing that the bottom was empty. "Can't be too careful with these kinds of things," he said with a grin as he stowed the boxes in the base of the barrel, then replaced the contents and the lid. "I will load this on my cart tonight and take it to the printer I know. We will print as many copies as we can and get them to whoever wants them. I have been wondering for years if this story was incomplete. I can't believe you found the real story!" he said, his eyes widening slightly in excitement.

Lance smiled. "Me too, my friend." They embraced, and Lance said, "The captain gives you his best."

The man smiled. "And I him."

With that, we headed out of the house and back toward the *Lyonsword*'s secret docking port, eager to get off the island as soon as possible.

Only about ten yards from the meeting place, Solace stopped in her tracks. I looked back to see what was wrong and found that she was staring blankly at nothing, her face pale with fear. I ran to her. "Solace, what is it? What's the matter?" I asked urgently.

She looked at me and whispered, "They are here."

Suddenly, the feeling that someone was watching me returned. For a moment, I considered drawing the sword and fighting, but based on Solace's expression and our proximity to the meeting place with the contact still inside, I decided that might not turn out well. Instead, I grabbed Solace's hand and pulled her into a run. "Follow me. We have to get out of here!" I snapped at the others as Solace and I dashed past them.

We ran through town, dodging late-night travelers and weaving between houses. But as we approached the edge of town, I saw something up ahead—a figure partially concealed in shadow. For a moment, I didn't recognize it. Then I skidded to a halt and froze as the others did the same, just able to avoid running into me.

Standing before me, waiting at the point we had entered town, was someone I had not seen in a long time.

"My dear boy!" exclaimed General Delaney. "Where have you been? I have been looking everywhere for you!" he said, taking a few hasty steps forward to greet me.

I felt Ivan tense beside me and held my arm out to stop him from charging the general. "Everyone, stay back," I said with a calm I was not feeling. "What do you want?" I asked the general with a hint of a growl in my voice.

General Delaney halted and his brow creased in a confused frown. "Benjamin, what's wrong?" he asked with concern.

I watched him warily. "What do you mean what's wrong? You know the answer to that," I said coolly.

General Delaney held his hands up. "Benjamin, there has been a misunderstanding," he said with conviction. "Someone tried to kill me and steal that book you brought me. I had to weed out who it was. Valdra said it was you, but I didn't believe him." Concern filled his eyes. "You must believe me. I found out it was Valdra. He did this all on his own. He wants what I have made—my status in the Town," he insisted.

"Why are you here?" I demanded.

The general opened his mouth to speak as he took another confident step closer. I put my hand on the hilt of the sword, and he stopped and raised his hands a little higher. "Benjamin, I am telling the truth," he pleaded. "Valdra was the one who sent people into the Forest to kill you and your friends. I had nothing to do with it. As soon as I found out what he did, I came looking for you." General Delaney glanced at the others. "Think about it. All of you," he said. "I have been trying to help you. It is one of the reasons Valdra has not caught you yet. I can stop him. If you just tell me what you are trying to do, I can help you."

I stared at the general and thought back to everything that had happened since he had first assigned me to retrieve the book. After I dropped the book off at his mansion, I had not seen General Delaney at any point during this mission. It was always Valdra. He had given me the lead that led us all into the Forest. He had apparently sent the doctor into the Forest to trick us and try to kill us. He had chased us throughout this whole journey. Never had I seen General Delaney do anything to hurt me. I frowned and closed my eyes for a second before opening them again, staring at nothing.

"Think about it," I heard General Delaney repeat. "I have never let you down."

"Ben," said Solace as she leaned closer to whisper to me. "Don't trust him."

I was so conflicted. But I couldn't think of any verifiable evidence against him. "He is right, Solace," I said. I turned to the others. "Tell me, have any of you seen him do anything to hurt us?"

Solace looked at the general, then let out a hard sigh. "No," she said as the others echoed her answer.

"And he let Ruth go, alive and unharmed," I added. They all nodded. I wasn't ready to completely trust him yet, but I couldn't just dismiss him. I looked Solace in the eye. "If he is telling the truth..." I started. But she knew the rest. She closed her eyes for a moment, reluctant to accept that he could be helpful. I turned to Ivan and Nadia. "Keep an eye on him," I whispered. They both nodded.

"Tell me what you need, Benjamin. I can help you," repeated General Delaney. "I am the only one who can help you fight Valdra," he added.

I turned to the general. "The book," I said. "The one you took from Ruth."

General Delaney nodded and lowered his hands, his posture relaxing, though I remained tense. "Yes. I remember. What about it?"

"Did you read it?" I asked, watching closely for his reaction.

He nodded. "Yes. Of course I did. It is a rare artifact. The story of life and the Kingdom, the long-lost city of light! I had been searching for it for my whole life!"

I nodded, then glanced around the group. They all held their lips pinned, prepared to follow my lead whether they agreed with my choice or not.

Finally, I turned back to General Delaney. "*The Story* is true," I said simply.

"What?" he exclaimed with wide eyes. "How do you know this?" he asked as he stepped forward again.

"I have seen the Prince myself," I said, continuing to watch closely for his reaction. "In the Woods," I added.

General Delaney stared at me in shock. "But I thought that the Woods were protected by—"

"That myth of the deadly boundary is not true," I interrupted. "The Creature put lies in *The Story* to throw people off so they would not find the truth that the Woods contain, that the Beast within them can reveal," I explained.

"Benjamin, do you know what this means?" said General Delaney with excitement. "It means that we can stop the beasts forever! We can end this all! Benjamin, you must help me learn how to get the Prince to help us. If that story is true, then he can kill the beasts!"

"I know," I said as I turned my back to him and started walking. "We are working on it."

Chapter 19

"WHAT DO YOU KNOW about *The Story*, Benjamin?" asked General Delaney as we headed toward the hidden port. "I have been studying this story my whole life. We can help each other."

I shook my head. "Don't think I trust you just yet," I snapped. I had decided to allow him to come along, but we were all a little tense about his being here. However, I knew the twins and Solace were on as high alert as I was and ready to fight by my side if he showed the slightest sign of betraying us. Lance and Otto, on the other hand, seemed completely unprepared for a fight.

"Benjamin, I am telling the truth. What more do you want to hear?" the general asked urgently.

"I want to know why you sent me to kill people every time they disobeyed you in the slightest. I want to know why I was so quick to accept that you were to blame for the attempt on our lives that day that day in the Forest," I growled. "I want to know how you managed to convince me that becoming a murderer was the road to take after my family died," I said darkly. "I want to know why you took advantage of me!"

General Delaney sighed. "I will admit that my approach was not the most sensitive. But you must understand, Benjamin, those people I sent you after were jeopardizing everything!"

"Really? What exactly did they do to deserve death?" I demand-ed, coming to an abrupt halt and spinning to face the general, as the others stopped as well. If I was going to trust General Delaney, I needed to hash this out, right here, right now.

General Delaney glanced around at the group of people who were clearly still hostile toward him, apart from Lance, who looked like he was stuck in the middle of a family fight.

The general turned back to me. "Benjamin. All I have ever want-ed to do is protect this land. I grew up in the Town. I watched my parents protect it and listened to my grandfather tell stories of wars with the beasts. It was my duty to protect the land and the people who live in it, and it still is!" he snapped. He paused and forced himself to take a deep, calming breath. Then he continued, his voice softer. "I watched the land get torn to pieces over and over and over again. I watched my father fall into hopelessness because he was powerless to do anything to stop it." General Delaney took one step closer. "I told you long before this all started that I lost him to a war just as you lost your father. All I have left is this story. It is the only thing that can save us from the beasts."

"So you deprived an old lady of her only possession?" I asked, raising my eyebrows and leaning forward slightly.

"To save us, yes!" he exclaimed, his frustration showing.

"Okay, then if you wanted the book so badly, why did you outlaw its print?" I said defiantly.

General Delaney pressed his thumb and middle finger into his temples as if trying to stave off a headache. "You know that was not my doing. It happened long before my time. That was my great-great-grandfather," he said, sounding defeated. "He was torn apart by what he thought was false hope. He was afraid that *The*

Story would spread that false hope to a people who were doomed to die at the hands of beasts he could not control."

I winced. I knew the feeling. That idea of false hope was one of the things that had initially prevented me from believing *The Story*. "Okay," I said, making sure to heed Solace's words to not trust him. "If we are going to let you come along, what do you have to offer us?" I asked as I crossed my arms.

Suddenly, the sound of a twig snapping pierced the silence somewhere behind us. We all froze, then slowly turned. Eight Martecytes materialized from the shadows among the foliage. Their coats floated about them like black fog, and their eyes held rage. Solace had been right. The armies of darkness were here.

"What did you do?" I yelled at General Delaney as I drew the sword in defense.

"It wasn't me, Benjamin!" he yelled back. "You must believe me! We need to get out of here!"

I wasn't sure what to believe about the general, but he was right about one thing—we needed to get out of here. We were evenly matched for the moment, but who knew how many more might be lurking nearby. "Run!" I yelled.

But as we turned to flee, the Martecytes moved with surprising speed to block our escape. Two of them cut off General Delaney, Solace, and me, and the others pushed the rest of our group away from us. I held the sword with both hands and tried to get Eye-thanoff's attention, but there was no response. Frustration flared within me yet again, but I forced myself to push it down and concentrate. *Fine, I will just do this on my own,* I told myself.

Solace and I stood back-to-back, leaving General Delaney to fend for himself. The first Martecyte leaped at me, his sword held high over his head, sweeping down. I lifted the sword to block the blow, and the clang of metal on metal seemed to launch us all into battle.

Solace was armed with a bow and arrow and started firing at our second attacker, but he dodged the arrows, swatting them away as if they were flies. As I crossed swords with the first Martecyte, two more appeared from the trees and closed in on us. As we fought, I was vaguely aware that Solace, the general, and I were being pushed back toward town and farther from the others, but there was nothing I could do about it.

Solace finally landed a shot, and one of the Martecytes pulled back in pain. Taking advantage of his retreat, I moved in for a killing blow, but to my surprise, General Delaney beat me to it. As the Martecyte stumbled backward, grasping to pull the arrow from a wound that was now leaking black fog, General Delaney appeared behind him. He reached around the Martecyte's head with both hands and plunged a knife into the front of his neck. As the Martecyte died, a scream rose from his lips, and I watched in horror as the darkness within him remained hovering in place as the Martecyte's body collapsed to the earth. The darkness hung motionless for a moment, casting a mysterious circular shadow below it. As my eyes remained reluctantly locked on the image before me, a dark soldier appeared over the shadow, seeming to materialize from the darkness above it, almost as if the shadow gave the dark soldier a place to exist.

"He didn't die!" I shouted. *What just happened?*

General Delaney grabbed my arm and pulled me away, back toward town. "What do you mean he didn't die? He's dead on the ground. Let's go!" he said as he urged me on.

I followed General Delaney and Solace as we raced for the cover of town, throwing frequent glances over my shoulder at our pursuers. "No, I can see it. He didn't die!" I insisted as Solace pulled me along.

"What are you talking about?" General Delaney said with a confused frown as we ran down a road with alleys along each side. He picked an alley to our right and waved us behind a stack of crates at its entrance. The moon was high overhead, filling the alley with light. Hopefully the crates would be enough to conceal us.

I set my jaw in frustration. "Never mind. We will have to figure it out later." I turned to Solace. "Are you okay?"

She nodded. "Yes, but I am running low on arrows."

"Okay. If we are careful, maybe we can make it out of here without you needing to fire another shot," I said as I peered around the edge of the crate. The Martecytes came into view to our left at the far end of the street that led past our alley, and I pulled back a little to make sure they couldn't see me. I held my index finger to my lips, and we remained silent as we watched them slowly approach, scanning the side streets and alleys as they passed them.

"We need to kill them all, or they will tell the others where we are headed," I whispered.

Solace shifted closer and lowered her voice as well. "Exactly what I was thinking. But what about the one that you said didn't die?"

Still holding the sword, I glanced over the group of approaching Martecytes and sighed with relief. "The dark soldier that took its shadow is still here. I don't know what happened, just that there are now two Martecytes and a dark soldier after us. Maybe they only die completely when they're killed with the sword," I suggested, crouching down and turning to face the others.

"Has anyone killed one before?" asked General Delaney.

Solace tilted her head, thinking. "No one but Ben has killed a dark soldier. I don't remember if anyone else has killed a Martecyte. Maybe Ben is right. Maybe you can only kill them with the sword."

I gripped the sword more tightly. "In that case, it's up to me. Stay close in case I need you."

They both nodded, and I turned back to the entrance of our alleyway. The Martecytes were much closer now, only a house length away, and still searching for us. I whispered to Solace and General Delaney. "You two create a distraction so I can get outside town."

"Good idea," said Solace. "You are more experienced in forested terrain. If you lure them to the trees, you should have the advantage."

"Good point," I said. "Move off to our right and I will head the opposite direction to the tree line. Meet me at the edge of town after I have taken them out."

Solace and General Delaney both nodded again. I gave a signal, and they took off, splitting up, with Solace running across the street, moving to our right from alley to alley. The Martecytes and the dark soldier followed her initially, then spotted General Delaney moving in a similar pattern down our side of the street. Both Solace and the general drew the Martecytes' attention as they moved, making sure not to get too far from each other in case one needed backup. As soon as the Martecytes had passed the entrance of our alleyway in pursuit, I slipped out and turned left, silently making my way down the long street toward the edge of town and the trees beyond.

Stopping where I was still within sight of the Martecytes, I raised the sword and yelled to them, "Come and get me!"

All three Martecytes and the soldier of darkness turned toward me in unison. For a moment, I hesitated, then we were all in motion. I ran for the trees with the Martecytes in tow and quickly spotted a small clearing surrounded by trees and plenty of cover. It would be the perfect place to ambush them. Though we were not yet at the hidden docking port, we were nearby, and as I ran, I noticed that the jungle-like terrain was getting rocky.

I darted behind a boulder and waited. Gripping the sword with both hands, I took a deep, slow breath and forced myself to concentrate. The first Martecyte came into view and passed the boulder. I sprang from my position and thrust the sword upward, driving the blade through the dark being's chest. He gripped the blade with his hands, and no sound came from his open mouth as blood poured from his lips. The Martecyte collapsed to his knees, but his eyes were wild and full of laughter until they, too, went dark. *No shadow. One down, three to go.*

Another Martecyte appeared just ahead of me in the trees, and I slid the blade from the dead Martecyte's chest and took cover behind some tall bushes. The second Martecyte scanned the foliage as he slowly approached. I inched my way from bush to bush until he was within range. But just before I could run him through, he must have sensed me. He spun, growling in anger, and lunged.

I slashed at the Martecyte, but he dodged my blade and drew his own. The two swords clanged together, drawing the attention of the third Martecyte and the dark soldier. They appeared behind me just as I managed to drive my blade through my current opponent's neck, killing him.

I pulled my blade free of the second Martecyte and ducked just in time to dodge the third Martecyte's attack. With the last standing Martecyte on one side and the dark soldier on the other, I swung my blade from one to the other, expertly blocking their blows. As the Martecyte angled his sword over his head, I raised my sword to meet it and took the opportunity to pull out a small dagger and stab the Martecyte in the stomach. The Martecyte grabbed at the wound as I spun to block the blade of the dark soldier. As I came out of the spin, I was behind the Martecyte, and I thrust the sword through his back, penetrating his heart. His body went limp, then fell dead at my feet.

With no time to delay, I pulled the sword from the corpse and swung it backward to block another blow from the dark soldier as he circled around me. Our swords clashed, and I found myself face-to-face with him. He grinned, revealing fang-like teeth. His eyes were somehow full of both rage and maniacal joy. The image of the dark soldier from my dreams came to me, and I felt my confidence falter.

Just as suddenly as that image appeared, the green eyes of the Beast of the Woods flashed through my mind, overtaking the image of darkness and restoring my confidence. Shaking off the memories of my visions and dreams, I shoved the dark soldier backward and swung my blade at him this way and that in an attempt to overwhelm him, but he just kept blocking. I thrust my knife toward his ribs, and he dodged it. I swung my sword at him again, and again he blocked it. But after a few blows, I began to see his pattern. He left himself open in anticipation of my movements, so I kept up the predictable moves until I finally saw an opening I could use.

As I lifted my sword for one last blow, he raised his sword to block mine. He stepped forward, moving his body into my blow, and brought his hands and our clashing swords downward toward his waist to close himself off to an attack to his midsection. In response, I stepped into his block and, in one swift motion, spun around behind him, driving my knife into his neck as I came to face his back. I cranked the knife, shoving it upward into his skull to ensure he was dead. Then I pulled the knife from the wound, allowing him to collapse to the ground, dead.

Not wasting any time, I left the dead soldiers and sprinted back into town to find Solace and General Delaney. Just as I reached the outskirts, another Martecyte darted out in front of me and thrust his sword toward my stomach. In my full-out sprint, I was vulnerable to that kind of attack, and I attempted to block by bringing my sword hand close to my waist for a two-handed grip. But the Martecyte's blow connected close to the hilt of my sword, sending it flying from my grasp.

"Ben!" I heard Solace's voice behind me, but I was locked on to the sight of the Martecyte coming in for a killing blow. I stepped back, dodging the swipe of his sword as the blade barely missed the front of my neck. Then, out of nowhere, General Delaney came to my defense. He picked up my sword and blocked the Martecyte's next blow, then stabbed him through the heart with his dagger before finishing him off with the sword to make sure he was really dead.

In shock, I stared at General Delaney standing over the dead Martecyte, the sword in his hand. For a moment, I thought I saw his shoulders tense in frustration. But before I could ask what was wrong, he turned and flashed a teasing smile. "I think you dropped this," he said, holding out the sword so I could grab its hilt.

I watched him closely for a moment, then reached out and took the sword. "Thank you," I said as Solace ran up to us.

"I can't believe you did that!" she said to General Delaney as she enveloped me in a loving embrace.

"I told you both, I am on your side!" he said reassuringly as he smoothed the front of his jacket.

I wiped the bloody blade clean on the Martecyte's clothes, then sheathed the sword and nodded, pondering once again whether the general could be trusted. "Well, we need to find the others," I said.

"They were pushed back into town as well," said Solace. "From what I saw, they were headed north."

With that, we headed off in search of them. Careful to stay close to the houses, we wove in and out of alleyways and streets once again. Each time we heard voices or footsteps, we hid. It didn't matter who found us at this point; if anyone saw us, they might give our position away to more Martecytes and soldiers of darkness without even realizing it.

As we moved along the streets, searching for the others, a thought occurred to me. I turned to General Delaney. "If you are really not the enemy, then why did you get so angry at Ruth when I first delivered the book to you?" I asked.

The general winced slightly with embarrassment. "I was hoping you hadn't noticed," he replied.

"Why? What happened?" asked Solace.

"When I brought Ruth to see him after getting the book, she clearly irritated him," I said, giving General Delaney a suspicious glare. "I recall you forgetting her name and being quite angry when she told you what it was the second time."

"Despite how it may have appeared, Ruth and I do have a history," he admitted.

"What history?" I asked. "I thought that was the first time you had met."

General Delaney shook his head. "No. We have actually known each other for years. I used to work for her. See, it was her who got me interested in the book in the first place. She told me about it when I was much younger and explained that it could help." He shook his head. "But I am afraid our friendship was fraught with challenges."

"What happened?" I asked with a frown.

The general sighed. "It was my fault, really. Still is," he said with a far-off look in his eyes. "See, the book meant a lot to her when she was younger, I assume because it contains information on the Prince and the Gate, both of which can help stop the beasts. But I wanted to use it, too, to end the wars with the beasts. We fought about it many times, and we eventually parted ways. I was angry that she kept the book to herself." He shook his head.

"Why did you get so angry about her name, then?" I asked skeptically.

"Honestly, seeing her again brought back some of that anger. It wasn't her name, really. She was being so calm...I might have pretended to forget her name just to spite her," he said with a look of guilt. "When she replied so calmly, it just irritated me. I was angry at her for not letting me have the book. It's...complicated," he explained. "But we spoke after you left, and she explained why she was so protective of the book."

"Why didn't she give it to you before?" I asked.

"She explained that it was the last one," he said matter-of-factly. "It was her duty to protect it, and back then, she was still learning how to do that. She was overly cautious." He shrugged. "I understood that, considering my family's history with the book. I was going to give the book back to her. But at the end of the meeting, she gave it to me. She said she knew better now and had actually been expecting me to come. Hoped I would," he finished, his expression soft.

I nodded. "She definitely knew someone was coming," I said, remembering the day I met her. Before I could tell her why I was there, she had suggested I was there for the book.

General Delaney placed a hand on my shoulder. "Benjamin, my boy, you must know that even though I have been tough in the past, I only wanted to make this world a better place," he said gently. "And I know that you have found a different life. When this is over, I promise you can return to your father's house and live however you wish. It is the least I can do after everything we have been through together."

I stepped away so his hand fell to his side. "I'll think about it," I said. All his explanations made sense and he had just saved my life, but for some reason, I was still on the fence about his intentions.

He sighed. "You still don't trust me," he observed, his shoulders sagging slightly in disappointment.

"We will see how the next few hours go. Then I will decide if I trust you," I said.

"Fair enough," replied General Delaney with a friendly smile. "And once you do, maybe Ruth will help us figure out the details of how the book can help us."

"Wait," said Solace. "You know where Ruth is?"

The general's eyebrows rose. "Yes. You don't?"

"No, we lost track of her after we got back from the Woods," I explained.

"Oh, that was months ago!" said General Delaney.

"We checked her home, but she wasn't there," I explained.

General Delaney nodded. "She came to me once and told me to hide the book from Valdra. Said she had a way to get it back in print, but she didn't want the original to be stolen, just in case something happened."

"Well, where is she now?" I asked.

"Last I saw her, she was heading back home," he said with a shrug.

"When was that?" asked Solace. "We checked there more than once."

General Delaney shook his head and clarified, "Not the home in the mountains. Her home near the Western Seaport on the Southern Continent."

"I didn't know she had a place there," I said in surprise.

"She rarely goes there now, but she grew up there. I used to spend a lot of time in that house of hers," General Delaney said with a far-off look and a small smile. "Anyway, where do you think your friends made off to?" he asked.

We had been searching the edge of town but had seen no sign of them. "If they survived, they would make sure to meet us somewhere familiar," I commented.

"We could head back to where we were separated. They might have gone back to look for us," suggested Solace.

"Good idea," I agreed. "Let's check there."

With that, we headed back out of town, careful not to be seen. Once we were in the trees, though, we went slower, making sure not to step on any twigs or rustle branches so as not to give away our position to anyone who might be nearby. As we moved closer to the place where we had been separated from the others, voices gradually came into earshot. We hunkered down and listened, but they were still too far off to understand what they were saying.

"That might be them," I said. "Let's go check it out."

We continued until we were close enough to make out the words. I held up a hand and we stopped short as soon as I realized the voices were unfamiliar. There were two people talking, and they were right in our path to the *Lyonsword*'s hidden port.

As I listened to the conversation, the gentle whisper of a night bird registered in my ear. The call repeated in a familiar pattern. *Ivan and Nadia,* I thought with a smile. "They are here. Follow me," I whispered.

We made our way toward the bird call as quietly as we could and came upon Ivan, Trixie, Otto, and Lance hidden in some bushes. Nadia was nowhere to be seen, but I knew she must be in a nearby tree, keeping an eye out. That was probably how they had spotted us.

"What happened to you?" I asked Ivan as we joined them in the bushes.

"Shhh," said Nadia as she descended from her tree. "They are headed in this direction. We need to move."

"How are we going to get past them?" asked Solace.

I turned to Lance. "Is there another route we could take?"

"Where are we going?" asked General Delaney.

Lance ignored him. "That is the only way," he said, gesturing in the direction of the secret port.

I nodded. "We will just have to fight them," I said with confidence. But before I could act on that, Solace spoke.

"Who exactly are they?" asked Solace.

"Some of the western king's soldiers who were dispatched to look for us in town," said Ivan. "Based on their conversation, they heard we arrived and are keeping an eye on things. Maybe someone in town spotted us leaving the town and told them. They might be checking other areas around town too," he added.

"Shhh," Nadia hissed again. "They are coming."

We fell silent, and the two voices grew louder. They were headed directly toward us. We all pulled farther back into the bushes and listened as they passed by.

"The western king wants them all captured before that man who works for General Delaney gets here," said one voice.

"Why?" asked the second voice.

"He said something fishy is going on right now. He is not sure what. But he doesn't trust people from the main continents," replied the first voice.

"How long till General Delaney's man gets here?" asked the second voice.

"Don't know. Just know he is on his way, and close," said the first voice as their footsteps faded into the distance.

Great, I thought. *Valdra is almost here. We need to get off this island now.*

Chapter 20

"WE MUST GET TO the ship and off this island before Valdra comes for us," I said, rushing past General Delaney in the direction of the *Lyonsword*.

"I have a ship," said the general. "It is docked in the main port. Where do you need to go?"

I stopped and turned back to him. "We already have a ship," I said. "You can take your ship and meet us at the Southern Continent. If Valdra finds out that we are working together, things will go sideways very fast."

"Things went sideways a long time ago, Benjamin," said General Delaney as worry creased his brow.

I sighed. "I still haven't decided to trust you. I will not put more people in danger. If you want to help, take your ship, and we will take ours. When we all arrive back on the Southern Continent, we will meet behind the Town at the base of the Cresent Hill," I said sternly. I turned to Lance. "Go let the captain know we are on our way." Lance nodded and ran off toward the *Lyonsword*, disappearing into the shadows.

General Delaney nodded, his lips pressed together in a thin line. "Okay. But I wouldn't go that way," he warned.

"Why?" I asked, placing my hands on my hips defiantly.

"Because there is a ship that I spotted coming in from the sea when I was over that direction earlier. I almost missed it because it was so well camouflaged, but it's there," he explained.

"And why would I need to be concerned about this ship?" I asked in frustration.

"It's the *Lyonsword*. Captain Nathaniel Bates's ship," he said, raising his eyebrows meaningfully.

I watched General Delaney, carefully trying to hide my surprise. "And who is Captain Nathaniel Bates?" I asked.

"He is an old friend of Valdra's. He is a dangerous con man that Valdra uses from time to time to get supplies to and from the Northern Continent. Normally I would say he is a good man. But he and Valdra grew up together. Now that I know Valdra is trying to take over, I'm afraid the captain is not to be trusted," he explained.

I glanced at Nadia. She frowned and stepped forward to whisper in my ear, "Be careful, Ben. We know the captain well. We have more reason to trust him than this man."

I nodded and turned back to General Delaney. "Thank you for the tip. Like I said, you take your ship, and I will take mine. We will meet up at the location I mentioned," I said, leaving no room for doubt in my decision.

General Delaney dipped his head submissively. "I will see you there, then." With that, he turned and headed off toward the shipyards.

I watched as he faded into the shadows of the night. Then I turned and led the others toward the *Lyonsword*.

Nadia came up next to me as we walked. "Don't trust him, Ben," she cautioned.

"I haven't decided what I am going to do," I said, glancing in the direction General Delaney had gone. I turned to Nadia. "Remember that first night we met the captain? When he found us in his shipment?" I asked.

Nadia thought for a moment, then nodded. "Yes," she stated skeptically.

"What was your first thought in that moment?" I asked.

Nadia frowned. "That he was a dangerous man who was about to shoot us all on the spot and dump our bodies into the ocean," she said, her shoulders sagging.

I nodded. "I also can't help but remember that we made it through two pirate attacks because of the captain," I pointed out. "That is either a really good thing—"

"Or he knew them all and planned it for some reason we don't yet understand," finished Nadia, catching on to my meaning.

I took a deep breath. "If the captain is working with Valdra, that means that Lance could be as well," I said. "We only trust him because the captain said we could."

"But if this is all true, then Valdra let us go on this journey. Why did he attack us if he was planning on letting us take *The Story* to the four corners of the earth?" she asked in confusion.

I glanced back toward town, toward the house where we had dropped *The Story* off. "Has anyone checked the pages to see if any copies have errors?" I asked.

Nadia shook her head. "Not that I know of. Did Lance load the text?" she asked.

I nodded. "Most of it. They might be trying to spread a false story."

"But why?" asked Nadia.

I shrugged. "I don't know...The other option is that they want us to find the armor for them," I suggested. Naida and I glanced at each other, then looked ahead in the direction Lance had gone. If that were the case, things were about to get much harder. "When we get to the *Lyonsword*, keep an eye on Lance and the captain, just in case," I told Nadia. "I will have to decide if we are getting back on that ship or changing plans. Whether they are both working with Valdra or not, Valdra might still be after the armor and *The Story*. We need to be cautious."

"Will do," said Nadia.

⁂

We continued through the rocky, forested terrain in silence, each of us lost in our own thoughts. When we finally arrived at the secret docking port, we all stopped short in shock at what we saw. Or, more accurately, what we didn't see. Before us lay the hidden alcove where we had left the ship. But it was empty. The *Lyonsword* was nowhere to be seen.

"It's gone!" exclaimed Otto, his voice slightly shrill with panic. "They left us!"

"It looks like that guy may have been right," said Trixie. "Who was he, anyway?"

I shook my head. "General Delaney. I used to work for him until he tried to have me and the rest of us here killed," I said as I rubbed my forehead. "At least, that is what I thought happened."

"And who is Valdra?" she probed.

"We used to work together. He is—or was—General Delaney's right-hand man," I explained as I surveyed the empty alcove. "It seems he has branched out on his own," I mumbled.

"Ben, this doesn't necessarily mean that General Delaney was telling the truth," Solace warned. "Maybe there is a reasonable explanation for why the captain left."

"We could check," suggested Otto.

"How?" I asked, turning to face him.

"We just have to find a high point and see if we can spot them," he said.

"Yes, we could do that," I said, "but there is no guarantee that we will be able to see the *Lyonsword*. It is designed to blend in at night." I felt a pained expression wash over my face as a headache began to pulse in my temple.

"I think we should at least try," said Solace.

I thought for a moment, then sighed. "Okay." I turned to Ivan. "Ivan, stay here with Otto and Trixie. Nadia, Solace, and I will check it out."

Ivan nodded. "Don't take too long. If they left, we are trapped on this island, and Valdra's soldiers will soon find us," he pointed out.

"I won't," I said, then turned and ran off to find high ground with Nadia and Solace in tow. We slipped from the hidden alcove out a small opening that led up a rocky slope. Once we were up high enough, we worked our way through the trees until we came upon a cliff that looked out over the island's eastern side. The ocean stretched out below us like a big, dark blue blanket, moonlight glistening on its surface. But the *Lyonsword* was nowhere in sight.

I heard rustling overhead and turned to see Nadia perched in the branches of a nearby tree, trying to see if she could get a better angle.

"Anything?" I asked.

"No," her voice came through the foliage.

I looked at Solace. "It looks like General Delaney was right."

Solace shook her head. "But it doesn't make sense!" she said in frustration. "Maybe you are the one who is right. Like you said, the *Lyonsword* is practically invisible at night," she reminded me. "Maybe it is there, and we just can't see it."

I could see worry in her eyes, and I suddenly remembered that Yuuki was aboard the ship. "Don't worry. We will find them and make sure Yuuki is safe," I said, my gaze locked on hers.

But worry churned in the pit of my stomach as well. If the captain was our enemy, there was no telling what might become of little Yuuki.

Nadia dropped down from the tree, landing in a gentle crouch before straightening. "She is right, Ben. It really doesn't make sense," she commented. "And we have all seen how well camouflaged that ship is at night. Not to mention the fact that if the captain's story is true, which, considering what happened tonight, I think we can say it is, the King fixed it with his Original Power. What would a ship like that be doing in the hands of an enemy of Eeffrayldour?"

"He could have stolen it," I suggested.

Nadia shrugged. "Still..."

I considered their points. "We should check *The Story* just in case. That is a good place to start."

"We will have to go back to town and get the one we dropped off," said Nadia. "The rest of the copies are on other islands or on the *Lyonsword*."

"Okay. But we need to be careful. This could be a trap," I said in warning.

Nadia rolled her eyes. "Ben, I think it is safe to assume that everything is a trap at this point. We might as well not let it stop us."

I smiled. "Good call. Let's go grab the others and head back to town to see if the contact is still there."

"Wait, how are we going to find him?" asked Solace. "He has probably left the meeting place."

"Good point." I rubbed my chin.

Nadia shook her head. "Maybe not."

Solace and I looked at her. "What you mean?" I asked.

"With all the guards running around looking for us and anyone connected to us, he might have decided to stay put," Nadia said with a shrug. "It would at least be worth looking into."

"She's right," I said, looking at Solace. "We don't know whether we will get off this island tonight or not. But either way, I would rather check while we still can. With the way things are going, we might not even make it off this island alive. I would hate to leave behind corrupted books if we could fix at least the one on this island."

Solace nodded. "Okay, let's go."

Nadia and I turned to begin the hike back down the rocks when I heard Solace behind me. "Um, Ben," she said hesitantly.

I turned around and saw that she was still standing near the edge of the cliff, looking out over the sea. "What is that?" she asked, pointing to a dark shape in the sky. The object was too far away to make out clearly. All I could see was that it was big, it was flying, and it was coming from the south.

"I don't know," I said as Nadia and I joined Solace near the cliff's edge.

We stood there for a moment, peering into the distance. As the object drew closer, more details began to come into view, and suddenly, it became clear what I was looking at.

"Run!" I snapped.

Nadia and Solace took off down the rocks while I brought up the rear. We scrambled our way back through the small opening into the hidden alcove and yelled at everyone to follow us.

"What's wrong?" asked a confused Ivan as we ran past them toward the main exit of the alcove, the others breaking into a run behind us.

As if in response to Ivan's question, a faint rumble came from somewhere in the distance. The sound grew until it swelled into a distant screech.

"What was that?" asked Ivan, looking wide-eyed to the sky.

Ignoring Ivan, I stopped at the edge of the trees, waving everyone by to ensure we were all together, and we sprinted toward town.

As we passed the first few houses, the sound came again. But this time, it was close. Too close. The rumble seemed to vibrate through the air, building into a screech that was somehow both high and low at the same time. Chills rippled down my spine, and the hair on my arms stood on end. The few townspeople in the streets froze as a shadow fell over us, outlined in the moonlight. The telltale shape of massive bat-like wings. The long neck and tail. Claws like an enormous lizard. We all looked to the sky. The colossal animal was covered in jet-black, rock-like scales. In the cracks between the scales, orange skin seemed to glow like lava. A dragon.

"Impossible," I heard Otto whisper. "I thought they were extinct."

The huge dragon opened its jaws, and fire burst from its throat. *The Fire Dragon!* I thought. *The Fire Dragon is alive!* The people of the Western Island Country scattered like ants. The fire engulfed the first house it struck, and the world around me seemed to slow. Memories of the Great Volcano and my father dying in my arms came crashing through my mind, followed by images of my family's home burning and Mary's lifeless body lying in a pile of charred rubble.

Suddenly, I felt Ivan grab my arm and yank me out of the horrible memories as the city around us began to burn. We ran through the streets as flames licked up shops and homes. Townspeople scattered around us, frantically searching for somewhere to hide, though it was clear the dragon intended to burn everything to the ground.

We began our own search for cover but were interrupted when the contact we had met with earlier suddenly appeared and beckoned toward us. "Come with me!" he yelled. We ran after him and entered what I assumed was his house, as it was not the place where we had met. He went to a secret hatch in the floor and opened it. "We will be safe in here," he said as we all piled into the underground room, which was already filled with people.

The hatch closed over us, and I drew the sword as we huddled under the staircase.

The room fell silent as we all held our breath, listening to the sounds of destruction overhead. I closed my eyes and felt Solace's hand on my arm. I covered it reassuringly with my own hand. When a loud thump came from above, my eyes snapped open as I released Solace's hand and grabbed the sword in a two-handed grip, ready for the worst.

But as I gripped the sword, images of my previous visions leaped to my mind, and I snapped my eyes shut again as a headache shot through my forehead. The images flashed by, one after the other. The green eyes and the tail of the Beast of the Woods. The breastplate. The path. The door. The Prince standing in the open doorway. *"Tsahreyethah meye,"* he said.

As each image passed through my mind once more, I heard the Ice Dragon's words. The Beast's tail that turned into a belt. *"Have hope, my friend, for the truth is a treasure worth knowing."* The breastplate. *"Be on guard, my friend, for your heart is a treasure worth protecting."* The shoes. *"Be ready, my friend, for* The Story *is a treasure worth following."*

With the dragon's last word, the sword grew light in my hand, and I opened my eyes. The world around me had transformed. The others were gone, the buildings had faded, and I stood at ground level. There was no one on the island but me and darkness amidst the fire, ash, and destruction. The sword seemed to call out to something stronger than it ever had before, and this time I could tell it was calling to something nearby, not in the distance.

As the world around me seemed to slow, I recalled what Trixie had said about the armor. The sword was attracted to other pieces. This time I knew for certain the sword was not leading me astray. It was leading me right where the Prince wanted me to go.

So, I chose to trust him.

I looked around in search of what the sword was trying to lead me to. But as I turned, I found myself face-to-face, once again, with the Ice Dragon.

"Where is the next piece of armor?" I asked her.

The Ice Dragon cocked her head to the side. "Remember what you have been given," she said. Then she pointed to me with a long, white talon. "Have faith, my friend, for the unseen is a treasure worth believing in."

In response to her words, I felt the sword in my hand again call out to something. But before I could see what it was, darkness closed in around me. I looked away from the Ice Dragon in time to see the dark soldier from my dreams and visions materialize from the darkness around me and attack. Instinctively, I grabbed the shield from its place on my back and held it up in defense. When nothing hit the shield, I straightened and looked around me. The vision had vanished, revealing the cellar I was hiding in.

"Ben?" I heard Solace saying. "Was it another vision?" she asked hopefully.

"Yes," I whispered. *I have to go out there.* The stray thought seemed to come from nowhere.

As I had defended against the soldier of darkness, I had realized something. Every time the dragon presented a new piece of armor, the dark soldier attacked. It was as if he didn't want me to find what the sword was leading me to. *I have to go out there.* The thought returned. I needed to find the next piece of armor, and for some reason, I felt as though I had to listen to this thought. I felt a strange urge to search outside of this cellar for what the sword was leading me too. *It is time,* I thought as the pit of my stomach churned. *I need to face the darkness head-on.*

Placing the shield at my back, I headed for the trapdoor, but Solace grabbed my arm. "Where are you going?" she asked in a worried tone.

I looked at her, trying to ignore the confused strangers crowded around us. "I have to go out there. The sword...It is calling to something again."

"But Eyethanoff has been busy," said Nadia. "He cannot help you. You will need our help," she insisted, and Ivan nodded in agreement.

Solace stared at me, the corners of her eyes creased with concern. "We can help you," she said as they all stood.

I shook my head. "No. I have to do this. Alone. Solace..." I let out a sigh. "Solace, I don't know what will happen, but I know I must find where this sword is trying to lead me. I have been letting my own fears stop me for too long. I have to do this."

"That dragon will kill you!" Solace snapped, tears welling in her eyes.

I shook my head. "I can do this, Solace. I know what I am doing. And none of us will make it out of here alive if someone doesn't distract that dragon. You must wait here until I can lure the dragon away, then get to General Delaney's ship and get off this island."

"What if he can't be trusted, though?" she asked, clearly grasping for excuses to stay and help me.

I shook my head. "Check the copies of the book we gave the contact. If they are wrong, let them burn," I said, an edge of frustration in my voice. "If not, and if I don't make it to the ship in time, you need to find Ruth. She will know what to do." With that, I turned and climbed the stairs to the trapdoor. As I opened the hatch, I felt Solace grab my coat, and I looked down.

"Ben, you do not have to fight this battle on your own. Have faith—Eyethanoff will come!" she said, holding my gaze.

I leaned down and kissed her. As our lips parted, I smiled. "I will."

With a reassuring nod, I turned and left the safety of the cellar. As I stepped into the main room of the house, I found myself surrounded by destruction. Three of the home's walls were still standing, but everything else was ash and crumbled stone. Flames danced through the city, and smoke filled the air. I approached the front door and opened it, the sword held tightly in my right hand and the shield on my back.

As I stepped out into the street, I looked around at the carnage. Houses burned. Even the king's castle in the near distance had flames grasping at its edges. Ash floated through the air as the dragon's shadow fell over the land again, and its call rumbled through the streets, hitting my chest like an invisible wave and causing my heart to leap into my throat.

I took in a deep breath and steadied my nerves. First things first, I had to lead the dragon away from the others.

I looked to the sky in search of the massive animal and quickly found what I was looking for. The dragon's dark scales were like living armor over its orange skin. Its eyes were red, aflame with malicious intent. I yelled to the dragon, and its gaze locked on to my tiny form.

I turned and ran for the edge of town, then headed toward a patch of beach near some rocky cliffs. When I reached the beach, I was out in the open, and I waved my sword and yelled again. The dragon, having followed my movements, descended upon me. As it swooped, I caught sight of the others making a break for the nearby shipyards, but, thankfully, the dragon ignored them.

Knowing that the others would make it to safety, I turned to face the dragon. It came at me head-on, black, leathery wings tucked close to its sides as it dove for the beach. When it came within range, it opened its mouth and let loose a whirl of fire straight at me.

I turned and ran through the shallow waves for the tiered cliffs that overlooked the city and the sea, diving behind a massive boulder just as the dragon's fire rained down. The fire struck the rock, barely missing me, and the dragon returned to the sky for another dive.

With no time to lose, I climbed the rocks to the highest point I could quickly reach. *I need to keep the dragon's attention and keep an eye on the others to make sure they get to the ship,* I told myself. Wiping sweat from my brow, I stepped onto a large rock at the edge of a cliff looking south over the burning town and braced myself for the dragon's next attack. Fear gripped me as the thought that I was facing something beyond my power to defeat tugged at my confidence. I searched for the others and spotted them not far from the docks. I gripped the sword and forced myself to focus. *Now that they are almost to safety, I just have to survive this long enough to find the next piece of armor.*

Suddenly the dragon called again, and I spun in search of its shadowy figure in the ashen night sky. But I did not see it. *It's taunting me,* I thought. *Otherwise, it surely would have attacked by now.* Then I felt it; the sword in my hand went light as if it were calling to something again. Immediately, I scanned the area below me in search of whatever it was trying to lead me to. But what I saw sent chills down my spine and chased all thought of the armor from my mind.

The dragon had swooped down over the city and was coming at me from below. I vaguely noticed the moonlight shining strangely through the ash-filled sky, but my attention was pulled to the city streets below. They were now empty of city dwellers. Instead, thirty or so soldiers of darkness seeped out of the shadows, creeping their way, like stalking wolves, toward the rock on which I stood.

Standing alone near the cliff's edge, I was filled with fear as I stared at the impossible odds against me. One against thirty soldiers of darkness. And a dragon. Having been distracted by the sight of the soldiers, I wasn't prepared for the dragon's swift approach as it swooped up toward me with a deafening cry. I jerked out of the way at the last second, but the dragon's wing made contact, sending me flying backward off the rock, and I tumbled to the ground. The cliff was covered in sandy dirt and grass, and I tried to dig my feet in as I stood, but my waterlogged boots turned the soil to mud, making the grass slippery.

As the dragon ascended to prepare for another attack, the soldiers of darkness seemed to disappear into the shadows at the base of the cliff. Then, suddenly, they began to materialize around me, closing in and blocking all escape routes. *Surely the dragon will deal the killing blow now,* I thought. My heart pounded and my stomach churned with panic as I stood alone on the slick ground, surrounded by darkness. The dragon let out another cry, and I looked up to see it circling overhead, apparently content to give the soldiers of darkness a turn at me.

As the first dark soldier attacked, I swung the sword in desperation. It clanged against the soldier's blade, and I immediately spun to block the attack of another soldier to my right. Overwhelmed, I desperately swung from dark blade to dark blade in an attempt to simply survive. *Help me!* I thought in anger at Eyethanoff. But there was no answer. There was only the dark soldiers, the dragon, fire, and destruction. All I saw was darkness.

I shoved aside all thought of Eyethanoff and gripped the sword more tightly. If Eyethanoff would not help me, then I would just have to find the next piece of armor and rely on it to protect me instead. As I lifted the sword to block another blow, the green eyes of the Beast of the Woods flashed in my mind's eye, and the Ice Dragon's words came back to me. *"Have faith, my friend, for the unseen is a treasure worth believing in."*

As I blocked another attack from a soldier of darkness, the dark dragon took a dive toward the city and swooped back up toward me, preparing to launch another stream of flames. With no place to run, I heard the Ice Dragon's words again. *"Have faith, my friend, for the unseen is a treasure worth believing in."*

As if in response to the words, the sword again grew light in my hand. I looked to my surroundings, but there was nothing but soldiers of darkness. As they closed in around me, I felt the sword call out even stronger, and again I realized it was not calling to something in the distance but something nearby.

Suddenly, the soldiers of darkness parted to reveal the dragon's fire headed straight for me. With no time to fight it and still no place to run, I grabbed the shield from my back and braced it before me to block the flames. As if in response to the shield, the sword felt normal again, almost as though the armor were that much closer to being complete.

The fire surrounded me on all sides, only broken by the shield I held in my hands. I slid backward on the slippery ground, the sheer force of the flames pushing me toward the next tier of the cliff that rose behind me. As the flames let up, the dragon passed overhead, looping up into the night sky to prepare for another attack.

Standing on ground that was now half rocky, half muddy, I felt sweat drip from my forehead into my eyes, burning them, but I didn't care. I stared at the shield in my hand, stunned that I was still alive. The shield was undamaged. It shone bright as if nothing had happened. I looked over my clothes—not a single singe. Not even the earth beneath my feet was scorched. In place around my waist was the belt from my visions, the breastplate covered my chest, and the shoes were on my feet. I had never seen this armor outside of a vision, and there was something so deeply reassuring about its presence, though it still felt as though some part of it was missing.

A screech from the dragon pulled my attention back to the sky as it swooped down upon me yet again. It blasted a new stream of fire in my direction, and once again, I held the shield before me. The fire hit the shield hard, and my feet, aided by the shoes of armor, dug into the ground for balance.

With new confidence that I could win, I let one knee sink to the earth and leaned into the force of the flames, grunting with the effort to hold them at bay. As the fire let up and the dragon swept upward, it tipped its wing toward me. I had been so focused on holding back the flames that I was caught off guard, and the dragon's wing caught the shield, sending me flying backward as if I weighed nothing. Laying on my back, I felt the armor vanish from its place, leaving me with only the sword and shield once again.

I forced myself to stand as the dragon circled back into the sky and the soldiers of darkness looked on with maniacal grins. *Why are they holding back?* I wondered. *Are they just going to take their time and kill me slowly?* My whole body aching, I gripped the sword in one hand and the shield in the other as I searched for the rest of the armor, wondering why it was no longer there. Anger flared within me. *This armor is useless!* I fumed. *It should function without whatever is still missing. It should at least protect me! I could fight this battle and win if only I had some kind of protection.*

"Why won't you help me?" I yelled. But this time, I was not yelling at Eyethanoff. I was yelling at the King. I knew he was there. I knew he had made the armor. If anything, he could send me something else to protect me or force Eyethanoff to answer me. And yet I had not seen Eyethanoff come to my aid since that day at the castle.

As I spun to block an attack from a dark soldier, the dragon dove at me from above yet again. I braced myself, the shield in my left hand and the sword in my right, poised to take on the advancing dragon.

As the dragon descended upon me, the soldiers of darkness scattered to give it room. But this time, it didn't spit fire. Instead, it attempted to hit me with a clawed foot. I dodged the attack and slashed at its throat with the sword, but the blade glanced off its hard scales. *Great. This sword is useless too!*

I blocked a blow from a dark soldier behind me and swung the sword diagonally to ward off a dark soldier before me. But as my sword came down, a brilliant beam of moonlight suddenly shone straight toward me and reflected off its blade, piercing the chest of a dark soldier who had been about to land a killing blow. The soldier crumpled to the ground, dead.

Suddenly I remembered seeing the moonlight shine strangely through the ash-filled sky. Now that I thought about it, it was odd that I could see the moonlight through all the smoke and ash. Then I remembered the beam of light on the ship that had blinded me, and I slowly began to come to a realization. One that I couldn't believe I had been too selfish not to think of before. It came with the memory of something Solace had told me weeks ago. *"Just because you can see something doesn't mean you have all the information."* Images from the past months flew through my mind. The Beast's green eyes, the Prince, Eyethanoff, the Ice Dragon, the dreams, the visions of the door. They were things I had seen in person or in a vision. But Solace's words brought a question to my mind. *What did I not see?* More memories flipped through my mind like the pages of a book. Eyethanoff's abrupt departure from the church, the push when I jumped from the cliff to the *Lyonsword*, the moonbeams dancing on the ocean, the beam of light that had blinded me on the boat. *Eyethanoff was protecting me from something I can't see!* I realized with sudden certainty.

My father's dying words rang in my ears, and I knew I had been wrong about Eyethanoff and the King. *"The war was won long ago, but we fought this battle alone and lost...Don't trust what this world tells you. Do not fight your battles alone."* I had been so focused on how I thought things worked, based on what I could see, that I had blamed the King and Eyethanoff for not doing things in a way that I understood. I had been fighting this battle alone. Or so I had thought. But they had been there all along. I just couldn't see them. It was so obvious now. *I am not alone!*

Chapter 21

I SCRAMBLED BACKWARD, TRYING to avoid the horde of dark soldiers closing in from all angles like a swarm of rats. But knowing that Eyethanoff was nearby gave me a spark of hope.

As if they could sense my change of heart, the soldiers of darkness suddenly attacked. I slashed at them, attempting to protect myself. But then those green eyes flashed in my mind's eye again, and I remembered the Ice Dragon's words. *"Have faith, my friend, for the unseen is a treasure worth believing in."*

A soldier of darkness lifted his sword, and I raised the shield to block his blow. His blade bounced off the shield with a loud clang, and the dark soldier stumbled backward.

I swung the sword at two soldiers of darkness on the brink of overpowering me just as Eyethanoff appeared! He twisted another moonbeam, sending it straight for my shield. It bounced off the gleaming metal and sliced through the heart of a dark soldier to my left.

As we fought side-by-side, I looked up to see the dragon descending from above, a dark soldier now riding on its back. The dragon's jaws opened, poised to spew flames at us. But suddenly, the dragon's attention was pulled to something else. The dark soldier on its back aimed the giant dragon toward the burning city, and I turned to see what it was after.

In the distance, I saw Solace, Nadia, Ivan, Trixie, and Otto making their way to the seaport, not much closer than the last time I had looked. *They should have been there by now!* I thought. But they weren't. They were running as fast as they could, trying to keep out of the dragon's sight. Something must have slowed them down or gotten in their way. And now they had been spotted.

"We have to keep the dragon from getting to them!" I yelled to Eyethanoff as I scrambled down the rocky cliff to the beach below.

"No!" yelled Eyethanoff with an outstretched hand, but I kept going. I had to protect them, or they would all die.

I ran across the sand, yelling and waving the sword in an attempt to pull the dragon and its rider's attention to me. Thankfully, the dragon paused its attack and circled back as I entered the town, headed for the seaport where General Delaney's ship was docked. But when I was nearing the last of the houses, the dragon again caught sight of the others just as they were making a final dash into the shipyards toward the ship. It was now on a collision course I could not stop. The dragon launched its flaming storm at Solace and the others, and in desperation, I cried out to them. But it was no use.

As the flames engulfed them, I fell to my knees in horror, dropping the shield and sword at my sides. The battle behind me and the city around me faded from my awareness, leaving nothing but ash and flame. The wall of fire that separated me from the people I loved so much began to fade as the dragon exhausted its breath and passed overhead.

As the fire receded, I could not believe my eyes. There stood Solace and the others, unharmed. Everything around them was scorched. But where they stood, the ground was untouched by fire. In shock, I rose and stared at them. But I knew what had happened, for I remembered how, in the Woods, I had seen the soldiers of light, the Lion's Sword, protecting others, not just me.

Suddenly, I heard the dragon call again, and I grabbed the sword and shield and rushed forward. As I neared the others, I spotted a soldier of the Lion's Sword standing, sword and shield held at the ready, at the boundary of the scorched ground.

I ran past the soldier of light, grabbing Solace by the arm. "Run!" I yelled.

We ran toward the ship, but the dragon's fire burned our path, hitting a ship next to the general's as it spewed its flaming breath, forcing us to retreat back the way we had come. As we ran inland in search of a place to hide, I saw more of the Lion's Sword soldiers take on the remaining soldiers of darkness. The dragon's shadow fell over the town as moonbeams shifted in the sky, bent by the soldiers of light. A battle only I could see.

Night was still upon us, but I knew it must almost be daybreak. Though it seemed like I would never see the sun again, I forced myself to look to the horizon. The sun would come soon.

Ivan found a house that was still mostly standing, and we all huddled in it, holding our breath. The earth shook as the massive dragon touched down and walked among the charred streets, leaving the soldiers to their battle. With each step it took, we shrank back into the shadows, hoping it would walk by.

As the dragon rounded a corner, its hot breath washed over the house, blowing ash through the broken windows. I closed my eyes to keep the ash out and gripped Solace's hand. In silence, we waited. The Lion's Sword would take care of the armies of darkness; we just had to make it past this dragon and onto General Delaney's ship. We had to find the Gate, or this darkness would spread and never leave.

The dragon paused outside the house. I breathed through my nose, trying not to cough, but the smoke was thick.

Suddenly, Trixie let out a small sneeze. We all looked at her. After a moment, I heard the dragon, on the other side of the wall, suck in a deep breath.

"Run!" I yelled for the third time that night.

We dashed out the door just as flames filled our vacated hiding place, and once again, we headed for the port. The dragon took to the air, and for a moment, I truly believed we would die by its fire. But at the last second, I spotted a soldier of light come to our aid. She bent a moonbeam toward the dragon, temporarily blinding it, giving us time to outrun it. This time we made it, slipping past the dragon and running back to the docks. We dodged shipping containers and scrambled over fallen debris as the soldier of light covered our escape.

General Delaney's ship was ready to depart, and standing at the base of the gangplank was the general himself. As soon as he saw us, he waved us over. He had waited for us.

Solace yelled out to me, "I don't feel good about getting on his ship, Ben. I don't like the idea of setting sail with that dragon still in the sky."

I turned back to her. "We don't have a choice. The *Lyonsword* is gone. If we stay here, we will die!" I said as I beckoned the group onto the ship, counting them as they all went by.

General Delaney and I boarded last, and he clasped me by the shoulder. "When I saw you fighting, I knew something was wrong. You should have been on your ship. So, I waited for you. But we are not out of the woods yet. Not that you haven't noticed, but dragons can fly," he said with a grin.

I nodded. "Trust me, I noticed," I said. "How are we going to get out of here with that dragon attacking us?"

"We have cannons and a lot of firepower; at the least, we should be able to scare it off. We will stay in port until we have won!" said the general.

Not sure this was the best course of action but feeling like I had no other choice, I nodded and got to work. We took up defensive positions as General Delaney's crew prepped cannons and flintlocks. The twins and Otto joined the gunners while Solace and I joined the rest of the crew, who had armed themselves with various kinds of flintlocks and matchlocks and other weapons they had on board.

The dragon spiraled into the sky before flipping over backward and diving for the ship. It plummeted quickly, then, at the last second, it suddenly spread its wings, thrusting them downward. The powerful wings created a draft big enough to move the ship, and I suddenly realized the dragon's previous attacks had burnt up the ropes that tethered it to the port. The ship began to drift away from the dock.

Several crew members rushed to find more ropes to tie it down, but they were too late; the dragon's wings had disrupted the water and moved the boat too far from the dock. The dragon lifted into the air again, its wings creating a strong enough wind to move the boat farther out to sea while it blocked any route back to the island.

As it lifted into the air, the dragon opened its mouth to release another torrent of fire, and I had the sudden feeling that I had been in this situation before. An impenetrable creature attacking us on a ship. No way to kill it. No weaknesses. I looked at the animal's large open jaws, and an image of the leviathan flashed through my mind's eye. As the dragon let loose its flames, everyone on deck scattered. A beam of light suddenly flashed in front of the dragon, blinding it yet again, and the huge animal pulled back, the fire mostly missing its target. *Eyethanoff!*

The topsail, which was still tied down, burst into flames, and crew members climbed up the masts with buckets of ocean water to douse it. With the destructive flames extinguished and the mainsail only partially damaged, I turned my gaze to the deck, searching for Nadia and Ivan. We might not be able to fight. If we didn't beat this dragon, we needed to get off the ship and fast.

As I ran from one section of the boat to another looking for them, cannons fired around me. I checked the sky and saw the dragon take another turn in the air and head straight for us before it pulled up short to avoid a barrage of cannonballs. The dragon screamed and ascended into the now early morning sky, preparing for yet another attack.

Not finding Ivan and Nadia, I ran into the captain's quarters, hoping they were with General Delaney. "Where are Ivan and Nadia?" I asked urgently as the noise of the battle was dampened slightly by the cabin's walls.

General Delaney was standing over the map table, his brown blouse free of his black jacket. His sleeves hung loose and damp, probably from helping the crew put out the dragon's fires. "We can still make it to the Southern Continent," he said in a distant voice as he stared at his maps. "We have just started this journey and still have to make it home before the ship falls apart. We can do that if we survive this and make sure we don't run into more trouble on the way."

"You don't get it!" I snapped. "We are losing this fight! If we do not abandon ship or somehow scare that dragon away, this ship is going down and us along with it!" I said sternly. "I need to find Ivan and Nadia!"

General Delaney looked up at me. After a moment of hesitation, he said, "You are right. I am sorry. It's just that I have been after this my whole life." Suddenly, he looked determined. "Ivan and Nadia are not here. Find them and tell them to do whatever it takes to get rid of that creature. It has blocked our path back to the port, so we have no choice but to attempt to run. I will do what I can to steer this ship farther out to sea."

With a nod, I found myself wondering why the dragon hadn't killed us yet. With the help of Eyethanoff and the other soldiers of light, we appeared to be faring surprisingly well. But still, it almost seemed like the dragon was just playing with us.

I left General Delany's quarters and finally found Ivan and Nadia helping the gunners on the ship's port side. I grabbed them. "We can't take it down with cannonballs!" I yelled over the sounds of war.

"How then?" asked Ivan.

"Remember the leviathan?" I asked.

The twins' expressions lit up with understanding. "We're on it!" yelled Nadia. While they ran off to find Solace and the necessary supplies, I searched for General Delaney's captain to tell him the plan.

Nadia, Ivan, and Solace soon returned with two harpoons. I was not able to find General Delaney's captain, so I joined Solace and helped prepare the weapons. Ivan and Nadia climbed on the gunwale and began waving their swords at the dragon to draw it within range and provoke it to spit fire. As the dragon neared the ship, I prayed it would come close enough that the harpoon could reach it. The dragon descended on us with anger in its eyes, and for the first time all night, I was happy to see its jaws agape. As the dragon neared, I held my position.

"What are you waiting for?" asked Solace.

"I am not getting in that thing's mouth!" shouted Ivan.

I shook my head. "It has to be in range!" I yelled.

As fire began to build in the back of the dragon's throat, Nadia grabbed a bow and began firing arrows toward its face, where they might hit soft flesh. An arrow struck at the base of the dragon's eye, and the animal pawed at the wound as it released a cry of pain, its fire momentarily extinguished.

The dragon maintained its forward momentum, though, and by the time it re-engaged with vigor, it was well within range. Its jaws opened once again, and I saw my chance. I fired. The harpoon flew through the air, headed straight for its mark, as it had with the leviathan. But suddenly, the animal tipped its wing as if expecting the weapon and rolled into a diving spiral as the harpoon whizzed past its head, glancing off its scaled, muscular shoulder.

With no time to think, I fired the second harpoon, but the massive creature saw it coming and dodged the weapon a second time. By the time the dragon had recovered, it was upon us. It reached forward with its clawed feet and landed on the side of the ship, pushing the vessel farther out to sea as it sunk its talons into the wooden hull and gunwale.

Everyone ran to the opposite side of the ship as it began to tip under the creature's weight. I dove for cover with Solace as Ivan, Nadia, and Otto did the same, and we clung to the ship's gunwale. The dragon turned on the ship's sails, letting loose a stream of fire that burned them to a crisp, leaving the ship dead in the water. Suddenly, lightning flashed, and I looked up to see dark clouds rolling in from the north. Thunder crashed as the ship rolled and shook, and a huge wave, seeming to appear out of nowhere, crashed into the hull.

"We need to get everyone off this ship!" I yelled. "The dragon is going to sink it!"

Solace shook her head. "There is nowhere safe to go. Do you see that massive cloud?" she said, pointing.

I shook my head. "That storm might put out the fires in town, but I know it will push this ship farther out to sea. We will be safer on land than out here."

The dragon suddenly spread its wings and thrust downward, sending it into the air and again pushing the ship farther from the harbor. The dragon rose only a short distance, then came crashing down once more, this time locking its claws onto the bow of the ship and biting off the foremast before tossing it into the waves. The ship began to creak and whine as the waves became stronger and it strained under the dragon's weight.

"We have no choice, Solace," said Ivan. "We have to abandon ship!"

I nodded. "Tell everyone to swim for shore!" I yelled over the growing winds.

We scattered around the ship, moving carefully across the tilted deck, telling any crew who hadn't already done so to jump into the water and try to swim to safety. As I moved on from one crewman to find others, I felt something touch my shoulder, and I turned around. But there was no one there. With a shudder, I glanced toward Solace. She had a strange, distant look in her eyes.

"Ben, I don't think we should leave," she said.

"Why?" I prompted urgently.

"Something is wrong. Something...dark is here," she said, meeting my gaze.

I glanced back at the island and wondered if the armies of darkness had somehow followed us out here. Then I remembered the dark soldier on the dragon's back. "It's the dragon, Solace. I saw a soldier of darkness riding it," I explained. *That has to be it.* "We don't have time to talk about this right now. We need to get out of here."

Suddenly, the dragon let loose another stream of fire. I grabbed the shield from my back, and we took cover behind it.

Solace gasped in amazement as the fire let up, leaving us completely unscathed. "The shield can do that?"

I nodded and said, "Get the others to safety. I will find General Delaney. Maybe he knows how to hold this thing off long enough for them to get ashore."

I headed toward General Delany, who was taking cover by the door to his quarters. "You have been fighting beasts for years," I said when I reached him. "That dragon isn't going away, so we have to fight until the others make it to safety. Do you have any ideas on how to defeat a dragon?"

"I've been thinking...Dragons with wings can't swim very well. Maybe if we could damage its wings, it would fall into the water and drown," he suggested.

I nodded. In reality, it was a long shot, but we didn't have any other options at this point, so I got to work.

With Solace still spreading the news to abandon ship, I rallied Ivan, Nadia, and any of the crew members left on board who were willing to fight, and we advanced toward the dragon. Falling automatically into our usual strategy, Ivan went in for an invasive distraction, charging straight ahead with his sword held high, yelling. But he soon discovered that his speed was no match for the dragon's fire. The dragon spit flames at Ivan, and he barely made it behind some cargo, which nearly disintegrated in the inferno, so he dove for cover behind a thicker stack of crates. But the dragon's fire was quickly spreading across the ship, leaving few places to hide.

While Ivan was keeping the dragon busy, the rest of us attacked, aiming for the dragon's wings. But arrows simply bounced off the thick, leathery skin, only angering the animal.

Nothing was working.

In a last-ditch effort, I grabbed the sword and shield and prepared to charge the dragon at full speed. But as I grasped the sword, the world around me erupted into the unseen battle between the soldiers of darkness and the soldiers of light. The battle flowed around me as the soldiers clashed. In the distance, I could see Eyethanoff battling with a soldier of darkness. Before I could look away, the image of the soldier of darkness who had stalked me and haunted my dreams flashed in the place of the soldier Eyethanoff was fighting. For a split second, I saw his eyes lock on to mine, and a smile spread over his lips before he turned back into a normal solder of darkness. Suddenly, the Beast's green eyes flashed through my mind, and the sword felt light again, seeming to pull my awareness to the shield.

As I glanced down at the shield in my hand, my attention was drawn to what little of the Lion's Sword symbol I could see from this angle. The silver symbol flickered with the reflection of the battle. Then I heard the Ice Dragon's voice. "Have faith, my friend, for the unseen is a treasure worth believing in." I looked up to see her standing before me on the ship. *A vision?* I wondered. In a trance, I went to her, forgetting the battle around me. *It must be.* The sword in my hand seemed to draw the other pieces of armor back to their rightful places. I could feel them, but when I looked down, they were not there. I glanced at the shield and wondered why the dragon and sword were bringing it to my attention again. I already knew of its power.

When I looked up to ask the Ice Dragon, she was gone, and I was standing in the Woods. For the first time in a while, the vision seemed organized and clear. As I felt the Beast's tail encircle my waist, I looked down and saw the belt in place. I touched it, wondering if it was real, and immediately, the vision of the Woods vanished, returning to the dark, confusing visions I'd had before. Their unsettling presence froze me in a state of fear.

This time, the storm of darkness was still. Silence fell. I could hear nothing but my own breathing as I took in the vision around me. Darkness surrounded me like a bubble. But I could barely see through it to the other side. The dim and hazy image was hard to identify at first, but I suddenly recognized it. I was surrounded by the Unseen Lands, kept out only by darkness. *The Story* played out within the Unseen Lands, barely visible just beyond the dark dome. A story of hope. A story of one who loved his betrothed and her people so much that he died to save them. As I watched, I realized what the Ice Dragon had meant. *"Have hope, my friend, for the truth is a treasure worth knowing."* *The Story* was a true story. But it wasn't just that. The fact that it was true gave it a power that this world had been so long without. The power of hope.

I suddenly felt the sensation of the breastplate, and I looked down to see it in place. The sight of it there made me feel safe, and I touched it unconsciously. As I did, the darkness grew thicker, swirling with images of my failures and the people I had killed for the general. But then the dragon's words suddenly made sense to me. *"Be on guard, my friend, for your heart is a treasure worth protecting."* The darkness within me formed an uncrossable barrier that separated me from hope. My heart was corrupt, just like the woman in *The Story*. *But how was she saved?* I wondered. Her heart was won by the Prince himself because he died...and because he returned. I suddenly understood something about *The Story* I had not comprehended before. The hope was not just in the Prince's death but in the fact that he had come back, by his father's power, and now stood as the only one who could allow the people of this dark land back into the safety of the Kingdom. A land of light, free of darkness. He was not just a symbol of hope. He was hope. And those who knew *The Story* gained true hope because it was clear—the Prince had defeated darkness.

As I began to understand the extent of the Prince's power, the sparkling path appeared before me, like a light in a dark tunnel. The belt and breastplate shone bright as the darkness tried to attack me, but it no longer could, for the armor was in place, right where it belonged. I felt the shoes materialize on my feet and

I looked down at them and the path beneath. Their reassuring presence seemed to free me from my fear, allowing me to move forward through the darkness, which no longer trapped me. Truth had shown me hope, and hope had shown me a way through the shadows—a way that could protect me from darkness.

I followed the path, one step at a time, until I found myself standing before a transparent door with no handle. The door from my previous vision. It stood on the boundary between the dark and the light, the only point of escape from this dome of darkness. I could barely glimpse what appeared to be the Unseen Lands on the other side, but there were no people or events playing out. Just a beautiful land filled with green hills, blue sky, and light. A land I found myself longing for deep within my soul.

The Prince appeared and opened the door. Then it seemed to spin before me, ending with me facing its side. The angle revealed the wooden door I had seen at the end of a vision, a small gap, then the transparent door. The Prince stepped through the open transparent door and knocked on the wooden door.

I felt the shield's presence in my hand as the doors shifted again until I faced the wooden door only. It had no handle either, but I felt drawn to what I knew was on the other side. *"Have faith, my friend, for the unseen is a treasure worth believing in."* Faith. That word stuck in my mind as I looked down at the shield, at the symbol that identified this armor as being of the Lion's Sword. I suddenly realized something about my fight with the dragon. During that fight, I had been desperate for something to protect me. I had believed this armor was not available to me unless I did something to make it work—unless I could see it. *But maybe it is the other way around,* I wondered. This armor had been given to me. It was no longer just Ruth's armor, I realized. It was mine too. Faith had made it that way. *Maybe it has been protecting me. Maybe the moments I saw it were not the moments it was protecting me but the moments I had faith that it was.* Because I chose to believe in the unseen, because I chose faith, that armor was mine. That symbol now identified me as a warrior of the King.

I looked back up at the door, a new purpose and fresh understanding in my heart, and reached for a handle I could not see but I had hope was there.

As I reached out, a handle appeared.

Suddenly, a scream rang out from somewhere nearby, and I felt worry clench my stomach. Something told me that scream was important.

The vision around me vanished as my attention shifted to the source of the scream. I looked around and found myself standing on the ship's deck, surrounded by nothing but fire and destruction. I reached for my chest and waist, but the armor was gone.

I turned to see where the scream had originated and saw Solace doing everything she could to get to me as Ivan and Nadia held her back. Tears streamed from her eyes as she reached for me, calling out to me in desperation. For a moment, I wondered why. Then everything came into focus, and I saw it.

The dragon was poised above me, its mouth opened wide. Its front paw had smashed through the deck of the ship, separating me from the others. Waves crashed against the battered ship, finishing what the dragon had started as they split the vessel in two.

Time seemed to slow around me as I looked up at the dragon, briefly glimpsing the malice in its eyes before it let loose a blaze of fire directly at me, and the sounds of battle and Solace's screams grew dull, overtaken by the faint sound of someone knocking on a door.

The Arlin Trilogy continues in Book 3
The Gate

About the Author

Ondrea Keigh grew up in the forested Pacific Northwest, in Washington State, before moving to live near the sandy beaches of Florida. She loves to write and will do so at any time and in nearly any place. Her first published story was a short story titled *The Night Rider Adventures: Episode 1 – The Night Rider*, and she has many more stories on the way! Ondrea graduated from Liberty University with a degree in psychology and also holds a certification in dog training. Before becoming an author, she worked as an animal trainer, and when she is not working on a new story, she can still occasionally be found training puppies!

ONDREAKEIGH.COM